• • • In a Wild Sanctuary

By William Harrison

IN A WILD SANCTUARY
THE THEOLOGIAN

··· In a Wild Sanctuary

BY WILLIAM HARRISON

William Morrow & Company, Inc.
New York
1969

TO MY CHILDREN
Laurie, Sean and Quentin

Preserve, within a wild sanctuary,
an inaccessible valley of reveries.

ELLEN GLASGOW

• • • 1

ADLER DROVE, looking down the stretch of highway,
his moist hands heavy on the steering wheel. He listened to
Clive talk and wondered why Clive always took advantage,
why he saved his most extravagant lies for such moments.
Those long sexual fantasies: it was curious, Adler felt, that
Clive kept them up. We'll all be perfectly stone cold dead
very soon, Adler told himself, so why does he keep trying to
impress me?

The tires hissed through patches of melted tar. Go, going,
gone, Adler mused. He wondered if any of the four of them
would actually do it, actually kill themselves as they had
vowed, or would Clive just go on telling his elaborate lies?
We probably won't do it, Adler decided. Here we are in
California, heading east, away from our manifest destiny,
traveling to Las Vegas, which, of course, is the rectum of

the continent, and probably none of us will ever honor that perfectly legal and respectable suicide pact at all. But wouldn't it be nice? Everybody goes this time, baby, Ishmael included. Ram it up your rammer, Ahaber; peg it up your queequeg; stubb it up your grubb; dick 'em up, Moby, the jig's up.

Clive, brown and handsome, sat talking about a girl named Jamie, a girl who allowed him to photograph her, once, with his Polaroid. They met, he told Adler, in India. Town of Delhi.

"With each snap of the shutter she grew more open to me, Addie, and more of a tease and finally I just fell on her with all those sticky photographs strewn all the hell around the bed. The dream of my innocent American lust. Ah. She slept naked against my backside and woke me with kisses, astride me, breasts in my face, tongue in my ear. Her thighs made a little popping noise, I remember, when she gave it to me. Like any of this? Shall I go on?"

Adler sighed. "Please, Clive," he said.

"Addie, be content with knowing my sexual history. How can you possibly know anything else? The vast reaches of my brain, all my comprehensive reading, the exotic lands I've seen and known? Allow me to keep it simple and tell you— ah, just this one facet of me. Her name wasn't even Jamie, if you want to know. I was lying to you about that. We were strangers and that was just my pseudonym for her. It was really some Indian name I could never pronounce very well, but it's always better, sex is, when there's a certain anonymity about it. Especially, Ad, when you're just eighteen years old as I was then. Anyway, we made love all day behind those paneled windows with the noises of the city just a few feet below us. There were always soft motes of sunlight in the room."

"Even at night?"

"Yes, Addie, always. Motes of sunlight."

How he can lie, Adler told himself as he watched the steady

horizon. It would be a pleasure, actually, he decided, to see Clive dead. Blissful silence. Or I'd gladly slit my throat to shut him out. Of course we'll never do it as planned, never just have done with it, without notes, not a single trace or testimony. Clive, please, you're giving me a headache.

"She never dressed. Just sat on the bed combing out her hair. Long black hair, it was, Addie, which fell down over those dark nipples and into the dent of her thighs. She would sit on the corner of the bed watching me, and she had a way of dipping one of her long brown fingers into the tea then touching it to her lips. I went off to Agra without her, left her flat, but the sweet thing followed me. I asked if she didn't know I'd leave her again, but she crooned something in Hindi I couldn't understand. Then one day we went out to the Taj by rickshaw. It was a bright summer morning, Addie, and the minarets caught the light perfectly."

Minarets. Now there you are, Addie said to himself. Clive can lie in brilliant detail. Credit him with a nice word. Minarets. We will leave not even a single note, not a one.

"So we walked up to the great dome of the Taj and Jamie grew very solemn, Addie, and grabbed my hand and held on like a child. Wouldn't let go until we passed through the marble arch. She was trying to say something to me, I learned later, but couldn't. But there were other strollers and Jamie nudged me when we passed an old English matron with rolled socks who was taking notes in a loose-leaf binder and gawking. Then Jamie walked out ahead of me. In spite of myself, I watched the sway of her hips. We went back to the hotel soon after that without uttering a word. All afternoon we were at it and all evening on the rooftop. Watching the dim lights out over the city and we stood against a wall and hawkers were yelling in the streets below. Selling brass. Up on the rooftops we went down on each other."

"You lie, Clive," Addie said. "The truth is not in you, sahib."

"Ah, well, true enough, you caught me again. True. It wasn't like that at all, Addie, you're right. It happened in Trenton, New Jersey, and it was my mother all the time. But there were a few exotic touches about Mom. Give me that much. She cooked a hell of a curry dish."

Adler gazed up the road. Leave no notes.

"I could tell you another story about my sister," Clive offered.

"Enough is enough. Please."

"No offense. Look there. A gasoline mecca among the palms."

Adler slowed down, aware of the change in tone of the tires. He suddenly felt dizzy with thirst. Slick with the blood of history, O Ishmael, the adventurers arriveth: Lewis and Clark, Smith and Hickok, Barnum and Bailey. Here we are, spraying a little gravel.

"Stop here, Addie."

"I'm stopping."

A small shopping center loomed up with a gas station, a merchandise mart with groceries and drugs, and a large, polished truck stop restaurant.

Adler stood at the postcard rack in casual observation. American buffalo hamburgers. Toy pistols. A rack of headlines. Clive was somewhere off in the crowd, he knew, stealing a few things he didn't want. A large noonday rush was on and no one paid attention to anyone else, and neither the clerks nor the floorwalker (bright green duster and weary brow) nor the boy servicing their Corvair bothered about either of them. Clive passed back and forth—Adler had lost count of the trips—loading things into the back seat. He doesn't even bother with his usual diversionary movements, Adler observed; just smiles and the boy with the gas hose grins back. Adler thought about how he usually helped out by talking to clerks, asking for menthol products, but this time Clive didn't need him.

A large sign hovered above them: SPANISH CORNERS/ONE STOP SHOPPING/OLD FASHIONED GENERAL STORE/TOURIST INFORMATION & ICE. The buildings were surrounded by brownish palms and stood beneath a single bright red Spanish roof. Adler sighed. He stood there perusing the postcards, scratching at his four-day growth of beard, and gazing beyond Clive and the attendant at the gas pump at the marker: LAS VEGAS, 89 MILES. We'll soon be there, go down like dominoes, and have done with it.

Clive entered the store again and moved toward the fruit aisle. A watermelon this time. Verily and forsooth. Adler closed his eyes for a moment, let his breath hiss from his teeth. Postcards: Death Valley. Clive was back outside again asking the attendant to load it into the trunk for him.

Clive doesn't look the part, of course, Adler knew, and that was why he always got away with it. Tall, handsome, over two hundred pounds, moves with a slow and heavy grace like an athlete, looks confident, says yessir and smiles like an All American: no one would dare stop him and question him. If I ever tried it once, of course, Adler knew, the store manager, floorwalker, clerks and carry-out boys would jump me. Pounce on that chubby little queer! Thief!

Without much humor, Adler strolled over and gazed into the car. Magazines, hair spray, a pencil sharpener, bags of fruit. Also, now, the watermelon in the trunk.

Rattling in his head were all the disjointed fragments of the literature course he had taken during the past semester and with those, too, all the books Stoker had loaned him to read. The Deerslayer. Verily. Who are the travelers in our land? The Green Bay Packers. Killers all. Morning, sir, my name is Charlie Starkweather, sir, and if you'll please, sir, be my travel agent, here's the little itinerary I have in mind: this little swing through the Midwest, sir, nothing much. Hear, O Ishmael.

As the attendant cheerfully wiped the windshield, Adler

picked up the two bags of fruit from the back seat. The large, asphalt parking lot was filled with puffy ladies with blue hair and young mothers with babies drooling on their shoulders. The sun blistered the top of Adler's head. He offered a passing woman a big lemon.

"I'm from your famous Sunco Fruit Company," he said. "Here you are. Free sample."

"You don't look like the regular man who gives free samples around here," she complained.

"Fruit companies have their own special pushers, lady," he explained, thrusting the lemon at her. She accepted it and dropped it into her purse.

He stood in the middle of the parking lot with the sun cooking his brain. Sadness descended on him. Nothing, he decided, is all that much fun anymore. Act with vigor, he reminded himself. Clive is over there busy as a bee, but I can't think about myself, not really, how I look or sound or anything. I'm an asthmatic pudge, that's what, and I'd better not even think about it very long or I might cry. No good, that. A Sunco man shouldn't weep on duty. But I'm not just Sunco either. I'm the one, verily, who went off to the university to become—guess what?—a dancer. Only I was a pudge and looked ridiculous in tights. So I became an English major with Stoker, but that was no good. So I became a botanist. Locked in that greenhouse, tending my plants, just an ugly little pudge among the vegetation, and that, verily, is what you call true manifest destiny. Students actually stop on the sidewalks and peer in at me as though I'm a beastie in a zoo. Sickening. I can't stand it any longer.

"Have an orange, mister. I'm with yr famous Sunco Fruit Company of Grand Rapids, Michigan."

"Your company has always had good oranges."

"Why thank you, sir. Take two."

Sadness beat against his temples. He stood there making a

droll face, perspiration edging toward his collar. The moisture forming in his whiskers felt like great hot tears.

"I've eaten your fruit—oh, for a couple of decades."

"By all means, have a lemon too."

"But is this all you have, son? Just two sacks?"

"There's more in a big truck out back."

"Wonderful stuff for the health, this fruit."

"Right you are. Now move along, dad. Next!"

Shoppers emerged from cars all around, but Adler didn't have the strength to call them over. He regretted the sun. He regretted his botany courses so full of lists for memorizing. I'll never go back, he told himself, and now, by God, I even grieve the good times, few though they were. No notes.

Two teen-aged girls approached.

"Hah, you two! Getcher free Sunco fruitio! Rat chere, you two. Don't dodge me. Getcher free samples!"

"What sort?" the skinny one bravely asked.

"Juicy lemons and seedless oranges! My last two bags! But of course, ladies, I have to see yr drivers' licenses."

"What for? Why?"

"Mean to tell me that neither of you are licensed drivers?"

"Jill is," the skinny one offered.

"Fine. Lay it on me, honey, I got to make sure."

The girls giggled and Jill, freckled and Amazonian, handed Adler a crisp new license. He inspected it carefully, turning it over with elaborate care, reading with his lips. Impress them, he reminded himself. I regret, O Ishmael, the bloody trap of the sun; here I am without sextant or compass, adrift on an asphalt sea. Mermaids linger close.

"The whole bag? Both bags? You want us to have it *all?*"

"But of course," Adler called to them, and he walked on toward the car where Clive was signing his aunt's name to the credit card.

Soon they were gone from the parking lot, Clive driving,

and once they were riding in the desert again Adler picked up the cans of hair spray and aimed them back behind the car like jets. Emptied, they were committed to the roadside; the highway receded behind them. One by one, then, the magazines were discharged to the wind: *Life, Look, Time, Cosmopolitan.*

"Addie," Clive said. "I think you're a little hysterical today. Right?"

Adler didn't answer.

"Shall I tell you a nice story about Jackie now?"

"No, Clive, please, tell me nothing."

Adler moved down in the seat, closed his eyes, and fell into summary of himself. The greenhouse beastie. I will become a part of the wind-waving grass of the prairies, he told himself, a beast of the field buried beneath my century with flowers sprouting out of my eyes. My Pequod goeth down in the grass of time. Starbuckle yr seat belts, all hands on deck, pass the flask and lash the tashtego! Into the bowels of the western stars we go down. Hear, O Ishmael, the waters that flow beneath the world, and hear, O Clive, dear talker, and know this: that we have sailed hard and now we can properly and melodramatically die, having harpooned the whale of misfortune with our last breath. Manifest destiny, verily: the good guys are all asleep on the prairie: Kennedy, Hemingway, Bogart, Eliot and Walt Disney. We will meet them in the gopher holes of Idaho and the great plateaus. Just the four of us without a single note, a single farewell. Stoker: ye of the long sexual hang-up. Pless: ye of the intellectual vices. Clive: ye cunning Ahab, old voyeur, old voyager.

The desert wind whistled around his ears, Clive's voice was still for a moment, and Adler sat in summary. He saw a momentary set of images: all the books Stoker had loaned him gathering dust on his shelf back at the university, and also the pot plants (lovely *anthurium* from Hawaii and tiny duckweed) that he had given Stoker in exchange—all of them dead and withered along the window sill of Stoker's empty room. Then the summary commenced once more. Lo, out of the Ozarks the boy beastie came. He envisioned the farm house, warped slat sides and truck garden beyond the shimmering kitchen windowpane: it had imprisoned him for seventeen years. I might have been chained to a bleak attic bedstead like an idiot son, he told himself. Mouth adrool. Meals brought up on a tray and shoved into my grasp. But it was worse. My father saluted me with grimaces and shame rode in his eye. I took his old Winchester, of course, and walked those hedgerows as I knew he wanted me to do. The dutiful man child. But the sport wasn't in me; I had dreamt of Nijinski's ghost and of leaping, of brilliant pirouettes hovering like flame. Father, I finally said, I've been giving some thought to dancing. Good deal, son. Get you a gal and shag off come Saturday night. No, Dad, at the university. In tights. Like Nureyev with long hair, with ballerinas on my shoulder, with *Swan Lake* playing from the pit. The swan lake swan song I gave him: grimace and goodbye. What good can come out of Arkansas? Can a blossom grow in the cracks of these rocks? Hell no, son, it caint. Try studying business administration. Try engineering.

Toward the east twilight gathered. Far off, across the rim of the mountains, the lights of Vegas, Adler believed, already made neons of the clouds. His thoughts went astray. Memories of his father's place in northwest Arkansas: I'm right glad, son, that you've taken up botany. Good deal, I say. Man workin' with the soil, that's what it is. Go suck yr green thumb, Dad, I wanted to tell him. Join me in a dance through the seedling boxes. Consider Phlebas, papa, who was once handsome and as tall as you. Tereu.

As the horizon seemed to draw them on, Adler pretended sleep. If Clive had the chance, he knew, they'd talk again and so he lay back, wind in his whiskers, and tried to recall some of the things Pless had told him, the rationalizations which festered in him now, which muddled his consciousness. Pless adores the fateful generalizations, he told himself, but I always agree with him. We are a people who butchered our way toward the Pacific and who eventually, once there, suffered frustration with no place else to go, Pless once told them. (One of those late night sessions last spring, it was. The dorm silent. Clive had raved for a couple of hours, then Pless, as usual, had begun filling in the endless blanks of their rambling dialogue, stitching the loose ends, making seams of their evening talk, casually giving them the coat of ideas they would take to bed and wear around the campus the next weeks.) There was nothing more to slaughter, nothing else to climb, nothing more to cut down and forge, he had told them. The Cherokees and Sioux, bison and bear: everything had gone down, and we had acquired our taste for destruction. We stood at the Pacific, the peaceful bay, and wept. Nowhere to go. Wagons stranded on the wharves of Frisco; the tears of the axles turned to rust. And Adler remembered an Arkansas winter when the hunting was especially good, when his father and cousins had urged him into the field with them every afternoon to draw a bead on the helpless critters in the hedgerows around that dilapidated farm. No satisfaction in it, but his father's tone had been all hyperbole, strident, saying: There Is Too. Ah, Ishmael, the blood lust, Adler thought. It sleeps in our marrow like Pless tells us. Think of the letters of Thomas Wolfe, which Stoker lent me: he wandered the length of the country, old hunter, until his brain burned up. I've made a long voyage and have been to a strange country, he dribbled on his last page, and I've seen the dark man very close. Ah lost. In Seattle, it was.

The twilight deepened around them as they drove. Soon the lights of Las Vegas were glimmering on the clouds. The lure of East Egg, Adler decided; the dream of dreams.

It seemed as though there ought to be something left to

kill, for violence, as Pless so cogently put it and as Clive concurred, is western progress. The wars are temporary, alas, though, and what next? We are actionists, but where is our enemy? We will leave no notes.

"You know, Addie boy," Clive suddenly said. "I've been thinking about our little pact. The university is the place to do it. The whole scene is better there."

"It makes no difference," Adler answered.

He sensed that they meant it. A silly agreement had become serious, had calcified: they had decided one evening to end themselves, to draw lots and follow a designated order, to go one by one and leave no notes, not a single statement by which anyone could rationalize or moralize. Let it be pure spite, Pless had advised when everyone was excited with the prospect and elaborating. Let the four of us, bright minds all, turn off the lights; the deans and fathers and bishops can stumble around in the darkness, he said, and fuck them. We drank to it. Clive's eyes glowed like coals. We said it aloud and there it was, irrevocable, and Stoker's hands were trembling, like mine, Adler recalled, and now we have this rendezvous in Vegas. But we won't do it there, no. At school later, as Clive suggests, so the silly citadel can ponder us. Our Pequod goeth down, and I'm ready, Ishmael, let the iceman cometh; I'm sick enough, and a vein I shall open, verily, to the prairie winds. Tereu. Clive whistles as he drives. A bad note. Even his music is a lie.

THE COLONEL GOT OUT OF BED as soon as he awoke, dressed in a pair of shorts, mixed his first daiquiri in the kitchen, and went into his yard. His large haven: he liked the slope of the terrace and the sound of the filter humming at his pool. And there it lay: his elaborate toy, the racetrack. Yards of five-lane black track, red and yellow racing cars, starter gates, switches, miniature bridges and tunnels and straightaways flowered all around him, and he sat there beside his tool box, sipping his daiquiri, and became the master tinkerer again. He tinkered—and readily admitted this himself—because he didn't want to think. It was early morning, Nevada, August. Turning, he gazed up at the corner bedroom window and repeated the names of the two boys who had arrived late last evening: Clive and Adler. Pless and Stoke, his son, were not yet there.

Sipping his daiquiri, he suffered some old assurances: it was summer, the second summer alone without his wife, Cassie; the war was still on; Charlie Miller, an old acquaintance, had gone down over Haiphong in his F4C. Small griefs piled up. He was also overweight, his old arm injury had been acting up for more than a week, and he needed a good screw in the worst way. Too much to think about, he told himself, and he threw the switch and waited, placing his head down on the tracks. The layout was cool to his cheek. Then the little racers came whipping around the far turn and buzzed toward him. Whoa! He raised his head as they sped by. Close call. Switch off.

His eyes gravitated to the Kincannon house next door, and he wondered if they saw him watching them, sleuthing their divorced daughter who was home visiting. He decided on another daiquiri; at breakfast he always had a sweet tooth.

The letter from the draft board was there in the wire rack waiting for Stoker. More trouble and friction ahead and he dreaded it. There it sat: official government stationery. Another reminder.

The house was already too much a reminder of Cassie and for that reason he had stayed mostly at the base apartment during the last year. Cassie's breath was still in the rooms and when he stayed long periods at home all his weaknesses seemed to beset him; he drank and ate too much, became listless with regret. He tinkered and hated himself for it. That day she simply ran off with her young engineer, he recalled, he sat down for twenty hours in these rooms, drinking in solitude, allowing that he couldn't much blame her, and then he began his tinkering in earnest. He took apart his fishing reels over and over, went out to Lake Mead and peered into the motor of the cabin cruiser, made a life out of grass seed and lawn furniture, domestic repairs, and finally built that elaborate and sad toy—he called it that, Stoker did—which curled around the lawn.

Now Stoker, he knew, would come home and try to draw him into another argument about the war. Stoker wanted him to render some unequivocal military opinion, but the colonel knew that he would probably manage to field all of his son's morality and affirm the national interest with the usual evasions. Among doves, a hawk; among hawks, a dove; it was a blight, the colonel considered, having odd views or ever trying to take sides with balance and common sense. He remembered how Stoker mimicked him: "Wal, now, there's this new F4C out there on the runway, you see, kid, and it sure is a killer and there's orders to be obeyed and there's always the war and you damn well fight it!" All opinions seemed to lend themselves to parody in this mess. And he was especially tender-skinned since Cassie left, he knew. Mixing himself his second drink, he wandered back outside, letting the screen door slap behind him. He wondered if Stoker had brought his friends just to stack the argument in his favor. Interesting pair, those two upstairs. Well. It's going to be a long August, he sighed, knowing that Stoker might continue hazardous in his thinking and might not accept his orders to report for induction or review with the draft board. Stoker had said as much. A damned long August.

The garden was lush. Perfume of gardenia so strong that the colonel felt he could cry. Kneeling, he tried not to look at the Kincannon house. He put his hands in the dirt.

Memory: the landscape of Tennessee. Always plenty of rain there. The trees and hills around Franklin brought to mind words like *bower, glade, valley*. The peaceful shades of green.

Memory: old Grandfather Bo and the landscapes of Franklin, Tennessee, which time has mostly eroded. During those long depression years the old grandfather sat there on the farm eating mush for breakfast, reading the Bible and sometimes Thoreau all morning, eating mush again for lunch, taking his afternoon stroll through the fields around the Confederate graveyard, then eating fried potatoes and biscuits and more mush for supper. In the evenings he butted into conversations, told his endless stories, and the house of women and the single young boy—the colonel remembered himself as thin and useless—was completely defenseless against him. He repeated those stories again and again.

The colonel's father died in—oh, he couldn't remember—perhaps early 1922. Effects of the mustard gas he breathed in France. Mother was frail and silly: always full of snuff and a little whiskey and talk of ghosts lurking in those fields beyond the clouded glass of her bedroom window. She tended a meager garden, the colonel remembered, no larger than this one he worked in Vegas. Had her Christian pretenses, but more than that a passion for superstitions: salt over the shoulder, rhymed incantations, even, once, a werewolf tale. Neddie, the sister, looked after the boy and explained things without any such nonsense. Explained Bo and mama, explained herself, explained the useless, thin brother. Dear Nedra, my lost sister. Ned.

Grandfather Bo explained everything else in his own way, or tried to. His endless stories. Told how the Union Army marched past the Confederates during the night before the local battle. Told that one over and over. Old Bo had been a makeshift schoolteacher with no formal training. Told how he lectured until the chalk dust swirled around him and he was caught up in the swirl with his poor country students. Snuff bubbling on Mama's lip as she listened.

Memory: at times, when the old coot launched into a new story—it amazed them all that after so many repetitions there would occasionally be a new one—a kind of magic would settle on the dining room. That room: its peeling, maple-leafed wallpaper. And Bo would sit there, fingering the last of the fried potatoes, his enthusiasm gathering, and the stories, bizarre as always, would come spewing out. Concoctions, the colonel remembered, with no particular point. "Now figger that one out," Old Bo would say, and the last phrases would get repeated, echoed, as his voice trailed off. Stories: about a duel in which the contestants shot each other blind and were left to feel their way around the wilderness where they had gone to do battle without aides or seconds; about a country dance where two lovers danced themselves insane, spinning madly in each other's arms until they were reduced to idiots while their stupefied neighbors looked on; about an old hermit who lived on an island in the river, who in a fit of anger killed his beloved dog, then fell into despair and a week later took his own life, leaving a long and nearly illiterate note on the ills of humanity. Several renditions of those stories—including the contents of the hermit's note—were offered up over the years.

The colonel cooled his hands in the dirt, turning it. How different, he thought, from the black soil of Tennessee. His eyes darted toward the Kincannon place, then back. Vigaro. He plucked out a weed.

Memory: beyond the farm and a mile through the rolling fields lay the Civil War cemetery. There while the army under Sherman crashed southward, the Confederate John B. Hood (name embossed on a marker outside of Franklin) determined to save one last and great victory for the South. For days— all this blurred now in the colonel's recollection—his 40,000 troops chased the 30,000 Union troops under Schofield. Caught them at last at Franklin. Old Bo used to tell the story over and over, as if searching for some fragment, some detail, some meaning of meanings. November, 1864. Grandfather Bo had been only eleven years old, not nearly old enough to recall any of it with accuracy and tucked away in Nashville with his mother besides, but always allowed that the story was his to tell, as much his as anyone's and damn the exact facts. Six thousand Confederate dead. The Harpeth River red with blood. Blood, said Bo, is the gingerbread of history. The metaphor escaped the colonel, but he recalled it. Two thousand Union dead. Details of all this again and again: how the Union Army evaded a fight at Spring Hill by marching past Hood's army in the night; how Hood's forces caught them at Franklin; how they swarmed up the Lewisburg Pike toward the Gin House and Carter House; how all the Southern generals—how many? five? more?—died on the battlements; how the press of bodies grew so great that the newly dead had no place to fall and remained upright.

The colonel recalled walking at his grandfather's side in 1934—God, long ago, he told himself—as they went slowly across the fields, as if measuring their steps, and the ghosts his mother complained about seemed to linger in those broken rows. They walked beside Carnton House where, after the battle, the owner had offered his family's burial ground to 1,500 of the Rebel dead. His grandfather's voice was a husky drawl, slow and patient as his footfall during those strolls, and in the cemetery the old man's fingers would trace lightly over the markers as they passed, and he would go on telling stories about it all, the one about young Captain Tod Carter, perhaps, who died there in his home town after three bloody years of fighting elsewhere, brought home to irony, valor and death. Or Hood weeping in his tent, his ambitions shattered. The colonel could remember straining to understand, but Bo's messages seemed blurred, all shot with paradox, and he could never quite fathom them. Old Bo kept a diary, too, which Neddie always wanted to read, but none of them ever managed to see it and when the old man died it was never found. It gave the house a legacy of mystery. Hidden truth. The colonel felt perspiration beading on his temples as he bent over a nest of flowers.

No one up at the Kincannons'. Don't think about it, he told himself. Think of Bo and the dirt of Tennessee, about Stoker and the month that lies ahead. Look somewhere else, to the mountains where the mirage of the past forms dimly: that dining room with its peeling wallpaper, the grits dripping down old Bo's flannel shirt, the shape of sweet Neddie beside the stove, and, beyond, through the window, the ghostly furrows.

His hands grimy, the colonel rose to take his shower and to get himself ready for a needless morning at the base. Again, he glanced up at the bedroom window. A big one, that Clive, he told himself, and he went back inside the house again.

He took a lukewarm shower. There: the healing waters come down. Don't let the past encroach, he warned himself; memory will beset the best of us. Cassie's pale scent in these rooms will waylay me; I'll get listless and indecisive again and Stoker'll get mad at me.

His closet full of uniforms: everything hung at rigid attention. His neatness confronted him.

Cassie's pale scent in the rooms, same as ever, so that I feel the past dragging behind me like an anvil, he thought, drawing his underpants on. No movement and no thought without it: there it comes again like a too-friendly monster, nodding its head, full of itself. It makes me reticent and the officers at the base—Callagan and Morris and the others—have long ago interpreted this as weakness. So did Cassie. So, in part, has Stoker. But there it is: memory: a ballast in every consideration now, for the first time in my life, and it seems to grow heavier each time it visits me, seems to begin somewhere long ago, with Grandfather Bo, perhaps, and to come forward to all the mistakes and bunglings of my life. Each morning I button this uniform and give myself a place in the present: Martin Heisler Stoker, Colonel, USAF, Nellis AFB, Las Vegas, Nevada. Divorced. Father of M. H. Stoker II. Stoke. Grandson of Boland Richmond Heisler, etc. Born Franklin, Tennessee. Educated Vanderbilt. Various memberships, etc. The scent of Cassie everywhere.

He returned to the kitchen, dressed, wondering if she really went off to Europe with her young engineer. He also wondered why he wondered anymore, if in this fiftieth year he had begun to slip a few gears, if senility would soon set in and swallow him up. Another daiquiri.

Seven months, he mused, since I finished my tour in Vietnam. The war is all done for me, gone, gone. There were moments, though, when I didn't give a damn how screwed up the politics were, nor who won, nor whether I chalked up missions or not because, damnit, there I sat in the old *Cercle Sportif* in the midst of Saigon, my second MIG-21 (three jiggers Scotch, one j. Drambuie) under my belt, drunk as hell, talking with Bosan and King and Miller (burned to a crisp three days ago) and Vermont and all the others. It was winter and we could talk shop. The Barrel around Hanoi. Knocking out SAM sites. The boys up at Takhli. All the sweet lingo of it. At least I *got* there. Well, of course they rotate almost everybody now. But I went and managed to improve my tennis game, to fly a dozen raids, to go into that village which had been bombed and explain to that old man, the town father, how it had to be done. A dozen raids, all routine, not a single interception, not one fucking MIG in the skies, nothing. And now Cassie's goddamned scent is even here in the kitchen. Everywhere.

The colonel popped a vanilla wafer into his mouth. Why not? Something for the daiquiris to sop with, he told himself. Then, impulsively, his eyes falling on Stoker's letter again, he slipped it out of sight into a drawer.

Memory: Saigon is a bruise, he told himself, but I touch it affectionately, like a bruise from the last big game of my football seasons. Something well earned, the blue badge of one's appearance in the game. I lost Cassie while I was over there shoptalking, of course, but would've lost her anyway. If not her dear Richard, someone else. Some young cock. And sure enough, there's the Kincannon house over there. Allie, the divorced daughter, visiting for the month of August. Divorced, doesn't wear many clothes, and, please, my dear, I want something very simple from you. Just: "How do you do, my dear, you remind me of my ex-wife, Cassie, right down to your name and your little ass, and would you mind, please, stepping over this little hedge to my house? There. Nice. Thank you and cheers." But of course it's never so simple. Sadly. I'd never say it that way because the necessary overtures just don't seem to be in me anymore. The anvil of my private history comes bumping behind me, embarrassing me, and the words don't come. Also, matter of fact, she'd say no. Forget it.

Driving along Cheyenne Drive toward the base, flashes of other cars entered the periphery of the colonel's vacant gaze. In this familiar habit, driving to his work, he let his mind go blank.

Early that morning he arranged to take a flight. He went to the locker room, got into a suit, managed a few crisp sentences to the men on the line. He sat sweltering in his flight suit as he waited for takeoff; his fingers twitched on the varishaped dials and knobs just beside his left elbow and his eyes squinted into the sheen of the runway. Then, soon, he was high over the desert with nothing for miles around, not even a lost prospector, and he was absolutely alone, zipped up tight and hot in his gear, and all the garbled images of the last months rode with him and he felt dizzy with time, out of focus. He put his bird into a few rolls, but his head wouldn't clear. Neddie/Cassie/Allie: the woman I love has been many women, he told himself, and I've been many men. Charlie, old buddy, who rode with me here, who confessed that you once kissed my Cassie at a squadron party at Luke, who sat with me those few weeks at the *Sportif* in Saigon, you are burned to a crisp over Haiphong. Stoke, my heart's blood, you are probably Bo's true descendant. The colonel sighed, knowing that even if he put his bird into a series of rolls and climbed out fresh at 15,000 feet and suffered the hot bath of the cockpit and checked the air speed and touched all the familiar instruments it would do no good. The ship, of course, would respond as always. The bird would feel true to his touch, but his certainty would not ebb back. Years ago, perhaps, before memory bruised him so thoroughly, he considered, a few rolls and maybe a long, hard, cross-country tour would've done it. But no more. His certainty, he knew, would probably never come back again.

···3

STOKER WATCHED PLESS' MOTHER, Verna, swaying around the kitchen fixing breakfast. She was still trying to make conversation, but he sat there thinking, no, she doesn't have a parental shape at all, not at all; I would like to eat my scrambled eggs this morning right off her slender neck; I would like to eat her, like cherry pie, juice and all; I would, in fact, like to do such a favor for all my friends and eat up all their tasty mothers; slurp; I would like to take her shapely legs and push them down my throat like a sword swallower does it, freckled inch by freckled inch; I'll bet Pless' poor dead papa, the stunt-flying major, went to his grave with a smile for sweet Verna. Her shape isn't the least paternal nor maternal, not a bit. Think of something else now, Stoker told himself. That pine tree outside the window. Concentrate.

Verna moistened her lips and spoke. "Does your father ever go on cross-country flights anymore?" she asked. She had asked, in turn, how Stoker enjoyed the hot Arizona summer, how his father was getting along, how he liked her nice rented bungalow, how he liked going back to school, and he had answered everything with a polite lie.

"Some," he answered now.

"Does he fly around to visit the old crowd much?"

"We really don't talk about it much." Stoker gazed up toward the stairway, wishing that Pless would come down to breakfast, wishing that they could soon leave for Vegas. He planned to meet, as planned, with Clive and Addie—but only for the shortest possible time. He didn't want to watch the colonel wallow too long in his weakness.

The pine tree just outside the window of the breakfast nook looked like a prop, out of place in Arizona. Stoker sipped his coffee, listened to Verna, but kept his eyes averted.

He was glad to be with Pless, glad they were traveling together again, for Pless, luckily, Stoker felt, had stumbled into his character and knew himself. Things had happened to make him know, while Stoker felt that his own life always see-sawed, that he had pulled himself together, fallen apart, then pulled himself together again time after time. But Pless' father had gotten himself killed down in Florida when the two boys were in high school together and since then, steadily, Pless had come into focus. Your daddums made a nice gesture, Stoker wanted to say: there he was cutting up out there over the bay with that other pilot, doing a silly, cutting a nice riff, and their wings brushed lightly and down they went near the bridge, taking half of the city's power lines with them, and you, Pless, know all about yourself because of it. Your Father Was a Good Man. Stable and True. And Stoker recalled that his own father, the colonel, got nicely drunk that evening and remarked that the major should have known better, and the city mourned in mandatory darkness that night, its power lines popped loose, robbed of its television programs for a whole evening. Verna came back to Phoenix and went to work six months after the crash, working for a chain of sporting goods stores, seeing the other widows for lunch and bridge, taking up with the men of the city, becoming alcoholic and beautiful. Unstable and Untrue.

"Did the two of you have a good time last night?" Verna asked.

"Wonderful." Another lie. Very frustrating, Verna, and bad, he wanted to tell her. They had gone to an itinerant carnival with their dates and Stoker—jolly all night and witty—had not gotten with it. The girl's name was Rhue Anne. He knew all about her from Pless' accumulated scouting reports: she had just finished a long tiring year at San Diego State during which she frisked in bed with young professors, undergraduates, an assistant dean, a milkman, and whoever, in short, knocked. She was willing to leave the carnival, too, and travel to the parking lot, but Stoker didn't ask. He kept talking, firing off adolescent witticisms which he deplored. She dripped chocolate ice cream on his shirt and gushed that her daddy loved her and that her daddy had once described her as having a Botticelli smile and a Chagall heart. Gushy daddums talk all night. She asked if he and Pless were really geniuses, gushing all the time and dripping on him, and if they were really the top students at their university and did they ever go to football games. Our school has no football team, Stoker assured her, and she gushed that she had a wonderful foreign student lover last year, a nice boy who played the drums—she didn't say what country he was from —and who argued on the side of Red China and had all sorts of voices like Jonathan Winters and Pless. Velly cute fellah, she said. Velly noisy drums. Stoker took her hand late in the evening—he wished he could tell Verna this—and dropped his voice into a sincere octave. He told her that he was part of a nice suicide pact, that he would kill himself with the others and leave not a single note. Rhue Anne gushed with laughter when he told her and squeezed his chocolated arm.

"Pless and I had lovely dates," Stoker told Verna. "Real sweethearts. We finally made a bet with them that they wouldn't ride the big double ferris wheel while blindfolded. Bet them five dollars. Of course they took the damned bet and when they got up in the air, all blindfolded with our handkerchiefs, we left them. Ran back to the parking lot, jumped in the car, and cut out."

Verna looked at him prettily. She moistened her lips again before speaking; the habit drove Stoker wild. "I don't believe you did that at all," she said. "You're putting me on again."

"After that we went out and got drunk."

"Oh? You and Pless? And what did you drink?"

"One sasperoonie, one black absinthe, one gin fizz, a straight Coke and a small furniture polish nightcap."

"A fib. You know damn well that Pless can't drink even a single beer without snuffing out like a light."

"I was lying about the furniture polish."

"How many eggs?"

"Two. Please."

Stoker gazed at the pine tree, lavished his gaze on it, and tried not to think of Verna's wet lips, her freckles, or Clive, or the Great Pact, or Rhue Anne, or the colonel.

"Have you heard anything from Cassie?" Verna asked, still pumping the conversation. She never liked Cassie, Stoker knew, doesn't now, but asks anyway.

"No, nothing," Stoker lied again. A letter bulged in his wallet, one he saved to show the colonel. Cassie had cunningly enclosed a photograph of herself in a bikini; she stood with some anonymous man in the photo, not her sweet Richard, some stranger who stood peering down into her abundant cleavage. One corner of the picture was gone where perhaps some writing appeared.

Stoker, not wanting to think about Cassie any more than he wanted to think about Clive or the colonel, mused about Pless. A friend with his personal history all neat. Lucky bastard. The right things happened to you, Stoker decided. Once when Pless had been seventeen, Stoker recalled, the major had given him a mere twenty-five dollars and had ordered him to hitchhike across the continent from Florida to Los Angeles. Get there, the major told him, and give your daddums a collect call and he'll send you the money to get home. A pleasant challenge which, of course, Pless accepted. So he made it with five dollars to spare and telephoned from Hollywood after treating himself to a seafood platter and a tour of the movie stars' homes. I'm ready to come back now, old daddums, he said. The major, of course, told him to get home on his own, said that it would make a man of him, then hung up and wouldn't accept any further calls. The next part of the story was the best, and Stoker remembered it, grinning. Pless had gone down to a supermarket, bought several boxes of nutmeg and oregano, mixed them, then had gone down to the hippie section of town. There he met four gullible high-school students from Ohio who were touring around, saying, "Yeah, man, O that's so cool," and things like that. Eager to buy some marijuana, they finally paid him one hundred dollars for the package. The major met him at the airport when he flew back, first class.

Then all the odd jobs at the university. Pless was the great anachronism: the poor boy, bright and willing, who would not be a burden to his widowed mother and who worked his way through school. He tended yards around the high-rise dorms, worked as a plumber's assistant (*not,* he insisted, as a plumber's *helper*), and stacked trays in the cafeteria. He also showed up at almost every social function on campus where there might be free food, and the girls of Ida Noyes Hall sent him back to his room with sandwiches and hors d'oeuvres in sacks. And out of all this he invented himself. He became known. The campus blades dropped by the room—and some of the losers, like Adler—and there was much oration, Stoker recalled, and little rationale. And, of course, the student gambits: a group of them one night composed for the literary competition the most thoroughly obscene sonnet in the language, they affirmed, give or take a few inversions or perversions; that year some of them also had their arms tattooed and Pless won the honors with an upper right arm beautifully etched with a single word: TATTOO. Set in a field of yellow roses and adorned with a blue saber, it became Pless' principal vanity. Also, around Christmas recess that senior year Pless set a cask of Pernod on his bookshelf (the tattoo remains, Stoker reminded himself, but the Pernod is long gone), proclaiming that it was the only civilized liquor in the world, his very favorite. Pless, of course, was never a drinker.

Then next year Clive appeared.

Stoker didn't want to think about that bloody bastard at all. Nor about Cassie and her anonymous fat man. Nor about Verna's movements, which were set before him like a tasty dish.

"You're not listening to what I'm saying," she told him, smiling and setting a plate of fruit beside his arm.

"Sorry."

"I asked if Cassie and her new husband are living in Europe. They said they were going to, didn't they?"

"I think so. That's right."

"Is your father okay? Does he still talk about her, I mean?"

"We don't mention it," Stoker explained.

"Well, the two of you *should* talk." Verna turned toward the stairway just beyond the door. "I've got to get him out of bed. Here's your eggs, though. Eat them while they're hot and don't bother waiting on Pless."

Stoker smiled and accepted his plate. Pless who knoweth thyself, he thought. He wondered how Pless could fall for Clive's continual pop-off. Then, rapidly, his thoughts bent back to Florida again, to the days when he and Pless had gone fishing up in the bayous, when they slept on sandy blankets and Pless was the only one who ever caught fish.

Stoker had given Pless a Randal hunting knife as a graduation gift from high school, a slightly extravagant gift for the True and Practical Outdoorsman. They never camped out after that. Then, at college Pless went adrift in intellectual latitudes, enjoyed taking the wild tacks—the zanier the ideas the better, he said himself—and Clive was the natural consequence: an eerie light that draws the inquisitive wayfarer.

Verna occupied herself at the kitchen counter as Stoker devoured an egg in four bites. Turning to glimpse her freckled legs again, he saw her lift a shot of morning whiskey to her lips, but turned back before she saw him watching. Alas, he thought, poor Verna. I knew her fell. In the breakfast nook, nook, nookie.

Never you worry, he wanted to tell her. I'm just a lot of hot air. I've gone bad in my balls along with everyone else and that's what your son and his friends have in common, truth be told: they've all gone bad in their balls. Too much sex, too little, the wrong kind. Anyway, Verna, love, I'm not dangerous; just a minor lecher. Preoccupied. The Naked and the Bed. Annabel Lee: I remember that I faintly recall that I once knew a girl in summer camp. Lolita she was: a shill, schiller, schillest. Love is feminine, passion is masculine, lust is animal, need is vegetable. And, by way of corollary, in November of 1895, Verna, Oscar Wilde stood in his prison clothes on the platform at Clapham Junction, waiting for the train to whisk him off to his misery, while the onlookers, aware of poor Oscar's circumstances, onlooked. In short, a flower is a flower is finally, hammered out, perfumed pulp, the death of western romance. Then it's kiss me, Lady Brett, my lips are cold and stony. All that. Verna, I live in the dry vagina of the times; have no fear of me and let me gaze. I couldn't rape Arizona's most insistent nympho. Of course you give rise to thoughts. Juliet of my Spirit, wherefore art thou? Care to perform a little Fellini with me? All that. Your undulations in the kitchen, Verna, maketh me jabber.

The stairway creaked under a slow footfall. Pless descended. He entered, nodded, and finally dropped himself at the table like a bundle of morning laundry.

He accepted his mother's kiss, coffee, and orange juice.

Deftly, he reached over and rapped hello on the top of Stoker's hand with a fork.

His uncombed hair tufted at his ears, fell over his brow, and he clearly resembled, Stoker felt, the major: heavy jaw, pale eyes, a face good for the telling of jokes, an American normalcy. Usually a freckled and alert face, this morning the stations of his brain still slept.

The morning headlines beside his plate informed him that Air Force planes accidentally destroyed another Vietnam village. "Ah so," he mumbled, rubbing his eyes with his fists.

Stoker returned his weak grin, thinking: it's always good seeing him.

"Well now," Verna said, still making conversation. "Since you two are going back to school so early this year, you must be looking forward to it."

"Truly, Mother, we are, we truly are," Pless as Boy Scout answered. Sipping his coffee, he dropped into mimicry. "This year the merit badges are ours. Let's go, Stoke. Let's bolt down this meager breakfast and have at it." Then, in a different tone, warmer: "Hey, hon, sit down here and talk to us and don't ask such silly questions."

Verna sat down. Her lips made a nice smile.

"You'll like it this year," she assured him. "Now that you have an assistantship and you'll be making money, you'll have your best year ever."

"True," Pless said, patting her arm.

"He should be proud of himself for the assistantship, shouldn't he, Stoke?" Verna asked. "Not everybody gets honored like that."

"Definitely. He should be very proud," Stoker said. He watched Verna's lovely moist mouth.

Pless as Storm Trooper: "I take care of ze rats for ze

mad professors. Dot is all it means, mein frau." He talked into his coffee cup, sulking, full of understatement.

"Rats?"

"I don' tell you? Zees year I clean out ze cages, halp herr doctors who use rats in experiments. Und ven experiments finished, I—vell, zees is de sad part, fräulein—I exterminate ze little creatures."

"They pay you money for killing rats?"

"I put a dozen or so in the large laboratory trash can," Pless went on. "Then pour in some chloroform. Then, calmly, I sit on the lid. I'm thinking of writing a manual, as a matter of fact, on all these procedures. Anyway, after repeating this simple duty several times, Mama, I take the filled trash can over to the furnace. Like Büchenwald. Listen, hon, it's really wonderful in the scientific community. I always feel like young Leibnitz."

Verna looked at him blankly.

"Well," he said, "us blackshirts have to start somewhere!" He pushed a bite of egg into his mouth.

Verna sighed, moistened her lips again. "You kill the rats after each experiment? The professors don't use the same rats over again?"

Pless as Viscount: "Oh, no, bad show, old girl. Nothing but splendid virgin rats for the good professors! Who'd think of using the bloody same rats twice?"

"I don't believe any of this," Verna added.

Pless continued, his face straight and drowsy. "If you don't properly kill the little bastards, Mama, they might sneak out of the ash can and make their way back to their cages. Then they might get involved in the next experiment, you see, and we can't have experienced rats messing up our experiments, can we?"

"Oh, I don't believe any of this."

"You'd better believe it, hon. The rat-killer always gets the biggest assistantship on campus."

Verna offered him a blank stare. Finally, Pless grinned. For a moment Verna's expression deepened, then she laughed, accepting Pless' smile as the admission of a joke. Then the two of them began talking about money, about their budget for the school year, the clothes Pless would need, and Stoker sipped his lukewarm coffee and watched them with a certain warm envy.

Then, later in the mid-afternoon sunlight, they stood out on the driveway saying their goodbyes. Verna clutched Pless' arm and seemed near tears, her pucker, Stoker felt, looking considerably more maternal, as Pless instructed her to be happy.

"Oh, I will, yes, don't worry about me," she told him, muttering against his shoulder and reaching up to kiss his cheek again. Her mouth tried to make another smile, but this time it couldn't.

Soon Pless and Stoker were driving out the freeway in silence, Pless at the wheel. Stoker fretted. Poor Verna, he decided, would soon be preparing for her evening drunk; the colonel would be up in Vegas introspecting his private troops; a bland summer was almost gone. Everything seemed to hang in the future tense: the inevitable meeting with the draft board, all the explanations, the new school term, and Clive. Most of all, somehow, Clive.

Stoker thought of Clive as his rival, his nemesis. The bastard goes over to the library, he reminded himself, and finds everything remote and esoteric to use on us. Bullies us with information. Tells those ornate lies. And you're wrong as hell, Pless, he wanted to say, about Clive being full of good-natured put-on; he's an intellectual bully. Stoker recalled a night last spring—not the night in which they made their pact, but another—when they were drinking and when Adler, swooning in his cups, referred to Clive's ideas as "the darkest side of the moon." A drunken compliment and a fabrication, but Clive had enjoyed it. Not so, either, Stoker wanted to say. Clive's ideas were jumbled borrowings, hodgepodge. Brigid

Brophy and the neo-Freudian hacks. Sophomore sensational-isms. Obscure existential cynicisms. Genet and Super de Sade. Drunken blithering, most of it. But what bothered Stoker and angered him and gnawed at him—the only thing—was that Pless seemed to like it all so much.

Stoker sat thinking as they passed the city limits, heading toward a reunion he didn't particularly relish at Vegas. I sit here quietly, he told himself, because one doesn't want to appear jealous, does one? So one keeps one's mouth clammed. Last semester is not mentioned. The pact is not mentioned. Clive remains sacrosanct.

Then, as they passed into the desert country, into a bowl of open country, though, Stoker couldn't keep silent.

"Do you think Clive and Addie will already be there?" he asked as casually as possible.

"They said they would."

"Do you think so, though?"

"Oh, I suppose they will."

"At the first of the summer you said you felt they might not show."

"I said it, but now don't you think Clive'll want his audience again?"

The landscape broadened around them like the sea, like that gulf with its shimmering horizons of water which the two of them had shared years ago, when they were younger than their youth in their fishing days in Florida. A few mountain ridges fixed themselves in the distance.

"How do you think he will be?" Stoker finally asked, imagin-ing Pless would know what he was asking.

"Clive will probably still be talking about it," Pless told him. "Also, he'll probably have poor Addie so goofy by this time that he won't be able to sleep at night unless someone holds his hand. Since you ask, that's what I think. And Clive will have all new angles, wait and see. Maybe some god-awful new book. Something to keep us worried."

$$\cdots 4$$

PLESS TRIED TO SMILE, tried to give Stoker at least the partial assurance of a grin, but it didn't work. Stoker looked grave: hunched down in his seat, staring off at the prairie, all bothered.

"We'll be in Vegas soon," Pless told him, but Stoker only sighed.

Las Vegas. Something for nothing, the American dream, adventures expensive and cheap, the call of the wild, all bets off. Pless thought about their summer, which they had divided between the colonel in Vegas and Verna in Phoenix, between idle and odd-jobbed days, between restlessness and those busy days in Phoenix when they had worked during the vacation periods for some of the other employees of the chain of sporting goods stores. Now, at summer's end, they were going back to Vegas, then on back to school, meeting Adler and

Clive first. In Pless' thoughts were all the myriad leftover images of the first part of the summer: Caesar's Palace with its great hollow manikins; all the ornamented girls who populated the Strip; the grim glitter. During June he or Stoker would wake up in the middle of the night, wander around the rooms at the colonel's house, restless, and finally would wake the other. They didn't especially want to go down to the Strip, but always went. They would drive down for the 59¢ breakfast at the Silver Slipper or go to Denny's. By 4 A.M. the showgirls would have dumped their sugar daddies of the evening—the old men who had the price, but nothing to cut it with—and the casinos would be full of cruisers, the girls who wanted more. A few of them would drift back to the tables to work as shills, but mostly they just cruised around, hunting, sizing up the young men in the room before they finally made their move. Stoker, of course, was always hopeful, always philosophical about being in the wrong place at the wrong time. Usually, Pless supposed, the girls tapped some airman from out at the base. Or some football player type. Clive would have done well in the casinos at 4 A.M. because of his looks, Pless allowed, except of course, Clive has little or no sexual urge beyond his tall tales. But the room keys were dangled and accepted. Nothing was subtle in Vegas, and everything was either for sale or a gift to the skin. So the two of them would get out of bed and go downtown or out on the Strip, into the midst of the weary carnival, which they didn't particularly want to do. Even after they had seen it a hundred times, they went again, for there it was: a town that behaved very much like a clumsy magician, one whose tricks all show, but who gets you hooked so that you can't stop watching. Fake, you tell yourself, but you can't leave it alone. Or it's like a neon light, Pless considered. You don't want to read it, but of course you do and that's the trick of it. The ultimate formula of Western civilization resided in Vegas, it seemed: dazzle and then seduce. Salesmanship. The auto industry.

Chrome and eyeshadow. If you have no resistance, the dazzle lulls you; if you resist, it rapes you, and either way you lose. So they would get up in the middle of the night—the colonel mostly stayed out at his base apartment those weeks—and accept their fate.

They were broke during those weeks, so didn't gamble, but that was no great matter. Whether it was keno, craps, baccarat, roulette or neon, Pless felt, it was much the same: they were willing voyeurs. After spending a few hours touring around the casinos, they would drive back to the colonel's house where they would sleep until noon. At lunch, then, they would talk, applying their blitzed faculties to all that they had seen, agreeing that it was all perfectly phony, all tasteless, but then their day would start again and they'd swim, perhaps, or read, then have dinner with the colonel or take a drive out to the mountains, and eventually, after a few games of rummy or hearts they'd climb back into bed, dream fitfully for a few hours, grow restless once more, and finally get up to return to it all. It lured us, Pless admitted, and we hated it.

He thought about Vegas, he admitted further, as a moralist. He risked hyperbole, thinking: it is a place of death. And he wondered if Clive could smell it. I wonder, he asked himself, if he'll inhale the essence of the city as I did? He has a nose for death. Even money he will.

On Cheyenne Road toward the air base lay all the litter, the worn merchandise of a transient people who have thrown off their ballast. There on the desert along the roadside were washing machines, refrigerators, sofas, husks of autos, lamps, hair dryers, bedsteads, a whole junkyard for the residents of the city too much in a hurry to take their things with them. A graveyard for the ungrieved goods of the times. Easily explainable, perhaps, since Vegas was far out in the desert and too much of a problem for the big junk dealers of Los Angeles or elsewhere, but there it was, always slightly embarrassing and disturbing: everything turning to rust among the cactus and tumbleweed.

There were also the vacant houses of the city. Row after row of cheap bungalows and frowtsy frame houses—all built at low cost, made to fall apart—had been boarded up. A building boom got out of hand, the colonel explained, and houses were taken off the market and boarded up so that rent prices in the rest of the city would stay high. Whole suburbs of empty houses, Pless remembered. North of Cheyenne Road there was a newly built addition with curbed streets, an impressive lighting system, landscaping, everything except houses. Some visionary builder had dreamt of Paradise Homes, but his dream had turned to sand; nothing remained except some sewers in the desert.

Then the downtown, the cluster of buildings around The Mint and the Diamond Horseshoe. These were the less expensive casinos where the crowds could play nickel roulette and stand for hours before a nickel slot pulling for the daydream. The neons bulged the streets with light: WE CASH PAYCHECKS/ THE WORKING MAN'S CASINO: DOUBLE YOUR PAYCHECK HERE. The housewives stayed up late in this part of town and, at times, cruised a little themselves. There were shop girls, waiters off the late shift, local plumbers and hairdressers and clerks. Stoker felt that these were probably the happiest gamblers in the city. They had their favorite dealers at the blackjack tables, waitresses whom they called by first names, and always a pleasant and dogged lust to familiarize themselves with a certain casino or a particular machine or game, as if they might eventually fathom a peculiarity which would make the difference between tepid hope and true fortune. They smiled and dribbled away their wages a nickel and dime at a time. "Like having a panther as a pet," said an old lady, beaded and rouged, who sat playing keno one night as they watched. "It moves with grace, boys, and captivates you, and you love watching it, but it's damn well going to eat you." The truisms of Vegas. Everybody in town resided in a personal metaphor.

Now here we are driving toward it again, Pless told himself. Wanderers of the plain returning to mecca. Clouds building off on the horizon. Rain. Stoker with his head thrown back, his mouth agape in sleep. He has anxious dreams, Pless knew, of the rendezvous ahead.

The Strip, of course, is the common virus of the city, he mused. Gambling is an aristocratic germ—a rare fever only the select can suffer. But in Vegas it gets injected into the giddy middle class. Barbers and hardware store owners and car salesmen transform themselves, momentarily, into dukes and counts of the vice, and come forward in their somber masks determined to play it cool. They play hard in order to lose. Always to lose. Their forebrains, naturally, dream of castles and the golden goose, but they come to play hari-kari, to get blackjacked, to get crapped on, to get aced. They mix with all the tuxedoed musicians, brokers who own gleaming mansions on Long Island, oil magnates from Tulsa and Dallas, aging debutantes from Atlanta and Pittsburgh. For a few hours they feel integrated. The caste system breaks down. They are smiled upon like members of the team and the croupiers attend them with polite haste, knowing that these one-night swingers from the suburbs pay the bills of the casinos. No Monte Carlo, that place. For one roll of the dice or one agonizing turn of the wheel, the lowly experience that delicious illness that only the very rich survive. Here I am: the moralist again. But screw it. Vegas is such a ripe and stinking place. He remembered an old professional gambler he saw one night puffing his little cigarette stub at the Dunes. Sick as a leper with his art. A champion carrier of the sweet disease: the tourists gathered around him, touched his sleeve, patted him, tried to rub off a little of his germ, gave him the high sign. The old gambler's face was a sack of wrinkles. He didn't give a damn. The high roller is a novice suicide.

Names on the marquees loomed eight feet high: Buddy Hatchett, Sergio Smashi, Bob Blueheart, Vic the Groan, Phyllis Killer and Ann Margaret of the House of No Name. Eight-feet loomers. All the sleepless nights they had wandered in Limbotown came to mind: all those dinky small trade places around and off the Strip. The nitty-gritty redneck gamblers occupied those. Poker games. Hair of the dog. Double or goddamn nothing. Grim rodeo riders with their thin hips crimped in their jeans, square-jawed as Jawn Wayne, squint-eyed as Bawb Mitchum. El Cortez and the Bonanza and all those places. The tune was always "Your Cheatin' Heart."

The twilight gathered. Pless watched Stoker and wondered at his dreams, wondered if he dreamt of the colonel (who wanted to be Hanoi Harry the Mad MIG Shooter) or Cassie (who had successfully turned herself into Alice in Wonderland). The odor of rain excited the desert as they drove, and Pless looked forward to Hoover Dam. He loved the descent into that canyon. It was like the laboratory of the giants with all those high wires and transformers.

He thought of Stoker and Addie and how they traded books and pot plants and how Addie had grown a passion for literature while Stoke had gotten fatherly toward all vegetation. He thought of Vegas again. The fates really resided, he felt, out at Nellis Air Force Base where good ole Colonel Stoker helped nudge disaster on its merry quest. The weapons-testing center. Witty jet pilots. Interesting new bombs. Modified radar sights and gatling-type cannons. Rockets galore. He remembered a Saturday morning when the colonel took them on an unofficial inspection tour. The colonel was at his military best that June morning, touring them around as though they were two fat senators, supplying them with sergeants and a few captains to shake hands with. And there was Nellis, an act that paled, it seemed, the dazzle of the Strip. Evil Disneyland.

A curious man, Stoker's father. I have the feeling, at times, Pless allowed, that he feels. His eyes seem to warm. He perhaps loved his Cassie, as Stoker says. If so, perhaps his oven heated up and there are a few warm cinders left over for the world. Even so, we've never talked. Pity. And so he was unofficially officious that morning at the base. Parade manners. Spit and polish.

"Cluster Bomblet Unit," the colonel explained to them. "That's what it's called, yes, and it's a large weapon as you see. It's filled with small grenades and it's used for, well, for attacking the enemy in the field and so forth." Et cetera. He watched the boys, his son and his son's friend, as he delivered the information, trying to gauge their emotions, but they kept their faces comfortably blank. "And the grenades," he went on, "are filled with little darts. The CBU spreads them around, you see, and the darts can cover, oh, about a quarter of a mile strip. Very effective field ordnance. And the darts can be poisoned. There are all sorts of chemical variations possible." He had watched the two of them all morning, but with a certain kindliness so that Pless had wondered, at times, if he didn't sense all the ironies he uttered.

"And here are the new land mines," he went on. "We drop these out of planes, you see, and they don't explode when they hit. They bury themselves in rice paddies and in the soft earth, see, and later a vehicle or a nearby footfall will set them off. They're actually pretty sensitive. Each one has a dry cell battery in it—are you sure you want to see all this?"

They assured him they did.

"All right. Dry cell battery. When it finally expires, the mine activates and explodes. That's what we hope, anyway. Wouldn't want to have the damned thing lying around and blowing up some innocent peasant ten years from now, you see. Of course, hell, you can't estimate the life of a dry cell battery and with things the way they are—hell, who *knows?*— the war *might* be finished before they've all blown off." Et cetera. The colonel delivered most of this information mechanically, in what Pless decided was a practiced tone.

They talked with others that morning too. A major with a red mustache said, "Sure. Five hundred pound bomb? Yes, I've dropped 'em. There was a slight hitch, remember, when we first used these. Damn things bounced back up and knocked out a couple of our planes on low-level scoops. We had to put fins on 'em and float 'em down. But let me tell you how deadly these babies are! I saw recon photos of a mission I flew with these things and, listen, guess what I did? Blew up a bicycle! That's right. Five hundred pounds of explosives and I blew hell out of a bicycle! Let me tell ya: you don't need these big babies out there much because you can't find six gooks huddled together to use 'em on. And you know what? You can't blow up a rope bridge with 'em either. I tried it. Two nearly direct hits and the damned rope bridge just swayed back an' forth. Screw it, I say, boys, we ought to whip 'em with clubs."

The sergeant behind the desk gave them an aside, too, while the colonel went off to the water cooler. "They beat us with them damn pongee sticks," the sergeant said. "Pongee sticks dipped in shit. Step on one of them and yer in the hospital six weeks sure. That's what got ole Major Warden when he got shot down. Pongee right in the instep. 'Course when the Jolly Green picked him up, they didn't do him much good either. Copter came down in a hurry under fire, put him in harness, and dragged him through all them briars. He might 'swell been caught an' tortured."

The colonel moved them from place to place, introducing them, and the images stacked up in Pless' memory: oily rags in a neat, folded, military pile in one of the hangars; those big aluminum darts used for aerial target practice, gleaming silver in the late morning sunlight, a few gaping 85mm holes in them; the cockpit of the F105.

"This is the dial-a-weapons system, you see," the colonel explained. Beads of sweat tumbled from his hairline; his cap was soaked and his collar was opened with no tie. "You just switch this little dial around and you get your cannon, rockets, bomb releases. These knobs over here on the left-hand side, you notice, are all different shapes. This is so the pilot won't have to look for them, so he'll know everything by touch. This is your radar sight. When you lock in on an enemy aircraft, you press this. Makes your bird follow wherever he goes and keeps him in your gunsights. In other words, when you lock in on Charlie, he's dead." The sun glared back at them from the sheen of the plane's metal. They squinted at each other. "The name of the game," he went on, "is get behind Charlie before he gets behind you." Neither Stoker nor Pless answered anything, nor asked questions, and when they climbed down from the cockpit the colonel waited, watched them, and his hand made a fist.

That morning: all normal at the base. The tennis courts thrived, the swimming pool was noisy with wives and children, pilots shop-talked in the bars, the PX buzzed with shoppers. They walked among buildings familiar to both Stoker and Pless, the artifacts of military community, everything labeled: TAC COMMAND HQTS/OFFICER'S MESS/ENLISTED MEN'S CLUB/ BASE EXCHANGE. They even strolled by one Quonset that morning, Pless remembered long afterward, with a sign out front reading: PERSONAL PROBLEMS. He thought at the time, oh, Colonel, does the shrinker in there know all about your Cassie? Is that the room where they put the band-aid on your heart? Meanwhile, the colonel walked on and kept talking, filled with the morning's euphemisms: fire bombs, not napalm; ordnance, not weapons; zap, not kill; boonies, not battleground; limited encounter, not war. Eventually they went to the officer's club where the colonel had his daiquiris and Stoke and Pless drank beers.

In there amid the mahogany and the quietness, the colonel wanted to explain further. "Southeast Asia is so awful," he said, "and so *important*." The blender whirred with ice, limes and rum. Pless wanted to say yes, it seemed important *because* it was awful, because men died out there, but such logic, he knew, would have scuttled his host. So the colonel's mouth vexed itself and he repeated, "All this is important in our history, boys, it really is. You'll see." Et cetera.

Nellis looked like a model city that morning, Pless recalled, with the officers sipping around them, babies riding on their mothers' hips out in the base stores, everyone friendly and warm under the indifferent morning glare. Domestic. Normal.

An enigmatic month of June, full of many such days, days in which he had watched the colonel watching them. Sometimes there seemed to be a deep nostalgia in the colonel's gaze, as if he perhaps searched for himself as a child of Tennessee, as the boy lover of Cassie, as a young lieutenant with his brass all neatly shined. There were many long afternoons that June with the three of them at poolside or at meals together; they managed, always, to talk and say nothing. The colonel, Pless finally decided, was afraid of them. He was guilty for having lost Cassie—he had lost her for Stoker, too, which compounded the guilt—and for the war, it seemed, and for his hundred personal indecisions. As it turned out, Pless was so courteous that he felt he was finally rude. By avoiding friction, the boys treated the colonel with indifference —all in the name of good manners.

Love your son, Pless had sometimes wanted to say. He thought of breaking silence with that sweet cliché: love your son. But he kept his silence and now he and Stoker were riding back there, going back to a scene dominated, probably, by Clive so that, in the end, he and the colonel would not likely ever talk together as he felt they should.

June in Vegas: the colonel had slept at his base apartment more and more as the days passed, unable to say what he wanted, unable to listen. Then July in Phoenix: working with Verna in the sporting goods store. And now August. Time runneth short, Pless reminded himself. Already the days of last year at school rattled in his head and he thought of going back and he could see and hear it all: Clive's voice, the frozen wind off Lake Michigan, the drab buildings and classrooms, Addie's lost face staring out of the greenhouse, the icy sidewalks over in Washington Park, Verna's plaintive letters, Stoke's grin, the war, Clive's voice again, the bell that tolls for thee. He wanted to have something important to say of it all, some password to utter, but he didn't. Stoker had accused him of having his life in order, but it wasn't true; he had known, once, who he was—when he had been only a slightly eccentric adolescent, deliberately different in small ways. But now he felt himself waiting and watching, and he wondered if he should keep a diary, if he should write down all that waylaid his senses in the guise of normalcy this summer.

Clive and Addie were supposed to tour around San Francisco before joining them at Vegas; by now, Pless calculated, they had made that scene, seeing all those high school types (remember the oregano!) who went out to the coast to search for brothers, lovers, and the beginnings of a new and dreamy family. The magazines had made it all normal out there too, all those swell kids gathering at the ocean to pin flowers on each other, to go adream. Normal. And the armies continued to gather in Cambodia. Normal. And the neons of Vegas gleam in the desert of time. And mother, sweet Verna, resides in the arms of the bachelors of Phoenix. And Stoker, dear heart, wonders if Clive puts him on. Everything normal.

He thought of Hoover Dam, which they approached. He thought of his father, then, the major, who always understood that leisure is a distress, who was always, as he said himself, the restless driver of a supersonic bus. He was always a man with a gentle way, the most thoughtful person Pless had ever known. He watched people, the major did, and made sure that their glasses were filled and listened when they talked. One of the great listeners—unlike the colonel, who sometimes tuned out Stoker in mid-sentence. The major created talk, and in the old days back at Eglin AFB in Florida Pless could recall how they sat out in the yard at night and watched the sentimental stars and the unfeeling satellites swimming overhead and how they gushed and philosophized together, Verna too, until one of them would eventually fall asleep and break the spell of the evening. "I seem to have too much time now," the major used to say as they sat there. "My thoughts go astray. I think it's probably the life I live as an executive mechanic. That's all this pilot business is. If I had it to do over again, I'd become a reader of books. I just don't read enough, Pless, not nearly so much as you do. It's a fault."

The major had been a gambler, too, and lucky. He won four thousand dollars that year he spent in Vietnam. Liked to go TDY once or twice a year in Las Vegas so he could play the tables. Liked to push his luck, too, Pless supposed, for there it was, suddenly: high above the bay at Fort Walton Beach, pushing it a little, laughing (Pless always imagined that he was laughing hard at the time, his head thrown back in his usual way), his wingtip had caught reality and had brought him down. He probably died worrying about Phillips in the other plane, wondering if poor Phillips got out. No, perhaps not. He died, probably, pinned in the centrifugal force of his spin, full of a final disbelief. All was not normal, papa, Pless could say now, no matter how it looked.

Think of something else, Pless commanded himself. Don't let the major cobweb your thoughts. Think of something— not Verna either, if you can help it, because her life is a temporary mire where one shouldn't make estimates. Watch and wait. But in spite of himself, he made estimates, concluding: she didn't love the major enough, couldn't get over being a little annoyed by his thoughtfulness and his goodness, and that knowledge burns her. She screws all the willing wingmen of Phoenix in order to punish herself in that knowledge. So sad. Such sad and elemental psychology. In truth, the major awed and appalled people, Verna certainly included, with his kindness, and now Verna, thirty-nine lovely years old, was the victim of psychic hangover.

Pless remembered an evening in mid-July when he went with Verna to a restaurant in the mountains north of town, an evening of psychic wounds all around when one of her jealous flyboys stopped at the table. The young officer was scarcely older than Pless and full of angry glances. He wouldn't sit down and he wouldn't leave, just kept lingering, tactful and chatty. Then Verna introduced Pless as her son, and the young man's face rose in bright relief. He leaned on the table, flirted with Verna, stood there waiting to be invited to sit down. Name's Peter Boudreau, he told them merrily. Pete Boudreau, fellah, glad to meetcha. That's my moniker. 'Scuse me, but yer lookin' awful sweet, Verna, babe. Finally, Pless had looked up and delivered his one line: "Buzz off, you asshole," he told him. It surprised everyone, even Pless, coming out like that. His Bogart routine.

Driving home that evening he had expected his mother to have plenty to say, but she sat in the car drawing on her cigarette, no expression in her eyes at all. This, of course, was her pattern: when Pless needed her to keep silent, she usually jabbered; when he expected her to jabber, she usually crawled into herself and shut a tiny but impassable door. Sometimes she talked much as the colonel did that morning at Nellis, telling Pless and Stoker things they had known all their lives, talking mostly to assure herself that she was there, that the boys were there. In spite of himself, then, Pless made estimates of Verna. Jack Daniels, Johnny Walker, Ezra Brooks and all those gentlemen of the rocks and soda set had ruined her complexion. Also she smoked too much.

Think of something else, he decided. Hoover Dam. He found that they had arrived, that they were going down into the bowels of that phenomenon. Think of poor Addie, he told himself, the thread of his overworked brain almost snapped;

think of Stoker, leaning against me, all konked, deep in his innocent sleep; think of Clive all dressed in black. We converge at Vegas, and it somehow fits. Think of the four of us, sad and hung-up, and it somehow fits as we go down to Hoover Dam, taking these canyon turns like the daredevil major would do it, like Mario Andretti of the Arizona strip. Stoker tilted first one way and then the other. Tock.

Clive: he seems—and Pless searched for a metaphor—like a one-eyed man. With one eye he was blind to others and to everything: a bore, a talker who never listened, a cheap showman, an intellectual vulture, insensitive as hell, a blunderer. But with his good eye, ah, it was as though he could see through steel. He saw the dung of the dynasty. He saw his colleagues. He even saw himself. He was a one-eyed seer, giddy with his own inexhaustible ego, perhaps, but giddy, too, with the demons. I give my puny self to others little by little, Pless concluded, full of tact and timidity, but Clive has a way of exploding into rooms; he accosts the innocent and makes them listen. Tells his endless stories. The truth of untruth lurks in his words, and oh, Pless admitted, I usually believe him, all his dripping images about his corrupt sister, Jackie, and his bedeviled papa and his awful childhood. His obsessions, his genius at the chessboard, the terrors that stride behind his eyes, his maniac beauty: I see and believe it all. Naturally he's crazy as hell. A boring black prophet, but, unfortunately, I believe him: all his fabrications. It suits me. And his poor lost self hides down there, of course, in the bullrushes of his lies, for down deep, below his bellicose tales, he's a child, abandoned and hungry, and full of ravings. Ah shit, I'm softhearted, of course; I'm probably the only person in the world who feels sorry for Clive. He addles poor Addie and stokes Stoker's fires. Yet he fits the classical psychological basket case: the outcast and exiled son (oh me, fathers & sons again) turned avenger. He has all the natural gifts, but doesn't seem to care about money or good looks or the accepted patterns of intelligence, all those assets honored in our land. Clive: obvious and mysterious.

Pless listened and heard the turbines grinding in the twilight. He nudged Stoker.

"Wake up if you want to see the dam," he said.

"I've seen it," Stoker mumbled.

"I'm stopping for a rest. You going to stay asleep or come out and spectate with me?"

"I'll sleep," Stoker mumbled tersely.

The air around Pless seemed charged and crisp. He leaned over the edge of the lookout point and saw the Colorado River like a black viper below in the twilight mist. Not many tourists walked there in the parking area, only one arm-locked couple at the spyglass. Put yr dime in the slot and get a close-up view of man's miracle! See Hoover nee Boulder, sparkplug of the continent! See how all rivers run to the sea. It's a long way to the bottom, Pless mused, a hell of a drop. A man could get wiped. Oh, me, Lazarus, if I'm ever reincarnated I want to come back as an eagle; we could wing around these canyons—the high-rolling, jackrolling, hard-eight any-craps major and I—and if our wings brushed, what's a mere feather lost to the wind? Time, as a poet somewhere uttered, is the mercy of eternity. Time, Pless ruminated, is the holy spirit. We all go down before it. He peered across to Lake Mead beyond. Awesome.

He peered off into the soft summer night. God, he asked himself, how many feet down there? Someone, he decided, probably knew exactly. Someone had counted the inches and had published the statistic in a 25¢ brochure which probably sold at the Hoover Dam souvenir stands. A long way down, whatever; distance is measured in time and time is the great god who swallows us.

He thought of the last semester at the university, those long evenings when so many students had dropped around to hear Clive rant. I was good for one or two parries myself, Pless admitted, and Addie squirmed nicely and Stoker wore his mask of winsome passion, but it was Clive, of course, who generated, Clive who stood in the middle of the room like colossus bombarding everyone with his loud esoterica. He gave us quotes from the classics, from the mystics, from old periodicals turned pastel with age which he had scoured from the library. He strutted. He brought a large blue alarm clock into the room so that even in the momentary silences it intimidated us. Tock. With his fists in the air, he directed the conversational traffic in the room; with a mere finger raised, he conducted every rebuttal. Bludgeoned the undergraduates who drifted in. When he was wrong, he was exceedingly loud; when he was right, even louder. He put everyone down arm wrestling. And he never stopped talking, as if he were afraid the pall of silence might betray his disjointed logic. Out of Clive's hurt, he hurt everyone's eardrums. And there were times, true, and Clive damn well knew it, when the drone of his voice grew almost hypnotic.

On such a night the pact was made.

Don't worry, Stoke, Pless wanted to say, we won't do ourselves in, not ever so neatly. We'll all probably live to be senile and to zap out in the grips of palsy, old men, our fingers twitching. Or perhaps we'll evaporate in the cosmic minidust of World War V. But such a night as that one last semester won't take us—just a piece of our sanity, at most, and I figure we've still got a little of that to spare. I trust our equilibrium. I have to.

But it had been a night of nights. They had gotten drunk early at Clive's apartment and had stayed drunk (it was just after the first wave of exams) long before Clive took out his big shiny razor and clipped his wrist. He had cut all the way around his wrist. It looked like a bright, red bracelet. And he had talked, then, about the long sweet sleep and about how long it would take for his body to go into shock, about twenty minutes, he said, and everyone had sat there watching his blood ooze into the wastebasket. Tock. He damn well had us, Pless admitted. You had us. We weren't grinning any longer, not even me—perhaps because I was whacked out on my usual limit of two whiskies. Good show, Clive. A hard act to follow, Stoker said. Ah, you crazy bastard. A long way down. The turbines hum in the deepened twilight.

They had sat there—Pless tried hard to remember each gesture, each detail—watching the thin trickle. Then, finally, Clive had grabbed his wrist—even so, a little kept bubbling out—and the four, mesmerized in this drama, had talked. They named all the American literary suicides they could think of: Hart Crane, Hemingway, Vachel Lindsay, Sara Teasdale, Sylvia Plath, Ross Lockridge. Then they couldn't think of any more. Too drunk. The wife of Henry Adams, Stoker added. Then other suspicious ones, even Faulkner; then they couldn't think of any of those either.

But they were on the subject. Pless recalled with regret that he himself had been the one with the plan. Sorry, Stoke, he wanted to say, I should've never uttered it.

"Now we could all give testimony by killing ourselves," he had said that night, though, and they had begun to speculate on how to do it.

Adler suggested a manifesto, but the idea was vetoed.

"Clive, dear heart, you look a little pale. Look as though you have that tired, washed-out feeling. Iron-poor blood. Have my hanky for your dripping wrist, won't you?"

"Don't mind if I do, Stoke. Thanks."

"Hell of a nice pulse you have there, by the way."

"I do the best I can."

"But donna nobody looka da wastebasket, jocko, or you getta sick in your stomick."

They were on the subject. Quotes from Cato and Camus lurched into the conversation.

"Actually," Pless added, rising to his wobbly feet, "we shouldn't leave a note of any sort. It ought to be a pure act.

Old-fashioned nihilism. We don't want to sermonize, after all, senators, so tell you what: we'll zap ourselves out one by one, see, so that everyone on campus will begin to get the idea slowly, but we'll leave no messages. No essays."

For a while they discussed what was meant by old-fashioned nihilism. It was usually too romantic, Stoker argued.

"One by one," Clive muttered from beneath his heavy lids. "Charming idea."

A cold April wind rapped at the window and so Stoker got up and walked a crooked path to the thermostat, saying, "Let's have one more round here, mates, and work out the fine details."

When the bottle toured around again, Pless declined. Addie nodded jerkily and accepted a mouthful. Clive and Stoker took dainty swigs.

"Cheers."

"Let's do it," Addie began to whimper. "I really want to do it."

"Of course we're going to do it," Stoker told him. "Don't be impatient and don't cry. You're getting so you can turn on tears like a faucet. This'll take time to develop."

Clive's eyes suddenly glowed; his adrenalin was up. "We'll draw lots," he said. "We'll put four numbers into a hat and draw. And this will be the good part: we'll keep our numbers secret from each other. Number one will be committed to die first, then two, and so on. The old honor system. When your number comes up, you go."

"Other rules?" Stoker asked.

"Well, yes, none of us should be the one to find the poor victim. Bad form. Too much shushpicion involved. Everyone will get the idea soon enough: there will be an obvious string of suicides. Ought to give rise to thoughts, shouldn't it?"

"You said *shushpicion*. I do believe you're whacked."

The subject boiled in the room. Addie's eyes were puffed and he whimpered, Stoker made a gray face. Clive's adrenalin poured and he loved every minute of it, and Pless—he remembered this distinctly—felt both guilty for having brought it up and also like a giddy Count Dracula hiding behind his cape, all filled with Gothic excitement.

"When do we begin?" Addie insisted.

"When the leaves begin to fall," Pless growled, thrusting a finger into the air like a vampire orator.

"When the leaves next fall off the trees," Stoker chanted. "When the leaves next fall off the trees . . ."

The handkerchief bit into Clive's purple wrist. Tock.

"It's a bargain, then. Solemn honor. Shall we write our names in blood?"

"Absolutely!"

"Oh, I do love a good black mass."

"Say, Clive, would you mind terribly if we use your blood? It's so available, you know."

"Be my guests."

"Shall we draw lots?"

"By all means. Let there be formalities and red tape."

"Yes, draw lots. Does anyone have a hat?"

"Here's an old stocking cap. Let us improvise!"

A cold April wind talked to them from the windowsill. Adler, trying to keep afloat of the patter, sobbed something unintelligible. Dipping their fingers into Clive's wounds, then, everyone made his mark. "Your best act of the season, Clive," Stoker noted, making his mark. Then everything was solemn. Stoker watched Clive, mesmerized, and licked his pinky clean. P: the seal of Pless. While the wind rattled the window again with soft applause, Clive, smiling, tore off four scraps from the piece of notebook paper which had served as their document and numbered them with his gore. Folding them, he stuffed them into the cap. Stoker gave him a grim glance, and Pless—he felt this now, too, driving across the desert toward Vegas—wanted to halt it all, saying, ah, dear souls, never mind; this is too much. But he kept silent.

Clive gloated and held the cap aloft. He stood up to his full height, then on his tiptoes so that he towered above them, reaching high so they could barely reach into the cap. The bottle went around for a last libation; the wind howled outside, bringing another snow to the campus, to the lakes beyond, to the whole Midwest, and there, snug in Clive's apartment, the wastebasket gave off a slight stench.

Adler stifled a sob. He was deliriously drunk and Pless, watching him, felt he could become a professional wailer that season, one who could hire himself out to funerals. A large hot tear plopped into Adler's scraggly beard and Pless grinned.

Then Clive stood up tall on his tiptoes, reaching up, the cap dangling above their heads, and they had to jump and grab their numbers from him. Pless remembered plucking out his number, wheeling around, covering it with his body so the others wouldn't see, then opening it. Number Three. Beautiful. He remembered what he thought: *I'll never have to sweat it*. And he recalled laughing aloud.

Clive went to the bathroom and returned with a can of lighter fluid. When he emptied it into the wastebasket and touched a match to it, everyone burned his number. The flames devoured all traces as Addie sniffed.

A night of nights. It had about it, Pless recalled, a certain formalized rhythm, as if somewhere in the midst of the pact, all giddy and filled with its excitement and newness and crude sensationalism, they spoke lines that seemed already written for them; or it was as if they played assigned roles, exchanging roles momentarily perhaps, but played out old parts, long rehearsed: priest, wailer, lamb, believer.

Now he stood listening to the faint hum of the turbines, thinking: this is a sad height (curse, bless me now) and all this rumination is sad and morbid and I shouldn't indulge in it. Yet there had been something about that frantic put-on of last semester, he knew, which had kept Stoker fretful, which had drawn Adler closer to his somewhat natural hysteria, which had occupied Clive and himself, all of them, so that the summer had been defined by a strained silence and ambivalence.

Slowly, Pless trudged back to the car where Stoker, sleeping heavily, curled against the door. He started the motor and turned back onto the highway toward Vegas, going toward the rendezvous with a feeling of concern and disquiet and—more than he knew he wanted to admit—anticipation.

··· 5

IT CAME TO VERNA ONCE AGAIN: a feeling that had clawed around in her for hours, since the boys left. She surveyed her bedroom in order to get her mind off it. There sits the world's most truthful mirror, she told herself; there stands the window with the curtains drawn against another night; there lie my clothes in a soft pool on the floor; and here I am abed, waiting. Nine o'clock. Her lieutenant was coming soon, but she lay there thinking of calling the colonel in Las Vegas. Yet, for what? To say what?

Thought: Pless has his own style now, something all his, a way that he cocks his head when he teases me. I love you, Pless, but I'm seriously afraid you've ruined my evening.

Thought: Lieutenant Boudreau, you're in for a paltry good time. I do not love you, Lieutenant Boudreau, and I never will; it is truly delicious, Lieutenant, to admit that I don't love you at all—especially this evening. I have this awful feeling, if you want to know, Lieutenant, as if I'm being transported, as if I'm riding in orbit around the earth and moon, my soul all broken loose and floating free. An odd and grisly sensation. I think it's death.

Thought: one needs a drink, one does. The room really reeks with my breath now and one needs a Pepsodent scrub, but one needs a drink worse. Velvet slippers for my icy feet. I go naked in velvet slippers on this stairway and it's too bad you're not arriving until ten, Lieutenant, because I might let you watch. You say you never see enough of me. Well, here it sways. I'm not really so bad—a bit heavy in the stomach lately, perhaps—for an old lady. Pless, I love you.

The glare of the kitchen lights weakened her and she sat down to investigate the remains of the bourbon. Three fingers and then futility, she told herself, and she wondered whether or not to call the colonel. He'd say it wasn't like her calling that way, being motherly, but she could say, oh, well, the boys had late dates last night and so I just wanted to make sure that they got there all right. Not exactly the truth, of course, but she reasoned that she could say it anyway; the colonel's life was mostly a pack of lies and he wouldn't know the truth if he heard it. He and Cassie had lived on lies, they had eaten lies like honey, and had died, both of them, of diabetes of the heart. Even so, she wanted to call.

Thought: I wonder what he's like now that Cassie's gone and he's a little thick in the belly too? Poor dear liar. I think I'll call him. I love you, Pless, and I really have to.

She ambled back upstairs to Pless' room. The address book was somewhere in the desk, but the room was so strewn and the desk so piled high with papers that she sighed with frustration. It was unlike him to leave his room junked up.

He had gone off again leaving behind all that he was and isn't, she felt—all the remnants of his teens and early college years, the litter that accumulates, and she was ashamed at how much she cherished every scrap. Astronomy books and mystery novels. An Encyclopedia of Famous Men inscribed by his father: a gift of Christmas, 1959. A briefcase, another Christmas gift, all stiff and unused, somehow too much of a stigma of the white collar class for him to actually carry it around campus. The photograph of the major on the bureau. Wings in a silver box, also inscribed. The paperweight bullet. The old meerschaum. Pless, she concluded, was just as sentimental as she was, and she decided to tell him so. There were also jeans and sport coats hanging in the closet, all too small for him, and cuff links in a plastic box which sat precariously on the top closet shelf.

Rummaging in the drawer, she found the leatherette address book. 702-944-4640 c/o Col Marty Stoker.

Thought: the name evokes a few memories, doesn't it, Verna? Admit it: time goes by so fast that one has to remember to remember.

She went to the living room and dialed, thinking that she'd just say she was worried since the boys had so little sleep. The phone buzzed and clicked in her ear, and she listened to the faint voices behind the buzzing, conversations off on another part of the continent full of the usual messages: family news, distress signals, why we have to save money this month, why we can't see each other anymore, why sales are down this quarter, why your voice means so much. With direct dialing, she was suddenly in Vegas.

"Hello. Marty? This is Verna."

He repeated her name dumbly.

"I'm just calling to see if the boys got there all right."

Yes, he said, they were there. They were out at the pool having a drink—all except one of them—and Pless looked fine, as if his job at the store didn't hurt him any.

"I was just worried about the drive. They stayed up so late

last night." It wasn't what she wanted to say, but she couldn't say more, couldn't tell him what a strange sensation she bore. "How're you, Marty?"

He said he was fine.

"I suppose Pless will tell you all about me. I'm still working on the same job, as you know, and I really don't see much of the old gang anymore. That was the reason I moved back here, but I really don't visit with them much and they've mostly all left Luke now. Oh, Tom Breckenridge called one day last week and mentioned seeing you." She realized how chatty she sounded, how false.

He asked about old General Barlow.

"Oh, sure, he's still here, but I heard from someone he might get another rotation back to Vietnam. Is that what's happening now? Are all of you going to get two trips out of this war?"

"Verna," he said, "I don't know a damn thing." He sounded forlorn.

"I never asked you about your year in Saigon. Was it too bad over there?"

Silence gathered on the line. A soft hum.

The colonel said it was all right, that he played a lot of tennis, actually. Then: "Listen, Verna, hearing your voice like this—well, it sets me thinking. I'll be down to Phoenix in the next few weeks. Do you think we could have a drink together? Or supper?"

Silence again, this time from Verna.

"I suppose we could," she finally said.

He asked if they could make it more specific.

"I'm home by six in the evenings," she said. "Call me again before you fly down."

"Listen," he told her, "could we say—ah, let me check. I'm looking into my little notebook. Could we say two weeks from Friday night?"

"All right, Marty."

Silence. His voice sounded so plaintive.

"I'll call when I get into town," he went on. "And, hey, I've invited the boys to stay here a few days. They can have the run of the house and a maid to take care of their meals because I can stay at the base apartment. I have this extra place out on the base."

"Pless told me."

"The boys want to go back to the university, but there's nothing up there at the end of the summer like this, I told them. Just a lot of empty buildings. I could show them a good time right here in town, if they'd let me, but you know how they are."

"That's right, I know: independent."

Another silence.

"Pless and Stoker liked being in Phoenix with you this last six weeks," he said, trying to start the conversation again.

"Did they say that?"

"No, but they enjoyed themselves."

"I appreciated how you looked after them during June," she added.

"I wish I could get them to stay now."

"Well, Marty, I'll be going. I only wanted to see that they got there safely."

"Two weeks from Friday I'll call," he said. "Don't forget."

They said their goodbyes. Poor Marty, she felt. He would come and make a plaintive proposition.

She walked back to the kitchen, thinking: I've got to put all these pans and rags and all the tag ends of my life back in place soon. She couldn't recall his voice ever being quite like that.

Going back down the hallway with a fresh drink in her hand, she had the feeling again—a small gnawing, one she was certain of having felt before, an almost mystic twitch. She tried to remember her pregnancy, tried to recall that strange feeling; it was awful: like the touch of a hand there on a tender inner part. The telephone call hadn't gotten rid of it.

I just don't think I can get dressed for you, Lieutenant Boudreau, she told herself, in spite of the fact that I need to keep our dinner date because I'm hungry and because I need a crowd around me and a few drinks and, for that matter, probably even a little of what you need yourself. What's the matter with me? The colonel's voice? His plaintive tone—not what I remember at all, and it touched me, I admit. Let's see, I saw him once after he and Cassie split, just for a moment at the base bar one night when I was with, oh, Larry Menchevee, I think it was, and he came over to our table all buttoned up, looking like a colonel, heavy tummy and all, and he seemed all in control. Like Stoke too: dark and good-looking, yet something fragile about him—just like Stoke—though both of them are, well, all man, and no doubt about it. Marty has his hair still, even some nice grey streaks which I always like. That feeling. It comes and goes in waves, and I could never describe it to anyone because it's nearly metaphysical; I feel transported, floating off.

Verna got dressed—not, she decided, for Peter Boudreau —but the feeling would not go away. Pulling on her dress she decided that poor Peter ought to find the house all dark tonight, that she should go out and have a few Manhattans alone. Then, lingering beside her mirror where she brushed her hair, the feeling battered her; she felt remote and terribly lonely and sick at heart, and she knew it was the feeling she had once had down in Florida in those curious days before the major went down in the bay. She knew that this morning, even before Pless came down to breakfast, while Stoker sat there looking at her legs, she had to have a few shots to face it, that awful tinge. There was no semblance of logic to it; she couldn't utter it because the logic of sentences could never hold it, not at all, but there it was. Oh, she told herself, I wish you were down here already, Marty, even tonight, because I'd probably try and tell you about this if I were with you. You're an old friend who fits like a glove and I'd probably try to spill this out. It'd be silly as hell, of course, but I would try, and oh, Pless, be safe. I love you and I have this feeling.

THE COLONEL TALKED ON and Clive listened, heard the whole story of his life—interrupted by that single telephone call—in a series of drunken vignettes. He sat there not saying much, hearing a monologue packed with the basic egotisms, he felt, all about the colonel's house, maid, travels, possessions.

Meanwhile one of the artifacts of the colonel's life sat beside them: a lovely chess set, ivory and ebony pieces on an inlaid board. Earlier in the evening the colonel had removed it from the cabinet (Clive had mentioned his playing, but only casually) and had set it up on the coffee table; he had told Clive about bargaining for it in a Saigon market, admitting that he had never learned the game himself. So it sat there gleaming its defiance at the colonel while he talked, Clive felt, and of course it was plain: the colonel knew nothing of games at all. Clive sat biding his time until his host faltered, waiting while the colonel discussed his son and Pless then, and not far away the murmurs of the boys themselves out at the poolside punctuated the colonel's voice. Yes, Clive answered, Stoke and Pless are very intelligent boys indeed, and, yes, Addie was a little disgruntled tonight and has gone wheezing off to bed slightly tipsy, yes, and Stoker should settle his problems with the draft board without delay, yes, and go back to the university and have himself a fine year. Nodding agreement with all this, Clive reached over occasionally and fingered the black bishop. It was properly weighted. The colonel talked on, claiming he had paid only fifty dollars for the set, ivory pieces and all. Then he began talking about the famous TFX, about how it was soon "going operational" and Clive sat listening, speculating that the colonel had no real sense of his own game.

"Our first active squadron is going over to Vietnam soon, and this is really a hell of a plane," the colonel said, "though not especially efficient for this war. No, what I mean is: up to 1.4 MOC it just isn't very spectacular in acceleration." He sipped his daiquiri.

What an evening, Clive told himself. Stoker's voice drifted in from the patio, and Clive thought: there they sit out there indulging their Great Pals Act, yes, and I wonder why Pless bothers with him. The colonel explains the butterfly pattern making his hands swoop around in the air with unsteady swoops because he's tanked with high octane daiquiri. Explains shooting the dart a light metal target pulled by a tow plane on a fifteen hundred foot cable the young pilots shoot at it, yes, and it measures sixteen and five feet and it's so hard to hit, boy, the competition is rough among those kid pilots. The colonel's whole creaming life is a game but the rules, yes, he doesn't really know the rules his student fighters fly around in the glee of air tactics but the great game baffles him and I can tell.

The colonel talked on, mentioning the Thunderbird Squadron, a close-formation flying outfit.

Stunt flying, yes, and air tricks all daredevils they go around to air shows and create good public relations for the corps (corpse) and, yes, colonel, it's a game but you haven't grabbed it so here we sit with the ebony squares gleaming. And yes, I hear what you're saying: the Thunderbird Hotel and Casino of Las Vegas, Nevada, tried to make a gift of a new Thunderbird sports car, yes, to each member of the famed Thunderbird Air Force Squadron, but the brass squelched that one, yes, and for more than two hours now we've had this sort of thing: petty military politics and all your toys and gimmicks. The good colonel is taller than Stoke, gray at the temples and getting good and smashed now, yes, because of the way his tongue labors in his mouth I can tell.

I'd explain the greater games to you, Colonel, but you'll find out for yourself soon enough just as in chess you'll learn to get the white team then manage to make the first moves and create your own strategies and patterns then arrange to never lose the advantage. You learn to stay one move ahead always politic and your patterns on the board finally begin to look like reality to your opponent, colonel, so that it becomes almost impossible for him to stare into your pattern and imagine anything outside it. Well, the metaphor breaks down because all is not chess and there are sometimes more rules in chess, truth be told, then in some of the greater games but in all cases the principle holds: there are patterns set there are leaders and followers movers and zombies winners and losers. Oh it gives me pleasure.

"These are terrible times," the colonel said. "Let me tell you some things that have happened right here in town."

Yes. Wives on the base, you say, are getting crank calls nowadays from sadists and untrustworthy Americans who ring in the middle of the night and say Your Husband Is Dead Over There, Baby, and We're All Glad the Killer Went Down.

Like that. Right in the middle of the night and you don't know what the world is coming to, you have your doubts about this era just the same as Stoke or anyone else but what's the world coming to? You spill a sip down your collar, colonel, and shake your head, and I nod and say I don't know what's what either, though I do: we're in the midst of the greater games of course and the rules are written by hands few of us can see or touch.

"A drink, Clive? A small one?"

"No, nothing."

Now the greater game comes only occasionally, of course, and one sits waiting for that rarity, sitting idly by like a substitute player on the old chess team half hoping that illness befalls one of the members of the main squad so that he can get into action. One waits. (Oh, me, yes, the chess team long ago my prodigy years.)

The colonel rambled, talking about the TFX or F-111 again. The supersonic topic strays back into the monologue, Clive sighed to himself.

But watch my hands of course because I'm working an art. Adler my scientific colleague and Stoker, your son and my dear friend of letters, promise that they will someday write (perhaps even a long novel, Stoker once said, full of seductions, deductions and brittle sentences) but I compose at the greater game. Make no mistake of it. I compose right now. Occasionally the great script and the great director find themselves together almost mysteriously and the great game is on; I've seen myself working this art the last few months if you want to know, old tippler, and I've conducted conversation in a room as though I waved a baton at an orchestra of mediocre talkers making them say what I wanted and feel what I wanted them to. The pleasure of it. Monstrosity. And chess is just mere apprenticeship in comparison these last few weeks in San Francisco with rooms filled with flower children and Adler sitting there like Igor the Mad Assistant.

I held sway. That night last spring in Chicago, too, yes, and now, even here there are two kinds either winners or losers and you prevail or you don't and even now as you jabber on I know you'll loll back against your chair finally, sigh, and surrender to my devices. Your drunken resistence will drop. Take on the authority in the room, always, I say, and beat him, then watch the others follow. The great game. Training rules forever of course: stay cool, drink nothing nor shoot anything into the system that might injure the faculties, abstain and concentrate, enjoy, if it happens, the psychic storm. So watch my hands, old sot, I don't intend losing the move ever; I've lost before and it does not please.

"A student pilot was killed just a few days ago on the bombing range," the colonel was saying. "He was flying a fourteen-year-old bird due to the shortage of planes with the war on. The thing just disintegrated."

Yes, Clive thought, watching the colonel's eyelids droop with the ninth or tenth daiquiri that sloshed inside of him, I hear all you say, all about how his wing came off, yes, and though you're no pacifist like your grandfather you do, yes, have a humanitarian sense too and after all, yes, we live in a barbaric world. Lovely, your muddled views. It's time to make my first small move. Castle and check.

"I suppose you've seen a lot of violent death, haven't you, Colonel?"

"Yes," he answered, "all kinds of death. Pieces of bodies strewn around the desert. All things." He pronounced the name of God.

"When I lived with my father and sister in Ankara," Clive began slowly, "there used to be public executions. Have you ever been to Ankara by any chance?"

The colonel said no, only to parts of the Far East, England, and once, briefly, to North Africa.

"Well, Ankara is a glutted city. It has its new buildings and habits, but a lot of the Turks are on dope, as you've probably heard. But more than that—the city has a narcotic aura."

The colonel, his face struggling for control, flushed with drink and weariness, mentioned hearing of the Turks in the Korean war, how they cut off the hands of thieves in their camps and went out at night with knives in their teeth when the gooks had the nerve to disrupt their dances and singing with a stray mortar shell.

Clive nodded, smiled, and dismissed the story. "We had an apartment down in the old part of Ankara. The old fort area. There were shutters on the windows and motes of sunlight floating in the room. It was always hot."

The colonel asked about Clive's father, his business and the reasons why he went to Turkey. A bad question.

"Imports and exports," Clive explained hurriedly. "He took up permanent residence in Ankara after he divorced my mother. I was over there two years—actually, a little longer—and roamed around Greece and the islands with him."

The colonel nodded, fighting against his drowsiness.

"It was always hot and the plumbing never worked. In fact, there were few services of any sort in the city. The waiters were poor. And in Turkey everyone masters the machine by letting it lie dead—once it breaks down. Nothing gets repaired. The roadsides are packed with abandoned automobiles. So anytime something broke down in our apartment, we had to fix it ourselves."

The colonel nodded.

"The Turks like things broken and helpless. Destruction is a form of possession. That idea. It gives them a hell of a satisfaction."

Stoker and Pless suddenly appeared in the doorway, Stoker yawning. Pless broke into Clive's rhythm with: "What're you giving the colonel there, Clive? The old Turkish delight?"

"The same," Clive said. He smiled, not wanting to appear annoyed.

"He's never been to Turkey," Pless informed their host.

"I don't think the colonel minds," Clive answered.

"Haven't been there?" The colonel looked up, scuttled.

"A put-on," Stoker added. "He's psyching you, Papa."

Clive, weighing the turn of events and sensing the need to grow more elaborate, said: "I was about to tell you about the public executions, Colonel."

Stoker and Pless moved wearily across the room. Before they turned upstairs toward bed, Pless paused in the doorway.

"I was about to tell you, Colonel, how I went to this hanging. They pulled the thief up by oxen, you see, and that's a slow way of going. So tradition allows anyone in the poor victim's family—a brother, a cousin—to force his way through the police guard and run and jump on the man's legs. That breaks his neck, you see, as an act of mercy. Well, naturally, there I was standing in the crowd near the front when this man behind me starts trying to fight his way through. I was just trying to help the policemen who were all around, so I grabbed this frantic spectator and held him. Service to the law, you see. And all the time the poor devil on the end of the rope was turning blue and wiggling like a fish."

The colonel watched blankly, trying to make this out.

"Bravo, Clive," Pless put in.

"He pulleth your leg, faithful Father," Stoker added, and he turned and went upstairs.

"The Turk *is* a slimy devil," Clive continued. "Always grinning at you and holding a knife behind his back. That's a true picture."

"You haven't been to Turkey?" the colonel asked, frowning.

"And the belly dancers," Clive went on. He paused, giving the colonel an opportunity to interrupt, but the colonel, he knew, would want to hear about the belly dancers and wouldn't break in. "A good belly dance is like a rape," he said. "Overpowering."

"See you in the morning," Pless called.

"How is it like a rape?" the colonel wanted to know.

With the others gone, Clive sighed, finished the dregs of his cold coffee, languished in a long pause, then began on the colonel once more. The colonel looked at him oddly, some-what askance, but Clive paid that no attention.

"Forget all I said about Ankara," he said generously. "There are other matters for you and me. I feel that we can talk. Right?"

The colonel smiled a drunken crooked grin. "You're a lot like my grandfather," he said, and Clive thought what a stupid thing it was to say.

"Oh? How's that?"

"Well, he was a storyteller too. Liked the whoppers."

"But you like stories, don't you, sir?"

"Of course. Go on. I was just observing."

Pless in the Bathroom/Clive, oh, Clive. You'll keep the poor colonel bobbing like a cork. You have him nodding in agreement with everything you say and he knows you're lying. Oh me, here I sit on this cold, cold john and I'm not at all sure we can go from A to B. I take out my colored pencil and sketch a flower on the wall above the toilet tissue. There. Just like I learned to draw the American Beauty rose in elementary school. Stem and all, like my tattoo. Very decora-tive. I'm half asleep and the bath mat pattern blurs and hypnotizes me; ah, it suits me. And what have we here? The daily paper and *Time* issuing the late reports: Cross My Napalm with a Little Hard Cash. Local Couple Nabbed While Indulging in Marat/Sodomy. Golden Gate Bridge Snaps. Jesus Back. Empire State Crumbles & Angers Four Doormen & Mayor. Hootenanny Scheduled. This Here Genuine Western Style Bar-B-Q Set in Yr Cecil Price Range. Big Roundup of JFK Assassins: Sam the Sham, Minnesota Fats, Ringo Starr and Zorro. General Motors Declares War on Lithuania. Polaroid up One Fifth. Assistant Professors Publish and Perish. Arnold Palmer Sucks Nine Irons. H. Rap Brown Eats Collards. Kill a Commie for Christ. All Reveres Ride to the Sea. Philosophize with Me on All This, please sir. Oh No, I Just Kant. Oh, dear Clive, Stoker worries about you, Addie worries about you, and now the colonel will worry too. You're just worrisome. Let there be a flower (red) above the toilet tissue (white) in the colonel's bathroom (yellow). There.

Adler in Asthmatic Insomnia/God Is Dead. America and Europe Are Dead. Love Is Dead. The Sky Is Dead. Oceans and Flowers: Dead. The Month of August: Dead. State of Nevada: Dead. Lake Michigan: Dead. Everything Is Dead except Death. List of things I will count before three o'clock in the morning, which is now, by my estimation, one hour and twenty minutes away: the sad, reddish whiskers on my father's slovenly chin, the shotguns in his basement and the hedgerows around the farm, seedling boxes in my greenhouse, cans of frozen daiquiri mix in the downstairs refrigerator, pores in my skin, number of words uttered by Clive since last Wednesday, the foolish grins of Pless, the corners of this room, the crevices of my heart, the colonel's brass buttons, the stars beyond the window, the tender ticktock of the new ice age, the entries on this list. I wheeze like a broken computer. Tereu.

Stoker, Undressing/My body is a citadel of petty vices; why did I have to get off here in the sewing room alone? I should have slept in a room with someone else as a safeguard. Now I'll take myself fondly in hand, squander myself in the dream of a few lewd nudes, and jack-be-nimble off I'll go. The old sewing room. Except Cassie never sewed a stitch in here; she didn't even read or watch her portable television set. She primped. Primped in the sewing basket mirror, darkened a lash or made her mouth with that little lipstick brush and compact which she kept among the spools. Tonight when I gave the colonel her letter, casually, of course, he looked at me and asked where I planned to sleep. In the sewing room, I said, and he shrugged. We play house around here as if it isn't haunted. So down in the living room the colonel sits under Clive's bombardment, that letter crushed in his hip pocket and festering under him like a sore—because no matter how drunk he gets he knows it's there and he'll jerk it out and sniff it and read it when he finally staggers off and out of Clive's range. He'll find something in it to cry about, something to worry over, something to pity, to hate, to laugh at, to spit on. A fragile thing, that letter: it's like a leaf pressed in an old book that falls out occasionally to vex us. I'm undressing now, but not for bed; I'll never sleep. Perhaps I'll slip on a pair of bathing trunks and take a swim. Perhaps go window shopping next door where the colonel tells me the daughter of the family loves to parade divorced and bare-assed from window to window. Pless will read himself to sleep, as usual. Addie will be propped up on three or four pillows, rasping with asthma, cursing himself. (I heard him sneeze when I passed his door a moment ago. No one sneezes in his sleep, so I know he's awake.) And Clive: he'll go on talking until the colonel fades on him; then he'll slump upstairs and take his nocturnal body to bed. And after my swim I'll trudge back here. The sewing room. I feel guilty for everything, for Cassie and the colonel and myself, for Pless and Addie, for tolerating Clive, for not taking myself in hand and, conversely, for doing it too often. Guilt: I feel it for those things for which I'm absolutely innocent, even for innocence itself. For instance I know—though I haven't done very well with girls— that I'm no homosexual. True, I'm dependent on Pless, but is every relationship necessarily sexual just as Clive and my psychology instructor insist? And is old Professor Coulter right when he says that one inevitably affirms those things he imagines he denies—just as all atheists unwittingly affirm God? What sort of reasoning is that? What logic? Screw it. So there's guilt for everything, all those sweeping international disorders Pless and Addie ponder, sure, I worry about them, but mostly I suffer myself, all my puny relationships and inadequacies. Here I am with the colonel again. We always vie for the Great Guilt Championship. And Cassie used to be in the act: always overwhelmed by those things she most adored: her body, her face, her freedom, her occasional sexual gluttony. She hated the colonel and felt guilty for that. Once, in a fury, she detailed for me just how much she despised him, how his piddling annoyed her, how his military neatness sickened her, and how his constant mismanagement of money frustrated her. Then for a year after that outburst, of course, she tried to atone with me for that moment of lost control. She felt guilty for feeling guilty. Once, I remember, I found them in bed together. I was about sixteen years old; it must have been in Florida while we were stationed at Eglin. There they were in the middle of the afternoon, Cassie and the colonel, thrashing around atop the sheets like young colts. Cassie was mortified for weeks after I walked in, up tight with guilt again. "Forget what you think you saw!" she commanded me, and in spite of myself I laughed. Then, later, when she asked my opinion (she shouldn't have asked, I told her) I said yes, yes you should probably divorce him. So I shared that neat decision—and her tremors of conscience. And now poor Cassie—who never sewed in the sewing room—is spending her life and her young Richard's fortune diverting herself. Always guilt. And so I undress; the sewing room stares at me and I stare back. I'll go swimming.

Adler in Drowsy Hostility/The famed *Fédération Internationale des Echecs* announces the Main Event of the Evening: Bobby Fischer vs Chicago's Own Boy Wonder and Meanest Man in the World, Clive. Ten Rounds or Less. Weapons: Chain and Mace, chosen by the challenger. One pace, six inches. Added Tag Team Match: HH Holmes and Howie Unruh vs Charlie Whitman and Dick Speck. Special Event: Erasmus High School vs the Detroit Riot Squad. Opening Bout: Lightweights: Mocha Dick (White Hooded Again, By Popular Demand) vs Clive's Sister, Jackie. Let me think on the violent possibilities. I will go downstairs after everyone is asleep and break all the umbrellas in the colonel's hallway rack. I'll snap their spines and set them around on the lawn like black petunias. Then, lo, I'll throw my arms to the sky and pray for the descent of the demons, like Clive in one of his mystic trances: pour forth, ye sweet St. Elmo's fire! I'll draw my hand slowly up my thigh while I lie here in bed, slowly, then I'll pounce and rape myself. I'll invent an elaborate toy with directions for easy use: lie in bed and pull the string; string travels across pulley into kitchen where it flicks the switch on the stove; burner #3 then heats kettle of water; steam spews from kettle's narrow neck, burns rope (cut nearly through) and rope breaks; pulley snaps and flatiron falls on seesaw apparatus; acid tablet springs into air, lands in bucket; bucket of acid spews and fumes burn string attached to second flatiron; flatiron, attached to shotgun trigger, falls to floor and shotgun discharges, blowing a hole in the wall here beside my head. Shit, but science is a farce.

Pless in the Colonel's Library/The colonel's books don't lie: he's an absolute romantic. Yet I might be one too. Clive is about as sentimental as a python; Stoker loves the flesh, but believes lust is purer than sentiment, and only during a few Otis Redding songs have I ever seen him really soul it; and Addie is a naked soul, an open wound, but not the optimist all good romantics are required to be. The colonel's books tell his life. Civil War, history of military campaigns, Philip Wylie, John Steinbeck, French maid easy, and oops, the tattered paperbacked Frank Harris. The colonel wants a little Horatio Alger sex, of course, but he's the nostalgic sort, too, which none of us are. Oh, perhaps I am with thoughts of the major always fumbling around in my brain, but none of the four of us make friends easily nor even have friends outside of ourselves, nor stand for the usual student drivel, all the sophomorish emotional cramps like: "Oh, alack, Pless, I have this reality crisis!" Most of the other students at school reek with softness and sanity, and they complain about it, worry that they ought to be somehow more garbled. Perhaps we are different, the four of us, as Clive insists. Perhaps we'll do it: pull the stopper and all go down together. Perhaps.

Clive sat back, still talking, pleased that the colonel had managed to stay awake. In the past hour they had run a whole gamut of talk, Clive assuming most of the burden, and now he was concluding some stories about the belly dancers of Ankara, how they could be hired—he added this casually and watched the colonel's droopy eyes widen—for private dining rooms. "They'll dance naked for the customers in there, you know, and pick up coins off the table with their slits, if such acrobatics are appreciated. Or they'll dance right down on top of your hammer, I'm told, and bring you off without missing a beat of the music. But, well, I didn't go to those places much because, truthfully, the damned food was always too highly seasoned. My whole time in Turkey I had indigestion." He yawned, but watched the colonel carefully for any response.

His gambit was simple: to keep the old boy guessing and thinking, to impale him with variations on a theme.

Violence, then: "Of course those Turks are rabid in almost everything, sir. They'll stab each other over a glass of arak. All sex is rape and all violence is sexual to them too, I believe."

The colonel asked what he meant.

"Well, they kill each other a lot. And they love to read about murder in their newspapers much as we do. And this proxy experience is a sort of sexual thing, a voyeurism, you see, just as we have in our country: everybody loves the murderer because he does it *for* us. The thrill of the newspaper details! You know what I mean. We like to know all the interesting bits about our murderers' lives, where they spend their last night, what they had for supper before the fatal moment, what their mothers were like."

The colonel gave him a blank and sleepy look.

"Sex and death are actually one," Clive went on. "It's just clearer in some cultures than in others, and in Turkey it seemed obvious. All weapons are phallic, I mean. And the love act and the act of violent death have amazing continuities, always. And in Latin, for instance, the words for *sheath* and *vagina* are the same."

Clive rose from his chair, ambled toward the colonel, and stood beside his chair. The colonel's head went slowly back and he gazed up as Clive drew himself up to his full height. It was exactly the effect Clive wanted: a subtle intimidation. He wanted to be very tall, very large, and coldly logical and lucid with his host.

"War," he went on, "is the great sexual game. You could say that castration is the goal. And enemies are always, in a sense, lovers. They experience an interesting comradeship in their fear. And the true soldier—the real killer—is always glad to have an object to murder. He wants to put his training to work and mate with his victim in a little dance of death, you see."

Standing above the colonel, slumped indifferently, Clive looked down and smiled.

"Or you can say it another way," he went on. "In death, lovers and enemies both enjoy a union—a sort of oneness in the act. Sex is a little death and the orgasm—you've heard this many times—is a small dying."

The colonel leaned back, gawking.

"Ah, those Turks," Clive said, moving away. He stood across the room grinning, then returned to an earlier image of the evening: the story about the man who tried to break through the crowd during the hanging. Repeating part of this, Clive smirked and shook his head and the colonel, nervously, tried to smile.

Soon Clive changed topics, telling the colonel about his father and sister. "Jackie was my mother's daughter by a previous marriage," he explained, "and so it was something of a trauma when she joined my father and me in Ankara. I was only fourteen years old, barely pubic, and the whole mess—I'm trying not to exaggerate this or dismiss it—affected me. They had more than a little incestuous taste, I'm afraid, sir. Everyone started touring through that apartment: a young chauffeur for an American diplomat, a shepherd boy, a few assorted nymphets, an old lady who did tricks with a big mirror, all sorts."

Clive went over, paused for effect beside the colonel again, took the colonel's glass, walked back across the room and refilled it. The colonel sat forward in his chair now, listening. He was doing a little instant psychoanalysis, Clive knew, and so Clive allowed the silence to gather in the room for a moment. He speculated on just how much reality to mix in. The colonel folded his hands under his chin and leaned forward.

"My father had been in business here in America," he went on, "but things in the family snapped apart so he decided to get away, to visit his business interests on the other side. Well, we went over to Turkey and got slovenly inside and out. I'll try and describe him for you: he wore blue jeans and Wellington boots and a turban and sunglasses. Also he almost immediately lost his hair. Shaved irregularly. Drank too damned much. And, in short, he lost his business, and he was in a bad way long before Jackie arrived, true, but she was also the last rock that took him to the bottom. My sister is one of the really bad people on earth. Her juices poison people."

The colonel rested his chin on his hands and watched Clive dreamily.

"Did you ever by any chance have a sister of your own?" Clive asked. He felt his temples pulsing slightly as he watched the colonel.

Yes, the colonel nodded. Name of Neddie.

"Then you can understand a little," Clive went on, "about

how mixed my feelings have always been. I loved Jackie, but there she was: all venom and bile. Not that I'm making any comparison, sir, between our sisters. I'm sure your Neddie was a normal girl. And good. But not Jackie. Even Mother saw the dreadful cycle with Jackie: all of her own mistakes and horrors come round again. Mother had four marriages, you see. My father drifted in the misty flats. And I went to Ankara —I'm trying to explain all this to you in a capsule, of course, sir—trying to salvage, selfishly, someone in my family for myself, but it just didn't work out that way. In fact, I became the family photographer. Jackie always wanted to pose with my father. Constantly. They loved to study their bodies on film."

"You mean they posed together nude?" the colonel wanted to know.

Clive poured himself a third cup of coffee, measuring it out deliberately, and didn't answer.

"Jackie on the balcony above the city, on the bed with the young chauffeur, with the old lady's mirror, in a room of mosaic tile: I learned her moods with a camera. She called me her shuttercock."

"Oh, come on," the colonel said. "I can't believe it was at all like that."

"Here, then," Clive said, and he opened his wallet and flashed a photo before the colonel: a girl astride a beach ball, naked breasts glistening in the harsh sunny glare of the Black Sea. "I took this at a resort we visited."

The colonel studied it, his eyes diving into the pores of her skin. He wondered if it were really Clive's sister; drowsy, befuddled, his eyes burning, he continued to listen.

Clive snapped the wallet shut and started another gambit: an appeal to the colonel's fatherly instincts. First he talked about how his father had become a sort of hippie, a middle-aged one, with his hair and beard overgrown, his clothes a mixture of East and West, male, female, and neuter. Then he said: "You may also notice how Stoke lets his hair grow nowadays. It's really part of a subtle death drive, as I see it: the yearning for a kind of asexual identity, a form of dropping out, of accepting no role. My father got like that, sir, and it was pitiful to see. I told Stoke only a few days before school was out last semester: 'Get yourself a haircut. Straighten up.' Because I recognized the signs. I'd seen them with my own father."

The colonel didn't exactly see the connection and said so. His brow knitted.

"Stoker," Clive told him, "is very near a serious nervous disorder. He's a hung-up boy. I mean everyone likes him, of course, and thinks he's superintelligent and all that, but you know him, sir—there are signs. He has his troubles."

The colonel nodded drunkenly and fell silent.

Clive then went on to the next subject: money. Once again, the colonel stirred and listened.

"After my father's business failed we just toured around the Mediterranean, taking trips over to Athens and Cyprus and Alexandria."

"Didn't you say your father went bankrupt?" the colonel interrupted.

"Well, yes, but it was a *planned* bankruptcy," Clive answered. "How can a rich American with any foresight at all really go bankrupt these days? He stashed a little money, signed over some properties to others for safekeeping, even made Jackie and me partners and shareholders. Actually we had more real money after he stopped his trade."

"Er, how much?" The colonel cleared his throat, surprised at himself for taking the direct approach. He wanted to know, though; he always wanted to know about money, how others handled it while he always botched it.

"Money," Clive said, not really answering him again. "I'm only interested in it insofar as it buys me time or travel.

Possessions I don't need. Oh, a good camera and a few clothes, but not much."

"That's a good way of looking at it," the colonel assured him. "A young man ought to kick around, study, think about life and who he is."

Clive told him how they traveled to Russia and Arabia. "Jackie was always with us," he said.

"I'd like to have a nice lodge in the mountains," the colonel said. "Bear rugs and all that."

"I don't need possessions, nor places for very long. Both places and things weight the body."

"Listen, Clive, I've never handled money very well. I admit it. As a result, I've spent half my goddamned life worrying over it. Take my advice. If your father passes any cash your way, teach yourself a business sense." The colonel's eyes glazed, and for a moment Clive wondered if he might pull out his bank book or his gold watch.

Another topic. Clive ruminated on his early life for the colonel, telling him about the days when he used to play chess. "We lived in Arlington Heights, Illinois," he began. "In those days my father owned little shops there and in Evanston. This was before he decided to handle all his imports himself and before Mother aged him with all her extramarital antics and before Jackie started getting into trouble in the back seats of automobiles and on blanket dates up at the Fox River marinas. Everything was tense, you know, but simple. Father had only one lawyer, mother had only one lover. But then all my first trouble started."

The colonel yawned, but paid attention.

"I became obsessed with cleanliness, for instance, and kept washing my hands. Several times a day. And rubbed my lips with tissue sometimes until they bled. And became terrified of all my blemishes and pimples." Clive watched his host, observed him psyching him again, and he went on, casually, as drowsiness seemed to settle on the colonel like a fog. "I joined a chess club," he continued, "and played tournaments down near the old Chicago armory. There were lots of good junior players in those days, mostly from the universities and from the night schools down in the Loop. And I soon envied hell out of the students. They were all cool and older and tough. That's probably why I'm still in school, because of those early instincts. Chess and the academe burrowed into me. In those days, you see, I had such little control—and those students seemed to have so much. They knew everything and I knew nothing; they had things too. Clothes and cars. Only at chess could I ever become their equal, I suppose, so that's why I learned quickly and beat them. Soon I was the king directing my board. Hell, I *became* a chessman. Are you listening?"

"Of course, go on."

"About that time I picked up my taste for travel too. I went to the junior tournaments in Oklahoma City and St. Louis and won. And I discovered that the only way to handle the riot inside my family was to get cold and canny too. Then when my mother and father split, Jackie went reeling off on her own and I ended up living with my aunt. She indulged me and still does. I have her credit cards with me still and she never complains. But all this probably doesn't lead anywhere and you're sleepy, aren't you?"

"I'm listening," he said with palsied politeness.

"Then after Ankara, finally, I went back to Chicago and lived sort of half and half with my aunt and Jackie."

"You lived with that sister of yours?"

"Mostly with the aunt. Aunt Leslie—a conveniently masculine name because I've always been able to sign her name to bills in a pinch. Anyway, Jackie was in Chicago, yes, and I watched her glut herself. She had a number of jobs, got on the bottle, took the Lesbos special, took all rides—and not really a joyride in the whole itinerary. So I bounced back and forth between Aunt Leslie's Gothic life and Jackie. Oh, it was lovely, sir. Aunt Leslie kept two old dusty bicycles parked in the parlor of her flat; Jackie had an apartment of mirrors."

"And whatever happened to your sister?" the colonel asked.

"Oh, she travels again. At present she's the wicked witch of the south. Buenos Aires. Rio. Hell, I don't think I know exactly."

The colonel yawned again, hiccoughed, and Clive started another subject, this time, briefly, the arts and music. "Would you mind slipping some music on the phonograph for us, sir?" he began.

"Huh? Oh, wouldn't mind at all. What would you like to hear?" The colonel shuffled toward his over-chromed stereo set with the last dregs of his energy.

"Anything will do," Clive said. "Music is one of the minor arts, but I always like a little of it before bedtime." The colonel nodded, and Clive was pleased with himself for suggesting this; putting a record onto the turntable, the colonel seemed to revive. "I think of music as a minor art," Clive went on, "because it lacks the blackness that, say, literature has. Music is beauty: all harmony and rhythm—with the exception of a few discordant modern pieces that never catch on. But life is pretty much discord and chaos. Art ought to reflect that, it seems to me. An aesthetic point, true, but my opinion. What sort of music do you like, Colonel?"

"Oh, all kinds." The colonel yawned again. By this time, Clive estimated, his host was beyond discourse.

The subject didn't last much longer. Soon Clive was talking about sex again and about Jackie. "She based her whole exotica on music," he explained. "Especially the music of certain non-Western instruments like the sitar or the balalaika or the zither. I suppose she felt the bizarre was superior. And she had elaborate stereo equipment, like you, sir, and moved it around from apartment to apartment as she got tired of places. She moved every six months or so, by the time the walls got dirty and the neighboring husbands and bachelors had been ruined. Her principal occupation, see, was always ruining lives."

"She sounds complicated," the colonel managed.

"There were nights when I stayed with her—that would be when I was, oh, fifteen or sixteen years old—and her music would bang around the walls of my room and I would lie in bed and listen to her lovers visit. They always played the stereo loud and had to yell above the music, shout at each other. Those apartment-house residents—they'd come sneaking across the patios, usually escaping their wives' kitchens, and Jackie would ruin them one by one. They became addicted to her. She had music, incense, and all the bizarre tricks of Ankara."

"Well," the colonel said uneasily. "I'd like to meet your sister. If it's all that." He ventured a weak laugh.

Meanwhile, the turntable clicked and music began to trickle from the colonel's ensemble: guitar music, Charlie Byrd.

"Now, then, sir, do you keep yourself in shape?" Clive asked, rising to his feet again. This was his final maneuver and he gave the colonel a manly grin. "You ever do the old Air Force calisthenics anymore?"

"I'm not exactly in shape, no," the colonel admitted. "Tell you the honest truth, son, I'm a little drunk. What'd you have in mind?"

"A little hand-wrestling. Why don't we just loosen the old muscles?"

"I thought you liked music before bedtime. Something soothing," the colonel said.

"Here on the coffee table is fine," Clive said, removing the chess set.

"Oh, none of that for me. Too late in the evening." The colonel demurred and waved his daiquiri at Clive. "You're a tough kid, is that it? You want to make the old man hurt?"

"It'll loosen the muscles, really."

"I'll get sore. I won't be able to pull the throttle."

"I do this every day," Clive said. "When I can find an opponent. It makes the blood run."

Clive fixed him with a stare and finally the colonel rolled up his sleeve and dropped down on his knees beside the table; both their arms were thick and brown with dark hair and their knuckles were large. The colonel removed his wristwatch ceremoniously, talking all the time. He said it was late and they should get to bed. They felt each other's grip.

"You're a big guy," the colonel observed.

"Count of three all right with you, sir?"

The colonel's hand went steadily backward and down. "I never did much of this," he said.

Then they went again. Sweat glistened on the colonel's forehead as he tried to turn Clive's hand over, but Clive held, patiently, until their entire arms and shoulders ached, until minutes had passed away on the colonel's idle wristwatch which lay beside the fallen ebony knight. Then Clive bore down slowly, and the colonel's hand went back, slowly, back and down. *And down. I've eaten him alive now,* Clive told himself.

When it was finished Clive suggested that they go to bed.

"Yes, good," the colonel said. "It's half way to morning." His smile seemed bent and forced and his arms hung limp at his sides.

$\cdots 7$

Stoker at a Lighted Window/She has not appeared. My father's lovely neighbor hasn't come loping into my gaze; she has struck no poses on yonder sofa; she has not stalked my dream, though it has stalked her and a hundred like her. Somewhere in this vast house she languishes out of my sight and I stand here like the dumb drooler waiting for the music from a farther room. Goodness, but my life is an awkward phase. I am, in truth, lonely, oh, truly true, and my bathing trunks are damp.

I have seen the windows of the International House, the withered apartments on Drexel Street near the university, the rooms of Noyes Hall, all the dormitories fair and brown; in all of them my darkened face, too handsome for such ventures, I admit, stares back at me. Wistful skaters glide along the frozen Midway Plaisance; solemn dreamers, sweet couples, stroll hand in hand along the Lake Michigan shore, and I have tuned them in, all of them, like distant stations on my mind's dial. Most of the acts I've witnessed have been, of course, dull: scenes rehearsed badly in dingy apartments over on Blackstone Avenue.

I tire of looking in. I tire of the blurred windows of the past: Cassie stroking her thighs in a twilit room in Florida; my briefly-dated Laura; other loners like myself who, I imagine, gaze at other windows this hour. Whatever, Father's alleged neighbor, allegedly comely and wanton, has not come forth.

The poor colonel probably misunderstood. His neighbor probably teased him, telling him that she went naked inside the house just to give him a small preoccupation this long summer. You're a slow man at best, Papa, and at worst gullible. Clive is in there with you sacking your brain with a fancy exhibition, and you probably want to hear more of him. Careful, Papa, for I know his tactic: he'll get you leaning, leaning, then he'll tell you the big truth that will shove you over. He'll scuttle you, Colonel sir.

Enough is enough, so I take my leave. With my usual luck, she'll appear in the next sixteen seconds after I'm gone from the window, disrobe, and do her evening exercises; with my luck, she'll be beautiful; with my luck the colonel will meet her tomorrow in the supermarket, carry home a sack of bread for her, invite her over for an afternoon cocktail, greet her in his satin robe, and nail her on the kitchen floor before he even blends the first round of daiquiris.

I walk away and stroll my colonel's garden. Old worrier. I'll put his mind at ease and report for talks with the people at the draft board; if I admit I'm of this world and country, he'll be happy. No matter. I'll never soldier for anybody, so no matter. It's expedient. I can apply for and receive a student deferment, and so there's no sense making an issue of the matter at all. I'll zap myself later, probably, so why fight anything now?

Oh, of course I won't do that. Just think about it.

The Colonel Unfolds a Letter/That big one Clive: now there's a queer one, that one, all show and blow. He condescends to me slightly when he smiles, but I like him. Charm. He stayed late and talked, give him that, and so he must have thought there was something worthy about me. Mixed up, of course, and snowed by his awful family situation.

Well, this is it: Cassie's famous scrawl. She practices being illegible. I'll just sit here on the toilet and read, if I can, between is lines. Postmarked Amersterdammer. So. Her Richard took her abroad after all.

July 12, 1967

Dear sweet: Know yr having a good time this summer with yr daddy, Pless & all. Been busy over here because Richrd's company has us visiting all their European offices. But good news! Will locate back in Detroit for about a year, be there in late November & naturally will drop over to the school to see you. Sorry but Xmas is out, so we'll make a whing-ding of it Thnksgivng, if possible. Guess where the company sends us Xmas? Florida! Suppose yr daddy will fly down to Eglin and buzz us? Ha! We'll be in Miami anyway.

Hope yr enjoying yr friends & having fun & enclosed is a nice fat little check to see you thru and get you back fall semester. Buy clothes. If you buy booze with this, baby, I'll really want to swat you good in Nov. & I mean it!

Will send dates of arrival in Chicago by telegram later. Rich looks frwrd to meeting you during the holiday in spite of his busy schedule. Also enclosed are photos made in Stockholm. Thats yr mama in the bikini if you can believe it. Not bad still, huh?

by now & kisses,
yr mother,
Cassie

She said *photos*, but there's just this one. She's with this man, not her Richard, I'm sure, and the two of them have their arms entwined, and she's biting on her lip—the old coy bite—and the man looks damned uneasy, I'd say, as though somebody is about to jump him. Perhaps it's her poor Richard off camera. And behind them: ah: very much in the photograph: this fat man in paisley bathing trunks. The beach looks pretty ordinary. But Cass, oh: she's still damned endowed, isn't she? Even her bulges look good. One month more or less since Stoke got this and he shows it to me tonight.

I wonder why he waited? And how much money did she enclose? And how much should I probably give him now?

I'm damned glad he didn't see me arm-wrestling.

The draft board: I need to reason with him coldly about that. Or I could bribe him. He could work things out, except he's stubborn.

Stoker: ah hell. Clive's right about his hair being too long.

My son wants to ruin himself.

Adler Removing the Watermelon from the Car's Trunk/The stars are out, my Pequod sails tomorrow, the umbrellas are all broken, and there goes poor Stoker sneaking across the lawn back into the patio doorway. He wanders all night long full of stealth and stamina; like Clive, he never wants to sleep, just jacks around after midnight, puttering, thinking about his gonads and the call of the wild. Pless too: his nightlamp still lights a page upstairs. And the colonel has occupied the bathroom for half an hour. And Clive has probably turned himself into a bat and hangs upside down from the moon, wherever it is. The house is topsy-turvy, unusually full of life; hell, it must be getting toward four in the morning and none of us can sleep.

There we are. I feel, actually, that we owe the colonel this one gift and mystery. So I'll just plop the watermelon down here among the gardenias and stick its little fuse in the ground.

There. True and behold: there's a miracle under the gardenia bush! It's a Tennessee miracle, Colonel, sugar, suh: one of them big round striped 'uns.

Stoker has been prowling again.

Over there a strange apparition: the toy racetrack curls around the trunks of those trees like a cobra.

The greenhouse beastie ponders the far heavens: Orion and the Bear hide in the moonless sky.

The pact. I haven't drawn the first number, no, but I'm ready. Verily and tereu.

Watermelon sprouts in desert garden. So be it.

I wheeze.

It's going to be morning soon.

Pless and the Miseries/The newspaper lists it all this morning, lists it all. The four horsemen, evil-eyed, are, in order: Vietnam, the lie of the assassination, the truth of race, the boredom of the young. And the poor are always with us, of course, so these things are the vulgar vultures that will snip out our eyes and gnaw our corpse. Don't know why I read it anymore. Along the rice paddies we hover to deliver jellied gasoline; we swoop on river shanties and strafe; we spray land mines like confetti; guava bombs are the fruit of the trees; the hooch lines and canals get barbequed; miniguns are fashionable this season. Or: a semi-autonomous CIA clique with Minuteman and right-wing connections which had been profiteering in Cuban gun-running and narcotic smuggling and of which Lee (Leon) Oswald and ole Jack Rubenstein and a good ole dozen others including Dallas police officers and a secret Oil Man and two other dozen dopesters (all dead now) did the whole thing. They shot our best man dead. Or: the rape of the cities is set, daddy O, next summer evenin' at, O, bout June teenth, keep the faith you mother, O, ass right, O swing low sweet lariat and Overcome Whitey, O, we shall, O dig my grave you blackeyed spade. Or: the children are gathering beside the ocean to be flower bowered and they have hoisted emblems and the wings of dove, and here comes the motorcycled rowdy-dowdies, coming to smash the sweet jaws, to break the sweet-smiling teeth, to snap spines all around, and they're revving up their engines and humping the beaded sweet nymphs, and they're shoving the emblems up the guru's ass and sniffing C through dollar bills, and they're counting the dead and maimed, and now they're running, all of them, circling toward the sea. Too much. The miseries tend to descend.

The Colonel Folding the Letter into His Rear Pocket/He glanced up on the bathroom wall beside the roll of toilet tissue. The rose, delicately formed, presented itself.

"Well I'll be goddamned," he said. "Who would do a stupid goddamned thing like that?"

He went into the hallway and met Stoker.

"What're you doing up so late, Dad? You look tired out."

"I am tired out. But come look at this!"

Stoker followed him into the bathroom. Above the toilet, neatly drawn, he felt, was one of Pless' roses. "That's really sort of nice," he told the colonel.

"Nice? You call drawing on the walls of someone's house *nice?*"

"It's a pretty flower, I mean."

"Pretty flower?"

"It could have been something pornographic."

"And what're you doing up at this hour?"

"I haven't been to bed. I took a swim."

"But it's four o'clock!"

Stoker returned his father's gaze with a conciliatory grin. "Listen," he said, "I've decided to do something sensible about my draft situation. I'll go down and talk to the board members after all. I think I can probably win a student deferment."

The colonel's mouth went agape. "What made you decide that?"

"It's what you wanted, isn't it?"

"Don't tell me you did it for *me*."

"Not altogether. But you did want that."

"Of course. I kept telling you: either prepare to be drafted or make arrangements to stay in school. But you held out so long that I can't figure why you've decided to do this now."

"I'll go down Monday morning before we leave for school," Stoker assured him.

The colonel broke into a grin. "Miracle of miracles," he said.

Clive at Poolside/Things I hate about the colonel: his money his age his witless nodding face. A whole list flowers in my head. Sometimes I despise them all: Adler because his bones are jelly and because he lets me handle him too much Stoker because he resists me more than anyone and Pless just because, oh, Pless is the prize he certainly is. I shouldn't envy him but I do and not because he's a better student, not that, though he is, but because he has his moments of rare saccharine bliss. He loves his stupid life. The thought blisters me and I admit it. Horrendous. He has affection and it impowers him I've seen his professors gaze on him fondly and actually listen while he talked he doesn't have to push it either just glides into dialogues and takes his way. A natural. Power seems unjustly given to some, just an outright gift, while some of us have to connive and conjure to get our little part of it, yes, Pless works a beguiling will on people and everyone imagines love for Pless. The thought blisters.

I think the old man was something like Pless, affectionate, but lacking the power and of course he had no money or position at all, no sexual power, no intellectual depth and he didn't send for me. I lie my way toward the truth with you, Colonel, yes, that's right I didn't go to Ankara because, yes, I wasn't summoned. Spent those years with Aunt Leslie there on the Chicago southside. City of my grief where the postcards arrived full of happy questions like: "How's the chess club doing, old pal. Bet it's fun. Love, Dad." I stayed at the apartment, though, with those two ancient dust-covered bikes idling in the parlor with the empty candelabra and with the smell of brownies and fudge and the chocolated afternoons numbing me. Aunt Leslie would say invite your friends over, dear, but the days passed along and I used to take walks, yes, imagining apartments that might be Jackie's or father's imagining how they lived over in Turkey wondering if they took trips to the lovely ruins or ever went to museums or if they ever really did sleep together. Mother too: she was off in LA by that time with someone named Henry Paschal. Loss Angel. So I had lots of picture and travel books of Greece, Turkey, the Aegean I read lots of those and articles from *Holiday* and *National Geographic* which Aunt Leslie subscribed to. Also read odd tag ends of books in those days: psychology, the occult, body building, skin magazines, crossword puzzles and chess problems. My sickness unto death. He didn't send for me. Ankara, then, was invented in the year 1960 somewhere between the old Armory where I went for my chess matches and Aunt Leslie's drab premises. And chess of course, Colonel, was a game for the Chicago poor and those of us at the armory trudged there in patches and tatters riding the buses or the El and there was an odor of sour bodies in the winter so that sometimes I had to get up from the table after a game and go outside with the smokers (never indulging myself) and breathe a little fresh air during those matches we hunched over all those weak-legged card tables under bad lamps and the man in charge was schizoid always coming in with different clothes one week a suit and vest all pin-striped and the next week a sweat shirt because he could never make up his mind if he was an athletic director or a professor. We were a surly bunch all loners and I never made friends there just familiar opponents. Then came my slow rocking ride home on the bus again. I used to bump along south on Michigan Avenue and cogitate and remember my mistakes of the evening, if any, thinking of Jackie and Mother dreaming of other girls with mysterious mouths and sometimes about the late evening meal I knew Aunt Leslie would be preparing she always fed me hearty, give her that. I put on weight those years, yes, and took my exercises every morning and late evening, lifting barbells that had belonged to my uncle. Also had the bicycle fixed and peddled my legs into shape and it all changed me when my neck bulled out, yes, and my arms developed. I thought of walking home from the chess society and mugging a few old sots for a few old dollars thought about it hard but never did it. Didn't do it because it wasn't smart and, oh, how I wanted listen, Colonel, you ought to know the truth about chess players in the city, how chess is a game for the cunning and withdrawn poor. Reduce life to a playing board and master it at that puny level: you know the syndrome. My clothes were from Robert Hall and worse one time Aunt Leslie told me to take this money and buy myself a good sport coat but I spent the money on books (Flaubert, a pornographic paperback or two) and bought a cheap green jacket with the remainder. Got caught in the rain waiting for the bus one Thursday night and the damned thing ran all over me—oh, Colonel, I remember this one so clearly—and my arms and chest turned bright green and I looked a sight and Aunt Leslie was furious when she saw what had happened and she checked the label of the coat but I had torn it out.

He never sent for me. I haven't seen him since those years when we lived as a facsimile of a family in Arlington Heights before his business failed and before everyone split and I moved down on the southside with Aunt Leslie, my mother's ugly sister, who kept bringing out five dollars here and there for me to spend and finally gave me the gasoline credit card while I went to the university though of course I had no car. And of course we're a bit better off now I manage to get a few dollars from Mother, Jackie, Aunt Leslie and even, once, that small postal order mailed from Alexandria. My old man, yes, was a lot like Pless, Colonel, in that he had natural affections and people responded to him, though they always cheated on him of course and threw him out and insulted him. And he took it and accepted that as how things would be and retired from American commerce, and from what I can piece together from his own sense of himself. I wrote to him saying You Send for Me Now I Can Earn Money in Chess Tournaments There and Help Us, but he never did.

Money: our maudlin poverty always pricked at me more than anything else. There was no cash to save the business, to rescue the marriage, none to pay my ticket to Ankara, none to buy a single paltry dream for the future and so I begged from Aunt Leslie, from Jackie and bummed coffee from the stupes I beat at chess and wandered around Chicago, pockets empty, stealing newspapers. The affluent society, yes, heckled me with gaudy clothes and cars and gave me degrading stares and those student players down at the armory with their meershaums and their alpacas, all dilettante and cool: I hated their asses. And Pless is just like them, of course, armed with all his aristocratic gifts, all his poise and opportunity.

But there are, yes, greater games if you bother to fathom their rules and the wistful flats of childhood fade. And Jackie hocked herself in order to buy ship passage to see the old man, yet when the time came that I could finally do the same I didn't go. By that time the gentlemen who sponsored the chess tournaments had discovered me and they imagined that since I was ragged and lived in Aunt Leslie's slummy neighborhood and played a good end game that I was smart, yes, and so they paid my way into the university, tuition and all. Into the greater game I went and I became—it took me months to convince myself, but I did—too busy and too intellectual and too aloof to think of Ankara anymore and in truth too hostile because he never sent for me let him spin out of my memory like a dervish screw him. Good riddance. A shade of morning lurks in the east and I hear noises in the house, yes, and the dull hum of the pump lulls me.

The colonel, bumping drowsily down the hall, encountered Pless and Adler.

"Isn't anyone sleeping around here?"

"Plenty of time for sleep later, sir. How about breakfast now?"

"Good idea, Pless. I'll throw a few things on the stove. How do you like your eggs, Adler?"

Adler winked one eye then the other rapidly. "Hard-boiled, sir."

"Omelette? Cheese omelettes? Do either of you like those?" They both nodded.

"Is Stoke awake? And Clive? Is everyone still up?"

"Stoke's konked out," Pless reported. "Clive's outside walking around the pool."

"An omelette for four, then. And I'll fix hash browns too."

"We're going after medicine for Addie right now," Pless told him. As he spoke, he drew on his T shirt and fastened his belt. "He has the bad wheezes and needs adrenalin."

"Asthma," Adler rasped, tapping himself on the chest. He stood in the hallway in his undershorts and a red nightcap. He looked, the colonel decided, like a fireplug.

The colonel explained how they could get to the nearest all-night drugstore. He gave elaborate directions, sensing they weren't listening.

"Get your pants on, Addie," Pless said.

"Someone marked on my bathroom wall last night," the colonel added, and with that he turned downstairs.

Stoker, awake and listening, heard Addie rasp loudly then sneeze. It was a three-part sneeze which said, roughly, Stoker imagined, Ho Chi Minh. Lying awake and staring into the cool dark corners of the sewing room, Stoker considered putting on his socks. I ought to go talk with the colonel in the kitchen, he told himself; but he closed his eyes and tried for sleep again.

Clive arrived in the kitchen and began his morning gambit.

"That's very good, sir, the way you break those eggs with one hand," he said.

"Ah, hello, Clive. Get any sleep?"

"Not yet, no. I'm strolling around your pool this morning and musing a little. By the way, sir, that's a neat racetrack you have out there."

"Thanks." The colonel stopped a smile.

"It's a replica of Sebring, isn't it?"

"That's right."

"All that detail cost you something too. Flags, signals, pit stops, nice little cars—all the stuff. You'll have to give us a demonstration, sir, when you have time. Is there any orange juice, by the way?"

"Orange juice. Yes. Right here."

"And the curves are nicely banked, too. I see you built up the lawn around the embankments. Very authentic. Took some time with that layout, didn't you, sir?"

"Well, yes." The colonel poured the juice, frowned, and it seemed for a moment to Clive that he might defend himself. He obviously didn't want to continue about his toy anymore, so Clive pressed on.

"Did you take the trouble to replant the grass around those embankments, sir? It all looks so trim, I mean."

"That's right," the colonel said uneasily, sighing. "I built up the lawn and did some re-seeding. But I had the time. I don't go out much socially in town and I don't like the casinos so I stay home and work in the yard. It's not much, but it keeps me out of trouble." A weak grin edged onto the colonel's mouth.

"Looks like the beginning of a fine omelette there, sir."

"You don't have to call me *sir*," the colonel told him.

"I see you have the *Escoffier*," Clive went on, picking up the colonel's cookbook.

"Why yes. You know cooking?"

"Just eating," Clive assured him. He realized how easy it

was to regain the advantage on the colonel. "The eastern Mediterranean might not have good plumbing, but it has food. I'll tell you about dishes I've eaten in Aleppo sometime. That's where I gained so much weight—got up to around two-forty once." The colonel blinked; he still didn't know whether or not to believe the stories of the last hours, Clive supposed. "But I can help with this if you'd like me to, sir. Are you heating the butter? I could make a Mornay sauce, if you have the right cheeses."

The colonel offered another quizzical stare. "I really don't know what we have," he said. "Some ham, maybe." He seemed tired and his Tennessee drawl was more pronounced.

"*Omelette à la Fermière,* good," Clive said. Then, as an afterthought: "Or we could just have good ole ham 'n' eggs. The boys might like that rather than something fancy."

Stoker entered, rubbed his hands together, and delivered his opener. "Hey, Dad," he said, picking up the blender off the kitchen counter. "Very nice! Four speeds!"

The colonel narrowed his eyes.

"You have some nice things all right," Clive added. "A blender, an *Escoffier,* a nice racetrack."

"A four-speed blender!" Stoker marveled.

"Come on," the colonel said, and he turned and started beating a bowlful of eggs with a fork.

Stoker laughed and leaned against the refrigerator.

"Did you get some sleep, son?"

"Not a bit, Dad. I went next door and got acquainted with your neighbor instead."

"The one I told you about?"

"That's right," Stoker told him nonchalantly. "Not a bad piece, really. A little old for me, you know, but she has some nice moves."

"You're feeding me a bunch," the colonel surmised.

"There is a watermelon in your flower garden, though," Clive added.

"What's that?"

"A watermelon. I saw it while I walked around your pool."

"What're you guys pulling?" the colonel asked, only half humorously. When the boys didn't immediately respond, he stepped over to the window and fired a glance toward his garden. Meanwhile he continued beating the eggs, sloshing a few specks on his robe.

"I suspect the upstairs maid," Stoker said thoughtfully. "Has she any suspicious characteristics, sir?"

"Betty Mae? Why no."

"Well, there's some strange things around here," Stoker said, listing with his fingers. "Clive says there's a watermelon out there among the gardenias. There's that sketch on the bathroom wall. And I hate to tell you this, Dad, but all that's not the worst. There are a few broken umbrellas out in the front yard."

"Broken umbrellas?" the colonel asked, whipping the eggs.

After breakfast started, Pless and Adler returned with the adrenalin. Adler perched himself on the kitchen counter beside the four-speed blender while Pless prepared the injection while Clive sat at the bar, the legs of his stool aslant, and double-talked the colonel on the metaphysics of being a math major. Because the pitch of the morning conversation hadn't lessened, the colonel showed definite signs of weariness, munching at his toast carelessly as he listened to Clive's meditations.

"Now to grasp math and physics—and ultimately aerodynamics, Colonel, which should especially interest you— you've simply got to come to grips with the Vinogradoff number. That's a mysterious number whose existence—and I'm not kidding about this—has never been established. Sort of like the planet Pluto: we're sure it's there, but we really don't see it. Anyway, it was named after the theorist I. M. Vinogradoff. Well, call this number V. Every successor of this number V is the sum of at most four primes. Vinogradoff tried to prove, that is, that only a finite number of integers exist which aren't the sum of at most four primes. You understand?"

"I'm a little rusty on my math," the colonel admitted sadly.

Pless groped like a blind interne over Adler's arm, seized a pudgy vein, and jabbed the needle in. Adler wheezed, winced, and made a thankful sound.

"There are other mathematicians, of course, who don't believe that the V number is real. But for me this is a lovely reality, sir. It's a number that provides a key to all numbers. Am I boring you, sir?"

"Not at all," the colonel said, finishing his toast. His face was slightly wary, however, and he glanced around at the others trying to test their attitudes.

"Feel anything yet, Addie?"

"Negative, Pless, dear heart."

Clive continued to jabber and the colonel, fidgeting with his coffee cup, tried to read his son's face to see if the conversation might have meanings that were escaping him. In succession, the boys had talked about the war in Vietnam, the tailoring of the colonel's uniform, the umbrellas, the watermelon, the racetrack, terminal illness, and now the mysteries of Clive's knowledge. Slightly confounded yet still the amicable host, the colonel heard Adler's wheeze subside and smiled. Adler sat there, the adrenalin pulsing around the corners of his heart, his hand shaking as he lifted a tumbler of orange juice to his lips. Pless lifted a brow in a question: feel it now? Adler's eyelids closed slowly saying yes.

"Think of it, sir," Clive tripped on. "Four prime numbers and a mystic number that solves the ultimate and infinite equations." His voice boomed around the porcelain of the kitchen and the colonel grinned weakly.

"When I get back to my laboratory," Pless put in, "I'm going to take all the electrodes that are implanted in the skulls of our rats and I'm going to plug them into a central switchboard. That way each rat can read all the others' minds."

"I'm going directly to the greenhouse," Adler said, "and threaten my plants with a torch. You can make plants beautifully neurotic, you know."

"When I get back," Stoker said, "I'm going to write a nice theme on my summer vacation."

"I'm going to produce the Vinogradoff number," Clive said. "Then I'm going to eat it."

"I'm also going to send my handsome photograph," Adler affirmed, "to the girls of Ida Noyes Hall. It will be the first mass proxy rape in history. They'll tear open the envelope, each excited little coed will, see my old hunker, and fall on the floor in mad spasms."

"I shall take the four of us," Pless swore, "and build us into a team. Strict training rules under Clive's famous abstinence system. Then we'll go to South Bend, Indiana, and become the new four horsemen of the apocalypse."

The colonel marveled, sighed, and finished his coffee.

Stoker: "Or I shall shoot a little straight LSD into my left eyeball with a medium stub fountain pen."

Clive: "Don't be gross."

Pless: "Feeling better, Addie? Had a nice fixie-poo?"

Adler: "I'm all a-tremble. S'wonderful."

Pless asked for another egg and the colonel gratefully began tending to his wish.

"What we're really going to do," Adler suddenly said, "is zap ourselves. When we go back to school we're going to zap ourselves one by one without even a single trace."

Silence impregnated the room. Mouths opened. Then, slowly, the sound of the colonel's laughter trickled among them. He cracked an egg one-handed, slipped it into the frying pan, and chuckled.

"You boys are really full of it," he offered.

Stoker tentatively joined his father's weak laughter. Clive, though, sensing some cosmic advantage, took up the admission. "That's right," he said. His face was encircled by a wisp of smoke and he blew a neat ring into the sweet and greasy atmosphere of breakfast. "One by one. And let us leave not a single note. We shall go deadie-bye without so much as a farewell or a single ta-ta. Lovely."

The colonel smirked. By this time, clearly, he was having no more of their patter.

"We could draw numbers from a hat," Stoker said eagerly.

"Splendid," Clive announced.

"You could do it all together," the colonel suggested. "You could hold hands and go jump into Lake Michigan."

Everyone laughed. Adler's was a high, staccato yelp.

"You don't love us," Pless said dolefully.

The colonel grinned and sat egg and toast before Pless. Then he turned to the greater business of the day: his first batch of daiquiris.

···8

THE GRAY CHICAGO WEATHER came early and hung on, and by mid-October Stoker had settled into his old moods. He took occasional bursts of pride in his studies, but only really wanted to make his grades. The listless summer was over, a listless autumn had started, and he sometimes just couldn't remember those energetic semesters of his undergraduate days. He was mostly alone. Pless had started school with his usual flurry and was always busy. Addie had come back from the rendezvous at Vegas to disappear into the foliage of his greenhouse. Clive, after that tedious trip back to Chicago, had dropped by only infrequently during September, just barely enough to keep Stoker's antagonisms alive, stopping over to give his monotone a workout, Stoker felt, to make his familiar fatalistic rumbles and to keep the old poison flowing. So most days Stoker walked to class and back and sensed that the colonel's dull habits had probably invaded him, that he was learning to piddle and waste away his time.

He sat beside his window, then, in his small room one afternoon with more anticipation that he expected to have for a planned dinner and evening together. Trapping his thoughts, he tried to make the hours pass. The buildings beyond the window were gray, the sky was gray, the gray rain falls down on the gray day, he told himself. Enough to despair the best of us. He wondered if it were true what was said of the Scandinavians, how they caught the galloping melancholies over the long winter, how the snow and ice seemed to freeze their arteries and souls so that they went around blowing their brains out, jumping into fjords, dangling themselves off barn doors, and wandering off to lose themselves in the dark and forbidding forests. One thing he knew: he had never seen much sun in any of his Chicago winters, not down on this lakefront where the mist and smog always painted the streets pastel. The windowpane was cold against his cheek as he watched a coed prancing along his Woodlawn Avenue, her thighs all minibare.

She disappeared, angling out of his view up the street, and he regretted turning back to face the room. His lavatory sat against the far wall like a pale white eye.

I shall read, he decided, my afternoon magazines. Updork has a new one in *The New Yorker*. Bubu the Guru has opened a new Indian Boutique. Ah, the latest literary gossip: writer and art cryptic Mr. McKuen McLuhan has gone off to Europe with his friendly homosexual-interior-decorator-hairdresser-pompomboy. They have retreated, ah, to a small villa @ $6,000 a month, linens and servants extra. Newsfronts of the world: Otis Redding, aw, dead. Glen Campbell drawled toward Albuquerque. Moshe Dayan has winked again in the desert of time and the Syrians are taking advantage. Another

H bomb lost, somewhere, it is supposed, near the Isle of Man. New York sanitation strike turns city into a trash heap, but mayor proposes the ultimate solution: pave over everything, including garbage cans, loose cartons and paper, rats and children. Vilayat Khan, the noted sitar player, signs with the Montreal Canadiens.

It's such a gray day that I just can't bring myself to study or even read, he finally told himself. Besides, he thought, the others probably feel the same pall. It's probably because we won't mention the pact though of course we think about it all the time and tonight, probably, we'll get together in the old way, eat a dull meal, start on wine, move along to the heavier stuff, and end on beer. A pall over us. Very likely even Clive's harangues will be lackluster, though perhaps that might be the calm before the storm; Clive's moods rise and fall in definite emotional tides, perhaps because he's a math student and his equations behave in the same way, just lie there on the page for a few weeks, dormant and unsolved, then finally come to life, make sense, and contribute to the big bangs of the world. And Addie, of course, is dormant too, adream beneath the *ficius pumila* of his greenhouse, growing like a tender orchid, perhaps into something stronger and perhaps not. And I: adrift, ah me, in literature, all mired in the secondhand life.

My room: gray, grayer, grave. Addie's gifts (pot plants) which he exchanged for my gifts (paperback novels) sit there on my sill. The *mimosa pudica*: that small fern from Guatemala that folds in on itself and wilts at the least touch. Timid cowardly plant. Like (pardon me for the instant symbolism) myself.

Just can't read. The pall upon me.

The works of the masters sit there on my shelves waiting to be read and appreciated, and, true enough, they all reduce to sex. Such an oblique variety that it disappoints me. Those pages are like the windows of 56th Street: there is never so much life in them as I hope. Oh, the bleeding pathos of my secondhandedness, the waste, the criminal shame of it.

Tomorrow, of course, I'll go to class. The Good Doctor will discourse on Hawthorne and I'll sit there listening, thinking of all the girls I've known, all of them with *A* for *A*wful embroidered on their bosoms. Hawthorne's sex must've been something like Henry James': completely lost in the folds of his pinstriped trousers and cravats, rubbed raw by his starched underbritches. Tomorrow, perhaps, the Good Doctor will say: "Let us begin Thoreau. I'm really very fond of Walden Pond," he'll say in iambic pentameter. Hell, I don't enjoy reading anymore.

At five, shaved and ready to join the others at Pless' apartment, Stoker answered Addie's knock at the door. Adler stood there, pants bagging, his old ballerina slippers on. In his outstretched hand he bore another potted plant.

"This one you'll like," he said. "It's *kalanchoe*. These long leaves produce little plantlets, you see, which finally fall off and take root themselves. It's an interesting reproductive process."

Adler came inside and shut the door behind him. He moved soundlessly in his slippers and with agility, like the dancer he wasn't.

"Yes, very sexy," Stoker said, accepting the gift. He looked closely at Adler, trying to determine anything: drunkenness, despair, the present mood. "And what did you do with your day today?" he asked, not sure of what he saw in Adler's eyes.

"The campus minister descended on me," Adler said, taking a seat. "I'll take a little drink, by the way, if you have one, Stoke. I need at least three more before I'm tucked in for supper."

"I'll get what I have. Campus minister, you said?"

"One of the soft-spoken sorts, yes, though at rock bottom he was just another Elmer Gumtree, I believe. I had walked home from work, see, all the way from the greenhouse and I was wheezing like a locomotive. He came in on me—just barely knocked then popped in—and I didn't have enough energy to defend myself. He must've rattled off a mile of theological jargon."

"Why'd he pick on you?" Stoker asked, pouring a light gin and bitters.

"I didn't fill out the religious preference line when I made out the registration forms this term. My name is high in the alphabet. I think this one—I never really got his denomination—plans to attack each infidel on campus in alphabetical order. Ah, good liquid. Thanks, Stoke, I need it."

"That's all that happened today?" Stoker watched, thinking that Adler seldom drank much unless his equilibrium wavered. He tried to estimate how far along Adler already was, but couldn't. Two drinks? Three? He smiled and waited.

"Absolutely all," Adler assured him. "Ah ha, your cluttered shelves. Have you got anything really juicy, old pornographer?"

"Take your pick," Stoker said, waving his arm.

"What's this? A letter from your mother?"

"That's right, but don't read it. Stick to my books."

"Never worry. I need only light reading this season."

Stoker smiled at him and left him perusing the shelves while he went to the bathroom and dusted some shaving powder on his chin. He could hear Adler grumbling among the books. A little tipsy, yes, he told himself, and he knew that Adler would choose, probably, either another Herman Melville or a Faulkner, something less ponderous and full of funny Snopeses.

"I'm also bringing you some *kudzu*," Adler called to him.

"What sort of plant is that?"

"A big leafy one from the Orient. It'll take over this room in a few short weeks. You'll get lost in it."

Stoker combed his hair again and patted his collar into place.

"If you'll fix me another quick gin," Adler went on, "I'll tell you about the entire plant kingdom."

"You knocked that one down already?"

"Plants—remember this, Stoke—have to live, unlike people, together. In communities." Stoker took his glass, went for a refill, and called that he was still listening. "They have to live where the soil permits. Plants even have to help each other."

In a moment Stoker returned with the gin, stronger this time because the bitters bottle was empty. As he handed it to him he asked outright: "Are you okay tonight, Addie?"

"I'm in a very good mood as you can certainly see." He took the drink, smiled over the rim, and sipped. "Only don't sympathize with me or I might bawl like a maudlin drunk, of course." He sipped more heavily, then wiped a pudgy hand over his lips. He looks, Stoker decided, like young Charles Laughton. "Communities of plants, yes, I'll tell you all about them, Stoke. Now naturally some plants—*kudzu* is one, matter of fact—take advantage. *Kudzu* covers the ground, see, and sometimes climbs up trees and grows around them like a giant hand. Gives them a nice green kill."

"Addie, stop," Stoker reproached him. "No metaphors."

"That's the lesson in its entirety." He sipped again, letting an ice cube fill his mouth when he finished. "Actually," he said, "I'm growing fond of little growing things. I've decided that I probably wasn't meant to be a dancer after all, no. Just wasn't meant to go flashing around in the air. I was probably made for the old soil."

Stoker smirked. "You weren't meant for anything."

"My ole daddy was right all righty when he said a man needs a little dirt 'neath his fingernails. I'm meant for the earth. Ashes to ashes and dust to dust: here lies a dancer gone to bust."

Stoker watched him closely. He suggested they go to dinner. "Pless wants to eat Cantonese tonight," he said. "That all right with you?"

"Turns out this idiot pastor who came around to my place didn't want to talk about God after all," Adler went on, not answering. "Oh, he made a few of the old pitches, you know, because, hell, that's his business, but the first embarrassing overtures passed away."

Adler's hand fumbled his drink briefly and recovered.

"I told him what you said once," he went on. "You remember this, Stoke? How metaphysics can never be successfully, ah, put into the human system? Just as a computer can't be programed for certain nonsense information without suffering a breakdown in its circuits. Theology is intellectual smoke, I told him. Quoting you, of course. Wispy stuff. But then it materializes itself and becomes introspective gum sometimes too—and stops our machine."

"What did he say to that?"

"I think I saddened him. He got a far-off look in his eye. Then before he left he admitted that he was seeing a psychiatrist himself. Ah, shit, I can't bear those types."

"Did he wear a collar?"

"No collar. Just a freestyle swimmer in the deep waters. I wish you could've been there for him, Stoke. He needed you. You have a straight head sometimes."

"Pless might have enjoyed him," Stoker said.

Adler sloshed his ice in his glass, then sat it down on the bookshelf, sighed, and put his fists into his eyes.

"Let's go for dinner," Stoker suggested again.

When Adler removed his fists there were bubbling hot tears.

"Addie," Stoker said, not knowing what to do or say, "just take it easy."

"Listen, tell me something."

"What?"

"Tell me what number you drew out of the cap last spring."

"Addie, forget it!"

"You haven't forgotten! Don't say you have!"

"But it's better if we *do* forget it." Stoker tried to remain calm.

"I just want to know who got number one. Was it you?"

"Forget those goddamned numbers!"

"Are you going to tell me or not?"

"No. I'm not even going to talk about it."

"None of you will," he said accusingly. He bit hard on his lower lip. His plump cheeks were moist and shiny.

"It's a lot better that way," Stoker said, not knowing if he meant it.

"I won't go to dinner until you tell me your number!" Addie said.

"Then you'll have to go hungry tonight," Stoker answered him softly.

After the evening meal they went to Pless' new rooms at the Blackstone Towers. His major professor, Kildrick, had managed to get him into the building, a large, pleasant apartment hotel usually reserved for faculty members, quiet, with no one paying attention to who came and went. There were double doors flanked by two black gargoyles which led into the lobby which contained four white leather couches, ferns, and a fake fireplace. Down one wing was the desk and mailboxes and, beyond, two elevators inlaid with mosaic designs; down the other wing were the coke machines, always empty, but bearing the strategic sign: Rents Payable 10th of the Month. Beyond lay the truck entrance and fallout shelter and beyond that was the outer court, trashcans idling under walls adorned with two large observations: HONKIES ARE WHITE/WHITE PEOPLE ARE SHIT. There were also bicycles, locked and chained to the railings.

Pless lived on the sixth floor, half way up the building. That night they went up and looked out his windows across the mild evening, talked about his place briefly, then went on up to the roof. Addie insisted that he felt much better after his meal, but wanted to urinate on someone. No unwary pedestrian lurked below. A cool mist rolled in from the lake, obliterating the shoreline.

They went on talking about Pless' new apartment until Stoker became bored. Clive had lived in the fancy apartment last year, Stoker recalled, while the rest of them had been packed into the narrow dorm rooms on the quad. At present they all had small apartments—set out at about a half mile from each other in a rough square—except for Pless, who had it plush.

They talked about Pless' apartment, even its furniture, until Stoker felt he wanted to leave, then the conversation lurched into gear, as it usually did, and Clive and Pless were talking about dissent: how there were so many protest groups, but how they were all so ineffective. Stoker listened without adding anything, at least not bored anymore, and saw Adler leaning on the railing and looking out absently across the campus. There was a faint glow from his greenhouse, and Stoker wondered if Addie was thinking of going back to work late as he sometimes did.

"We've worked out a system to defeat dissent," Pless was saying. His voice wafted on the rooftop, reaching Stoker as if from far away; it was not the sort of talk, if there was any talk at all, he wanted. He felt that Pless and Clive were wrapped in cellophane, all sanitary and abstract and safely shut off from him. "We do the trick in the mass media," Pless went on. "We take the poor hippie and put him on the cover of *Time* and *Newsweek* and this has the effect of bringing him into the establishment. Or we take the leading Leftist and interview him and pay him good cash for his trouble or we take the pacifist and say, 'Yes indeed, your views are certainly interesting,' and we print every word he utters, but of course this changes nothing. Just gives us a certain moral satisfaction because we imagine we're being democratic and tolerant. The country goes right along like a giant snail—proceeding as it wills. Dissent alters its real course none at all."

"It's a way of keeping the dissenters from becoming violent," Clive offered. "We give them a certain due. We listen politely and destroy them with courteous publicity."

"That's a thesis," Stoker said. "You really think so, though?"

"That way they don't become revolutionaries until—well, until too late," Clive said.

"That's exactly how it's done," Pless went on. "That's our peculiar form of mass democracy. We listen to everyone, we actually heed no one."

Stoker shrugged and said maybe so.

"The San Francisco North Beach crowd," Clive told him. "They stand around in their beads and jeans and beards while the entrepreneurs cash in on them. They're so pliable. I could've stayed on out there as guru-in-residence, right, Addie?"

Adler didn't answer, just stood gazing, leaning on the rail.

"It's getting cold up here," Stoker said. He suggested that they go back to the apartment and so they moved toward the elevator, Clive feeding as much fuel to the discussion as possible. It was the sort of conversation, Stoker knew, that Pless enjoyed. Clive would indulge it as long as possible.

Inside the apartment again, everyone had another drink and Clive predictably tried to get intense. As they talked, Stoker strolled around the room, a large room with pleasant oak tables, everything made familiar by the presence of Pless' things. On the desk opened a copy of *An Analysis of Variance* by Sheffé which contained as a bookmark a small note in Pless' low, elongated handwriting:

> Physics! Save me from
> metaphysics!
> —ISAAC NEWTON

Suddenly, once more, Stoker listened to Clive and Pless talk as if they were at the other end of a long tunnel. Their words seemed muffled and indistinct and Stoker knew he had to leave. There's no reason why we should ever do this again, he found himself thinking. Clive's monologues make me weary, Adler is so neurotic he's going to jump out of his skin, and I'm even tired of Pless.

He announced his exit and received a mild protest. Politely, he accepted a nightcap, a double which he didn't need, then departed. As he closed the door behind himself, Clive was starting up again; he figured they'd soon be analyzing the war again and he was glad to be leaving.

Giddy with the last drink, he weaved his way along the darkened streets. Deciding he should probably get very drunk, he went up Dorchester Avenue toward a bar he knew on 55th Street. He walked along thinking about the colonel, the unusually large amount of money he had offered (because of Cassie's check) before all of them had left Vegas, how hard the colonel always tried. Cassie came to mind too, briefly, in the image of a dead queen, alabaster, floating on a barge down the rivers of a male body. He ached: the old familiar yearning, sustained so long that he could sometimes grow unaware of it for hours, even days, pounded inside him.

He thought of ways to zap out. Rilke died of infection from being pricked on the finger by the thorn of a rose. An exquisite poet's death. One young man, out for an evening turn on his motorcycle, caught a beetle in the forehead while whipping along at ninety. They found the bug embedded in his brain. He thought of a poem about an airline stewardess, too, who was sucked out the opened door of a plane, fell, peeling off her clothes as she descended, freeing herself like a lovely bird, opening her breasts to the wind, floating earthward in a fatal striptease.

Then Cassie again: the alabaster castrater. He recalled how she always touched his knee, his arm, and could never keep her hands to herself. She seemed to delight in his slight sexual frustration in that, too, and felt flattered that she could turn him on, her own son, and sometimes she actually flirted, patronized him, trying her tested gestures and gazes on him as if he were just someone else to seduce; then, again, she took care to put him down, to remind him that he was a mere boy and no physical match for her. It was because she didn't know what to do with men, of course, because she couldn't even distinguish son from father or lover from friend in her silliness. The bitch. He recalled all the horror stories Clive told about his mother, too, and supposed they had endured the same problem: they had watched a sick woman flower like a tumor in the family. The sick infect. Mental disorder and disease is as contagious as the Black Death, Stoker reminded himself. The colonel, therefore, is a ghost; I am a yearner; Clive is full of worms.

He was glad to have escaped the evening's conversations.

At three in the morning he emerged, his weave more pronounced, from the dingy Whalespout Inn. For two hours he had sat in tipsy dialogue with an old merchant seaman in a hooded parka; the old man, one of those who came to the tavern from the nearby docks, careened one way then another on his barstool, rambled on about his days in the war, about women and latitudes, and his face moved back into the shadows of that hood, eerily, so that Stoker sometimes became engrossed in watching him and didn't listen. Afterward as Stoker went along the street with his head reeling and his legs turned to noodles, he tried to piece together their conversation. But it had been vague. The old sailor had spent his last years on the Great Lakes and had seen the cities of the new-foundland all aglitter and had somehow become filled with right-wing prophecies, as best as Stoker could tell, though the connections were obscure. Stoker had talked about expatriate writers, novelists who had gone to sea. There was just talk, then, and little meeting of minds. The old salt just grinned, hid behind his parka, and didn't make much sense, but it was almost enough, Stoker felt, that he wasn't Clive. Once, winking and nodding at Stoker from inside that hood, the old man said, "Listen, kid, and I'll tell you this: nothing is more beautiful than Vesuvius erupting." Stoker had no idea what he meant. Or what they were even talking about at the time. It was a small nightmare, both of them stoned.

His steps led him down Ellis Avenue, onto 57th, and on toward his Woodlawn flat. The greenhouse sat there a block away like a luminescent giant, all pulsing and glowing, and the thoughts flew: Addie, the old sailor, Cassie again. Motherhood, he tried to cogently explain for himself, was always a ballast of confusion for Cassie. She was one of those women who suffered it by accident and who never adjusted. And something even more devastating: she was a woman who grew more beautiful as she grew older. The colonel had married a country girl who simply liked men in uniform; then he had watched her grow into a creature graceful in high heels, into a cocktail cock, smiling and saying the right things, giving men the laying on of hands techniques. By the time of her thirtieth birthday Cassie sensed her impact on men for the first time and it came as a startling revelation for her. Sex was soon a marital problem, a general social problem, a Cassie problem, and for her, afterward, nothing was easy—not even a grown and throbbing male child around the house. Then, in that interim before she actually moved out of the house, while the colonel was sleeping at the base apartment, Stoker remembered how he stood outside her window while he sprinkled the colonel's garden. There she stood in the center of her bedroom, brilliantly white she was, her arms pulled up as she brushed her hair, her breasts high, her feet planted apart on the soft rug. And what of such moments? Do they come to everyone, Stoker wondered, to all the salty travelers on the lakes, to reproof all the emotional rules? What of such strange new viruses? One thing he knew:

he hadn't looked away. And Cassie hadn't minded—or didn't know.

Drunk, he lurched off a curb.

What of such lunacy? His mind was a turnstile, whirling.

Stoker turned suddenly and headed back for Ellis Avenue. The nightmist turned to phlegm in him and he thought of poor Addie, probably abed, gasping for just one good un-asthmatic breath before dawn. Ellis Avenue: he turned, retracing his steps, going back in search of the plaque. The campus was shrouded in silence.

He wanted to read the plaque, but couldn't find it, couldn't even remember whether it was there or if it stood inside a building or hung on a fence. As he pondered this, he lost his balance, toppled, and crunched into a graveled mudhole in the street. A cliché tumble, he told himself: drunk in a ditch. The criminal shame of it, the waste, the bleeding pathos.

Later, toward dawn, he felt the angels coming to get him. Their voices were like prayers, all feminine. They took him softly beneath the arms and lifted him up; their fingers fluttered around his head. One of them even spoke his name. Mister, another called him, and her breath was full of cloves and myrrh.

···9

AFTER STOKER LEFT THAT NIGHT, Adler went to the greenhouse to work, but found Cogdill there. Cogdill was the young instructor in charge of lab equipment —the autoclaves, the ultracentrifuge machine, the electro-microscopes. He didn't like Adler, always watched him, and that night was particularly sullen.

"What do you plan to do here so late?" he wanted to know.

"I've come to keep an eye on you," Adler said. He knew that he shouldn't have said it. Cogdill was humorless and liked to be called Dr. Cogdill and came up there late at night sometimes, truth be told, Adler thought, to hide in his office and masturbate. He was a poor lonely devil who hid in his work—the same as everyone—but just couldn't be friendly.

"I don't like you young graduate assistants messing around

expensive equipment," Cogdill blurted out, probably more angrily than he meant.

"The equipment is here to be used," Adler told him.

"Not by incompetents."

"All day long," Adler said, "the instructors and grad students with priority use the damn machines. There's a fucking line waiting to use the machines. I have to come up here after midnight and half the time you've locked everything up."

"If I had my way I'd lock everything up at five o'clock each afternoon."

"That sure as hell figures," Adler said, his voice high. Sensing now that he was into the argument, his hands trembled.

"Since we've begun this little discussion," Cogdill continued, "you can tell me just what you *are* doing up here so much at night."

"It's very simple," Adler said, trying to calm himself. He felt his small wheeze murmur in his chest. "I don't like doing the stupid goddamned exercises required of the first year graduate students. I want to work on other things, something important. In the fine print in the university catalog, individual research is encouraged."

He didn't mean to sound so brave. But there it was: the words hung in the gaudy silence. Cogdill tightened his mouth.

"I want to study the effects of atomic radiation on plants," he said, this time more calmly. "Plants, you see, sir, are the principal receptacles of radiation. In the northlands, for instance, the caribou eat the plants, the Eskimos eat the caribou, and suddenly the radiation in the bones of the poor Eskimos is a thousand times more than it should be."

He could see that Cogdill was even madder. He didn't want to lecture the poor bastard, but couldn't say anything right.

"Anyway," he went on, "that's why I need the ultra-centrafuge machine—which is always busy in the daytime."

"Well," Cogdill said. "It turns out you're a bleeding humanist, doesn't it." Adler didn't answer. "It turns out that you're Pierre Curie all the time, isn't that right?"

Adler didn't say anything, but almost shrugged.

"Well, let me tell you something," Cogdill went on. "I'm leaving tonight. And the place is unlocked and all the machines are available. But if anything happens tonight—or any night, Adler—I'll have your ass."

"There are fifty other grad students," Adler reminded him.

"But it's you—you're the turd in the bowl, my friend. I don't like you. No one likes you. You and your ballerina slippers. And if there's *ever* anything wrong around here, Adler, you can count on catching trouble."

"I'll remember that."

"You damn well better remember it. And don't get into any of my classes. I don't want to see your face while I lecture."

"Don't worry about that."

"Good night, Adler. And watch your step. In fact, if you know what's smart, you won't bother coming around here late at night. I'm not kidding about this: anything goes wrong and I've got my man. I mean it."

Cogdill turned, put on his beret, and started for the door.

"Thank you for the advice, sir," Adler said. "And by the way, sir, fuck you." It slipped out before he could stop it.

"I ought to take care of you right now," Cogdill said, giving him a threatening look.

"I wouldn't, sir. I keep a hatpin inside my trousers here. I'd be glad to stick it in your eye while you worked up enough courage to hit me."

Cogdill, shaken, clenched a fist. "You know what's wrong with you, Adler? You've got no respect for authority. You can't stand not having your way. You don't understand the concept of your apprenticeship here. But let me say this again: I'll have your ass. You can't keep away from me around here forever—not after this. Your wise mouth: it'll catch up with you. You wait and see."

Adler walked away from him. By this time his hands were twitching violently and he felt sick at his stomach. He walked down the long row of seedling boxes toward the back office, deliberately not looking back, and when he finally did Cogdill was gone.

He sat down at the desk where two of the six drawers were assigned to him as an office. Sighing, trying for control, he tried to think about his work, but the argument with Cogdill had made him weak. The poor bastard probably went to graduate school under the same conditions he now tried to impose, Adler knew: snobbishness, generally uncooperative instructors, rigid rules and regulations, the grinding exhaustion and humorless fog of assignments.

After a few minutes Adler went back through the maze of large-leafed plants toward the old storage room. Except for the slow gurgling of the water in the goldfish tank the greenhouse sat in silence and his footfall echoed slightly on the flagstone aisle.

He felt rich with hostility and a vision of Cogdill came to him: Cogdill strangled in the clutches of an exotic vine or impaled on a cactus. He saw, also, the colonel standing in the desert with broken umbrellas all around him, and his own father walking among the rocky, drab fields of Arkansas on one of his lonely hunts. Suicide, he told himself, is just murder turned inside out; it's inward hostility, hatred that comes round like a boomerang.

The door to the old storage room was open and he went inside, flicked on a light, and found the shelves of glassware before him. After a search he had what he wanted: the largest glass vats, some tubing, a workable Bunson burner, everything for trouble. Give Cogdill something to worry about, he decided.

The glassware was dulled by dust and age, but sufficient: slowly he built the apparatus, everything in place and working and waiting for the alcohol which he would bring, he decided, tomorrow. Behind the shelves piled high with boxes and plastic bags filled with preserved snakes and octopi and worn charts and clumsily painted models of earthworms he built it: his small but perfectly workable distillery. I'll make a killer brew, he decided, a vintage white lightning that will choke Cogdill with its odor if he ever ventures in here. Something one of Pappy's neighbors would be proud of. He laughed, bit his fingers with excitement, then left the old room, taking one of the medium-sized canisters with him.

On the way back to his room he flung it against a telephone pole and it shattered in a thousand tinkling pieces.

··· 10

THE ODOR OF COFFEE awakened Stoker. He sat slowly up in bed, felt the naked rustle of his body beneath the sheet, and tried to comprehend the room.

A girl in white (nurse? keeper? angel?) stood across the room at a hot plate, her back turned. The steam haloed her.

Stoker gave her a slight ahem.

She gave him back a quick glance over her shoulder, but said nothing.

He was in another flat like his own, perhaps smaller, with newer curtains over the closet, a lavatory less anguished, chairs less strewn. Two beds, quilt tossed, stood facing an opened cupboard packed with canned soup and cracker boxes. Red and white labels addressed him.

The girl was full of automatic movements. Sleepily, she sat down at the table, gulped at her coffee, and bit into a large, sticky cinnamon roll. She watched Stoker as she chewed and he became sure that she would say something when her bite was finished. He decided that she was a nurse and he remembered Laura, whom he had dated briefly more than a year ago, a nurse who distinguished herself as his fourteenth or fifteenth sexual failure, another good thing—how many others? —gone wrong. The girl with the cinnamon roll, though, was definitely not Laura. For one thing this child of the continental breakfast was too pretty. Her teeth were fully in her mouth. Laura had been abundantly toothy and though surprisingly lovely of body (he had only one occasion for proof) a dull and charmless girl in the face.

He sent forth another ahem and tried to smile, but his face felt like marble, so numb that he slid a hand to his cheek to feel how swollen it was.

"Laura," the girl with the cinnamon roll said, "will be back at four. You're to wait."

Laura, yes. He sighed with satisfaction at how cogent his mind and memory seemed to function and the girl lowered her eyes slowly, saying with her droll lids that everything was all right, saying stay cool. She savaged the remainder of her roll, then, and dabbed her mouth with a paper napkin.

After this Stoker watched her rattle the pans and dishes into place and wipe the hot plate with the apron before she hung it back above the sink. Then she put on her coat and nurse's cap.

"You're to wait, be sure," she said at the door.

"What time is it now?" he managed.

"After one," she said. "Just lie easy. Your face really took it in that fall last night."

So. He lay back on the pillow, listened to her footfall fade on the stairway, felt his jaw twitch in pain. The afternoon slept peacefully again, malingered.

Twice, later, he got out of bed, his head and face throbbing, and went touching his way around the room, fingering the coffee pot, a loose pair of panties on the shower rod, the spray of pencils sticking up from the elephant-hide container on the small desk. Both times he went back to bed and pulled the covers under his chin. Sweet Laura, my sweet and nearly vague Laura: did you really find me and take care of me last night? He recalled her as a stranger, someone he had met long ago before he was quite himself, a year ago at a party.

Image: they had gone arm-in-arming across the quadrangle from that party, into the nurses' quarters, boldly up the stairs, down a few miles of brightly lit corridors, high on their tiptoes and whispering admonishments to each other, and finally through the door and into her room. They kissed as they leaned against the inside of the door and they never switched on the lights. Her kiss was all teeth, but moist.

Image: they had gone spiraling into bed full of the usual dread and enthusiasm, and dread had won out. Once again, he failed his minimal expectations and while they dressed she asked if he were a virgin. No, he said sadly, without the least bluff, not at all, Laura, just zero for thirteen, if you want to know, and he kissed her neck goodnight. Once again that winter he decided to try it again with her—after having two additional futile rounds with others. He called and met her at the bookstore, they went to a proper dinner, talked, tried to go to Clive's apartment, couldn't get in, and walked over to the Exeter Motel where he couldn't go through with it. They were standing underneath the neon, he remembered, with the T blown out and he tried to cop out with a witticism: "Bed will just come to worse," he told her, but she didn't laugh much. Poor Laura.

Now the afternoon dreamt itself away. He lay in bed with his limp sexual history, speculating on how the girls had brought him there, if he had managed to walk a little or if they had gotten male assistance or if either or both of them, Laura and the cinnamon-roll girl, had undressed him. Also: was the jaw broken? how many classes missed? should I gamble and have something to eat or am I too ill? what time is it now? why am I staying?

Later that afternoon he found four aspirins at his bedside. He struggled up once again, found the refrigerator beneath the sink, washed down the aspirin with a beer, and went to sleep again.

At half-past four, then, he awoke with Laura sitting on the side of his bed. Her hand was placed professionally on his forehead, but she wore a tell-tale smirk of a smile.

"What're you going to do for your next act?" she drawled, and he remembered that she was from Louisiana.

The slanting light from the window illuminated her reddish hair; her smile was still slightly toothy, but provocative, like a happy Leslie Caron's, and she gazed down on him with half-closed eyes and a reproachful turn of the head.

"Now, Laura, if you've had second thoughts about all this," he said to her solemnly, "then just give me back my ring and we can always be friends."

She laughed.

Then she did a surprising thing: she bent down and held his head tenderly and pressed her cheek gently on his.

"Oh, Stoke," she said simply.

His senses broke apart.

He later learned that Laura and the cinnamon-roll girl, who wore the name PARKER on the small plastic tag of her nurse's uniform and preferred to be called only that, had managed to get him up to their room and tend his bloody face. This last, he later also knew, Laura had enjoyed, for Laura nursed, he became sure, out of a maternal and physical affection for the world. At any rate they had pulled him up a flight of stairs while he, hair matted with blood, gravel embedded in his cheek, and every ounce of his one hundred and seventy pounds presenting them with a dead weight, babbled on about his mother, about life on the Erie Canal, and about a vague plaque. They had gotten him into bed

· · · 129

and—Laura giggled when she confided this—had eagerly undressed him.

Now he sat on that same bed. Two adventurous days had passed and he watched Laura, stirring her over-simmering soup, and she looked back at him. Already they were strangely comfortable.

It had taken him those two days just to remember what he knew of her, and now, having remembered it, he had fallen into this curiously fond feeling, this relaxation. It was unlike anything he had ever felt before—even with Pless.

"Are you hungry?" she asked.

"Not much, but I'll join you." He watched her movements, the turn she gave at her slender waist.

She was raised in New Orleans, attended Loyola there, and became herself, she told him, reading while lying on a blanket over in Audubon Park, stretched out in the sunshine with either a copy of *Tess* or *Tender Is the Night* or *Lady Chatterley* and a bottle of tepid Coke and, frequently, one of the boys from Tulane. One was finally the young med student she followed to Chicago. She adored him, she told Stoker, and became a nursing student because of him, but their love ended —not, she admitted, as casually as it began.

Now in this October of her senior year she had found him lying on the curb near her apartment house. Less than forty hours ago she had come home from duty at the hospital clinic, too, and had slipped into sudden familiarity with him (it was, Stoker conceded, as though they had been married a decade), and had crawled between those now-accustomed pea-green blankets where Stoker, once again true to form, hadn't made it with her. Yet from the start he had felt at ease, even leisurely.

"Listen," she drawled on, "we can have something a little more substantial than soup, but soup is my principal food around here because I usually study while I'm eating. With meat and potatoes you have to pay attention to what you're doing, but with soup you can just keep on reading, and spooning it in."

"I know you lazy eaters," Stoker told her. "Usually you like okra too. Because you can just lay it on your tongue and let it crawl down your throat."

"Okra's my very favorite," she lied. She came and sat beside him on the bed, saying: "And I don't want soup. Let's go to the grocery store and push a basket around the aisles and buy better groceries. We can take them to your place, if you want. I'd like that: go shopping, be wifely, do a wifely thing or two for you. I eat too much soup with Parker. We deserve better."

She had a way of drawling without stopping perceptibly for breath. She placed her cheek on his again, softly.

"Also, you're tired," she said. "I can tell you're really fatigued. So let's go to the grocery store. It sounds unlikely, I know, but grocery stores can cheer a person up."

He dressed and they went downstairs together. The street was filled with students and traffic and Laura's car, parked at the curb, wore a ticket, a pink badge placed there by the campus policeman. She laughed and stuffed it into her purse and seemed to Stoker someone that he had found, someone he hadn't known he had lost.

For the next few days Stoker didn't once think of Clive and the others. His room, in spite of Laura's frequent presence, sat tidy and uncluttered. He walked to class through the lapping leaves, the gutters rattling with music.

Laura, he concluded, was probably taking him as a course in therapeutic sex. Improving her altruistic techniques on his body. She was a sweet clown, unlike he recalled her a year ago, all full of pipe dreams and tender calisthenics, riding him, nudging, urging him on. And the years which had been so bathed in past tense seemed to funnel into a precious now; all the books and dead narratives, all his musings of Cassie and his drab backward meanderings broke and dissolved on Laura's silken stomach, on the insides of her thighs, in her pleasant bucktoothed kiss. He felt wonderful as he walked to his classes. The leaves scattered before him, announcing his graduation.

A foxy coed traveled toward him, nearing him with sweater bobbing, loins swaying, and passing in a whiff of angora and perfume to set him wondering. He asked himself if Laura might set him free. Free to diddle with the world from which I've never had my fill, he asked himself, for that's it: I've never quite had enough and I could copulate with these trees along the campus walks, stick my princely dagger in yonder gothic windows, go through the dorms like a masked rapist, like Addie said he'd like to do. Ah, Addie, you're pockmarked with sex too, all mauled and scarred, and it's probably in your genes, bless you.

He walked toward his class, cutting through a swirl of dying leaves toward the greenhouse.

Will Laura set me free, he wondered, or will she keep us for ourselves? He could imagine eternal marriage. Man is a mating creature: truism. Skin on skin is a moral good: truism. To turn over in the mornings and have her there; this morning, before the cold of the room or hunger or even the slightest sexual appetite beset me, I had the supreme pleasure: the purring touch of her sleeping backside. A languid pause. I was afraid to breathe on her.

The greenhouse loomed up and he opened the door and went inside. Passing down the aisle, he watched the gold light of the autumn noon filter through the panes overhead. An attendant, white-frocked and grim, nodded as he passed.

Approaching Addie's shared office, a small glass cubicle at the rear of the first large room, Stoker stopped at the goldfish tank. They were there, Addie told him, to be infected with fungi; no better off than the rats Pless kept. What's your name, he asked, my little fish of this garden spot? Shall I call you Rappacinni? You like that?

Moving toward the office again, he looked up to see Clive. He stood beside Addie's desk inspecting a cluster of buttons and wires along the wall.

"Stoker, hello," Clive said when he saw his visitor. He smiled a smile that looked planned. "I was just testing this automatic window control. Works by a thermostat."

"Don't tell me. You were going to open all the windows so that the plants will die."

"Fine idea, but, no, just inspecting. Where's our Addie?"

"I came looking for him myself. How've you been, Clive?"

"I could tell you stories about it."

"Please, don't. Have you seen Pless?"

"He's not feeling well."

"The flu?"

"No, it's more like the melancholia. He had to kill his first batch of rats. Also his mother has been in the hospital this last week—drying out. I'd forgotten she was on the bottle."

"Well, Pless gets into moods and he gets out of them," Stoker said. "We've known each other a long time and I've watched him: he handles himself all right."

"Does he?"

"I think so."

"I think you ought to go around and see him."

"Really? Oh, I don't think so. Believe me, Pless is one of the tough guys." Stoker despised how Clive always tried to dramatize crisis.

"But I think Pless has the first number," Clive added, not looking at Stoker as he said it.

Stoker fixed him with a stare. Then, looking through the glass walls of the office, he saw Adler coming toward them; he waddled in sandals and a dirty apron down between the rows of seedlings, his head buried in a paperback.

"Either you have it or Pless has it," Clive added quickly.

"What the hell difference does it make?"

"None at all," he said. "Hello, Addie."

Adler stopped between them, seemed to sense something tense, said hello, then asked if there was any trouble.

"We've just come to breathe the fragrant insecticides," Clive told him.

When Stoker asked him to go for coffee, then, Adler said he couldn't, removed his apron, flung it on the desk, and started complaining to them. He told them about Cogdill and the ultracentrafuge machine and his neck reddened as he talked. Stoker became amused and decided that anyone so angry was good and sane, that Adler was probably doing much better this week.

"Keep bitter," Stoker told him. "It becomes you."

They sat around the office for a few minutes while Adler told them about an experiment he wanted to run, and as they listened Stoker enjoyed himself, thinking how casually Addie delivered his information—unlike Clive, who used information like a mace.

At last Stoker said he had to go to class, and Adler strolled out of the office with him to say goodbye. When they were out of earshot from Clive, Adler said, "There's nothing wrong with Pless, is there?"

"Why do you ask?"

"You and Clive looked like ghosts when I came in. I thought something had happened."

"Nothing has happened, Addie. Nothing's going to happen. I've got to go to class now, but let's have coffee—maybe tomorrow. All right?"

Adler nodded, waved, and returned to the office where Clive sat waiting.

By the time Stoker left the greenhouse, his thoughts began to accelerate. Of course he wasn't sure nothing would happen. Clive had mentioned the pact and he had felt the hair rise on the back of his neck. The thought lingered. He strolled toward the Classics Building thinking of Pless, his mood thickening.

In class, while the professor droned on, he couldn't stop thinking about things. He decided to pick up Laura at the clinic at four o'clock. Have the four of us ever really been friends, he asked himself, even Pless and I? He muddled. It seemed to him they had nurtured an idea of friendship, fondled it, talked about it, and clung to it in such an intellectual way that each of them possibly had only an *idea* of friendship instead of a single friend. Like theology is what you're left with after God is gone, he decided. Reality fades, but the idea of reality lingers—and you try, always with a certain futility, to get a little nourishment from it. He concluded that he could probably only count on Laura, only her.

When his class dismissed, he went over to the clinic and waited for her. She came out shortly after four, all white and official, prettier than he had expected to find her. They went out to her car, kissed, and she asked him what was wrong.

"Nothing," he told her. "I'm just preoccupied about seeing a friend of mine. I want to go by my apartment and pick up my laundry. There's a laundry room at his place. That's my thought: pretty mundane."

"Very domestic," Laura said approvingly.

Driving toward his apartment, he reached over, touched her, and felt her take his hand and move it onto her breast.

"You're sure there's nothing wrong?" she asked again.

"Not a thing."

"Are you in a big hurry to do your laundry, then?"

In his room he noted a surprising number of Laura's articles as he went around bundling his dirty laundry: her clothes, cosmetics, books and note pads. He breathed her faint perfume and wanted to thank her for every trace. Then as she dallied in the bathroom he started thinking again about the others, about the pact, and he wondered if he should talk with Laura about any of it, or if those tiny distress signals generating from Addie and Clive had any sense to them, anything that could be communicated. His speculations multiplied and he gazed out of his window onto Woodlawn Avenue where the afternoon was turning from green, once more, to gray.

Then Laura came out of the bathroom, beautifully naked, and curled on his bed without a word. His reverie perished.

More than a day later Stoker managed to visit Pless at the Blackstone Apartments. It was a dark and rainy day, but Pless was in a buoyant mood without a trace of the melancholy Clive warned Stoker about.

They sat and talked for more than an hour, the conversation following Pless' whimsy. He had been reading Haldane's elaborate theory that both John Keats and Emily Brontë inherited fatal genes which gave them at once their literary talents and made them susceptible to tuberculosis, and wanted to test the theory on Stoker. Pless had undergone an intellectual shift, Stoker discerned: this year he was a geneticist rather than an environmentalist. Finally, they got around to personal things.

"I have a girl," Stoker told him outright. He had planned to drop this news casually, but it fell clumsily into the conversation. "She's staying at my room."

"Stoke, that's great," Pless said, and his enthusiasm seemed genuine so that Stoker broke into a grin in spite of himself.

"As a matter of fact, it *is* great," Stoker allowed.

Pless then wanted to know how it went, but had trouble framing the sentence. "Ah, does she, did you . . ."

"We're working on it," Stoker told him. "It's going to be all right. She's a nurse and believes that sex is a word that belongs with a vocabulary of words like *hygiene, therapy* and *tension.* She tells me that screwing is a good health habit."

Pless asked questions and Stoker told him as much as he could: that Laura was the same girl he had met at a party last year, the nurse; that she was literate and appreciated his knowledge of literary trivia; that she owned a beat-up Austin-

Healy and wore her hair short. By way of telling Pless about Laura's apartment, Stoker also mentioned Parker, who, he added, was lovely.

"I have this thing going," Pless announced. "One of the secretaries over at Green Hall. She visits me in the rat room and leans on me."

For a while, then, it was like old times: a conversation resembling a letter from an old friend who offers a roundup of his domestic trials. Stoker asked about Verna, who, it turned out, did go to a hospital briefly for a drying out.

"How did Clive know about it?"

"How does our mystic Clive know about anything?" Stoker replied. He hoped Pless might venture something mildly critical of Clive, but the moment passed. Then they talked about Addie, how listless he seemed, and Stoker mentioned finding him mad about his work in the greenhouse and interpreted that as a good sign.

"He's still soft and manic," Pless said in summary. "The same as always."

"I think Clive needles him. I don't like that," Stoker added.

"What about?"

"About the pact—since you ask."

"What's the matter? Has Addie drawn number one?"

"I hope to hell you're kidding," Stoker said with astonishment.

There was a strained, momentary silence. "But of course I'm kidding, Stoke. What'd you think?"

Pless smiled and Stoker found it hard to read him, more difficult in that moment, he suddenly felt, than ever before. For a second, in fact, it crossed his mind that Pless, Adler and Clive were all insane together.

Once again their conversation moved off into a safe latitude. Pless went to his desk, stacked some notecards into place, and told Stoker about some incidents in his laboratory—odds and ends of his routine.

"Clive told me something else," Stoker finally broke in. "He told me *you* were brooding. Is it so?"

"Let's go down to the laundry room and wash your clothes," Pless said, putting him off. "Come on. We'll talk down there."

Caught in the harsh fluorescent glare of the basement laundry room with the whine of the washing machines all around them, Pless did begin to talk and Stoker listened, as always, with respect. Pless always made sense, never bored, seldom got esoteric and vague. Over their years together Pless had talked of many things: automation (which he maintained was fearfully crucial), the Negro (who was alive, he said, and named Zarathustra), genetics (which would microfrankenstein us), the university (which, like God, was a functional fiction), psychology (which would one day largely be gobbled up into chemistry) and the war, the nature of art, pussy, urban life, liquor and drugs, music, jurisprudence, architecture and time. In the laundry room, then, Stoker gave him his usual audience. As Pless removed Stoker's wet wash and tossed it into the mouth of the dryer, he went about articulating the present mood and phase of the emotional moon.

"Forget the pact," he began. "That was just an evening's sophormorism."

Stoker watched his face, wondering if perhaps Pless was giving him a slight put on. Could it be so?

At any rate, he answered Pless with candor. "It's our sophomorism, Pless, that kills us all."

Silence. Pless accepted the rebuttal. "But see what's happened," he added. "We're back at school, all of us working. You're going to be a writer. Your girl will probably inspire your first chapter. I'm going to be a *good* psychologist. Adler is simply brilliant in his field—I've heard you say it yourself. They wouldn't let him run all those labs at the greenhouse if it weren't so. And Clive: his grades have been off in past semesters, but talk to any of his profs—Lebovitz or Zygmund or Lashof, any of them."

"It's not Clive's equations I fear."

"How can he intimidate you? He's such a bluff, such an innocent! He came out of the goddamned Chicago ghetto, Stoke, you know that and he has only inferiority feelings bulging his pockets. He's a poor boy and hostile about it and his mother and father split on him. And his sister—hell, who knows what she did to him? Of course he's a bag of lies and paranoia!"

"No analysis, please."

"All I'm saying is this: you have to overlook a few adolescent evenings. We're the sanest of the sane."

"You seem awfully sure."

"Well, how can *anyone* be sure? But I think so." He smiled, shrugged, and tried by his charm, his old friendly manner, to make everything knit together, but Stoker wasn't sure.

"You ought to distrust yourself," Stoker told him. "Do me the favor, at least, of distrusting some of your instincts. I don't really think—to begin with—you're so sure of yourself. And who can be sure of Clive? Least of all, you, baby, because half the time the two of you have your little rapture going. And I've seen more of Addie than you have—and he's balancing on a ball, swaying with every slight emotional breeze."

"Who is analyzing who tonight?"

"It's all right. Let it be my turn for a change. I want you to reassure me about everything, of course, but let me ask you, for instance: have you ever had a homosexual experience?"

"That's a neat turn! What's it got to do with anything?"

"Just answer. Tell the truth."

"Almost everyone has some sort of experience that could be interpreted as homosexual," Pless answered.

"Lately?" Stoker tried for a casual tone.

"Oh, hell no. Years back. What of it?"

"You always experiment with yourself," Stoker said, "confident as hell that you'll surface. And up until now—this is my point—you might have been all right, but how can you keep on with such certainty?"

"Christ, Stoke, I was eleven years old! My cousin came to stay with us, slept with me, and fondled me. That was it."

"But you went along with it, didn't you?"

Pless gave him a smirk.

"Look, when Clive told me that you were in a low mood, guess what? I believed him. And I seldom do. And I expected to find you guarded tonight—but guess what again? I think you've been low. Right?"

"Everyone gets depressed. The tide goes in and out."

"What is it? Verna?"

"It's mostly finitude. I'm not as brilliant as I need to be, I suppose. What else does it need to be?"

"It could be the war, your dead daddy, anything. I *know* you. Why disguise anything?"

"I'm really all right," Pless said. By his tone Stoker felt he wasn't trying to fake him out.

The dryer stopped whirring. While Stoker unloaded his clothes and pushed them into a paper sack, he let the dialogue slip back into mild waters. He talked about Laura again and asked Pless if he'd have a meal with them soon.

"I'm really glad about Laura," Pless said as they went back to the lobby.

They stood waiting before those mosaic elevator doors while, beyond, the cables made a slight twanging noise.

"You have a real palace," Stoker said, making talk.

"Good old Kildrick. He even got me my room in this place at a discount, you know. But don't worry. I'll never lose contact with you simple folk."

When the elevator door opened, Pless stepped inside, smiled, and was gone. Puzzled, Stoker went back across the campus. He felt a thousand miles and years from Pless, unbelievably lost, and he wanted to talk to Laura about the feeling.

She wasn't at his room, though, when he returned.

Disappointed, Stoker walked down to the phone booth on the corner and called. After several rings, Parker answered, cooing into the receiver, obviously expecting someone else. When Stoker asked for Laura, he was told to wait.

Then he and Laura had a long, rambling phone conversation in which he complained at finding her gone and she told him that she had to go back to her room sometime and that, also, Parker would worry and that, no, it was nothing between them, that everything was the same. He suggested that they go have a beer or something because it wasn't even midnight yet, but she said no, she was already in pajamas and exhausted. Then he asked about having breakfast and she said yes, at the quad, yes, but make it late. When he hung up, silence rushed into the booth.

He ambled back to his room, went in, took off his clothes and stretched out on the bed. Thankfully, a few things of Laura's were still in the room: a compact, a ball point pen, and, folded neatly on his towel rack in the bathroom, her uniform. After brushing his teeth he picked up the uniform, touched it to his nostrils and breathed it in.

The bed again: I'll just bury myself in it tonight, he told himself. No lovemaker, I. The bed tonight will be for dreaming anyway, so I'll lie here, let my worries parade briefly before me, sort themselves out, then let Laura, resplendently naked, dominate all the other images that lurk in my head. Eyes closed: I see her rib cage, the arch of her back, the jut of her nipples; we are in the library, hiding in an Eden of books; we are in Pless' rat room, she leans on me, she pipes and I follow her to Hamlin town; we are in this room, in rooms across Lake Michigan, across the world, and my dreams fold me under.

Stoker walked over to the quad the next morning. The night wind had swept the trees mostly bare and a new chilled breeze rippled off the lake.

The crowd in the bookstore jostled him and he jostled back, feeling good in the press of people. By the time he reached breakfast with Laura he was in unusually good spirits.

"There's a party tonight," she told him as she crunched her toast. "The kids across the hall are openin' their door and we're openin' ours and we're just goin' to let everybody flow around." Her drawl was more pronounced early in the day, he decided, before she mingled with all those Yankee nurses. "So bring boys," she said. "Every horny nurse in the hospital will probably stop in. And bring a bottle of something. A big bottle."

"Leave it to me," he promised.

"And, oh, Stoke, I won't be able to go back to your place after it's over. It just won't break up until nearly morning, if I know this bunch, and I'll have to help clean up. Understand?"

He said yes and touched her hand. A small sense of possession fluttered in him, and though he wanted to argue with her he didn't.

After breakfast he trudged over to Wieboldt Hall for his seminar. Just before he stepped into the classroom Professor Skidmore caught his arm, drew him aside, and put on his charm—which consisted of a thin, almost painful half-smile, the same sort he usually reserved for moments of the greatest literary folly on the part of one of his students. "Oh, by the bye," he began, and Stoker winced and tried to look pleasant. "There's the student literary magazine. The deadline is near, Stoker, and I've been meaning to ask you about a contribution. You mentioned last year you might consent to do a story for us."

Stoker promised that he'd try and submit something.

"As faculty adviser," Skidmore said, "I can push the deadline until Thanksgiving. But that's absolute. Try and hand in something. I promised the student staff I'd query you." He pursed his lips.

In his class Stoker hunched over his desk, having long ago

mastered the art of attentiveness to such men as Skidmore, and made a hawk-face while his thoughts, of course, ran rampant. The discussion was Miss Dickinson's poetry. Skidmore picked out a few random biographical footnotes: how the poetess was so shy, for instance, that she talked to her visitors around corners and door facings so there would be no direct confrontations.

Stoker's timid self loomed on him as Skidmore danced among his facts. For years, he accused himself, I've been timid, lost in adolescent silence. He thought of how he had always tried to pick reality and unreality away from each other like weeds and flowers in a silly, dualistic bouquet. Also, he admitted, he had made some stupid surmises: he had concluded that the colonel was a fool, that Cassie was a whore and a monster, that Pless was a rationalist, that this university was a smart place to be, that art was safe while life was a bog. In picking out the flowers of reality, he sensed, the poisoned mushrooms filled his basket. And all the while, he told himself, I kept withdrawing to a safety I imagined; I became a dreamer, feeling that eventually—though I uttered this to almost no one—I'd become a writer. I thought of myself as one at work on a desert island, sending out scraps of my wit and opinion to the mainland by bottle, and getting, always, a return bottle saying simply: That Last Message Was Beautiful and True. We Love You.

Well, screw all that. I was beginning to find pleasure in my timid window peeping, in playing the silent and wise youth with the colonel, in suffering verses and pages that weren't even written yet. Screw that. Laura is real and I'm real enough; let unreality settle like scum to the bottom and don't fret over it.

Skidmore pursed his lips while Miss Sherry, another student, delivered her usual symbolic explanation—this time of Miss Dickinson's punctuation. Critics are boors, Stoker decided, down to the last student morsel.

Even last night, he told himself—I made it through. I was

unhappy and disappointed, but I went to bed and slept instead of window-hopping around the campus or twiddling myself on the counterpane. And now, perhaps, I'll even make plans. I'll write a story for Skidmore and the local hippie literati, perhaps, and even suffer its probable failure. I'll take my master's degree, perhaps, and begin writing a book, some sort of book. Take a job at Penwiper State College, teach comp to idiot football players until enough of my own dear pages are paperclipped together. Plans, yes: let young Stoker make his way. I'll do it.

"Did you laugh, Stoker?" Skidmore asked. Lips apurse.

"Ah, no sir. Sorry."

"Did you have anything to add to the discussion?"

A pause. The class and world, Stoker felt, waited. "Well," he said, "yes. I have several things to say. Could I begin with my classmate's—excuse me, Miss Sherry—elaborate and if I might say so, sir, insipid little theory?"

As breath drew in all around him, he went forth.

After class he picked up a treasure at the campus post office: two postcards from the colonel, a perfumed note from Cassie, a dun from the registrar, and a letter from Dick Ramsdale, an acquaintance who was working on his dissertation while touring Europe.

When he looked up, there stood Clive. He was pawing a small set of photographs which he had just removed from an envelope. Before Stoker could speak, Clive stuffed them into his nylon jacket.

"There's a party tonight," Stoker blurted out. Immediately, he wondered about himself, but he went on. "Hot-blooded nurses. Leave your pants in the foyer. I was told to solicit all able-bodied gentlemen students."

Clive looked down on him with some disdain as he supplied the address. It's right to invite him, Stoker decided, because such specific sexual opportunity ought to scuttle him. His stories are all tall tales of tail.

"I had a nurse once," Clive puffed. "Friend of mine had shacked up with her over on Ellis Avenue, in fact, and I dropped around one afternoon. He just jerked his thumb back toward the bedroom as I came in. Glenda, her name was. She had a large bruise—in fact, a blue breast. Put me off a little. Blue breasts have a way of putting me off."

"Stop, Clive, please."

"Go have a cup of coffee with me. I have stories to blow your innocent mind."

"Can't do it," Stoker told him. "What sort of photos did you stuff in your pocket? Latest pornography?"

"Manner of speaking, yes. My sister Jackie."

"Let me see the famous sister."

"They're nothing. Snaps from Rio and points south."

"Let me see."

Clive sighed and produced them. There she was: a plain Jane with an anachronistic sultriness, a look on her face one might see on late television movies in parts played by Maria Montez or some forgotten starlet. She stands before a fountain or sits on a high terrace above Copa beach, this sister of his, photographically disappointing, but there: a counterpart, at least, to all his grisly stories.

"Very nice, Clive," Stoker managed, giving the photos back. He sensed a definite upper hand with his tormentor this noon.

They said goodbye. As Stoker walked back across the campus, he gave Clive certain credit; there was always enough verisimilitude about his stories to keep one wondering. Perhaps Glenda, a nurse, would appear at the party, her bluish breasts exposed. Perhaps some wild relationship with Jackie did exist for poor Clive.

Stoker opened his letter from Dick Ramsdale and found it rich with cliché. Among the ruins, the oversized castles, the lonely villas, the Parisian alleyways, Ramsdale went about discovering himself. Stoker turned to the colonel's basic prose, a postcard from Phoenix with: "Shot a nice round of golf here (see photo) in steaming weather. Tell Pless I'm taking V. to dinner. Pay your book bill early this semester & don't get behind. Call collect anytime as I'm not going TDY anymore this month. Ever, Dad."

Glancing up, Stoker saw a kite lashing out above the trees; he tried to follow the string to its source, but couldn't.

As he reached the apartment house he gave Cassie's monogrammed envelope a quick look. Inside, taking off his shoes, he let the letter lie on a table, then he slipped it, unopened, into the pages of a novel which protruded from his shelf.

· · · 11

CLIVE ROAMED THE LIBRARY that afternoon
in search of books on South American geography and some
tidbits of esoterica. He didn't want to go to the party that
night, but couldn't ignore Stoker's invitation and therefore
couldn't go unarmed. Above all else, this: he had to have
some intellectual scrap iron to bludgeon them with; otherwise
he knew he might let a simple match of arm wrestling boil
over into real violence; he might get giddy with rage and clean
the room of Stoker's new friends—the nurses and that crowd.
He knew what they'd be—pampered and weak—and he
wanted to maul them.

First, though, he thought of Jackie. He toured through an
atlas of South American countries familiarizing himself with
cities, rivers, mountain ranges, and all the places she had
recently visited. That done, he skimmed a history of Indian

religions along the equator. When he found an interesting page, he removed the razor blade from the fold of paper in his wallet and cut it out. Severed pages stacked up at his elbow and when his craving subsided he tucked them into his jacket pockets. He'd not use this research in his letters to Jackie, he knew, but just wanted to have it.

Next he gathered the disparate loose ends of his party talk: bits on the Dreyfus affair, animal behavior (pigs and dolphins, he read, were the most intelligent), and some voodoo items gleaned from his browsings on Central and South America and the islands. Anything would do, he knew, because he would use an old tactic: he would toss it all in the air and let his listeners ponder his sudden shifts of thought—a phenomenon they usually took as a sign of his volatile and superior intelligence. Idiots.

He found something else he liked, a book on Shinto. His razor blade flashed again and he smiled.

Wandering down the rows of books he let his finger trail across the titles. This is a lovely arsenal, he told himself, and I'm an intellectual commando—no regular soldier in organized classroom battle, no, but something slightly deadlier I like to think: a free lancer. Oh true, I don't make very good grades, not as brilliantly topnotch as dear P & S, but, ah, they listen and watch and wonder where I'll lead. Power: that's the thing. And he thought of Adler with his mundane hostilities, how Adler rebelled against the established order of things with no sense of the greater game, no imagination, and, at best, an impotent sort of bitterness. Adler wasted his anger on his instructors. He was the sort, Clive decided, who made marks on the walls of public toilets because he didn't have the gutty good sense to do anything more.

He stopped again at some oversized volumes of maps, opened one, and found a detailed map of Argentina. Out came his razor. His thoughts idled, meanwhile, and he didn't see the student assistant who moved up behind him.

Quickly, he slammed the volume shut, turning his body so that he shielded the razor blade, but he already knew he was too late.

"Hey, what're you doing there?" the student said.

Clive turned and fixed the boy with a stare. He immediately recognized his type as one of the assistant librarians: steel-rimmed glasses, a thin pallor, soft hands and eyes. At the moment, though, the student's chin jutted out with a certain authority.

"Nothing," Clive said, grinning, and without trying to hide his movements he folded his razor blade back into its paper sheath and placed it in his wallet.

"You were about to cut that map."

"Did you see me do that?"

"You were going to." The student turned hurriedly and began walking away. Clive took two long steps and caught him by the arm.

"Where are you going, friend?" He smiled.

"To report you. I saw what you were doing."

"Let's think about this," Clive told him. "When you get back here I won't *have* a razor blade and won't be anywhere near the maps. If you manage to incriminate me in spite of that, chances are I won't be found guilty. Who would make the judgment? The librarian? Some stupid violations committee? And, all right, suppose they decided you were telling the truth: what would they do to me? Chances are they'd do nothing. There's not much evidence, is there? So it would come down between you and me. Where it is already. Understand?"

"Let go of my arm," the student said.

Clive drew their faces close together. "Now look here," he said. "Don't cause me any trouble."

"Bastard."

Just as suddenly, then, Clive gave him another faint smile and released him. "If someone comes down here after me," he said, "then I'll find out your name. And you'll find mine out too, and you'll never forget it."

The student pushed his glasses high on his nose and left.

Clive walked back to the carrel where he had left the stack of cut pages. He trembled slightly, but felt exhilarated and couldn't help smiling to himself. Even so, he knew he couldn't take his cuttings out of the library and so he folded them and stuffed them into an air vent which had a loose grating. Then he checked his notebook, still smiling, his hands still tingling, to make sure that he hadn't left a telltale scrap there. His gaze fell on a schedule in the back section of his notebook.

> P: leaving: 8:39, 8:42, 8:15, 7:55, 8:31 p.m.
>   returning: 11:16, 11:52, 12:21, 11:09, 11:16
>
> A: leaving: 9:05, 9:22, 7:36, 9:04, 8:20
>   returning: 12:47, 2:10, 1:36, 2:19, 3:05 a.m.

The evening work habits of Pless and Adler in tentative form. Clive looked down at the page, still excited from the incident with the assistant, and felt the blood pulsing around his temples.

The schedule. He sighed, closed the notebook, and gathered up his things.

Slowly, he walked out of the library, stopping at the guard's desk to have his materials checked. No problem. He went slowly across the quad, pacing his steps toward Stoker's place, but then he changed his mind and turned around. He headed back toward his room, suddenly wanting to be alone. I'll start on Stoker's schedule tomorrow, he told himself, but for now I'd better rest for the party, rest and think. Tomorrow I'll get back to their simple little habits: when they rise, where they eat, their class hours, where they spend their leisure this year. Never has disgust been so scientific. I'll learn them out of existence.

He reached his room, an L-shaped cupboard on Kimbark

Avenue which he had filled with his barbells, stolen books and phonograph albums, and candles. He had candles everywhere: varisized tapers for his every mood and reverie. As he spread himself out on the bed a question began to knock in his head. Why do I hate them so much? A multiplicity of reasons, he answered himself: because, for all their small griefs, they're more affluent and more privileged. He pondered that as he gazed around his room, a small and dingy room which made him recall the nice rooms he had rented last year, rooms so expensive that he had gone into debt keeping them up.

He got up, turned over the stack of records, then returned to the bed.

No, he decided, that's not altogether it. He tried to think about it, but the fierce reasons for his disgust wouldn't be located. He fell back, finally, on an admission he frequently made: that he hated almost everything with the same hot disgust, not just those three minor players—simple Stoker, awful Addie and popular Pless—but nearly the whole sick texture of his life.

Turning, he grabbed up a book of matches and lit the fat candle which was wedged onto a saucer on his nightstand. His eyes glazed momentarily before the flame, and he decided that perhaps he just hated out of boredom, because hate was such a sweet liquor, a liquor, after all, that could really keep you drunk.

···12

THE PARTY WAS LARGER than Stoker expected. When he arrived he went upstairs and into Laura's apartment, but she wasn't there. He found Parker, who told him that Laura was across the hall, but the crush of students was too great for him to attempt to cross the room again so he settled down atop a cold radiator with a glass of Scotch. Parker kissed him lightly on the cheek for bringing two quarts of Vat 69, then disappeared into the throng, leaving him to survey a field of torsos and to wish that he could make his way toward Laura's arms.

He analyzed the crowd, giving it a hasty sociological eye. There were four groups, he concluded. First the uninteresting intellectuals. They stood or sat mostly in one place, looked over their horned-rimmers, nodded, and made cautious sounds. To an extent—because of his record, he decided—he was one of them, but he admitted that he was really more a part of the second group, the brooders. These were the bright and talented ones, mostly, but they loved their hang-ups, enjoyed being alienated, and fluttered about how hard it was to communicate. Unlike the intellectuals, who obeyed the system except in certain accepted modes of defiance, the brooders bucked almost everyone, especially their professors, and so usually suffered bad grades, academic enemies, melodramatic love affairs, social disdain, chronic maladjustment, and also usually body odor and bad teeth. They were always stalking off in anger from the university and they were always coming back—back from San Francisco, Europe, Mexico, and the second-rate schools where they went to bolster their grades. They made a life, in short, of being misunderstood. The third group consisted of the nurses, and this party, Stoker's best hopes whispered, would possibly find them prevailing. They were the only ones with a genuine sense of humor, he felt, because they were basically vulgar. They were all laid in high school where they wept, pulled their hair, and got all that over with early in their careers; in college they already knew enough to avoid the fraternity boys and so matriculated in and out of several beds, made good grades, and signed on to become nurses much like old sergeants re-enlist, out of a sense of proficiency and destiny and toughness; later, then, they found out that they enjoyed their work, even its most unromantic moments, and began to take pride in themselves. They were, in short, women. Stoker imagined that at this party they would swing and the brooders, who tried to sit back and say witty and sardonic things, would be dazzled by them. The last group consisted of the Uglies. If Adler were here, Stoker knew, he would be one of these. In the course of an evening the Uglies had the duties and temperaments of servants. They poured drinks and went after ice. They searched for the lost contact lens. They wiped up things. Since they expected little or nothing from such occasions, though, they'd probably not have the letdown, Stoker reasoned, which the brooders would suffer when everything was over.

He sat on the radiator wondering how he could even know all this. A short while ago—last spring—he had been a deeply driven brooder himself. He enjoyed his failure to communicate with the colonel, Cassie, his professors, anyone. Any new insight, he supposed, was because of Laura. He gulped down his drink and chewed up the ice cubes with confidence. Delicious.

Slowly, he edged toward the kitchen.

Parker was there pouring generous drinks from his bottles.

"I could just kiss you for bringing all this booze," she chirped.

"You did kiss me, but you can do it again," he teased.

A couple of nearby Uglies laughed nervously. Parker turned, arched herself up, took him around the shoulders, and laid one on him. The insides of her mouth tasted like cinnamon. Damn. She didn't let go. In response, he pretended he was a hairy Greek. Grabbing her, he pushed her back against the refrigerator. After a moment someone asked for an ice cube, but she was busy nibbling and sucking on him. He felt a thick bead of perspiration dive from under his arm down into his pants. Finally, with a certain exhaustion creeping into his lips and facial muscles, he quit her.

"I just came out here," he said in casual breathlessness, "for a little more whiskey."

Someone nearby applauded.

Parker materialized again and became a hostess.

Fragments of conversation wafted around Stoker and he tried not to listen. Someone said, "I hear that skirts are going nine inches above the knee next year," and someone answered, "Hell, most girls I know don't *have* nine inches above the knee."

He drifted out of the kitchen. As he did, a voice burrowed

into his ears from the outer circle: unmistakably Clive. Stretching, Stoker saw him standing tall above the admiring brooders. He was always a champion with them, working them like Mandrake the Magician worked his bunnies.

Yet it occurred to Stoker as he listened to that familiar voice that Clive, unquestionably, should probably seek out the company of the brooders even more than he actually did. Why not? Does Pless, Stoker wondered, and the challenge of our little group offer him more? He can bully anyone, but prefers our mixed bag: one brooder, one intellectual, one Ugly. Perhaps he took a campus survey, Stoker allowed, and found us—and works his magic on us just to test himself for greater conquests on greater scales. Stoker pondered him, thinking: tonight, having slightly gotten the best of him this afternoon in the post office, I feel a little more kindly. Over there across the room he is a bragging magpie, the grim weaver. A coed gazes up into his face; she has a cow-like stare, a mind ready to mythologize the young men she meets, and little idea that he would gladly take her into the alley and mutilate her nipples and flanks. Ah, true, dear heart, he's a sadist—that at least. Even so, he fascinates, and he's a force in any room where he stands.

Excusing himself, Stoker passed along into the hallway. The stairway was crowded with lovers: legs akimbo, lies flowing.

The next apartment belonged, obviously, to a girl who wasn't a nurse because there were Japanese lanterns everywhere and all the equipage of a young matron who had little else to do except decorate things. A papier-mâché candleholder. An ugly do-it-yourself tile table.

Laura was across the room in conversation with a stranger, a young man with a blue-shadowed chin and dark brows.

Stoker stood there until she noticed him. Then, flashing a smile, she came twisting through the crowd toward him, took his extended hands in hers, and full of public display gave him a greeting kiss. Not as potent as Parker's, he judged, but Laura smelled delicious and her lips felt wonderful on his rapidly more inebriated mouth.

"Where've you been?" she drawled.

Her arm linked in his and she led him back across the hallway, deliberately away from her friend, it seemed, but Stoker didn't mind. She greeted late arrivals as she hung on his arm, showing him off, and he smiled and nodded as they began pushing their way toward the bottles in the kitchen. When the traffic thickened, though, they halted.

"You wait here, darlin'," she told him. "I'll get us a refill."

He stood waiting. Darling.

The stereo erupted with "Judy in Disguise."

Jostled in the direction of Clive again, Stoker found that the hand-wrestling had already begun. A fat boy, creamy skinned and grinning, had positioned himself in the chair opposite Clive as the audience sipped and tittered. Clive was at his best, bragging and putting them on, making himself the loudmouth everyone would enjoy seeing beaten, except, of course, he'd win. He'll never get his from this round boy, Stoker knew.

As the two locked hands Clive fixed his stare on one of the coeds at the periphery of the circle. The girl moved her hand nervously to her cheek. Like the coed a few minutes earlier, she gazed at Clive with rapture. All behavior is sexual, Stoker remembered—or so Clive had said often enough—and here was the documentation.

Clive offered the fat boy a dictionary to put under his elbow for added height.

"Hell," the Ugly said, "you want to use both hands?"

"No, but *you* may," Clive said. "Of course I couldn't put you down if you used both hands, but you couldn't put me down either."

Everyone laughed nervously at his bravado, then waited.

The act itself was quick and comic. The fat boy's knuckles

cracked down so hard that the noise was heard outside the circle of Clive's audience.

"Come on, I wasn't ready," the Ugly complained. Uncontrollable laughter billowed up from the crowd and Parker, who came to stand at Stoker's side, asked what was going on.

Clive consented to give his opponent another try, and for a moment, perhaps because the fat boy's face showed definite signs of sincere involvement, a hush overtook the audience. But Clive was still filled with dramatics. "Tell you what," he said to the Ugly, "I'll give you a standoff for a minute or so." Then, turning to his enthralled coed: "You can tell me, dear, when I should gross him out. Give a signal." The hush became an undertone again, everyone whispering and muttering about Clive; nobody could stand him, Stoker decided, but nobody went uncaptivated. The coed squealed her affirmative and the next round began.

The fat boy tried too hard; sweat glistened momentarily on his creamy forehead as his lips tightened. Everyone regretted his loss of cool.

Then it happened again. The girl cried, "Now!" and Clive pressed forward, ever so simply, and—whack!—it was done. Parker approved by squeezing Stoker's arm.

"Where's Laura?" Stoker asked her.

"With her Max again, probably," Parker sighed. "Just leave her alone and let her work it out. It's her old steady."

Stoker felt his throat knot slightly. "Her doctor? The one she followed here from New Orleans?"

Parker answered yes by lowering her eyes.

Laura wasn't with Max nor anyone, though, for in a moment she came back with Stoker's drink and a passion to dance. He made all his excuses—there wasn't enough space on the floor, no proper music, his feet were uncommunicative —but they went whirling anyway. He tried to balance his drink and move a little as he watched her hips grind in a subtle counterbeat to the dim thump of the music. No good. He felt awkward. Shuffling toward her, he grabbed her waist and they went spinning out to the hallway.

"Let's go to the car far a while," he suggested.

"Later," she said. "There'll be even more people later and no one'll miss us."

In the next hour, then, Stoker resided in a state of expectant fantasy. His sexual history went weaving before his eyes in a tipsy parade. As Laura chatted with her acquaintances and laced her hand in his, he saw himself moving from window to window in the world; he saw a woman in a mauve room gazing at herself in a mirror, and her reflection was so lovely that it frightened him, but when she turned around her face was a map of pain and he turned away; to distant lighted windows he ran, but they darkened before he arrived; his dizzy heart gave him images: a girl on a Florida beach, a book from the Olympia Press, white Cassie in her bedroom, his own body with the skin peeling away from it so that he lay transformed, baking in the sun like a fat snake. His head reeled and he allowed some of his weight to go to Laura, saying, "Laura, don't let me drink anymore. I've had enough."

But he had a few more. Another hour passed and he met Clive standing in line for the bathroom, and of course he was trim and sober and smiled down with condescension, Stoker felt, and said everything with wondrous articulation.

"Good evening, Stoker," he enunciated.

Stoker managed to shrug and move his mouth without sound.

"I see you have yourself a girl," Clive went on. "Very nice. Is she the one you've picked out to grieve you when you're gone?"

Letting that sink in, Stoker rested his eyes on a fragment of the Japanese lantern which was now being kicked around the floor.

"Oh, you're a hostile fart," he said.

"Temper, Stoker. Please."

"Great sober pig. I'm not bothered by you anymore—one way or another. I want you to know that."

"I don't know what you're talking about," Clive said, smiling.

When the bathroom door opened, Stoker shoved on by. "Out of my way or I'll wet your coat tail," he said, then, turning, added: "All that bile of yours. No wonder Pless pities you."

Stoker heard Clive laughing at him after closing the door, and he found that his hands were shaking from that brief, open encounter. His lips grinned at me when I threw that last old garbled sentence at him, Stoker decided, but his eyes, ah, his eyes: they narrowed into slits.

With his hand propped high on the wall behind the toilet and his body tense and ready for delivery, Stoker waited, thinking: I cannot meditate, cogitate, enunciate, ruminate, or, now, when put to it, ejaculate. He thought of the stream of strangers Laura had introduced, but couldn't recall a single name. Concentrate. His face was mirrored in the bowl.

Finally finished, he returned to find that all those who had waited so long for him, Clive included, had disappeared.

Nearby, Laura's friend—Max, it was—was talking to Parker and his drawl was thicker than Laura's, a great syrupy sound.

"Oh, Stoke," Parker said as he passed by. "This is Max. Max: Stoker." Her introduction was rich with apprehension.

"Evening, Max," Stoker mumbled, leaning over to smell Parker's lush blonde hair. "Ah, sweet it is." She smiled and gave him a friendly jab with her little finger.

In the kitchen, pouring his last, Stoker eavesdropped on topics. Mayor Daley was preparing to give the rioters of the coming summer Comiskey Park, nine Lake Michigan barges, Arlington Park, Northwestern University and the Palmer House. Every nubile coed in the greater Chicago colleges and universities had also been asked to report to the nearest ghetto, find herself a malcontent buck, and solve, once and for all, the racial tension. With friendly concern the kitchen occupants tried to draw Stoker into their discussions, and he stood there trying to think what corner of his vast expertise he should expose to them. He thought of his knowledge of, in no order at all: the Third Reich, the American Indian, Modigliani's models, the phallic drawings of the eighteenth century, tennis, epicalyxes, movie trivia, current literary gossip, prosody, advanced grammar, astronomy, flamenco guitar and salt water fishing. None of it fits their mood, he concluded, and, besides, I'm no Clive.

When he moved back into the mainstream of the party he found Clive and Max, hands locked, about to do battle. Lo, it's too perfect, he told himself; he moved in to watch.

Again, much talk accompanied the performance, Clive boasting and Max drawling. The end, though, came quickly.

"Damn, you're strong," the drawler said, getting up and massaging his wrist.

At this point Parker was doing a bougalou with a mustached brooder. Her body seemed oiled, all parts in working order, and her eyes fell into Stoker's as she skated around her partner. Music knocked in the room, Stoker speculated on the curve of female hips, and Laura, softly, came to his side and took his hand.

"You potted?" she wanted to know. Then before he could answer: "I'll drive you home and put you to bed now, if you want. If you're tired of all this."

Never, he told her, had he been so weary.

It was a short drive over to his room and in those moments he tried to gain a sense of focus. Obvious conclusions came spewing forth: Laura, he affirmed, is slightly more self-conscious now than she was a few days ago; Clive is a ringing idiot and my enemy; Parker could go for me; the brooders are a sad lot, each and every one; Max is on old truelove and deadly. Leaning back on Laura's shoulder as she drove, he suddenly knew all this, but without premonition or a sense of crisis.

Laura meanwhile turned from East 56th into Woodlawn Avenue. Her thigh pressed on his, and although Clive's remark continued to nag at Stoker he just couldn't think about it.

Once inside his place, Laura sent him off to the bathroom to bathe, powder, and defumigate his liquored pores. He touched a match to the space heater, felt it warm his toes, and heard from the bedroom the soft sounds of his hacked-up record player doing The Doors in undertone. Laura, my muse, he told himself, please play me like a broken flute.

"What's going on in there?" she called.

"Just trying to take off my pants, Muse."

Towels. He dragged several off the shelf, chose a white one, fondled it, fixed it across his face like a hood, and played search for the soap.

"What're you doin' now?"

It pleased him to be safe in his apartment, to have Laura guarding him, and he enjoyed feeling around for the bar of soap on the cool floor of the shower stall. Clive's remark lingered. Prithee, Clive, thy sense of decorum lacks. I would smite thee. Like a knight fitting himself for a joust, he thought of his body as a steel spring, all armored and rigged, poised, driving all its will and strength toward the tip of the lance, thinking one thought, serving one thrust. Concentrate. A thousand times you've made yourself detour around such vitalities (remember the pine outside of Verna's kitchen?) and now you've got to force the semen down from your brain, he told himself, down the shaft of your troubled torso, slow white dicky droplets, each one, into your old handlebar, and out into Laura's vast galaxies.

He found the soap, removed his mask, and stepped gingerly into the shower. Water rattled around him and when it warmed he turned it on himself and let out a whoop. Concentrate. Pile-driving lance thou art. Great redheaded dragon. Concentrate on Laura's dainty little pocket; her heart is that hairy little mouth; she loves it, too, every push and nuzzle.

"Hurry," she called to him.

His lance saluted faintly. Weapon and celibate friend, he addressed it, I want this one thing from you; build me a new city, dreary old erector set; pay no attention to this drunken hulk of me. Let my stray thoughts settle on you, on every lovely blue vein. Concentrate! Ye who failed me in Florida and in a hundred air force bases of North America! Attention! A little military discipline now, please! There! Stand up and be counted! *Achtung!*

The towel whispered softly around his body as the bathroom heater quietly hissed his performance.

Think romantic images, he commanded himself: all those sea and tide images from D H Lawrence, those great rushing swells, passionate melodies of the surf as Mellors, bless his wee bonny arse, gets a piece of Constance Chatterley. Now the tide rushes in, plants a kiss on the shore. Think of wavering candlelight, a bottle of Montovani, moon river. Concentrate. Think of Henry Big Sur Millah popping for fun in Paris. No, more romantic than that: a lonely suntanned American lost on a distant isle, warm native girls for breakfast and lunch, bowls of fruit, hula humping, poignant *alohas* in the dying sun.

"What are you *doing?*" Laura appeared around the corner, smiling and nude, and shut off his bathroom heater.

"Thinking about you," Stoker told her.

"Is it so difficult? It's taking a long time." Laura locked her arms around his neck and flattened her breasts on his chest. "S' hot in here," she murmured.

Suddenly, as if their bodies hadn't moved, Stoker imagined, they were on the bathroom rug and all his pleasant levity was gone as she began her moves; she climbed around him like a vine, riding him, putting kisses on his temples. His fantasies, which usually ambushed him in the act, had no time to gather, and he momentarily sensed that they might be enemies after all, not allies, and he looked at Laura in the harsh bathroom glare, their every sound magnified into coarse reality by the surrounding porcelain fixtures, and Laura was suddenly a dear friend—she had always liked that word *friend* when speaking about them—doing an old, friendly act and service for him. His heart melted for her and he loved her for it and wanted to drive his magic and precious juices up inside her, thinking: ah, she rides, and my hands are full of her small white ass, and here I go, I go, I start to go, it comes pumping out of my marrow, out of my spine and the conduits of my heart, and the slap of our bodies is tender applause, oh, here it comes, booming now, like waters breaking a dam of ice up high in the mountains of me, and, oh, concentrate, I go, I go off, I'm coming, Laura, I tell her, and she rides hard and artful, never letting up, and I say oh stop it now, oh stop.

"Surprise," Laura said, watching his silly expression.

Then they lay in bed they talked about how quick and simple it had been, how it would be from then on, how it was always better—this was Laura's addition, but Stoker concurred—in strange rooms or cities or in moments that contained an element of surprise. They complimented each other on style (hers) and size (his) and slipped into a solid vernacular: a really good screw, they agreed. She became a part of the pulse beneath his arm, pressed against him with the covers up under their chins.

Then he was adream, floating in a euphoria, a dazed warmth.

In the middle of the night he grew enough awake to realize that she was gone and it took a moment for him to figure out that she had probably gone back to her guests at the party. He smiled and turned over, touching as much of his body as he possibly could to the sheets where her scent lingered. In his half-sleep he knew that he would sleep far into the next day, but that when consciousness came to him again Laura and the world would be there, the university would be there, Pless and the colonel would be there, and, among them, somewhere, himself. I'm alive, he knew; all is there, nothing is lost.

··· 13

PLESS AND ADLER BUZZED HIS ROOM until he woke up at noon the next day.

They waited while he staggered around getting dressed, found the keys to his car for him, then helped him outside and into the driver's seat so that he could take them down into the Loop for lunch. It was a bright day in late October, the sky all sapphire, and they traveled slowly down the Outer Drive along the lake watching girls in orange sweaters walking leashed puppies near the shore. A permanent smile curled Stoker's face, and he realized he was far less somber than either Pless or Addie. Addie reported that he was constipated —and also that he and young Cogdill had been snapping at each other again. Pless sighed frequently, so much that Stoker detected his thick sobriety even through the haze of his own hangover.

"What's the matter?" he asked him outright.

Pless as Young Hemingway: "I feel good. It is a good autumn day and I feel good. We all feel good. This is a good thing."

As they drove along the sun caught Adler's scraggly whiskers and Stoker thought he looked saintly. "Your beard is getting handsome," he said to him, hoping to boltser his feelings.

No answer.

They parked in the city lot and walked several chilly blocks into the center of the Saturday afternoon activities. At a window of a long, sterilized diner on State Street they stood for a moment watching a lanky Negro in an exaggerated chef's hat flipping steaks over a broiler. T-Bone, Big Ole Baked Potato, Salad and Coffee: $1.95/Quick Service/Everybody Gets a Seat.

"There, friends," Pless observed, "we have the degeneration of the steak dinner in our time."

In the next block they paused to inspect a male manikin in a leather suit. Six Hundred Dollars. They strolled over to Wabash, and beneath the shadows of the El they saw faces bending toward them from the buses halted in the traffic: bored, patient, ignorant faces. Stoker began to feel abnormally good, though he suspected that Pless and Addie had grimly planned this little excursion by way of promoting a little high morale—dragging him along because they imagined he needed his spirits lifted the same as they did. But the city did excite him this afternoon and seemed like a woman, all feminine, her streets opening like thighs, and he was adrift in her like a hopeless infatuate, seduced by her soot and camphors.

They ate at a small bar, McRafferty's, on Dearborn Street. Hungry and bolting down his food, Stoker reached for the butter and tipped over his beer. It ran off the edge of the table and spilled on Pless' pants before he could get up, and the waitress, a tired-looking girl with freckles, came dabbing at the mess with a towel.

"It's all right," Adler said, turning to him. "You're not spilling as many things as you used to."

Stoker gave him a quizzical look.

"You used to be awfully clumsy," Pless added.

"You never said anything about it," Stoker said.

"He was the worst fisherman in Florida," Pless said. "And he kept wanting to go hunting too, but I knew he'd trip over a log and shoot me in the back. It was enough pulling his fish-hooks out of our clothes when we went out into the gulf."

"I don't remember it that way at all," Stoker objected.

"Repression," Pless said.

The lunch put Stoker in an even better mood, for he felt some of his old warmth with Pless generating. They talked about classes, about shows and movies in town, some safe and friendly subjects.

Afterward they drifted down on State Street below Division. Stoker bought a shirt in one of the haberdasheries and then they ventured into a neighborhood of stag movie arcades. Each arcade offered a semicircle of booths with coin-operated machines. Slumped with resignation in the gaudiest of all these arcades was a vendor of change, a small sad man with drooping pants and a fistful of quarters.

They crowded into a narrow booth whose front floor was tilted like the floorboard of an automobile, and as Pless drew the curtain shut the darkness smelled stale, burnt and old. Adler fed a quarter into the machine and some brown film flickered before them on the dirty screen. A plump maiden sat on a bed removing her bra. Slowly, it peeled away. As a nipple appeared she looked suddenly surprised, as if she hadn't expected it, and a strained grin flashed her teeth. They sat watching, their legs propped up, Adler wheezing slightly.

"You know what this booth is?" Pless asked out of the side of his mouth, Cagney-like. "It's a masturbation booth."

The girl in the film smoothed her stockings, drawing her stubby fingers along her ample thigh. With a snap, then, the film ended.

"That's all I get for my quarter?" Addie complained.

"She'll never get those damned pants off anyway," Pless told him. Even so, he popped another quarter into the slot himself.

The girl continued to remove her stockings as the film rolled; then, without warning, another scene opened on a thin blonde beside a swimming pool. She wore lace underwear and changed poses rapidly, alternating smiles and barely detectable winces as she searched for a comfortable spot on the poolside tile. There was a dark mole on her shoulder and her eyebrows arched up into her hairline before falling sharply. That film ended with her waving at the camera daintily as she wiggled her legs in the air.

They drove back to the campus. Not much was said among them, so little that Stoker began to worry over them, but he drove along keeping his apprehensions to himself. He wanted to talk about Clive, about Laura, about any topic of mutual interest, but he sensed that the whole downtown trip had been a real fight for both of them, an effort to keep on the surface and a diversion. In silence they arrived at the Blackstone Towers where Pless went sulking away, thanking Stoker for the lift, and at the greenhouse Addie left without so much as a goodbye.

Let them stay in their funk, Stoker decided, and he went back to his room, read his assignments for the following week, attended to his lavatory which was pregnant with every dirty dish and utensil he owned, shaved, and finally, on impulse, sat down and wrote a note to Cassie.

Mother Dear: Having not heard from you, I assume, naturally, that plans haven't changed & that y'll be here for the Thanksgiving recess. Let us cranberry and giblet together.

Bring yr Richard & yr sweet pocketbook. I will then tell
you all the news, that I (a. have a girl, (b. could use additional funds, (c. am thinking of composing a long epic poem
about the American Way of Strife which will endear me all
over this land & make you proud.

Ever, S.

The envelope was peppermint flavored. Throwing on his
jacket, he walked down to the corner mailbox beside the phone
booth and deposited the note en route to see Laura.

It was early evening, and he walked, stars overhead, thinking: I am twenty-two years old, strong of body, no longer a
technical virgin. All things are richly sensual; the Loop this
afternoon was a voyeur's dream and now the campus windows, awake in their first light, beckon. The sound of my
corduroy walk is sexual; the plants of Addie's greenhouse
yearn with sex; all relationships are sexual, including mine to
Cassie, the colonel, Verna, Pless, Ad, Clive, Laura, Parker,
Ramsdale, Skidmore, and the occupants of those distant windows. All literature is sexual (you open books like thighs)
and all architecture (phallic buttresses and oversized vaginal
doorways) and we are placed on this earth for sensation—
which precedes and postscripts all cognitive value—and for
erotic passage, a dance and flight. Ah, such wisdom: it seems
mystical, as though it ought to be in the possession of ancient
seers, visionaries who reside in high mountain caves and eat
honey and bed down in bone, but I know it too. I know. And
my friends are in a funk, yes, but I feel the lilt of my muscles
inside my clothes as I walk. The plaque I never found that
fateful evening is only a block away, but I keep going; I can
see it another time; there's a new sculpture by Henry Moore
hovering with it, I've learned, and strange how I know where
everything is, how my mind maps the campus, the city, the
hemisphere, all space and the dangling stars.

At Laura's apartment, Stoker plodded steadily and noisily
upstairs. If she's not here, he told himself, then I'll settle

• • • 169

down and wait for her, perhaps with Parker to keep me company. It somehow pleased him that he hadn't seen her all day; it added to his expectantcy.

The door stood open.

"Whoa there! You startled me, old buddy!" At the table sat Max, his fingers spread out over a copy of *Life* magazine, and Stoker felt his throat contract. Words bubbled up, almost spilled out of him: her medical student, her doctor, her lover come back. Max wore a bathrobe (unidentifiable) and smoked a fat cigarette (probably Turkish) and looked like the room in which he sat (demolished). The room seemed in fact an empty still life of the party, Stoker felt: unwashed glasses, broken Japanese lanterns, mountains of cigarette butts and valleys of stains. And there sat Max, reading—or trying to. In an instant Stoker took it all in and his breath, in spite of all he could do, heaved in his throat so that he didn't even know if he could speak.

"Who're you looking for?" Max asked him. "Parker or Laura?" At that point, Stoker knew that he looked like a fool; his mouth probably dangled open. "They're both on shift," Max went on. "Won't be back until after ten." Then again: "Which one did you want to see?"

Stoker compounded his foolishness. "Parker," he managed, and he hated himself for it immediately, and felt sure that Max knew he was lying, that he knew exactly, and Stoker felt himself glued there, reverting to his old brooding form, timid and exiled, and realized he was biting his lip. "But look," he finally managed to say, "I'll come back. Uh. No use waiting all that time. What time is it now?"

"I don't have a watch," Max answered coldly.

"It doesn't matter. I'll come back later," he said, and turned away.

"Who shall I say called, old buddy?" Max yelled, but Stoker was already halfway downstairs again.

For hours he lay on his bed replaying that brief scene in

his mind, saying new things to an imaginary Max, letting his frustration take two directions: yearning for Laura and grieving for himself, afraid that he'd lose her and afraid that he might drop off into those misty flats where the brooders resided, where his caged adolescence had spent itself. A thing like this, he feared, could send him back to the windows of the world, peeping in at the timid fringes of existence.

Yet it was a comic scene, too, he explained to himself, with Stoker as the dupe. A curious vantage opened: he saw himself and Max in a whirling farce, cracking jokes, playing Noel and Coward in a witty and frothy one-act. They parried and parted. Who gets the girl, he wondered, and wins the scene and who, indeed, says what to whom?

After a while he could pep-talk himself no longer; his body began to sink under its ballast of disappointment and he dissolved onto the bed. Sleep is such a sweet release and refuge, he decided, and for a brief moment he meditated on the long and lovely sleep of death, the pact, all the ultimate acts of cowardice and retreat, then he wrestled such thoughts away, regained himself, and groped for more rational patterns. In the morning, he decided, I'll call Pless and ask him to go to breakfast (what's more rational, after all, than eggs and toast and the crisp Sunday newspaper?) and Pless, as always, will reason things out.

A long night. In fitful sleep, he got up often, his bladder aching, and stalked off to another few thoughtful seconds at the toilet. He stood above the unromantic lid bombarding himself with the metaphysics of boys and girls together, trying to lie to himself: nothing happened, that little meeting meant nothing to Max, go to your Laura. But his marrow argued with all such positive thinking.

Returning to bed, he saw his failures parading before him. Names and faces of heroines: Sharon, Patricia, Joan, Rhue Anne. All of them had been warm for his loins, had come to him in various stages of heat and undress in those cities where he had traveled with the colonel and Cassie. They had been too dumb to realize that his sexual wiring wasn't quite intact. Painfully, involuntarily, he reviewed them, and afterward he wanted the strength to go to Laura, to take her by reason or by rape. She's mine, rightfully, he argued with himself, because I love her so much.

A few hours later the infrequent sounds of Sunday cars echoing against the window beside his bed slowly waked him and he got up, shaved again, put on fresh clothes, and went down to the corner telephone booth. Locked in that warm plastic box in the glint of the morning sun, he looked across the campus as he dialed; in spite of himself he already felt that everything was in place, that he could make it. Standing there in that opaque booth, boxed like a tender orchid on display, he called Pless.

They met in the refectory of the theological seminary, a small basement room where the seminary students always crowded themselves in before chapel services on Sunday mornings to pounce into a few "meaningful" conversations and to enjoy the inexpensive coffee and rolls. It seemed fitting, Stoker supposed, that he and Pless should attend these premises for such heartbreaking confessions.

Actually, the moral issue was dim. As he tried to frame the situation for Pless, he bungled along even in that. He told him about the party, about Parker's luscious kiss, about Max, but then stopped. Pless urged him on, giving him a solidly professional gaze. Stoker finally told him about going up to Laura's place and finding Max sitting there in the rubble of the party. Then, Stoker's confession having gotten into gear at last, he even told Pless about saying he had come to see Parker.

Munching his breakfast roll, Pless listened attentively, his look grave but confident.

"Hmm, I see," he remarked, being Dr. Freud.

"In short," Stoker said, "I think I'm bounced."

"There's a very simple solution," Pless offered. He leaned back in his chair and drank off his coffee. "Go back over there and . . ."

"Oh no, I just can't. I'm not competitive enough."

"Let me finish. Go back over there, Stoke, and pay *Parker* a visit. You like Parker, don't you?"

"She gave me a hell of a kiss at the party," Stoker admitted. "And I like her, yes, but Laura—we've had a fine thing, Pless, really."

"I understand. But if that's so, this won't matter. Go ask Parker for a date."

"I don't know."

"That's how I'd do it. And you asked me, remember?"

"But sex is like a bowel movement for you," Stoker complained. "It's all easy and hygienic. That secretary you mentioned, for instance: I'll bet you've already laid her."

"We've broken up," Pless admitted.

"Say, that's not why you've been so low lately, is it?"

"Oh, hell no. My work hasn't been going too well. Listen, Stoke, play it rough. It's a big rough game. Barge in over there. Don't sulk around."

"I'll try and do something. I have to."

"What about last night after you went home? Everything all right?"

"I had a miserable time getting to sleep."

"But you didn't go window-shopping around campus?"

"No, that's all over."

"Good. Eat your breakfast then." Pless grinned, and Stoker gave him a wan smile in return.

After breakfast, though, he went back to his room and tried to work, without success. He came to his desk again and again, studied for only a few minutes, got up to divert himself, returned to study again until late that afternoon his hungers waylaid him: he needed another meal and his groin ached with energy.

Choosing to not flog his sexual instincts into submission and to instead indulge his other hunger, he went off in search of hamburgers and found them in that same greasy bar north of the campus where he had met the old sailor. There, sitting on a barstool, sandwich in hand, he entered a nearly formal reverie, drifting back into the gates of his childhood, passing into scenarios with his colonel, who, he concluded, had given him the legacy of mildness he now suffered. The colonel, he mused, took a few emotional bruises as he rose in the ranks, for he was never a man to push himself. Recollection: he taught me to drive a car when I was fifteen. There at Fort Walton Beach. We went to the Officer's Club and drove right on down to the surf in the old Dodge convertible, and I learned the gears and pedals as the wind whipped our hair. He sat there with his arm propped behind me, patiently explaining things while I jerked us forward toward Destin, and finally I opened it up with his permission, and there, he said, was the motivation for all the learning I'd do: that moment of absolute freedom and speed and control behind that wheel, those wonderful sensations, and I suddenly knew how much flying meant to him, how he probably endured all the shit and polish of his profession just to gain a few lonely moments in the air, gliding above the earth, beyond the voice and ambiguous touch of Cassie, into the distant horizons. We sped up the beach toward Destin at nearly eighty miles an hour, the surf roaring alongside us, and by the time we got there I was a driver. And now I see his face: every crevice of his forehead, the cut of his jaw; a sad man, lost among his strengths, unable to find them, perhaps, and wary of me. And I think of my obligation, if any, toward him; what can a generation ever give back? Mustn't one always make gifts to the future, giving, if anything, to one's own children because nothing can ever really be given back? Recollection: that day Pless' father went into the bay. At the time it was all abstract. Had it been the colonel, though, my years might have been spent just as Pless has spent his: trying to think back, trying to hear the voice of the ghost. That's his trouble, always: some form of nostalgia. We pay the living no homage. Ah, such a meandering of thought.

Stoker swung off the stool, paid his bill, and went out into another deepening twilight.

Going back toward his place, he stopped off at the plaque. He had seen it a few times before, though not adorned with the new Moore sculpture, the mushroom-shaped ornament that punctuated it. There it was, the grass worn away around it where so many students had come to meditate with it:

ON DECEMBER 2, 1942
MAN ACHIEVED HERE
THE FIRST SELF-SUSTAINING CHAIN REACTION
AND THEREBY INITIATED
THE CONTROLLED RELEASE OF NUCLEAR ENERGY

There it sat beside an old tennis court, a patchwork of other plaques added around it honoring Fermi and the others, honoring the donor who paid for the plaques, honoring the anniversary of the great event, honoring. The Moore piece sat there, roped off, like a stranger after the fact. It looked a bit like an octopus, he thought, or the tangled roots of a tree.

He felt his father's presence as he strolled home and wondered if by ESP or by Emerson's elaborate concept of the oversoul or by Jung's *spiritus mundi* minds leapt across continents. Does the colonel feel me now? Does he see my face as I see his? And do our images collide like separate telepathic waves somewhere in southwestern Kansas and do they possibly become one image there, features blended, son and father one?

At the corner telephone booth he stopped and put in a collect call. He listened as the wires clocked the stations between them, imagined his urgency passing Omaha, Kansas City, Colorado Springs, heading toward Vegas.

The colonel answered sleepily.

"Anything wrong?" he wanted to know.

"Nothing especially," Stoker said, talking a little too loudly into the phone. It was a good connection. "I just wanted to hear your voice."

It was the right opening. The colonel warmed immediately and they began to talk. He told Stoker that he had been winging down to Phoenix to see Verna—this right off. "If you've been sleeping with her, Dad, I'm jealous. I've always wanted to sleep with Verna," Stoker put in, and the colonel answered enthusiastically, "Be jealous then. Yes. Of course I have. She's wonderful. I'm in love with her. And she thinks I'm General Patton and that I've charged headlong into the enemy all my life and that, given time, we can probably marry. How's that grab you, son?" His voice was tinted with uncontrollable mirth and they began laughing together. Then they talked about seeing each other soon, and Stoker told the colonel about Cassie's promise to visit during the Thanksgiving recess and he told about writing her a note, something light, and said that curiously enough he wanted to see her, that he had some forgiveness for her. "Well, that's right," the colonel said. "You ought to forgive her. She's just a nice, stupid woman basically, and her stupidity has always been on the side of affection. She never meant me harm. She just gave too much away."

Stoker listened to his father's voice, trying to read his tone, and it was filled with sincerity, he decided, and he wondered if the colonel might forgive him as easily, if after all the planned alienation of his adolescence the colonel might be able to say, "He was just a stupid kid and meant no harm." In that moment affection seemed to burn Stoker's eyes; he wanted to cry out in the phone booth, but didn't. His usual reticence choked him off.

"Now tell me," the colonel finally said, "what made you call?"

In spite of all that Stoker felt, he kept cool. "It's nothing," he said, "to bother a colonel with. Could you put a corporal on the line?"

"It's something," the colonel persisted.

"You can always send money," Stoker said, wishing he hadn't.

"You really need cash?"

"No sir, just kidding."

"I'm *loaded*. How much you need?"

Anytime the colonel asked how much, Stoker knew, he didn't have much; he would always bet on a conservative answer. "A joke really, Dad," Stoker assured him. "Write me a letter about Verna. Tell me she's beautiful."

"She really is, son. It's a miracle with us two."

"Look," Stoker said, "I'm going to hang up now. But I'm glad I called. You sound fine."

"You called about some problem and I damn well know it, but if you won't talk about it then you won't. I love you, son. Say hello to Cassie when you see her."

They said their goodbyes, then, and for a moment Stoker listened to the sad hum of the wires before hanging up.

He walked back to his room, hands in his pockets.

His plans to study for another hour or two seemed scuttled. For one thing he wanted to see Pless and tell him the good news about the colonel and Verna, but when he thought of walking over to the Blackstone he felt too exhausted. Then he thought of seeing Laura, and his whole body tightened with the notion. He sat down, thinking: desk, papers, books, bed—all these things are a tomb and here I sit among them, drugged by my usual inaction, taking a small pleasure in the knowledge that Pless and the colonel do care a tiny damn for me. Thinking: I look into these pages of Thoreau like a mirror and just can't study. Summarizing: my name is Stoker (just that much I like) and I was born in Texas in the base hospital at Randolph Field twenty-two years ago; educated in public schools of Texas, New Mexico, and Florida and became, finally, Phi Beta Kappa (Bachelor of Arts, major in English and American Literature) at the University of Chicago. Scholarship recipient. Hobbies: none. Passions: Innumerable, but Partially Inclusive Of: Novels of Nabokov, Grass, Mishima and Cheever; Plays of Shakespeare Only; Poems of Auden, Thomas, Stevens and Dickey; Thighs and Breasts of Laura; Pizza, Brownies, Filet of Beef, Crabmeat and Cashews; Pine, Oak, Cedar; Silk, Velvet, Suede; Beer, Chablis, Port (Mateus) and Vat 69; Virna Lisi; The Beatles, Doors, Simon, Garfunkel, Peg Lee, Ray Charles; Cubs and White Sox; Morris Graves, Philip Levine and sometimes Wyeth; Autumn and Cleeping; the stories I've never written, all of them profound and witty.

It was dark, the particular darkness that came to his campus. The Gothic towers stood in mild relief against the heavy blue of the sky and the air seemed veiled as if something had stolen in from the lake—that great inland mystery out there—to encompass the bell towers, the deserted class buildings, the empty tennis courts, the labyrinth of the med center, the lonely quads. He stood momentarily at his window watching it.

He went to bed again, relieved himself, cleaned up his mess with a towel, then resolved to get up early armed with all his forces of literary judgment, to go to the examination and wax factual. In the afternoon, he supposed, he would probably go over to Laura's apartment—or Parker's or Max's or whoever—and try to get something started. And he had to see Pless. And Adler: he thought of Addie. Poor dear vegetable.

Later, deep in sleep, he heard the room shudder. Knocking at his door, he decided.

His bedcovers were gone and evaded his touch as he tried to find them. The knocking continued, and he felt he should find his covers before answering the door. He heard his name spoken by a voice from his dream: Laura's voice. Clumsily, he unwound himself from the bed and made his way toward the rapping at his door; the clock ticked off the dark predawn moments and he seemed to glide in soft slow-motion toward the door. He threw it open, but only a shaft of light was there, so harsh it seemed to blister his face. The pale hallway lightbulb. All else was emptiness. Laura wasn't there.

"Screw this," he told the empty hallway. "In the morning I'm going to get up sane and hearty."

···14

BEFORE CLASS THE NEXT MORNING he walked over to the Blackstone, but Pless had already gone.

He trudged on to the Classics Building, fitted himself into a desk, opened his bluebook at the given signal, and turned on. The ink boiled somewhere in his forebrain, traveled down his shoulder and arm, and flowed from the pen: the feeling he got when he was writing well. Everyone around him sat rigid and serious, pondering the American renaissance: mad Melville, Emerson the high-collared egoist, the nervous fairy Whitman, soulful Thoreau. Smoke spiraled from the pipes of the student traditionalists. Laura flitted around in his pre-consciousness.

The exam was designed to exhaust. It was one of those long, history-loaded quizzes that served, in time, to take the affection for literature out of the students and to leave them, at best, with pride in their supermemories. The poor theological students loved God, but had to read Averroes and Karl Barth; the young doctors dreamt of gallant service and spent their nights memorizing lists of words they would soon forget. The romance of learning: Stoker thought, it dieth like the swan, but I'll probably teach a little myself someday and run an ill-fated class through the paces too. One generation goeth, another cometh, and the crap abideth forever.

Finished at last, he walked out of the building into the sunlight. The colonel was on his mind again, and he wondered if one day soon he might be sending money in his letters home, money to see the old retired warrior through his senility.

At the corner of East 59th he paused. In one direction was Laura, in another Pless, nearby Addie, and also it was noon and the odors of spaghetti and cheeses wafted on the air. With mild resolution he turned toward his own place; moods were all around him, ready to waylay him, but he said to himself: You're sane and hearty this morning, boy, and you've just aced another quiz; don't sink back into fantasy and nightcrawling, don't.

Yet as he walked across the quad he felt the encroachment of gloom.

Great battlements of cloud rolled in from the lake. Rain in the air. Soon.

It came down hard so that his last leaping strides before he reached his apartment were above a series of familiar puddles. Inside his door, then, breathless, shaking the downpour off himself like an old dog, he bumped open his cantankerous hallway door with his shoulder.

A flash of lightning.

When he turned, there was Laura. She stood in shadow, backed up against the nameplates, withdrawn and small, saying hello only with her eyes. She had been smoking a cigarette—he'd never seen her smoking—and the odor hung around them.

A thunderbolt drowned out her only sentence. He took her hand and led her upstairs.

The next hours were built out of contradiction. While they made love insights overtook him in every nudge and caress, endings and beginnings loomed up everywhere; sex will always be physically easier now, he told himself once, yet he knew that all the awkward terrors would be replaced by another terror: he was entering the tough rooms of a manhood he didn't much like, into rooms of cold charade merely different from those before. Such a stupid and obvious revelation came to him: life was going to continue to be complicated. Yet it came like a profundity. They tangled in bed, pausing now and then to look at each other, to touch, then they tangled again; they spoke little, and certainly not about what festered to be said. Their smiles seemed marbled with pathos. And in every thrust and mouthing Stoker's future seemed to announce itself: life will sometimes get awful again. He had never expected such knowledge; in his adolescence—just this moment ended, he began to think—he had dreamt of eventually breaking through, coming to orgasm, wisdom, honesty, communication, equilibrium. This time, though, wrapped in Laura's arms, he knew that he was entering slowly, warmly, another maze.

The afternoon spent itself, dissipating in a series of booming thunderstorms that left the room damp and chilly. Laura took another cigarette from the bedside table, lit it, and blew the cold smoke above their heads. She turned to him again, her fingers resting on his neck. He knew that the sentences they'd have to utter would be full of contradictions; their lovemaking had been tender and almost abandoned, but he had felt the tact in it too, the small distance.

"Your man is back in your life," he said, almost questioning. He was trying to help her start.

"Not exactly."

"Yeah, he's back. And we're—well, we're dying off a little, aren't we?" This time his question was less a question.

"Who's to say?" she sighed. "If we make rules, Stoke, then we'll just break them and confuse ourselves. I've gone through it all before and I know." Her face creased. Pain in the eyes. Yet she was trying not to lecture, he decided.

As she buried her face beneath his arm, he regretted the melodrama.

Bravely, then, he came on. "Well, Laura dear, you were a great piece this rainy afternoon. Now let's go eat something. I'm awfully hungry."

She looked at him trying to see if his enthusiasm was genuine.

They watched each other dress. She put on her slip, but for some reason—perhaps to torture me, he guessed—left off the rest of her underwear.

"Sure you want to go out?"

"I'm really starved," he assured her.

Dressed, they went downstairs and got into her car. The streets were patched with icy evening pools, the first signs of winter.

They drove along, then, making conversation, but not really talking to each other.

"I wrote a good quiz a few hours ago," he said once.

"We ran a series of lab tests today," she said disjointedly. "I don't much like lab tests when I'm tired. The party tired me out."

At the edge of the Midway Plaisance Laura stopped the car and they rolled down the windows and listened at a student rally. The speaker had mounted himself on a fireplug and addressed a crowd of about two hundred students from his uneasy perch. He was shouting about the war and waving a tabloid, the folds of which flapped in the breeze, rattling in his hand so that he looked like a performer in a vague circus act. The faces around him were earnest. A girl with long hair stood near Laura's car with her fingers in her mouth. There was also an old professor who stood at the fringe loaded with books, his hat crushed down, his pipesmoke billowing out white beneath the pale glow of the streetlamp.

They drove on.

At the restaurant Stoker dripped spaghetti sauce on his shirt.

"You're so clumsy," Laura gushed, laughing at him.

"Me? Of course I'm not clumsy. You Americans just have no sense of continental eating styles. Always cutting your meat with the proper hand, switching the knife and fork, and eating with the improper hand. Do things right. First put a little sauce on your bib. Helps you get into the spirit of the gorge."

She laughed.

"Or, if you suspect someone's watching you with disapproval, just slip a meatball into your pocket. So."

"Oh, Stoker, stop it!"

"Or drape a little parsley in your hair."

"Stop it now!" Her head fell back in laughter. Lovely. She sat there, he knew, underwearless, in her sweet bucktoothed smile.

He wanted to keep it like this. "And did I tell you that I'm writing something for the literary mag, by the bye? A poem. An epic haiku."

Her smile was perfect, her laugh muffled by the hard bread she munched.

"And I've made a survey of the goings-on in windows around campus. The girls of Ida Noyes Hall, by and large, have thick thighs, or did I tell you that? Sociological research, this. Second-floor girls have large nostrils—or so it appears as one gazes up from one's ground-level vantage point. Listen, Laura, don't sit there laughing. This is ultrascientific."

"Tell me more, please."

"Oh my no, eat your ravioli. I'll watch you scientifically. Eat it before it gets cold."

When they went outside again, a cold rain was falling.

They kept talking. "When will we ever eat up all those groceries we went out and bought?" she asked.

"It was only six dollars' worth," he reminded her.

A few moments later: "Is your laundry all done? Do you still take it over to your friend who lives at the Blackstone?"

And moments later: "Parker talks about you now. She heard at the party that you have a big reputation among the underground lit set."

The edges of their talk seemed worn.

Laura drove slowly through the streets; the faint odor of Parmesan cheese rode with them.

"I know you're feeling gloomy," she said finally. "Don't."

He kissed her cheek, got out without saying anything, and gave her a wave goodbye. For a few minutes he stood looking down the street after her car was gone.

Slowly, then, he made his way upstairs. At his door he found a typed note attached to his door with cellophane tape.

> Stoke: I know you still must be in a bad
> mood. Come see me tonight & we'll talk.
> Pless

He welcomed it, but it confirmed what he felt, what Laura had observed of him, and he stood there in the hallway, leaning against his door with the note in his hand, and gave way to his feelings and began to cry.

Then he prowled the streets again, passing from tree to tree whose shadows darkened the already dark night. Cold, he pulled his collar around his ears as he moved window by window toward the Blackstone, not knowing why he wanted it, but stealing along, his eyes darting up streets and down alleys. He saw mundane lives: women in shawls, girls filing their nails while studying their textbooks, men calcified before their television sets, their faces immobile in the gray light.

All around him was the chill of winter. Far off a foghorn complained from the lake.

On Kenwood Avenue he passed a recessed alcove, then turned back to occupy it, to view a worn apartment decorated with travel posters and unframed lithographs. Two young men sat next to each other on a sofa, staring earnestly into each other's eyes as they talked, and they seemed like dancers in a static vignette, their hands rising in an occasional gesture, shrugging, offering each other small movements as they spoke the words Stoker couldn't hear. He became fascinated with them, seeing them with a curious objectivity as if he viewed them from the wrong end of a telescope which placed them at a far but focused distance. He didn't know why they interested him, but there he stood: his face just to the side of the window, his eyes cut sidelong at them for minute after minute. He'd tell Pless about stopping there, he supposed, just as he had told him about other scenes.

Watching, he grew sleepy.

Just as he was about to leave there was an old man beside him with a flashlight. It clicked on straight in his face.

"Ah!" he yelled, and jumped back. The light pinned him and blinded him, so he turned to run. The old man caught his sleeve.

"Gotcha!" the old voice rasped, and the grip was stronger than Stoker could account for. "I see you good, too!"

Stoker tried to wrench his arm free, but couldn't. As he jerked the old man yelled aloud and Stoker knew the two boys inside would be hurrying out to see what was the matter. He wrenched again and his jacket and shirt sleeve both tore loose and he was free.

"Come back!" the old man shouted. "I see you good!"

But Stoker was running, cutting down alleyways, vaulting fences he had learned over months and years.

He didn't stop until he reached the Blackstone. There he hurried past the two gargoyles, pushed the button for the elevator, and waited breathlessly. The sweat on his face had turned to ice.

··· 15

MOURNERS WERE STREWN AROUND, Adler felt, like the petals of flowers. They were mostly the courteously grim students who knew Stoker only slightly, but also present were: the colonel wearing a rack of medals, mother Cassie with her black-pleated minidress high on her thighs, Pless and his mother all drawn and white, Clive somber and aloof, and the sorrowful nurses.

Religious music groaned quietly in the background because the colonel had supposed it appropriate. There were sniffles and soft wailings. But Adler sat there watching it all with his tears dried up, seeing those strangers and spectres who choked the aisles and hunched in the pews, wondering at their reality and at himself, giddy and lost, but without tears.

Unreal. Of course it was. The cardboard minister extolled

in the proper hollow tone the properly hollow verities: the search for knowledge, the love of family and friends, the unselfish life. A proper eulogy, just unreal. The figures moving in the chapel were all inventions. Dust to dust. The light which slanted across the chancel, brilliantly green and yellow as it filtered through the glass torso of St. John of the Cross, lifted pigments into the pale November silence and settled them like soft unreal amens across the urn. And Stoker, Adler thought as he sat there, you are the most unreal now: gone by impact, gone by flame, gone, all gone.

The details of all this appeared almost too sordid and absolute to be denied, yet they seemed unreal to Adler too. Only a few days before he had seen Stoker in that rare good mood during their lunch in The Loop, and now, even with events apparently pieced together, a picture still didn't emerge; he simply couldn't imagine that dive, that long, arching fall. Twelve floors off the Blackstone: impossible. Now, although he found himself wanting to know every detail (the shoes were found in pieces, the story had it, but every tooth was intact and there wasn't a scratch on his head), Adler sensed that regardless of all he might learn he still wouldn't believe. Dust to dust. Unreal as that urn which now caught the colorful memorial light of St. John's windows.

Funerals were all so unreal too, Adler felt. Pagan, anachronistic, hopeful in the face of hopelessness. They made one turn the eyes and thoughts away in embarrassment, as I'm doing now, he told himself; images, the tag ends of gossip and fact, phrases and fantasies steal across the mind and divert. It had been a long two weeks for Stoker, that was the consensus: weeks in which he had finally found someone then lost her, in which he had gotten drunk and injured, had exploded in class, had written an unusually mediocre examination, had received a melancholy note from a friend, had written his mother and called his father, had visited Pless and perhaps a dozen others in his distress, and had finally been caught—he had escaped, but was recognized—while peeking into a local apartment house.

Dust and ash. Adler got up with the others as the music swelled. At the exit of the chapel he walked up on Pless, Verna, Cassie and her husband, and the colonel, all of whom were discussing the event, of course, and he slowed his steps, straining to listen, then stopped behind Pless. He hoped no one would notice him. The colonel's face: gray, like an old wound with the blood drained away.

Pless: "If I had been there for him, he wouldn't have done it."

Verna: "Oh, hon, quit it. You can't take any blame."

Cassie: "I don't understand why he was looking in that window!"

The Colonel: "Nobody's sure if that's accurate, Cass. That old coot probably just saw Stoke's photo in the newspaper and got excited."

Cassie: "Well, what *was* wrong?"

Pless: "Whatever it was, he was coming to see me about it. If we had just been able to talk!"

The Colonel: "There'll probably be things about this we'll never know. We can't settle it all now. Was it all right in there, Verna?"

Verna: "It was just right, Marty. The arrangements were perfect."

The Colonel: "I worry about it—as if it makes any difference."

Verna: "It was all in good taste. Don't fret. Can we go back to the hotel now?"

The Colonel: "Oh sure. Here, take my arm."

They dispersed, then, and Pless turned and saw Adler standing on the periphery and he reached out gently and took his sleeve. As he started to speak, though, Adler pulled away. For a moment their gazes met.

In his room, later, Adler took off his blue suit, slipped it back on the hanger, and went into the bathroom where he washed his face and hands. He wanted to talk to someone about it all—anyone except Clive—but knew he couldn't. Pless would be occupied with the parents, the nurses wouldn't know anything, and there wasn't any use writing home because the old man would simply say, "Ha! There you are! The goddamned colleges have gone crazy!" And in any case he never wrote home about anything, not about his research at the greenhouse, money, the Chicago weather, his visit to the Bolshoi, his trip to California, his thoughts on himself.

It was impossible, he knew, to correspond with a man who had never suffered a single philosophic malady, for whom life had always been perfectly simple: either you worked like hell or you went hungry. That essentially Depression-era attitude had dominated his father's thoughts even during the lush Eisenhower years when the farm prospered. There was no talking to an anachronism. He could recall seeing his father perched atop a new and expensive International tractor, leaning back, cigar fixed in his teeth, his hundred dollar boots propped up on the steering wheel, telling about the old days and all the hard times: how he had run away from home to work as a bellhop in Little Rock, how he had finally consented to return home to northwest Arkansas and help his father, Adler's grandfather, with a harvest—only to see the profits and part of the farm itself lost to a siege of smallpox—and how he ran away again, went to barber college for a few weeks, how his barber tools were stolen in Dallas, and how he wandered into Mississippi to pull cotton and on north to grub in the mines of Kentucky and Indiana. Tales, old man, Adler wanted to say, straight from Upton Sinclair, from the Joads, from the clichés and rhetoric of rock bottom.

His mother was just too much. She only wondered how he had managed to lose his faith—meaning her own emotional binges, those orgasms of belief which she gave herself in those slat-sided country churches. Of course he couldn't write to her either. She was another anachronism. Dust to dust.

Little wonder, he knew, that they gave up communicating with him; he had fought against them for so long, making efforts when he was no more than fourteen years old to cure himself of the family's rich Southern accent and to ridicule the monotonous hillbilly music that flooded the house. Later, when he went off for his first two years at the University of Arkansas, he styled himself as a dancer—for a short while, at least. Then, after a year of change during which he went from fine arts to literature to botany, he left for Chicago. That was it. He saw them only once after that, on Christmas day of 1964.

They considered him the lost black sheep, perhaps a slightly rabid one, and he thought of them as he knew they were: vain, materialistic in spite of their bloated religious values and filled with assorted prejudices. That Christmas morning, in fact, he came down to breakfast wearing his ballet slippers because they were comfortable and because he had seen no reason to throw them away when his dancing class had finished. "Now whut kind of dirty little queer have we here?" his father had bellowed, and Adler, in retaliation, had bounded back upstairs, put on an old purple shirt, a yellow ascot, and one of his mother's pendants. Then he came back downstairs to announce that he would grow a beard and sideburns as soon as he returned to Chicago. They ate that last turkey dinner in silence, then he was gone on the night train back to school, back to the greenhouse where the mute plants kept him company.

Now, though, he wanted someone to talk to, needed it in the worst way, just as his weary chest sometimes needed a shot of adrenalin. The unreality which came when he first read the news in the campus newspaper and which nearly choked him in that pollen-soaked chapel bore down on him.

Having no one, he decided to visit Stoker's apartment. He supposed it would be another day or two before anyone decided to clean out the drawers, pack the books and clothes, and attend the morbid chores there, and besides he knew where Stoker kept the extra key: there on the ledge beside the nameplates near the front door.

At dusk he walked across the campus to Woodlawn Avenue. He carried the remainder of the borrowed books.

Sure enough, the key was there. Also, the apartment house seemed conveniently empty, no one around to ask him what he wanted, and so he went up without any bother. The lock clanked loudly and he was inside.

There were signs of the girl everywhere. Her scent—a pale gardenia—seemed to fog the room, and her underwear and stockings dotted the furniture, thrown there on purpose, it seemed to Adler, just to announce themselves. The bed was quilt-tossed and haggard, a large inanimate victim of the lovemaking, and the room seemed thick with sex, perfumed and battered by it, so that Adler stood there with a curious first thought knocking at him: Why? Why after this? This is a room, he told himself, that's been thoroughly fucked in. He couldn't understand it all the more.

Of course, he admitted, sex is one thing for Pless, something else for Stoker, and another thing for me. For Pless it's easy, for Stoker it was always a trial, but for me it was always clearly impossible. Looking at the room he sensed the quality of his own yearning: he was the sort who lusted after an evening of good conversation, a few beers with an acquaintance or, at most, a few laughs in mixed company. A friend was improbable, a lover ridiculous—not that he felt particularly maudlin about it. It was just the way things were. Tonight, for instance: it would be nice to go sit in a booth at the quad with a cup of coffee warming the hands and someone there to say, "Ah, damn the shame. Stoker was such a simple, harmless guy." But here I am, he told himself: locked inside a foreign room, sniffing the tatters of another life, a life already gone cold, not a goddamned soul to say Poor Bastard or Up Yours. Well, sex was certainly out of the question. One could always walk six blocks over and buy a piece of black tail, but one never did—not me anyway, he admitted. After all, strangers in bars wince when they finally get a good look at my face; and the good-hearted whore is a literary myth; and one doesn't want to be condescended to by headwaiters, parents, professors and pieces of unidentifiable nookie, does one? One doesn't want to get put down for breakfast, lunch and supper, as it were, so here I am, the odor of friendly genitals surrounding me, embalmed in these silent traces of of gardenia and doom.

He walked across the room. On the dresser was a notebook which belonged to the girl, her name written on it in a wide, flat scrawl: Laura. There was also an address where the notebook was to be returned if found.

The room simply didn't fit. Another odd piece in the jigsaw. Stoker had a girl, Adler reasoned, and they made it together and stayed in each other's company for a short time and that was better than usual for old Stoke; he usually moped and bitched about the state of his balls. Disjointedly, then, the rationalizations bubbled up: Clive manipulates people, Adler thought, and Pless manipulates his grades and his professors and I manipulate (small green matter, though it is) the plants in the greenhouse troughs. But perhaps poor Stoke didn't have anything to manipulate. Is that it? If not, what? Pless usually has sex, Stoker sometimes had bad sex, Clive probably has no sex, and I have traveled far, seen much, but remain, alas, virginal. So was that it? No, it couldn't be that either, or could it? Well. Did he just draw the first number? Did that do it? Loyalty to the group? An antiphysical dare we must now obligate ourselves to accept? That can't be it either, can it?

Slowly, Adler reconstructed the fatal evening. The details came from three sources originally—the newspapers, a brief telephone call from Clive, a call which Adler made to Pless, and whispered lament. Yet, to make them balance: ah, that was the chore. Stoker had broken up with his girl (that much was even in the newspaper accounts) and had gone over to the Blackstone, probably depressed, to see Pless, stopping en route to grab a few quick glances in some neighborhood windows. (That activity was always pretty damned innocent, Adler allowed, and not as sick as the newspapers or Cassie imagined.) Then the old nightwatchman had pounced on him and Stoker had gotten away, gone to the Blackstone, waited around, and had finally gone up on the roof. About midnight he hit the plaza out front, according to the switchboard operator, a tall bearded pre-med student, and the noise was like "a rifle shot." Tereu. The sound of breaking bones.

Adler leaned on the dresser. Everything flapped through his head like a reel of broken film.

"There's something strange here, though," he told the room. "I feel it right here—in this sweet stench."

He decided to call Laura.

At the same corner telephone booth that Stoker always used, Adler looked up the number. The walls inside the booth were covered with numbers and annotations which he read as he dialed.

"Hello? Listen, this is a friend of Stoker's. Yes, I know. I just want to talk to someone about it. Just a moment, please, if you've got the time." The voice on the other end was soft and sad. "That's right, yes, I was at the service this afternoon. I'm a good friend. And I thought—you know, I don't want to talk right here. I'm in a telephone booth. I thought you might have a cup of coffee with me." He pictured the girl at the other end of the line: wistful eyes slightly swollen and red, blonde, breasts up firm underneath the white uniform. Then he erased the image and went on. "No, I wasn't at your party, but I've known—that is, I knew Stoke for nearly two years. That's right. Look, how about the snack bar at the quad? It's still open." The voice was tired and softly reluctant. "No, you've got me wrong," he said. "I'm not a crank at all. Promise, I'm an old friend of his. And to tell you the truth I'm all by myself tonight and can't get this thing off my mind. Look, *please*. Just one cup of coffee."

The voice consented and he repeated the instructions on where they would meet. Meanwhile, his eyes fell on snippets of information penciled around him: WH 6 9946/Ask for Annie. All nite burgers/DI 3 3411.

"Half an hour, right," he said. "Please be there."

He hung up and walked outside. A touch of snow. He pulled his muffler around his throat.

For some reason, then, he went back to Stoker's room. He had to look at it once more.

Having gone back, though, he detected nothing new, nothing of the revelation he wanted. He replaced the books he had borrowed, then checked the pot plants, mostly wilted, which sat in the window sill. Again the room almost seemed to speak to him, as if it wanted to tell him something, but he couldn't quite make out its voice.

He finally gave up trying and walked over to the quad in the gathering snow. The snow would drift down from the lakes, blanket all of Illinois and most of Missouri, then expend itself in the high pastures of the Ozarks where his father would grumble and toss another log on the fire and his mother, squinting, would peer through the frost of the kitchen window at the battered thermometer. In the hedgerows all the rabbits would twitch their noses as winter rode the air.

The booth he had designated in the quad was empty and so he sat down, ordered his first cup of coffee and began his wait. The room was unusually crowded, students shuffling from table to table, carrying trays of food, plucking old newspapers off vacant chairs.

After a while he saw a girl standing at the cashier's counter who seemed to be watching him. She stood there buying cigarettes, glancing back nervously at him as the cashier counted change into her palm. But then she left. He suddenly tried to recall if she had been among the nurses fluttering down the aisle of St. John's chapel in their white uniforms that afternoon, but couldn't remember her. Yet when she left without even looking back he had a definite sinking feeling. That was probably her, he told himself, and she looked me over and saw how ugly and suspicious-looking I am and probably thought I was some sort of ghoul wanting to savor poor Stoke's high dive and rites and just turned herself around and bailed out.

He ordered another cup of coffee, but his thoughts went astray and soon it was cold in his hands. Another twenty minutes passed, then he drank it in one gulp. After an hour had passed, he got up and went out.

"Okay, that's it then," he said, looking up into the soft swirl of winter.

By the time he reached his room his chest rattled with asthma. For a few minutes he stood inside his door, unmoving, rivulets of melting snow edging away from his shoes as he stood there dumfounded and giddy with himself, feeling a loneliness now that boiled inside him like liquor.

Snow. The cold Ozarks. Such a great neutral killer, winter is. And nature was always disappointing down home anyway, the roads all bogged and the house creaking and groaning and the pines standing around like stupid green sentries keeping me closeted and dull. The fields had no intelligence: just stood out there useless, full of rocks, so many rocks that the cows usually limped and nothing would grow. Small wonder my wit didn't turn to stone with it all.

He remembered how his father used to urge him out of the house and how he reluctantly went, how he always fell into the creek in the summers and snagged himself on some hidden strand of barbed wire in the autumns and how, in the spring-time, his allergies ambushed him and he sneezed and sputtered so that his mother once said to him, "Ah, son, you got all the sounds. Just like Spike Jones' band," and laughed at her own joke, throwing her dumb head back, her teeth yellow in her mouth.

He sat in his room, wheezing.

Piped in from Nashville on radio WSM was the culture of the house: Minnie Pearl, Ernest Tubb, Flatt & Scruggs; and over the hulking television set came Bonanza, Gunsmoke, Dennis the Menace and other delights; and out of the mailbox beside the road came *Sports Illustrated,* church bulletins, H. L. Hunt's *Life Lines* and assorted catalogs.

A far country. Once, trying to fit himself into nature, Adler had gone over to the White River alone, carrying a neat pack of his father's fishing gear on his back and a sturdy flyrod in his hand, but the elements were against him. The rains came. He shook a copperhead out of his sleeping bag before trying to sleep that first night and the next morning, drenched and purged, cruising downstream in a rented canoe, he failed to see the mean beauty he had set out to find. Only later, working in his greenhouse on the campus, did he find nature the least compatible—and then only because he exercised control.

Otherwise, it had always been unfriendly. And the house had been unfriendly, his flesh not of his flesh, his tenure at home something to be endured. The university had been unfriendly too, its library a great vault locked against him, guarded by prim assistants who were slow afoot and pre-occupied and brought him only a few volumes at a time and quoted him rules. Each semester he began in seats near the lecturer in his classrooms, but always faded back toward his proper obscurity in the back of the room. His dancing instructor, Mr. Jaynes, a slender fairy from New Jersey who tried to speak with a slight French accent and who clicked his heels together when he first greeted his students in the mornings, loved all the boys except Adler. He wanted to show them all body positions and to touch their torsos whenever possible and, of course, to suck them a little after hours, but he didn't care at all for Adler and piled ridicule on him and asked him to demonstrate the really impossible positions for the class. Humiliating. In frustration with that first year at the state university, Adler ate his blues away, gained weight, and finally because of Mr. Jaynes and his waistline turned in his tights. After that he knew he had to change schools. He decided on Chicago and spent half of the next semester carrying on correspondence, arranging his transcripts, and trying to make up his mind what to study next.

As an English major he felt for a while comfortably useless, so quit that too. After all there were students who for no reason at all enjoyed literary reputations on campus, who seemed to have read scores of books, to have thought through Shakespeare and Dante, to have in progress works of their own awaiting publication. Besides, the greenhouse did fascinate him—and his father approved of the more practical dirt-of-the-world goal. So he was then a botanist, but still friendless.

Chicago, Chicago, a toddlin' town. The change of schools helped not at all. His instructors were all like Jaynes or Cogdill or worse, bastards every one. For a year he hung around different groups of students (Pless and Stoker, when possible) trying to endear himself. But Chicago was never its old self, a large speakeasy filled with revelers and friendly bathtub gin; it was somber, crowded but mostly silent as if everyone tried to keep indoors, noisy but empty as if all those cars were ghosts passing along the streets. So for a while he simply tried to bluff it through, thinking to himself, ah well, all this will pass. But bluff failed. His mother sent him about that time a wry mountain symbol: one of those small ceramic trinkets found in every souvenir shop in the Ozarks: a little man flushing himself down a little toilet, the words GOODBYE

CRUEL WORLD inscribed on its base. It was his mother's dull acknowledgment of his plight and also a token of her artistic taste. By the time he received it his humor had totally fled.

I'll make my loneliness pure, he told himself. A martyrdom.

Yet in spite of this affirmation in his most secret heart he hoped that someone might notice him, that someone might appreciate his solitary study habits and long hours at the greenhouse—a professor, a fellow student, anyone. But another year passed. Nothing. He memorized plants in the troughs of that vast greenhouse, memorized Graf's *Exotica,* memorized the steps to his room and back, memorized his habits, desires, pains, classified himself and filed himself away.

Standing before his mirror and medicine chest, his wheeze was a dull motor idling inside him. Let it rasp. He placed the inhaler back on the shelf, thinking: Number Two. It's easy enough to think about, he admitted, because, after all, Stoker only had himself a couple of bad weeks—embarrassment, one might say, ranging from lost love to getting caught peeping—but I've had a lousy decade and there are good enough reasons for pulling the chain like the little ceramic man and going flush down the spout. Down the spout, into the alimentary canal of the nation, into the rivers of the continent, into the sleeping sea where the Pequod doth abide. Easy enough to say screw the whole gibberish and cosmos in its each and every part: Clive and his V number and all his candles and lies, all the rocks of the Arkansas plateaus, the umbrellas flowering in Vegas, my asthma and my soiled ballet slippers, daddy's drawl, the night-blooming cereus, sex dreams, dust to dust.

But first I'll talk to logical Pless once more. Not that he'll change anything, but Pless has an old-fashioned mind and likes to take flings at logically examining the illogical. So I'll talk to him. Then I'll turn giddy forever; madness deserves madness. Verily.

···16

INSIDE PLESS' APARTMENT at the Blackstone
Towers it was possible to look sideways out of the windows
behind the sofa and see the pavement below, but no one
looked. For a while that evening the adults—Verna and the
colonel, Cassie and Richard—formalized their feelings in
reserved silence, but then toward midnight they began to drink
more: daiquiris for the colonel, whiskey for everyone else.
Then Clive arrived and they began to loosen up, Cassie especially. She folded her legs underneath her on the sofa, exposing
a shapely patch of slightly veined thigh. Conversations
sprouted here and there and the mood altered.

Cassie: "Clive, goodness, you're such a very big boy."

Clive: "Actually, I'm an android."

Cassie: "Oh, where from? Mars or Venus?"

Pless searched around on the dial of his FM radio for some music and found Peter Duchin and some violins.

The colonel moved around trying to avoid looking at Richard, who was tall, tanned, and younger than Cassie. Richard, tipsy and casual with the stiff air of a businessman at an obligatory social, pulled at his ear as he spoke and seemed to feel, Pless decided, that he should say important things on such an occasion.

Richard: "Now what's wrong with the students nowadays? That's what I want to know."

Pless: "Well, I think we're just all solipsists."

Richard: "Now I'm not just talking, son, about how you dress."

Deliberately mixing weak drinks for Verna, Pless served everyone, moving through conversations, adding comments, listening, retreating. The liquor pulsed feebly in his head, but he couldn't get with it at first. Clive held forth on Helena Blavatsky's old plan: revolution through assassination. He was mostly for violence, he said, because it at least wasn't boring and usually turned people on. When the colonel disagreed Clive paid him a compliment, saying, "You're not a boring man, for instance, sir, up there breaking sound barriers in your jet and all that!" A weak compliment, but sufficient, and the colonel responded with a confused grin.

Richard: "You ought to come into the business world, son. That's the smart thing. Industrial psychologists make good money—and they're needed."

Pless: "My specialty is killing rats in a barrel."

Richard: "Perfect training. I can see you have a good head for industry. We could use you in Detroit."

Pless went back to the ice bucket. He took another drink, the one too many. No matter. Stoke deserves a proper wake, he decided, and he wished they could have a jazz combo: New Orleans niggers sweating on the mouthpieces of worn trombones and trumpets, blowing wild.

Cassie: "Now I'm going to tell you exactly, Verna, what I think of you. I mean it. And it's going to surprise you how much I admire you and look up to you. You're resilient and bounced back, going back to Phoenix like that and going to work. Under different circumstances, Verna, we could've been friends for years. And now, really, I know you're going to be happy with Marty, and I know this is going to sound false—I just know it probably will—but I'm sure that the two of you, assuming things work out and you get married, will be very happy. Bygones: let them be bygones! Isn't that right?"

Verna: a smirk and silence.

Peter Duchin gave way to Ray Charles and Pless reached over and turned up the volume on his radio. He wished he could open it up to about nine decibels.

Richard: "The newspapers are right: the whole damn country is sick. I read that J. Edgar Hoover thinks the communists are behind it all."

The Colonel: "And some believe that J. Edgar Hoover is behind it all."

Pless: "And wouldn't it be nice if just anyone were behind it all?"

Cassie rummaged through the books on a nearby shelf, reading titles with an inscrutable look on her face as if she were ciphering hieroglyphics in a tomb.

Clive to Verna: "Ah, our colleges are filled with injustice. Take the Eskimos, for instance. We don't teach their literature or pay much attention to their history. We neglect their scientists. And this is unjust and dangerous. We're not prepared in this country to fight off Eskimo viruses! We're ignorant of their hostile tribal mores! Let these poor people be first-class citizens! Nanook deserves his civil rights!"

Verna: "That's all interesting, yes, but could you get me another refill, please?"

Clive: "First, would you like to dance?"

Verna: "I'm not very good at your dances. And what's that music?"

Clive: "Handel's *Messiah,* I think. Just follow my movements."

They danced apart, moving against the beat, and Pless smiled at them, thinking how much better his mother managed it. Clive, graceless, finally stopped trying, and Pless realized, simply: no one knows what to do or say or how to act. It's going to be a long evening.

Cassie: "I thought he was a reasonable boy. As a matter of fact I thought he'd grow up solid and dull like his father."

Pless: "No, he liked to get high. Whenever he could."

Cassie: "Is that why he looked in windows?"

Pless: "That's why he did everything he did."

Richard: "Is that what you want too? To get high?"

Pless: "Sometimes."

Richard: "When you want that, what do you do?"

Pless: "There are all sorts of ways."

Cassie: "Tell the truth, Pless. Did any of you ever take drugs?"

Pless: "No, never. We didn't go for acid."

Richard: "Sex?"

Pless: "We're all sexual. That's one way to get there, yes, and drugs are another, but none of us were much for drugs."

Clive: "Let me explain. There are really two sorts of people in the world: the ones who want sobriety and reason and the calm pleasures of common sense and those who want a trip of some sort, an inebriation, and—well, ecstasy. We all have the two drives in us for these things, but one usually dominates us and you can call it whatever you want because it's just an old dualism that has lots of names: classicism and romanticism, conservatism and liberalism, square and hip."

Verna: "And what did Stoker want?"

The Colonel: "Don't get emotional, Vern."

Pless: "Let me get you a drink, hon."

Verna: "I'm not emotional, yes, I need another drink. And put a little bash in this one, please."

Cassie: "I'd like to know too. What did he want?"

Clive: "For any really complicated individual, as he was, a high doesn't come easy. You have to understand that. After a while it takes more and more in order to get kicks. But I didn't mean to start any of this, really, and to get us mulling over it. I've got to go to the bathroom. Sorry."

Cassie: "Listen, I want us to talk about this."

Verna: "I don't agree with you about Stoke. Not at all."

Pless: "You didn't know him very well, Mother."

Cassie: "No one knew him very well."

The Colonel: "That's what I can't believe: I thought I *did*. He called me on the phone—remember my saying that? We had a *good* talk."

Clive was gone and Pless excused himself too. He went into the hallway, took the elevator down to the lobby, and walked over to the telephones. He dialed the university operator, asked for the extension number at the greenhouse, then dialed Addie's number. The phone rang nine times before he hung up. He sighed. It seemed as though he had been locked into that disjointed party upstairs for hours and he hesitated, not much wanting to return. At last he dialed the number again, determined that Addie was probably there and just not answering. The phone rang another dozen times, then Addie answered.

"Come over," Pless said. "The parents and Clive are here. We're having some drinks."

"No, none of that," Adler snapped. He seemed preoccupied and grouchy. "I just can't cut that sort of scene tonight."

"You *ought* to come. It's not very pleasant, but I'm putting up with it."

"I can't do it. But I want us to talk later. There's something I want to try and say about Stoker. I was over at his room tonight and have a lot to say."

"Like what?"

"Oh, I can't talk over the goddamned telephone."

"Then come over. Everybody'll clear out before long and we can talk."

"I can't do it. I don't know what the hell you're doing over there, but my insides are in a knot. I'm not coming over for any cocktail hour. Screw that."

"Forget it, then. How's your work? Are you working tonight?"

"I'm working, yes. Barely. Oh, by the way, what does Stoker's girl friend look like? The nurse?"

"I never saw her. Why?"

"Was she blonde or what?"

"I just don't know."

"Well, no matter."

"Addie, you shouldn't stay by yourself if you really don't want to."

Silence. "I'm hanging up now, Pless. Okay? And we can talk later, can't we?"

"Of course we can. But you're not all right, are you?"

"Hell no. I'm not all right at all. But I'm not coming over there and watch his mother cry. Goodnight, Pless. Hang up now."

After placing the receiver back on the hook, Pless stood in the lobby for a moment. His impulse to call Adler still seemed right and he thought about going over to the greenhouse and seeing him. The thought was clearly there: what if he's number two? He couldn't help think it.

Richard was telling a story about an Irish wake when Pless went back to his apartment. "There was such a crowd at this little farmhouse," Richard went on, "that they had to take the corpse off the bed and stand him up in the corner with his *rigor mortis* showing. There were coats and drunks heaped on the bed, you see, and there were people celebrating upstairs and downstairs and crowding each other off the stairwell in between. Then the priest came and saw the cadaver standing up in the corner of the upstairs bedroom and he shouted, 'Praise be, now! What's the poor soul doin' standin' in the corner? Lay him out decent on the bed, will ya?' But the host said, 'Ah, but the bed's just too full. There's no damn room, father!' And so the priest says, 'Well, get the poor soul some chairs, then, and lay him out proper on those. Christ's holy blood, that's just no way to treat the dead!' And so the host obliges and yells downstairs: 'Three chairs for the corpse!' And everyone crowding around the punchbowl down there yells at once: 'Hip hip hooray! Hip hip hooray! Hip hip hooray!' "

The Colonel: "Now what the hell is a story like that supposed to mean on a night like this?"

Richard: "Not anything, I guess, but everybody's laughing."

The Colonel: "I'm sure as hell not."

Pless: "It's just a story about a wake. I don't think he meant anything by it. I had the same thought myself a while ago: we ought to have a celebration. Stoker wouldn't like us to be in the doldrums."

The Colonel: "How the hell do you know that? He might have wanted to hurt us, to hurt everybody."

Verna: "I don't think he meant anything by the story."

Pless: "He was just drunk."

The Colonel: "I'm pretty damn drunk myself, but I wouldn't tell a goddamned Irish joke tonight!"

Cassie: "Oh, come on now!"

The Colonel: "You stay out of this!"

Richard: "Now just wait a minute!"

The Colonel: "I ought to cream your fucking face."

Richard: "Look, I didn't mean any harm. I apologize."

The Colonel: "You sure as hell ought to."

Verna: "He *did*."

Cassie: "Three *chairs!* Oh, I see what you *meant*."

The Colonel: "I understand what was meant too. And I

understand the idea behind the old-fashioned Irish wake too: laugh it up and honor the dead by having yourself a good time. Isn't that it? But what the hell are we supposed to do on a night like this? After all, it was a goddamned suicide and he was sort of telling us all to go screw ourselves, wasn't he? I mean that's right, isn't it? Who's to say it isn't? So I don't see anything so goddamned comical."

The colonel's voice cracked with this last sentence and he turned abruptly and knocked over his pitcher of daiquiris. From the radio came the wailings of the Beatles: "You say hello I say goodbye!" Cassie plopped down on the sofa again with her thighs flashing white underneath her, Verna stooped and dabbed at the spilled daiquiri with a cloth, and nervously, Pless suggested a game of Botticelli.

Clive: "Although many people called me a monster and the possessor of the evil eye, I never took a single human life and just appreciated a good orgy now and then. In fact, I was murdered myself—given poison cakes to eat, shot several times, and dumped in an icy river. And I was just a good solid peasant. Oh, a little arrogant, yes, and I managed to take tea with prime ministers and give counsel to princesses. And my real name was Efimovich and one of my daughters left our native land to become a lion tamer in America. And I always liked the girls, true, and had a slightly gross style—grabbed them and unbuttoned them and squeezed their breasts before they could yell. And in the quiet moments of my life I found time for a little religious prophecy and my motto was always simple: sin is the first good step toward holiness. Who am I?"

Pless: "That's not how we play the game."

Clive: "You have no idea of who I am, do you?"

Pless: "You're Grigori Rasputin, naturally, but that's not how we play the game. We're supposed to ask you questions which you're supposed to answer with a simple yes or no."

Clive: "Well, you guessed me. But you can't expect Rasputin to play by the rules, can you?"

Verna: "No games, Pless, please. Not now."

Zither music began to plink and hum from the radio and Clive talked about two Russians he had played chess with. One was an old bum with a thick beard who used to visit the armory, he said, but could hardly play the game, in spite of his obvious talent, because he wanted to chat—especially about women and what a stud he was. The other Russian he met while traveling with his father, he went on. Around Lake Geneva. The Palace Hotel. "My father sized the man up: lots of charm, but a terrible egotist. But he was one of the better chess players I've ever challenged. Charmed me in a quick twenty moves that one time we played." Pless listened and smiled, glad to have Clive's voice to steady the room.

Cassie: "We've just come back from Europe. Isn't it wonderful traveling over there?"

Clive: "It's a graveyard."

Cassie: a weak smile.

The voices lulled; the zither music, louder now, twangy and homespun, unified the murmurs in the room and Pless, leaning against his bookcase, looked on everyone with contentment. Nothing bothered him, not Richard's misplaced story or the colonel's surliness or Cassie's banality and he was neither tired nor very sad. It was after one o'clock. Watching Clive and the others, he felt warmly aloof and contemplative, his arms all nicely heavy with his few drinks. Mood mingled music. Richard is: a pooh bear of the Western world, a member of Rotary-Kiwanis-Civitan-International-Elks, a man out of tune with zithers and madness. Our colonel is: fox trots, garters, cattle drives, nostalgias and assorted apple pies of honor and truth. Cassie is: a pair of seamless hose, a perennial starlet. Verna is: tears and daydreams. Clive is: an aphrodisiac for an evening all akimbo.

Centered in the room, arms outstretched, Clive lectured on the dervishes of Turkey. Then he began to spin, slowly, his hands unsteady in the air like two thick wings, easing themselves into his fluid turnings. He talked as he spun around, his voice slightly breathless. Mevlâna, he said. The mystic trance is the thing, he said; one doesn't do this to achieve unity with the divine, but to catch the soul in the centrifugal force and make it giddy. Pless instantly thought of the major, his father, tilting and rotating earthward. Across the room, more haggling.

Cassie: "He lived with you. Didn't you see this coming? Or was it living with you that made him mentally ill?"

The Colonel: "Your fault. You're the one who went away."

Pless watched Clive dance. The mammoth. He has no control for ordinary dances; when he danced with Verna he almost stepped on himself and had to quit, but now he glides like a hawk, moves like a giant ice skater; he must have practiced this in his room, his candles ablaze, stolen phonograph albums booming out some esoterica; poor Clive, poor all of us. He must have practiced for hours until, sufficiently transported, his dervish dreams took him spinning off to Ankara and thoughts of his wayward parent. Ah, watch him. His corny and hypnotic tactics. Mother.

Verna joined in, turning slowly and delicately at Clive's elbow, and their movements became two separate whirlpools which drew the gaze of everyone in the room inside. Verna's arms were high, her breasts flattened; her shoes lay in the corner beside the bookcase.

Clive, the giant Mahdi. He's a crude religious leader, Pless decided, who lends such hodge-podge evenings their rituals. Watch him, Pless told himself, then, turning, to the colonel: "Watch him now."

Meanwhile, slightly breathless, Clive kept talking about the dervishes, the ones who were cloistered at Konya and who did this sort of thing every day so that the crowds came out and watched and became mesmerized in their spinning. They wear large white skirts that billow around them, he said. And zither music is wrong. The dervishes have a single high pipe whining as they do their act. And, Pless thought, he's got them going now; the con is on. On will come all his indelicate metaphysics, every trick: the Vinogradoff number, his occult readings, the mystique of the chess board and even, if all else fails, his big blue alarm clock with its intimidating ticking.

Verna was lovely. Her movements were sensuously economical like those of an old gypsy and she was drunk, perfectly bombed, Pless knew, because her tongue was now permanently fixed on her lips, her eyes were closed in a cool rapture, and she just didn't give a damn. Like Clive, she pivoted on one foot and pushed herself into her dizzy trip with the other. The music heightened, grew louder, and Pless wondered if Clive had control over the radio, if it would ever end and some friendly disk jockey would come drooling into their ears, or if Clive had it conned too.

Cassie joined them. Reaching out, she touched the colonel's sleeve and he came spinning after her.

"You've got it!" Clive gasped, encouraging them.

Then Pless and Richard. It was crowded and knuckles slapped as they sailed their arms around. The sofa was pushed back. A table and lamp were moved, the lamp jostled then switched off. Semidarkness.

Cassie giggled, but Clive admonished her. "Quiet now," he said. "This is the trick: you're after a dizziness that lifts you up. You have to concentrate."

Richard, stolid and true but oiled just enough, gave it a serious try, tried to whirl too fast, and stumbled over the edge of the rug. Pless turned slowly so that he could watch it all. Cassie held her skirt needlessly high and took small, birdlike steps as she spun around. The music took on a high monotone.

Unable to keep from laughing, Pless made his turns slowly so that he could observe the other performances.

Suddenly the colonel, who had made a few tentative turns, sat down on the sofa and dropped his head between his legs.

On went Clive, picking up momentum and still jabbering although by this time no one really listened.

Verna's eyes rolled back as she spun around. She seemed almost in a swoon when Pless hurried to her side and caught her just before she went down.

"Steady," he told her. "You all right?"

"Slightly woozy," she said, placing a shaking hand somewhere between her stomach and heart.

Then the colonel went reeling off toward the bathroom. Cassie giggled at him.

Verna allowed Pless to guide her to the large chair beside the bookcase while Richard, clumping loudly, gained speed with the music.

Clive disappeared. He made a quick getaway to the darkened kitchen, moving out of the scene and leaving Richard and Cassie alone and slightly ridiculous, Pless felt, there on the floor. Then the music abruptly ended and they stopped too. The evening had spent itself.

One ritual led to another, then, and everyone was soon at the door putting on coats, searching for hats and purses, and saying good night. Clive reappeared, shaking hands with everyone like a politician, smiling, and directing traffic into the hallway. "See you tomorrow," Verna whispered, kissing Pless' cheek, and Cassie dabbed at her eyes with a handkerchief, sad, Pless determined, that the evening was ending. In the bright light of the hallway all of the colonel's medals flashed, but he appeared pale and worn behind their weight and Verna seemed haggard as she took his arm and went along toward the elevator. "You boys get some rest now," the colonel added, setting the brim of his cap, and Richard shot them an uneasy grin. "Enjoyed it, fellows," he said, and then: "And I hope we see you again soon—in better days." The deft optimism of the young corporation executive. Goodbye, they all said.

Take care. The elevator made its twanging noise, but wouldn't come. Careful of the rain—if it's still raining. Better button up. Good night. Then the four of them stepped inside the elevator doors, turned to Clive and Pless, and made a last face together.

··· 17

ADLER MADE A MENTAL LIST. He would talk to Pless briefly, avoid Clive, take care of his work at the greenhouse, then try and figure out how he would zap himself. How long would all this take? One day, perhaps two. At any rate, he told himself, I've gone all through tonight without sleeping and I won't sleep anymore until it's all over. That should do it: in forty-eight more hours or so I should be whacked and ready.

There were other matters to think about too: his parents down among the rocks in Arkansas, his beard (he somehow wondered if he should shave), his asthma (his wheeze was more pronounced now), Cogdill, so many small things. Yet, there was nothing to think about at all. He contemplated an ultimate solution to all such trash, he knew. Let it be simple.

Since he had decided not to sleep anymore, that morning

at five o'clock, the sky still dark and rainy, he made his way over to a little restaurant on 54th Street. Gobbling eggs and sausage and coffee, he began to wonder if he should leave a note. Of course that wasn't in the pact, but who said so? And I ought to put my signature on something, he decided, so that it can be puzzled over; after all, Stoke autographed the pavement with the weight and stain of his collision and the damned sandblasters will have to honor his effort with their toil now, will have to explode his traces from the plaza. Unreal. Stoker ought to come swaggering through the door, grinning his crooked grin, bearing a few dog-eared books under his arm, cursing Clive and the weather and the sandblasters are going to try and rub him out and the rains will come and mingle his ashes with the prairie soil. Everything in nature leaves a note. I've seen a young deer, a spike buck, making his mark on an elm up on the ridge above the old man's house, scraping his half-point horns there on the bark. And the hawks do their sky-writing, all their dives and arches. And the snails along the White River ribbon the rocks with their glistening scrawl. Stoker was going to write a story, but didn't; was going to get married and impregnate his truelove with a bit of himself, his image; was going to lecture to the dull students of future classrooms on how to author one's own name in literary history. Tereu. Pirouette and leap I wanted to make. Let my body initial the air like a sweet invisible ink. Then, after that was finished, I thought of a little rancid research: lengthy scholarly commentary on orchids, for instance. This is the *Stanhopea,* this the *Oncidium,* and this the *Epidendrum* (smaller and more delicate). Yrs truly, A. Adler, Ph.D. But I have not exactly made my mark. And what would a last note say? Goodbye cruel. Flush. Death by Water.

"Say, I'd like to have another plate of sausage and eggs. And is there a bathroom here?"

"Right back there, yeah. Another order? You must be hungry, kid."

Adler went back through a hallway to the men's rest room, which had a window open on an alleyway. Without stopping to relieve himself, he climbed atop the commode, unlatched the screen, opened it, and popped through. Within a minute he was two blocks away.

He crossed the width of the campus walking toward the park, then turned down 61st Street toward his room near the corner of Dorchester Avenue, not far from Clive's place on Kimbark. He walked warily those last blocks, looking for Clive, though he had no real notion that Clive would be awake at such an early hour, and keeping an eye out for the man at the restaurant, who might be following with a cleaver, tracing him by the sausage odor which still seemed to vapor his body. He thought of dancing with a coed when he was back at the University of Arkansas: a frail girl with long, dark hair and immense eyes. For a moment that afternoon she forgot his face; their bodies went blending in leaps and whorls and he tossed her up in a series of moves and although she didn't belong to him they both belonged to the choreography for a few precious minutes. Afterward everyone in class went off to a movie, but he somehow didn't go. He thought of the movies he had seen and counted his favorites, wondering if he might someday have a library of the films he enjoyed, things like *Lawrence of Arabia* and *Dr. Zhivago* and *Shoot the Piano Player*. But the future, he reminded himself, is approximately forty-eight hours long now. Wonder if people will own film libraries in a few years? Wonder if books will go out of style? Wonder if people will continue to sit alone in rooms and turn pages and have their private readings? A note. One ought to leave a line or two, something for the coroner to diddle with.

In his room he counted ways to kill himself. A gun, obviously. Clive owned a gun, an old Army surplus .45 which he had shoplifted from one of the stores down on lower State Street. I could ask to borrow it or just give it to him straight: I need it, Clive, so I can put a shot right here above my left ear. In that case, of course, Clive being such a grand guy, he'd loan it to me. Loaded. On the condition he could watch.

A wheeze broke from his chest.

Or I could give myself a gigantic adrenalin shot, he went on. A real blast that would make my heart pop out of my chest and go hopping across the floor. Or I could go into the room of succulent plants at the greenhouse and dive on a cactus, impaling myself. The *Schlumbergia,* perhaps, so that its red flowers would decorate my corpse. Or I could cut my throat shaving. A ripe beard I have now, true, only if I did it that way it might be taken as an accident, so where would I be? Who decided we couldn't leave notes anyway? Clive or Pless? This ought to look like what it is: Died by His Own Hand. All that. No, I'd better not do it with a razor in the event someone might imagine that my hand just slipped. Hanging, perhaps. Ah, here I am at daybreak pondering the whys and wherefores.

WHEN DAWN FINALLY ARRIVED Pless and Clive had been talking for hours. The conversation was at first about Stoker, then about the general topic of death, then Clive was musing about suicide. Listening and adding something occasionally, Pless got excited. He drank several cups of instant coffee—Clive took none—and let his thoughts free-fall. Once he took the floor to footnote Clive's ideas with some statistics: the unusually high suicide rates in the United States, Japan, and the Scandinavian countries. Another time he talked about how the universities, which were so carefully departmentalized and therefore dumb, couldn't deal with the phenomenon. The sociologists pointed to cultural pressures when a man killed himself, he told Clive, and the psychologists muttered about guilt and anxiety and the biologists about the chemical reactions in the body and the philosophers about the loss of reason.

They sat forward on the edge of their chairs and laughed. The radio music changed from the madcap zithers of early evening to stale violins.

Mostly Clive talked. His remarks were usually reflective of Stoker's high dive and the events of the last days, but his voice was full of different moods: detached speculation, argumentation, grief, urgency. Listening, Pless felt an old tingle, something of the danger he had felt with Clive when they first got acquainted. Clive of the perilous tones. Pless smiled, sipped his coffee, and filled in the occasional silences.

"There are at least three really *good* reasons for committing suicide," Clive went on. "And I'm not talking about the usual: someone getting disappointed and starting to feel sorry for himself and wanting to make everyone else sorry too. That's not the bad show I mean."

"You think that's why Stoker did it, by the way? Because a sudden straw broke his back—sort of instant despair? And he wanted us to feel it?"

"I hate to think it, but probably. It looked that way. Yet who knows? It was probably lots of things. Because he got recognized buzzing windows. Maybe even, in part, because he held the wrong number. But who's to say? And that's not what I'm talking about—even if it was the case."

"Go on. You were going to put in a good word for self-annihilation."

"Well, suicide is always messy, I think, but not so messy as going on living sometimes. And in so many cultures it's a perfectly acceptable way out—Japan, for instance. You were mentioning their high suicide rate. Of course that's because suicide is an acceptable social gesture there. In our country a man suffers a personal humiliation and he starts drinking and driving around like an idiot on the highways and involving others with his hang-ups. Suicide is a decent exit in comparison. Not that being decent is the best reason—that's just one of my reasons."

"I'm listening."

"Then there's this: suicide is the great escape. The big sleep theory. And in this god-awful escapist society what beats it? Drugs? Six movies a day? The gossip columns? We do almost everything we can, I mean, to get out of our own lives. Well, this is the last great trip. I got into a sleeping period in my life once—probably you did too. It was great. I didn't want to get out of bed for anything."

"I got interested in my dream life once," Pless admitted. "I slept fourteen hours a day sometimes—just so I could dream. This was just after puberty. I was also learning to play with myself under the covers."

"I was older. It was during the time I lived with my aunt here on the south side. I suppose I didn't want to admit that the family was busted and that the old man was in Europe and Jackie was freeloading on the world's traveling salesmen and I just crawled into the hammock—not to dream. To think of nothing. Another time in Ankara, too, I got like that. I was eating too much. Lots of milk, cheese, *baklava* and strong coffee in the mornings, then I'd just go back to bed and sleep through noon."

"You never stop about Turkey," Pless said, shaking his head.

"Everyone wants the big sleep sometime in his life," Clive went on, paying no attention. "But that's still not the best reason for taking your own life. Suicide, after all, is pretty damned *extreme* escapism."

"What else, then?"

"This will appeal to you—because you're a moralist. The best reason's this: in an insane age, suicide is the sane act."

Pless added some hot coffee to his cup and said nothing. Clive accepted his silence with a grin.

"You've said it often enough yourself," Clive went on. "This is the age when we learn that mental illness is contagious, when we have the great plague that proves it. So suicide, for one thing, is the ultimate social criticism. You zap yourself and in effect say: Look, everything is ridiculous, but I'm actually doing something sensible. It's the principle of the double negative making one positive. You go around doing sensible things in an insane environment and what have you got? Stupid absurdity. So you eat banana peels and throw away the fruit, you say things backwards so your mama won't understand, you play Russian roulette, you go down to your nearest cathedral, climb the walls, get way up there among the chapel rafters, then dive down and impale yourself on the brass crucifix. Oh, listen, I read something good lately: a few ancient Romans got this kick about drilling themselves a third eye. Right here. Drilled this hole right between and above their eyes into their forebrains."

"They died, of course."

"Of course. But some of them got this tremendous fix. A perpetual kick."

"Very permanent sounding."

"Oh, but did the Romans get high!"

Pless, mimicking: " 'Scuse me, buddy, but could I borrow your hand drill, please. That's right, I'd like to do the third-eye bit. A bit gory, yes, but I've had chariots and orgies this season.' "

"That's it: you zap yourself before you get zapped by your stupid order of things. It may be a little unnatural, but it's sensible."

"You accept that the age is mad, then?"

"Certainly. Absurd wars where cause and effect is obliterated and where we're all sent out to get killed for reasons that're forgotten and weren't very clear to begin with. Music has turned to noise. Sex has turned to shit. God has turned to Santa Claus and Santa has turned into Dracula with his finger up his ass. Sure, I believe it. I bought it from you, hero. It's your assessment of things."

In the kitchen, Pless splattered water into the coffee pot. Beyond the rooftops he could see the first rays of the sun.

"What else?" he called.

"What do you mean?"

"Keep talking. Tell me more."

"The sensible people are crazy. Your parents, for instance, or Stoke's. Did you catch that Cassie creature? Or buttoned-down Richard? And the colonel is all confusion—like a man with his hands full of broken glass who wants to build a fine crystal candlestick. Now your major, your old man. What made him *risk?* Listen, he knew death. It was probably like spice to him. It flavored life. But his insanity was really sensible—because he knew existence was pretty damned tasteless. Now the troops who were here this evening—your mama being an exception, perhaps—they believe that they understand things and they're zombies. I've listened to them discuss Stoke and his little act for three days now and none of them know that what looks insane is really sane. They have no inkling of that!"

"Wait, slow down. Don't you want just one cup of coffee?"

"Thanks, no." Clive hovered in the kitchen doorway. He carefully gauged his effect on Pless, smiled, took a deep breath, then started again. "My days playing chess taught me a lot about this," he went on. "The genius of the game is great risk, irrational gestures. Every champion plays an unconventional game. Then this idea began to creep out into my life. Madness is genius. Chaos is order. Paradox is the only viable form of truth. I learned it from my old man and sister—who always played by their own ridiculous and intuitive rules. The unhappiest time in my life was when I sat still here in Chicago and tried to figure out who I should be and what I should do. I was left here alone and wanted to be in Ankara with them, but I had accepted my assignment. Then I decided: no. I won't live a reactionary existence: I'll show up in Turkey and I'll make them deal with me and I'll never stop surprising them."

Pless, though he had even once heard Clive admit that he hadn't gone to join his father, wondered at the truth. In a way, he didn't care. As he poured his coffee, he nodded and Clive kept talking.

"There might have been a time when the reflective man didn't look silly in his society, but not now. Today he gets butchered. The rush of events is just too great and nothing is ever quite static enough for the mind to get hold of. So all reflective thought becomes an immediate anachronism. You follow?"

"I think so."

"It's like a man standing in a hurricane pondering the nature of storms. He might think intelligently, but he gets blown away. The only really meaningful thing he can do is something absurd—something almost mindless and comic."

"My father told me a story about a friend of his," Pless put in. "A guy who was captured in the World War and sent on a train to a concentration camp back deep into Germany. One day the train stopped and everyone looked out of the cattle cars they were riding in. The SS was shooting some peasants —Russians or Poles. The machine gun was ready and everybody was lined up. Then this one little peasant stuck up his hand. The captain went over to him and the peasant obviously asked if he could take a leak before getting shot. The captain shrugged and looked annoyed, but said all right. So the firing squad waited until the peasant relieved himself, buttoned himself back up, and took his place in line again. Then everybody was shot down. My father's friend said he just never made sense of it. He didn't know why the peasant bothered or why the captain let him take the trouble or why the whole incident provoked him as much as it did. But he thought about it, he told my father, all through the time he was imprisoned by the Nazis."

"That's right to the point, isn't it? Nothing is quite so human as that sort of stupid act. And, hell, those are the only acts that get our attention now anyway! We don't listen to our moralists or our prophets—that's certain. Marcuse and Heidegger and all the philosophers talk among themselves, I guess, but nobody hears them. Like our poets. They write poems that are read by other poets. Only the rare, irrational deeds prick us."

Pless stood gazing out of the window and Clive came over and stood beside him. They were close, arms touching. "It just doesn't seem possible about Stoke," Pless said softly.

Silence between them.

"It wasn't a stupid act," Clive said. "That's what we're saying. We just won't let it be." He almost said something more, and Pless turned to him, waiting, knowing that he was on the verge of saying something about the pact.

"Ah, listen," Clive finally said. "It's morning. We've got to get some sleep. But we'll talk more. Okay? We've just begun to say what we have to say, haven't we?"

"I suppose so," Pless answered.

They walked back through the living room. It smelled of stale cigarettes and rum. Yawning, Clive stood at the door and pulled a sweater over his head.

"We'll talk more," he repeated. "Maybe later today."

Pless idled in the hallway, leaning against the door while Clive waited for the elevator. There seemed to be a sudden communion between them.

"Look, Clive," he said, as the elevator doors slid open, "what number did you draw?"

"Four," Clive answered simply. "What about you?"

"Three."

"We'll talk later," Clive said, and the doors closed on him.

Pless went back to his kitchen window and looked out across the city at the pale morning light on the distant towers of The Loop. That's right, he told himself. More than anything else we don't want Stoke's act to be completely lost, a total waste. Then he thought of Adler. Number two. He knew that he had better see him right away—as soon as he could get some sleep.

··· 19

ADLER SHAVING. It gave him a sense of cleanliness and readiness as he watched his breath steam the mirror and concocted his last will and testament. He would leave dear Clive a few stalks of *diffenbachia:* that nasty plant from South America with all its poison juices. I'll do it up in ribbon, he decided, and label it: Sugar Cane for a Sweet Storyteller. When he bites into it, of course, the juices will inflame his mouth, gums, lips, throat, tongue and paralyze him. He'll vomit. Nauseous with pain. O ye. His lying voice will hush. Headhunters used that stuff for torture. Would like to hang around to see a little of that. Swollen, puffed up. He'd look like the adder he is. Like a blowfish.

Legacy. To my mother, dear creature: photographs. Baby pictures (with and without diapers), hunting snapshots

(Daddy's oversized vest packed with Remington shells and my face creased in the sunglare), and the dreadful gazes in my high school yearbooks. I always looked like a little gargoyle peeking from behind some maiden's shoulder. Didn't allow that crap when I got to the universities. Nothing for Mother these last years. Gone without a trace. Narry a photo except those first few—when they put me in front of a camera out of disbelief, to see if I looked that ugly in a reproduction.

Legacy. To my father, old straight shooter: books. Simple things like books of fairy tales for you, Dad, so you'll get the idea. What fairy tales? The giant Jack killed. The grandmother eaten by the wolf. The first two little piggies who were ravished. The wolf who got it from the friendly woodsman. The evil witch who gets hers. Nothing literary for you, Daddy dear; none of Stoker's gray paperbacks with their symbols of symbols and their purple passages of life's wretched term; nothing of Melville's monsters or the stupidities of Crane's heroines or Whitman's fairy self; nothing troublesome. Comic books, perhaps: the Dragon Lady and the hoods of Dick Tracy and Little Orphan Annie. Let Evil Be Black, pater, and Good Be White as Snow.

Adler wiped his face with a towel, pulled his topcoat on, and left his room unlocked. Frosted air off the lake met his face as he walked.

Legacy. To the colonel the mysterious umbrellas of existence. To Cogdill a turd in his desk drawer. To my Alma Mater, my school, my inspiration: the trouble of my carcass and the vacant post of one minor lab assistant, small of stature, hunkered and foul-looking, intelligent, unsexed, dutiful. To Pless a large volume explaining everything in behavioral terms. To Stoker. Ah me, imagine that dive, that arching fall, the slap of death. To Mr. Jaynes, wherever you are, my dear forgotten ballet instructor, my little ceramic man wrapped in a copy of my daddy's *Life Lines*.

He walked for an hour, musing. The blocks passed before

his eyes like pages in a strange book. Soon he came to a graveyard.

Headstones everywhere. TO OUR SHERRY ANN: FOUR MONTHS OLD. Buried no doubt in a hat box, poor chile. EMMA PALMER/WIFE, MOTHER, HYPOCHONDRIAC/NOW CURED OF ALL HER COMPLAINTS/1901–1949. Ah, that's a good one. PLATO, FAITHFUL PUPPY/1966. Dog to God. Dust to dust. Unreal how he could go twelve floors off the Blackstone like that. There it was in the newspapers, though, right down to the bittersweet details about how his head didn't seem hurt. Old joke: it wasn't the fall that killed him, baby, it was that sudden stop at the bottom. JOHN ARNOLD CURLEY, 1881–1935/OUR DEAR DRUNKARD. That's touching. Now I'm the neurotic and the real pushover in this pact, if you want to know. How did it happen? Clive cut his wrists, alas, and survived. Tough break, that. And what did we do? We were drinking and the snow was blowing up mad around the windows and that's why I got to whimpering, I think, because of how ominous the wind sounded outside. Like a voice urging us and we were drinking. Pless was whacked. Even Clive was touching the bottle to his lips and I had too much and Stoke had too much. Grinning his sideways style, he was. PROFESSOR HARLEY BATES, 1893–1959/FINALLY DEAD FROM THE NECK DOWN. Now there's a truism writ by his former students who doubtless napped and cheated on him. And how else was it? Oh, the wastebasket all gory and smelly. Clive suddenly very interested, getting up and fetching those pieces of notebook paper for us. Ever so helpful. He wrote our numbers. Slick as blood. Popped them into the hat and probably palmed his, if I know him, and held them up there in the stratosphere above me, dangling them, and up I went on my tiptoes drunk as shit and it was a stocking cap because my finger almost went through the bottom of the knitting before I found my Two. It was Pless making the rules. I can't even remember. Not to go around finding each other afterwards and no notes.

Well, screw that. I might write a letter to the *American* myself. Detailing those new fraternity rites out here. File under crank letters. I don't know why I got so sniffly and weepful that night, but I think it was the way the windows rattled with the wind off this lake. Jesus, it's cold out here. I've never seen this little cemetery before either, but here it is: soft and grassy (all brownish now) on this knoll above the surf of Michigan. TO AN OLD BOXER WHO FOUGHT HIS LAST ROUND WELL. Decorated with crossed gloves, this one. Nameless. Old-fashioned nihilism we said that night and the honor system and I suggested a manifesto and boo-hooed when they wouldn't do it. When I saw my number a sigh of relief, I remember, and I thought Ah no one will ever go firsties, but there you must be, Stoke, all cremated and flung over these waters: you and Detroit's sewage and a few thousand pounds of fish crap in our flouridated drinking water. Made our marks, we did, signed and sealed. Tears in my beard. And Clive burned the evidence—each scrap of paper. Nothing of the agreement remains, no nothing, except what stuck to our bones.

He felt himself dancing. Lilting among the gravemarkers, turning. His worn topcoat fell aside as he jumped across a headstone. He ran to the edge of the knoll, then, addressed his body to the waves of Lake Michigan and bowed low.

Thunderous applause, he told himself with a smirk. I dance adagio to doom. Up yours, Jaynes.

Oh, I feel the pressure, and why? One ought not to feel committed to doing something like this, but it's almost a sense of fate now, something I wear like a talisman, and why? Is it because Clive keeps pumping up memories of that night we made the pact? Or because Stoke did his part? Or just because I am what I am, wrapped and predestined with this obsession? No, I don't believe in fate, just feel it. JOHN R. GROSS. There's another old one. 1803–1849. Ah, it's cold out here for us dancers. How about death by pneumonia, all you happy ballet fans around here?

Running, jumping, turning, he retrieved his topcoat and swirled it around his head like a cape before settling it on his shoulders. If an officer catches sight of me, he'll lock me up sure. What's yr name, sonny? Pete Quince, officer, & what's yrs? Address? Rats alley, says I. Now look here, sonny, suicide and attempted suicide are criminal offenses in most of these here United States in case you don't know, so you'd better level with us about yr intentions. Et cetera. Ram it up yr Ahaber, officer. Stubb it up yr keelhauler.

One more short pirouette and his asthma bit into him again. He stopped, wheezing, his chest constricted and noisy.

He walked, slowly. SISTER ANNA CHRISTINA/BLESSED ARE THE MEEK. The enigmatic stones passed in review. MATTHEW O'CONNOR, 1879–1937/"BY HIS OWN PECULIAR PERVERSITY GOD MADE HIM A LIAR." God, god, god: he has used my chest cavity as his spitoon & that's why I wheeze like this.

There was a bench outside the cemetery where he sat for more than half an hour before going on toward Stoker's room again. His breathing restored, he started out, wanting to see and feel it once more. Snowflakes came down like cold confetti during his slow parade. Stoker's room: there was something about it. He felt he needed to see it again and needed to see that nurse, too, Stoke's girl, just had to, but knew that he probably wouldn't. Or Clive. He especially didn't want to see Clive. Or even Pless.

The downstairs door was ajar and he slipped in quietly and edged up the stairway wall toward Stoker's room. It was quiet in the old building, so that the rasp of his breathing was magnified; he tried to hold his breath, but choked slightly and coughed. Then he heard voices in the room and moved to the edge of the stairs so that his eyes fell even with the floor above. He could see into Stoke's room easily and there they were: the colonel and Pless' mother. They moved around like ghouls inside the room, touching the objects of the lost: books and toilet articles, all the paraphernalia of their grief; the bed, piled with clothes which had been taken from the closet, sagged with defeat. Yet, unmistakably, the gardenia odor still wafted around. For some reason he couldn't explain, sweat popped out on his forehead. He felt he had to get inside that room, had to feel what had been there, the sweet sexual perfume which had boggled his thoughts so much during his last visit. It was almost as if everything would be different, as if his very life depended on it, but the voices frustrated him; the colonel was taking his time. Verna was crying. "Look at this," the colonel said once, and the tone was so plaintive and so wretched Adler almost laughed. Ah shit, he told himself. He decided to forget it.

At the front door he caught sight of Pless coming down the street. Jerkily, he closed the door and ran down the hallway toward the back door. Of all things he didn't want to talk to anyone now and didn't want to be seen. But the back door was bolted and locked and he was no more than thirty feet from the front door where Pless would soon appear. Quickly he sagged down into the shadow of the staircase, hiding, and almost immediately the front door bumped open loudly and there was Pless. For a moment Adler was sure he was seen, but then Pless turned and called upstairs:

"Hello! Anyone here?"

An almost cheerful note. Then Pless followed his dull echo upstairs as the colonel called down.

"Come up. We're here."

Crouched down, sweating and wheezing, Adler rocked gently back and forth. He wanted to cry out, to go running upstairs to weep on the nearest shoulder, but he reminded himself that he had made too much of a habit of that. Humiliation rode around behind his eyes, burning him, and he rocked gently; he could smell his thin, dank body odor seeping up from his clothes and he hated it.

He sat there in the shadow for a long time, perhaps another half hour, until he almost toppled over into sleep. When he finally decided to make his getaway, there they were again, the three of them, coming downstairs. The colonel was telling Pless that there would be no need to take them to the airport.

"Let's see, I have the tickets right here," he said, producing them from the coat of his uniform as they reached the bottom of the stairs. "Flight 968. One stop back to Vegas. If you'll see about the rest of that gear up there, that'll be help enough. And the car: we're all settled about that, aren't we?"

"That's right," Pless answered.

"There's just so many things to think about," Verna said as she passed through the doorway. "Be all the help you can, hon."

"I will," Pless promised, and they were gone.

After waiting a few more minutes, Adler went upstairs again and tried the door. Only after finding it locked did he remember the key, but then he felt too weary to go after it, so just left. Outside, the ground was white and children on the block were making noise and snowballs.

By now it was afternoon and he felt hungry and for a moment considered going back to the same restaurant, ordering sausages and eggs again, and escaping through that same alley window. Then his thoughts turned to pizza, great mounds of spaghetti, and he decided to spend his remaining cash on a gorge. Death by obesity. Fill myself with ravioli and explode all over the walls. The American dream: cream pudding, pastries, butterballs and a small cardiac for dessert. Or I could always eat myself and die of psychological heartburn.

He took a booth in the window of a pizza shop and downed a nine-incher with spaghetti, meatballs and three lagers on the side. He matched the rhythm of the gathering snowstorm with his efforts at the table: as the swirls grew fiercer, he stuffed more in. Afterward as he walked toward the cashier, he felt a ballast of sleep, though, and thought of falling back into his booth, fingers curled around another lager so that the waitress wouldn't bother him, and sleeping until springtime. Belly tight under his topcoat, drowsy, he went out once more. Six blocks farther, plodding through the soft, new snow, he sighted the greenhouse.

Inside, everything was a cathedral of dark colors and silence. At the far end—which was nearly half a block away— an instructor and his students hovered over the violet-lit seedling boxes, but a moist solitude pervaded the rest of the greenhouse. The snow-covered glass overhead shut off the usual streamers of light so that the leaves wore solemn hues this afternoon and down the long corridors of ferns and flowers the eye fell into shadows. Small puddles melted around Adler's shoes as he stood in the doorway. I'm a plant, he told himself, and here's home. I'll do it here.

But as he shuffled down the aisle toward his office, he spotted Clive near the big kiln where all the greenhouse pots were baked. Adler stopped short, stepped behind a cluster of *cyperus,* and waited. Clive looked cocky and up to no good; he carried a sprig of morning glory in his fingers and seemed to be inspecting the kiln. Going to find its weakness, Adler decided, and punch a hole in it so it won't work anymore. Damned Clive. I don't know why I'm like this about him now, but I can't let him see me. Vulture. He wants to pick me clean. And I don't want to please anyone by zapping myself and know that it sure as hell would please Clive. No one cares for me, true, but Clive despises me. Stoker was the only one who ever cared a whit for me, come to think of it. Pless always busy and hot for Clive's bullshit. And Clive only tolerant of me so that he can badger me occasionally and make me cry. Ah shit, feeling sorry for myself; I can't even stand my own thoughts.

Clive looked around, checking to see if anyone watched, then filled his pockets with the tabs—wooden markers like ice cream sticks—which were used to identify the plants. Now what, Adler asked himself, does he want those for? He'll steal anything: that's it. He's probably wondering how he can get the bricks out of the kiln. He's probably wondering if all this green stuff will burn.

Soon, tired of waiting, Clive wandered away. Adler moved cautiously, moving the *cyperus* aside and peeking through, trying to make sure he was gone. He followed at a safe distance, crouched down behind one of the rows, until he saw Clive leave. Sighing, he went back to his office.

Hide 'n seek with Pless and Clive. Screw them. They're not friends. I don't have any friends.

He began to be very sorry for himself. Like someone deliberately letting go of a desperate hold on a cliff's edge, he let remembrances and thoughts flood in, everything hurtful.

> Beauty is only skin deep
> Ugly is to the bone
> Beauty always fades away
> But ugly holds its own.

Old Arkansas proverb. Sung to me, he recalled, by my pleasant classmates at the country school, damn their eyes. Well, true: I'm no hothouse flower, just a garden weed who turns up in unwanted places. Daddy, Jaynes, Pless, Cogdill—they're all the very same, the bunch of them: can't stand me. It's not so bad being repulsive to Clive, of course, because he hates dogs, kitties, children, America, Europe and the rosebuds of May and June. But the law of averages should have produced a single companion, someone. Stoker, perhaps, was it. Oh, Stoke. Such goddamned maudlin things I feel. Oh, Stoker, love.

He began to weep a little.

Legacy. To myself, my own raw and battered libido: memories of those ragamuffin Ozark kids who taunted me. Don't bother to dress up for Halloween, Addie, you've got it made, they said, or they dropped the handkerchief behind me and laughed when I waddled or they drew my face—good likeness, the teacher admitted—on the blackboard. The school was off Old Pike Road, an old slat-sided three-roomer held up by honeysuckle and long division and the sharp eyes of Mrs. Brown and Mr. Sidney. They detested me too. The old man made a deal for some bottom land and had himself a couple of good crops and bought that new tractor and told everyone he'd send his kid, ugly as he was, off to the university, so that some neighborly resentment got built into everyone's dislike of me. And puberty came too soon. I was scarcely used to being an ugly child, then I was an ugly sexual creature. Tommy Bolin asking me if my pecker was as ugly as my face. Girls not exactly looking at me when they had to speak. And the old man, for that matter, wincing every time he saw my mug. About as subtle as a razorback hog, my dear father. "Look, son," he said modifying the old joke, "you could get yourself a gunnysack to put over your head and then maybe them little girls'll let you in their panties up behind the schoolhouse on weekends." Old fart, saying that to me. I went bawling upstairs, not letting him see me do it, naturally, and took that long look at myself in the mirror hanging on the closet door in Mama's room. And there it all was, in truth: eyebrows that grew together like a black snake across my face, beady eyes, round nose and mouth all adroop. Such goddamned maudlin things I feel and I might as well let them in, might as well recollect because now, probably, all of it will help me do what I'm going to do. Let it come. Let it all hang out. Tereu.

My mother, bless her, asked me not to cough on her. That was when I had asthma so bad that winter. We were never a family to do much hugging and kissing, true, but there was a time I'd have liked a little touch here and there: some rubbing on my chest—although it wouldn't have done any good—or a hand on my forehead to test for fever, though I never had fever with my asthma unless it was running into pneumonia which it twice did. Well, the old lady *prayed* that asthma should be lifted from me. Give her that much. As though my wheezing were a curse, Jesus, she prayed to give herself a little soul protection and certainly never much helped me. Not a single palm laid to my forehead. And of course that was in the days before all the new spray mists and medicines for asthma. We had religious arguments, I recall, which she won until I was old enough to spend a year in college and arm myself with some outside reading on the subject. Then I came back one day and told her that Jesus was just a good Jew boy who tried his best to get rid of organized religion, but that his disciples and St. Paul, bumbling idiots to the last man, had made a religion out of him. She screamed at me for a while, then shut up. In fact, she never brought up the subject again, nor prayed for my asthma, nor touched me. Don't cough on me, son, she said. Bitch.

Adler sobbed quietly, his shoulders bumping with his crying, while the thick snow gathered on the glass above him and turned the room gray. Then, once more, he stopped, catching his breath in spasms. His wheeze was more pronounced.

Legacy. To myself in hibernation there among the books in the library at the university. I walled myself in with books. In fact, thinking it over, I was always more a reader than Stoke. He had all those paperbacks, but loaned a lot of them to me new. He wanted to write, not read—though of course that's not to say he wasn't literary because everyone knew that. But I've been a reader out of necessity; one has to hibernate somewhere. One cannot become a good weed without fodder and soil. Ah, poor Stoke. So I would read every night, especially when I was so tired from dancing in Jaynes' class; it was mostly history at that time, but later it was novels after I came here to Chicago and met Pless and Stoke. Mad Melville: I love the way he's so full of Shakespeare and the Bible; there's something downright elegant about his madness and his whale and his Billy Budd, poor loser. I think that's what I wanted with the ballet: a little elegance after all that hillbilly shit in my old man's house. The first time I ever saw the dance at Fayetteville I knew that was for me. A traveling troupe came through, I remember, and I went back every night, then met that lovely woman who ran the dance program at the university, Eleanor her name was, and she encouraged me, but it was Jaynes, damn him, that I had to suffer in class. Had I been able to stay with it, I could've taken dance from Miss Eleanor, but Jaynes and the old man discouraged me and I started eating heavy again and put on that quick thirty pounds and after that it was back to the books—any book, anything to keep my mind occupied—and I wore the ballet slippers like house shoes. Elegant it was, though, for a short time. I loved the notion of being onstage somewhere, springing through the air while the audience, dressed in tuxedoes and ball dresses, watched in awe from the darkness; and there I would be at a distance so that my face didn't matter so much, leaping like a fountain of muscle, suspended by air and music. I wonder if Stoke went down with a small sense of that aesthetic freedom, that glide momentarily beyond gravity. Poor love. The dream of elegance faded, whatever, and my figure became that of a jolly Austrian baker, one who wasn't so goddamned jolly. And so it was books. Then the plants, of whom I was one. Then more food and movies. Peter O'Toole I enjoyed all four times I saw that damned movie with his face getting lashed by sand and he was all screwed up in his sex, but a man of destiny. T. E. Lawrence's prose was never quite so good as Peter O'Toole's face. And after arriving here I sat in the back of my classrooms, of course, where I wouldn't be noticed; the good grades rolled in those first semesters, then I was a lab assistant, lovely, with power over those smart freshman kids; my old interests, of course, idling. I wanted to show that atomic waste is not diluted when stored up in plants —as was once the theory. But now I'll never do that, no. But I was a lab assistant with good grades, easily replaced, sure. Somewhere in a file cabinet in this great university there will be a card marked *deceased* and some tight-assed secretary will remark, "Oh say, listen, look at this kid's grades. Isn't he the one who zapped himself? Oh sure, these brainy kids are hung-up and always don't make it, I can tell you true. I seen too many." The old man will echo the same thing. The old lady will say it was lack of faith, the lack of belief everywhere, the whole world crumbling into atheism, communism and perversion.

Remember everything, he told himself. Everything that can possibly add to the needed misery.

He walked out into the greenhouse from his office and saw that the instructor and his pupils had abandoned the seedlings under the ultraviolet light. Dismissed class early, he speculated, because of the snowstorm. The giant room glowered with darkness now and in the silence he could hear only one thin noise: the bubbles in the nearby goldfish tank. He went over and peered in. Down among the moss the fish moved timidly, flashing softly; he looked up and saw a series of pulleys above the tank, chains and ropes which were occasionally used to move the larger specimens in the room and which once, before the installation of the new automatic window system, were used to pull open the windows during the summers. Above the ropes and chains the snow-blackened panes grew heavy. The afternoon wears on, he told himself. He wondered if he might eat a last meal, but decided against it and instead he wandered down one of the aisles, passing the *ficius pumila,* its leaves thick with latex. Then he moved on to the mushrooms, to the *morchella:* like a stubby penis.

Legacy. Think about the first time you met Pless and Stoke, he told himself, and think how they never really liked you, how they were just being tolerant, at most. There was the smoker for the first year grad students and Pless said hello and delivered, somewhat stiffly, a sort of speech. "My field is psychology," he announced, "but I have a lot of interests. Not botany, no, but I'd like to hear you talk about it sometime.

Mainly I'm interested in any ideas—and anything with a real kick, you know. I came to the university to talk and I think that's what an education is for: to get your brains scrambled, to hit all the far-out points of view." Pless never liked me. He was always credited with so much charm and so much intellectual depth, too, but I don't know. He's a little icy, a little spooked. His father got killed flying his jet and I just don't know about him; of course Stoker was all skin and soul and just wanted someone to stroke him, and for my money Stoke had body warmth, but Pless practiced cool. Ah, weighing the dead and the living. And Pless never liked me because I couldn't entertain him like Clive; that Clive gives him the fancy put-on and I just don't know if Pless buys all that shit or not, but one thing's sure: he never bothered much with me. Telephoning like that the other night doesn't fool me. Was that last night? Time is all gone now, all gone, I need sleep and I'll soon get it good. Pless always likes those sharp one-liners, but all I ever gave him were a few asthmatic sobs. He went out with me that time in Vegas to get adrenalin when my asthma was so bad, but only so he could feel paternal and superior, I believe, and so he could experience his cool while I gagged and coughed up wads of green phlegm. Aloof and cool and eclectic, that's what Pless wants; I believe he thinks there's a region where he can move off into cool objectivity, where he can escape the hard memories of the flesh like his daddy's crack-up and his mama's escapades; he plays that role hard, I can tell you, and I never fit into it very well at all. Us ugly ones is too real for him, I guess; we is too ugly to the bone. In my humble opinion he didn't care much for Stoke either, oh, they might have been good friends once, high school buddies and all, but Stoke had problems of the flesh, all old-fashioned hang-ups and just not esoteric enough for Pless because Pless believes that something has to be slightly vague and mysterious to be interesting. Like Clive. All angles and lies and whopping stories no one understands half the time. Clive is so fucking sick, if you want my humble; sicker than yrs truly the ex-ballet star, the prince of the pot plants, yr one & only fat boy who coughs on his mother.

It was Stoker who cared a little, remember that. Oh, think on that if you want to make misery this late afternoon.

His face that morning he came by asking me to go to coffee and Clive was in here bugging me: he knew I needed to talk to someone then, like tonight I should have seen that nurse, or last night. When? My mind is losing its grip, oh let it. Stoker cared he did and he's gone to bash. Those books, I know what they were: small epistles, every one, little messages he tried to reach me by. Stoke was subtle and full of tiny messages, very shy communications, and always pondering his sexual fate. And that's it about that room of his: the feeling that he made out okay with his nurselove, and that's what's so confusing about his zapping himself. Why would he do it? Or is there some awful psychological paradox I can't read? When you finally break through to people is that where superdespair starts rolling over you, when you discover that their bones are hollow and that communion is not much better than, say, the old alienation? Ah, I'm talking like Pless, and of course I'll never know about Stoker, only that he seemed slightly more genuine than either Pless or Clive—spilling his beer like that, ah, always trust a clumsy man—and he liked me, too, and is that possibly why I'm so blue now, because the one friend who I didn't even realize *was* so important is all gone, just a mark on the sidewalk for the sandblasters?

Adler made his way back toward the storage room in the gathering twilight. Outside, the snowstorm had turned into a blizzard and the wind moaned around the glass building; a solitary pedestrian leaned against the wind and for a moment Adler put his nose against the glass and watched until the steam of his wheezing breath broke his vision.

At his distillery. He had no alcohol, nothing to make his first batch, but he arranged all the equipment properly so that anyone could see what it was. It'll add to the mystery, he decided. (Oh, the vices that kid had! White lightning in the storage room, marijuana and poppies in the seedling boxes, dirty peectures in his desk drawer, and a big, handsome, homosexual bodyguard, yes, oh that Clive character with all his degenerate Turkish delights!) Carefully, when the glassware and Bunsen burner were all in place and successfully suspicious-looking, Adler locked the storage room door.

He went in search of a pencil. Rummaging from desk to desk, he found paperclips, matchbooks, old exam papers, but not a single pencil. The thought came to him that he should smash into Cogdill's office and write the suicide note on the top of the desk with a chisel, but he canceled the notion; Cogdill might stroll in later and interrupt things. He looked on. We have a fifty-thousand-dollar electromicroscope, he regretted, but no pencils. He considered opening a vein, but Clive had already staged that particular melodrama. The typewriter in Professor Wedgeworth's office. No, I can't type; I would fall asleep searching for letters on the keyboard. He toured his own coat pockets and found one ballpoint pen, inkless since last April. Legacy. To this great university, endowment more than three hundred million dollars, I bequeath one box of #2 pencils to be dispensed throughout the departments and divisions.

Dark outside and snowy. He sat beside the kiln and listened to the wind outside and the breath (raspy) inside himself.

Then he began measuring the goldfish tank. It was approximately four feet deep and seven feet square. Taking down a cluster of ropes and pulleys with a long hook, he made estimates. The problem was to get up there around the pulley and to get properly tied. He studied—and needed a pencil, he decided, in order to calculate. He went back to his office, picked up a yardstick, and returned.

Problems to the very end, he thought. Pencils and pulleys and zapping oneself is an act of sanity, after all, otherwise you wouldn't have the sense to figure out all the details. No one is coming tonight either, not Cogdill or anybody else because of the blizzard, and probably not Clive again. There's the phone over there, of course, but Pless probably won't call either. No one coming to save me. Think on, think about the hurt.

Stoker again: his looking in windows was a sign of health, if you ask me, because he just wanted to get next to people; strangers, acquaintances, dream girls, anyone he could see or hear or touch. Privacy killed him. He once asked Pless, I know, to share a room with him, but Pless wouldn't do it; then he was always trying to lure a girl into his bed and not altogether to get in her pants but just to sleep with her, to have her breathing beside him, I believe, and after all in the affluent society each man can buy so much more privacy and this is what kills him, I feel, this solitude which seems so sweet but which turns into loneliness before you know it. Well, I never had that problem and loneliness was never pure, not even when I wanted to make a martyrdom of it, I was always alone in my room and alone in sickness and alone in reading and alone at movies and never once, no, never did I want the luxury of deep friendship, never, or of the sex act, just someone around or some place where I could intrude on someone else's life. Oh, Stoke.

His tears started again. He wheezed and his eyes burned.

Then he remembered seeing a pencil stuck in the bin where the little walnut trees were planted, so he walked over, picked it up, and went back to his office and sharpened it. He wondered about the ropes and pulleys: whether it was really a mathematical problem or just a carpentry job.

I AM NUMBER TWO

He wrote it on a scrap of notebook paper and folded it into his pocket. There. Let the detectives and deans ponder it.

Struggling, then, he climbed the nearby steel girder and

inched his way over to the pulley. Disgusting details. He finally threw everything down beside the goldfish tank, made his way back down, and he started his calculations on the floor. Nine feet from the top of the tank to the pulley. Tank four feet deep. Using the yardstick, he measured out what he needed. I can knot the rope, he decided, so that it'll hang in the pulley. Perfect. One can estimate doom, after all. Death is physical. No one is coming because of the snowstorm.

After finishing, he sat down on the stool beside the kiln again. Now there's another possibility, he allowed: I could fire up the oven, rig up something to close and latch the door behind me, then dive in. No good, though. They'd never find a trace; they'd believe I skipped off to Canada to avoid the draft or gone back to the Ozarks to build bigger and better stills with my old man's neighbors. Ah, the goldfish trick is tricky enough; let the little shiners nibble out my eyes.

Remembrance: things I did with Stoker. Went to lunch in The Loop. Heard lectures in Mandel Hall. Literary discussion (limited) about Djuna Barnes. Went to sessions in Pless' room where Clive orated. Explained exotic pot plants which I gave him for his window sill. Asked what his number was.

Things I did with Pless. Listened to him discuss the social revolution and watched him getting baited by Clive. Went shopping for adrenalin in Vegas. Heard his voice crack, once, when he mentioned his dead daddy.

Things I did with Clive. Toured San Francisco and made the hip scene eating Chinese food and drinking out of that small Saki bottle. Heard eighty-nine variations of Jackie, his nymphomaniac sister who probably doesn't exist. Got a little turned on when he cut his wrists. Got frightened of him. No one is coming, not a single solitary soul.

For my last act, ladies and gentlemen, a variation on the leaping pratfall, one of the most difficult of all ballet gestures requiring control, muscle coordination, concentration and about twelve feet of rope and chain. This pratfall, dear members of the audience, consists of a leap spanning twenty-three years, beginning in the foothills of the Ozarks in Arkansas, United States, and concluding near Lake Michigan, town of Chicago, a distance of about seven hundred miles. Moreover, it will end in a splash, not a whimper. No applause, yet, please. And, please, your absolute silence. Snow, stop rattling around up there on the glass. Flowers, stop gasping for breath. Bubbles, no loud popping noises if you don't mind. No one coming.

He climbed up the girder again, panting hard under the strain, balancing a coil of rope on his shoulder as he pulled himself toward the overhanging beam where the pulley was attached. When he finally reached the pulley, he stopped. His wheeze battered him and he had to recover himself before going through with his plan. He sat there for half an hour, his chest rasping. Verily. I'm in bad physical shape, he told himself. But I'll be a lovely corpse. Should have left my body to the med center. They would have given me five hundred dollars or so, in fact, and then I could have had a last fling, perhaps a trip to Europe, a long journey. The thought's enough to make me start all over, but I'm not going to. Leave no notes, well, hell, screw that and tereu.

He tied his feet securely, looped the rope through the pulley and knotted it. After measuring it again, he began the difficult task of tying his hands behind his back while balancing himself on the narrow steel beam. The end of the rope slipped once, twice, a third time, and perspiration broke out on his neck and face.

Shortly after midnight the snow stopped falling and not long after that Clive put on his sweater and topcoat and walked across the Midway Plaisance, up Ellis Avenue, and through the heavy drifts that had accumulated around 57th Street near the greenhouse. The streets were empty. Softly, certain that Adler would be there, he opened the greenhouse door and made his way down the aisle and there, upside down in the goldfish tank, dangling by his feet from the overhead pulley, neatly submerged and drowned, was Adler. For several minutes Clive looked at everything, though he touched nothing. Adler had miscalculated his fall slightly, he noticed, and had smacked his head on the side of the tank before ending up inside. There was a smear of blood on the wall of the tank, a thin red ooze down there in the moss where Addie and the goldfish hid their faces.

Clive gave it all a last look, smiling at the apparatus: pulley, ropes, the clumsy but durable knots. Then he walked back to Addie's office and pushed the button of the automatic window control.

The next morning when Cogdill came to work he found Adler and all the plants in the greenhouse dead.

IT WAS ON HIS SECOND MORNING BACK
in Phoenix—he was going to fly back to Vegas for a staff
meeting that afternoon—that the colonel saw the item in the
newspaper.

Verna was still in bed, her long freckled legs brown and
uncovered on the sheets, but the colonel had waked up early,
as usual, and had gone down to the kitchen to make himself
a quick daiquiri and to start breakfast. Sausages and toast.
Eggs later. The beginnings of a vodka bloody for Verna.

He went out in his bathrobe for the morning paper. The
day was already well along, pleasantly brisk and filled with
the lingering autumn. He took pleasure in the touch of his
bare feet on the tiled porch, on the moist grass as he walked
out to the mailbox beside the gate, and on the warmth of the
cement driveway. He looked out to the mountains and took

a deep breath. Alive: death reminds us we're really alive, he told himself, and he could feel about Stoker this morning a little of what he had felt for all the pilots—Charlie Miller and all the others—who had perished all the years of his tour. There's always that moment after the bare grief is finished when life roars back; you feel the texture of things, you get inebriated with just breathing. Later, he decided, I'll go in and nuzzle Verna again.

He went back to the kitchen, turned the sausages, and opened the newspaper. He was turning to the sports pages when his eye caught the word *suicide* in a headline.

STUDENT SUICIDES RAISE
QUESTION OF CHICAGO PACT

His senses fell apart. Hurriedly, his eyes scanned. Adler dead. Dead two days. By drowning. Left a note: I Am Number Two. Then he read the story over and over—it was small, only four or five inches long in one column—and caught the important phrases like bullets. It was the first sentence that stung most: "The second suicide at a major Chicago university today raised the suspicion that two dead students and perhaps others are involved in a suicide pact."

The colonel went to Verna and shook her awake.

"I'm thinking of Pless," he told her when she had finished reading the item, "and of Stoker, too, of course. Of both of them."

"Oh, no, I don't think so," Verna said sleepily.

"I know more about this than you do, Vern. Listen, believe me."

"Let's think it out," she said, and she sat up in bed, her breasts falling loose, and wiggled her fingers toward her dressing gown until the colonel handed it to her.

"Last summer," he told her, "they were giving me this big put-on. You know how they do us: they feed us a lot of crap to see if we'll buy it. You know: lots of irony, lots of double meanings and little private jokes. Anyway, they were giving me all this big put-on about what they were going to do when they went back to school, and Adler—this kid, here—said that they were all going to kill themselves. Just said it outright."

"But they were just *kidding* you, hon. Weren't they?"

"That's what I thought *then*. But even then a little ripple went through them. We were having breakfast at my place. And Adler—hell, the important thing is this: Stoke is gone and now this kid is gone. They were all at my place mentioning this in August, too. Adler and the big kid, Clive, drove in from California, remember? And Pless and Stoke drove back from here to meet them."

"Of course I remember."

"They were all tense and nervous at my place. And now that I think about it—listen, Vern, there was a lot I didn't understand at the time. It might not make sense yet. But they were marking on my bathroom walls and they broke all the umbrellas in my rack and took my chess set, I think. Stuff like that."

"Why didn't you ever tell me about all this?"

"I just didn't. And there were other things I haven't been sure of—things that have a little more meaning now. Vern, I'm going to call the base and tell them I've got to have more personal leave. I'm going back to Chicago."

"Oh, hon, this *minute?* You're not *sure* of anything."

The colonel looked at her. "This just can't wait, Verna," he said. "I don't *know* much, true. But we just can't sit here!"

"I'm not even *sober*," she complained.

For a moment, a small feeling of disgust rose up in him. He had never felt anything like it for Verna, but there it was: slightly painful like the beginning of nausea.

"I've got to get up there. That's all there is to it. Better still, I've got to phone Pless right now."

"He doesn't have a phone."

"Damn!" The colonel smacked his fist into his opened palm. "Send a telegram."

"All right, but what? Get me something to write on. Let's see, it ought to be a *smart* telegram. Something simple. Something that will make him wait until I get there before he does anything."

"Oh, he's not going to *do* anything," Verna said.

The colonel watched her stroll across the room and rummage in the desk for a pencil and notebook. He knew she didn't believe him, that she somehow couldn't believe it.

He called his base and when the question of additional personal leave became sticky he got his general on the phone and read him the clipping from the morning newspaper. When his clearance came, he started another series of calls trying to get an F-85 so that he could fly to Chicago himself. As he talked, he wrote out a line and showed it to Verna: HOLD ON UNTIL I GET THERE. NEED TO TALK WITH YOU.

Verna shrugged and lit a cigarette. She had none of his desperation and he had to remind himself that he had seen them at his place in Vegas last summer, that he had suffered their games and gestures and had detected the worrisome undertones. Yet he was disappointed in her and his speculations about her grew; perhaps she has just had too goddamned much, he admitted.

He couldn't arrange for a jet out of Phoenix, so called about a commercial flight. As he fixed his schedule, he scribbled out several other messages. He decided on the direct approach, on a message with authority and a ring of command to it: ARRIVING O'HARE TWA FLT. 776 TONIGHT AT 6:21 PM. PICK ME UP IN STOKE'S CAR AND DON'T BE LATE.

"Yes, he'll come out to the airport," Verna assured him. "Why shouldn't he?"

"There's something going *on*," he tried to tell her again.

"Something, but *what?* And how do we know Pless is involved?"

"We didn't know about Stoker until it was too late," he argued. "And he *was* involved. Or has been falsely linked up with this shit up there. It's right here in the newspaper! And I'm going back to find out exactly what's what."

"Let's have breakfast and think about this some more," she managed.

Burned sausages, dry toast, heavy coffee. The colonel sat looking at the newspaper article, his face creased with worry. Verna had two Bloody Marys, then a straight shot of morning bourbon. After a cup of coffee, she took two aspirins and another shot. For the first time the colonel watched all her dosages with mild disapproval. Sitting there, a small pocket of silence holding them, the colonel could foresee troubles between them should they get married; it wouldn't be smooth, not at all. After all, since they had come back from Chicago they had stayed drunk together for almost a day and a night. They had been in bed most of the time, true, and she was a good woman, supple and talented, sexually gifted and un-inhibited; she went down on him a lot. Yet, now, the traces of her weaknesses were there and he couldn't help wonder if she weren't still burdened with the major's death, somehow, or if Stoker's suicide hadn't compounded her troubles, made her toughness fail her again, made her vulnerable to more hurt than she could bear. Her drinking: there wasn't much enjoyment in it, just a solid determination. So he began think-ing about her as he thought about everything: she had her good and bad points. Like so much else, she could be weighed and measured and graded. The colonel hated himself for viewing things like that—people especially and Verna in particular—yet he invariably did. For all my own personal washouts, he admitted, I'm mostly practical: I believe in good or bad or a mixture (in Vern's case) of a little of both. I believe in smart and stupid. In right or wrong—no matter how hard they are to figure. Like Stoke: what he did was wrong and stupid and hateful and no amount of philosophical explanation and no amount of discussion about how ambiguous things are nowadays will ever change that.

"I just don't think I can go with you," Verna said finally.

"Oh, Verna," he managed.

"I'm just too drunk, too down. Send the telegram and go without me. I'll follow in a day or two, if I can. But now it's impossible."

The colonel looked over his coffee cup at her.

"I know what you're thinking," she said. "He's *my* son. But you're not just going for Pless, Marty, but also for Stoke. You know that, don't you? You're going because you still can't accept what happened and you want better explanations. *Any* explanations."

"I'm going for Pless, too," he added.

"All right," she said. "But I can't go. I'm sorry."

"I'll tell Pless it's your job. I'll say you couldn't get away so soon after coming back home."

"You do that. Please. And I'm sorry, I am."

She just doesn't believe this, he told himself. He thought about another kitchen, his kitchen in Vegas that morning Adler had divulged everything. Breaths held. He tried to recall the expressions on their faces, but couldn't. If Verna had only seen and heard all that, he decided, then she'd get ready and come with me.

That afternoon, his safety belt firm around his waist, his fist closed around the stem of a daiquiri, stewardesses undulating along the aisles, it was difficult to hold his thoughts in balance. He worried about Verna, now, along with all the rest. But in his thoughts, predominately, was the university. A strange and awful place: he couldn't help feeling it. A flood of hatred ran over him and he felt himself swayed to distrust and violent solution toward it; it was a poison factory, a place where the mind was exposed to alien and harmful compounds, where taken a little at a time the poison could immunize and have a curative effect on the students, but where too much maimed and destroyed. He had sat in a hundred bars in the past few months where the student revolt was regarded with disdain and bitter hate by most of the officers, where there had always been at least one voice saying, Close the Damned Universities Down. The military solution: quick, physical action. Yet now he felt persuaded. Stoker was dry, scattered ashes. Something had gotten to him, some rot, some poisonous mold of the mind, and something so monstrous that its very source ought to be cut out of decent society. Suicide. An agreement to commit suicide. What vile shit was that?

He wished Verna were with him. From his small window he viewed the expanse of the Southwest. Turning back to his newspaper, he read the weather report. Chicago had fourteen inches of snow on the ground.

··· 21

AROUND THEM LAY Clive's familiar assortment of phonograph albums (Mozart, the Beatles, harpsichord selections), books, barbells, candles. Pless ambled around the room as he listened.

Clive was talking about a new phenomenon, the death of another student, a boy named Harry Khroeler. The boy had suffered from a terminal blood disorder, but had returned to the university for his junior year with his parents' consent, doomed, to attend classes with as much normalcy as possible before the inevitable happened. He hadn't told his classmates or professors about his condition, though, so although everything was quickly explained to the press it was rumored that he was part of the suicide pact. A sensation-minded Chicago radio station fixed the number of students in the pact at nine. A local television station managed to lure a university dean and a psychology professor into a discussion of self-inflicted deaths among college students and it was admitted, yes, that every year there were some twenty attempts on their campus alone. The Associated Press hovered over every new item now. The university had been caught in the uneasy attempt to announce the deaths of Stoker, Addie and Khroeler in their home towns by way of reducing the impact of all these events.

Clive savored it all. "A fortunate accident," he said proudly of Khroeler's death.

Pless shrugged.

"Anything to keep the fire kindled, so to speak," Clive went on. "Did you see these afternoon papers? A nice, big spread this time."

Pless looked over at the newspapers spread atop Clive's desk. The headlines seemed too large, overbearing.

"Everybody has his theory now," Clive kept on. "Lots of wild guesses. It wouldn't surprise me, by the way, if some junior dean comes knocking on our door soon. They're trying to trace everyone who might have known Stoke and Addie— so they can squelch any further rumors. Ah, I'll bet they wish they had a nice computer somewhere in the administration building with all such little bits of information in it."

"One can't have everything," Pless sighed.

"No, one can't." Clive smiled. "But this Khroeler thing really *is* fortunate. No one understands anything nowadays unless it's put into a headline—a big one. Our little agreement got big play today because of Khroeler. Stoke and Addie were both mentioned again. And there was that lovely denial by one of the minor academic deans that anything is happening on campus. Said all these lovely events were pure coincidence."

Pless gave him a look.

"Let the newspapers sing, Pless! Let them try and fit our little jigsaw together!"

"Does the jigsaw make a picture, old Cliver?"

"Such a pleasure you are, good Pless, of course! We've made our public gesture now. We've pricked the skin of the city. That's all-important. Even if you don't go through with your part, the gesture is made. No one can take that away."

Pless wondered if he and Clive were trapped in a put-on, if they would be sparring, now, until something between them realized itself. He studied Clive's expression, but found nothing. With some indecision, he decided to tell Clive about receiving the telegram.

"The colonel's coming back to town," he said. "That's one thing the publicity accomplished. He probably wants to know what in hell went on and what's going on."

"Let him come," Clive said bravely.

Pless felt that he saw a small distress in the corners of Clive's smile, but he tried not to read too much into it.

"What's done is done," Clive said. "What's coming is coming and not even Stoke's daddy can stop it either."

Pless went over, picked up his parka, and put it on. "Well," he said, "I'm going out to the airport to pick him up. Will I see you again later?"

"Do you want to?"

"I always want to see you." Sincerity invaded Pless' tone in spite of himself. "And now especially. If Stoker's old man gives me trouble, I don't know what I'll do."

On the freeway going out to O'Hare Airport, Pless wished he hadn't said that last to Clive. But there it was, whatever: he leaned on Clive and they both knew it. Addie had leaned on Stoke, Stoke on Pless, Pless on Clive, and Clive on his "greater game." And they would all go down like dominoes, leaning and tumbling. Pless gripped the wheel of the MG, closed his eyes, slowly counted to ten, then opened them— surprised, slightly, to find that he was still in the same lane. He thought about the poor colonel. The colonel wants his car. Wants his son back. Oh, the poor bastard. There have been moments in the past—thin, subtle moments they've been—when we've almost talked together. Too late now.

He didn't know if he could fake it with the colonel or not—or, for that matter, exactly what all his faking would be for.

He parked, walked through the terminal, and stood waiting on the concourse for the passengers to deplane. Soon the colonel emerged from the passengers' tunnel; he was fully uniformed, serious, preoccupied, and Pless waited, not raising a hand, until he was spotted.

"Have a good trip?" he asked, almost brightly. The colonel came directly up to him, took his elbow and led him away to the baggage counter. They stood there in silence as the porters sat around on the idle turnstile waiting for the unloading.

"Pless," the colonel finally said. "I want us to try and talk to each other. I've come all the way back to Chicago just to talk and I want you to try and level with me. Straight talk: that's really all I'm interested in. I need it in the worst way."

"Talk about what?"

"About what's in the newspapers, of course." At that moment the little gongs sounded over the intercom and the voice of a female announcer cooed a series of flight numbers. Then the bags arrived and the porters shoved them onto the conveyer. Tourists and weary businessmen lurched around, bumping shoulders, as they made their claims. The colonel watched Pless in profile. "I don't know what've got in your head," he went on, "or what Stoker had in his when he jumped. But these last few seconds have convinced me that I didn't fly back here for no reason at all."

"Convinced you? How?"

"I've been watching your face. You're putting me on—or off—already. You're screwing around."

It seemed incredible hearing the colonel invade this privacy of knowledge he enjoyed with Clive, and Pless felt his hands twitch slightly and he fought with himself over whether or not he should offer up a quick denial. "You shouldn't believe everything you read in the newspapers, sir," he did manage to answer.

"Stop it now," the colonel said, and he stepped forward, grabbed his suitcase, took Pless by the arm again, and moved them out toward the parking lot. "Just don't give me any of this goddamned runaround."

They drove out onto the freeway again into the tense traffic and Pless still tried to fake it, to put up a good front with the colonel, but the colonel seemed to puncture his defenses with everything he said. Pless hadn't expected that the colonel's mood would be this strong.

"I'm probably the only person in the world who knew more than he saw written in that newspaper." the colonel said. "And so I'm back to find out a few things—and don't think I won't."

Pless as Tough Private Eye: "Okay, kid, there's dirty business goin' on here and I mean to get to the bottom of it."

"Shut up that cheap shit," the colonel snapped. "Your sense of humor doesn't carry a hell of a lot of charm, if you want to know, and as a matter of fact you haven't got much humor about you and never have. All that mimicry is just a lot of superficial shit."

Pless, driving, stared down the freeway. He couldn't tell the colonel anything, he knew; he wouldn't.

"Where's Verna?" he asked, trying a delicate stall.

"Coming later." A slightly fretful tone in the colonel's voice. "It's her work," he added. "She couldn't just suddenly hop out of town again."

"How's she doing?"

"We can talk about her—if you want. But right now we've got more important things to say to each other."

Pless swallowed hard. Everything was going to be more difficult than he imagined. He wished Clive would be at the apartment.

They went to the Blackstone and the colonel moved right in. It became comic: Pless felt shadowed and hounded. Yet the colonel wasn't the bumbling guide he had been at Nellis that morning last summer when he struggled to do and say the right things; much of his old weakness and indecision seemed stripped away, and Pless tried to read him closely, tried to see if he was faking it, too. Life's poses. He wanted to laugh.

"What're you going to do? Sleep on my couch?"

"Fine, good idea. You don't mind do you?"

"Clive may be coming over later," Pless put in.

"Good. We'll all talk. That's what I'm here for."

"Okay, but there's really nothing to say," Pless insisted. "I mean, we're all sorry about Stoke, but what's in the newspapers —well, there's nothing to say about it except it's just—"

"What?"

"Sensationalism."

"None of it's true, then?"

"Well, no. Of course not."

"Let's talk about Stoke, then. Let's start at the beginning. Why do you think he killed himself?"

"I don't know. Lots of reasons."

"Things I don't know? What?"

They were in a restaurant, then, still talking. The colonel showed no exaggerated emotion, just a methodical pursuit of the subject, and Pless, summoning all his cool, tried to stay on top of things. At times he almost felt himself wilting. He wanted Clive. But the colonel pressed him and the food arrived at the table, was nibbled at, whisked away.

"Like sex," Pless tried to say in answer to the question. "Stoke couldn't make it with girls and that was part of the reason. He *did* look into windows. You probably don't want to hear any of this."

"What makes you think so?"

"Because you're straight and—oh, the solid citizen."

"But I want to know everything. That's why I'm asking."

"Well, there are lots of reasons why he might have done it. How are we going to isolate one cause? We're both too smart for that sort of procedure."

"Didn't he have a girl?"

"That's right. A nurse. A student nurse over at the university hospital."

"A nurse? Hell, he was going to bed with her wasn't he?"

"He said he was. I suppose he was telling the truth. But who knows?"

"What then? He couldn't make it with her?"

"His problems went back years—to you and Cassie. Hell, it's complex. He might have begun to make it with this girl. There were hopeful signs."

"Unravel it all for me, Pless. Use big words. You're the psychologist, aren't you? Trust me to understand a little."

Pless bit his lip.

"And try to make more sense than you have already," the colonel went on. "So far we've established that he had a sexual problem, but that he was making out with this girl, this nurse. Which means as far as I'm concerned that he *didn't* have such a big problem after all. Maybe a problem, sure, but not enough to make him dive off that building. So there must be something else. And I'm here to talk about it, now, Pless— and about anything else you want to talk about. Because I think there must be shit in your head—that's what I think. And if there is—and if Stoker had it in his head, too—then I want to see it, smell it, get my hands in it. That's why I came back. That's why Verna didn't come back right away, too, if you want to know the truth: because she couldn't stand to know too much right now. At least that's the feeling I got when I first showed her that newspaper article. But I can—" The colonel's voice broke. "This had better be good," he said. "This had all better be damned good."

Oh, Pless told himself. I wish Clive were here.

They drove across the campus going back to the apartment. Silence piled up like the snow along the streets.

"I may be wrong—I realize that," the colonel admitted as they drove. It was the first break in his mood since they had left the airport.

"It's all right, sir," Pless said.

"It's just that newspaper story I read this morning in Phoenix," the colonel said. "I can't tell you how it hit me."

"I know."

The colonel rubbed his eyes with his fists. "Do you remember what Adler said last summer while all of you were visiting me in Vegas? Do you recall his mentioning the pact? We were at breakfast that last morning."

"The thought of some sort of pact was probably in his mind for a long time," Pless said. "He was beset by problems. Full of fantasies. I don't know how to explain what happened to him."

"But there wasn't any sort of agreement between him and Stoke?"

"No, those are just the kind of stories that sell newspapers," Pless lied.

They returned to the Blackstone with the colonel more subdued. He seemed tired and somewhat comic again, Pless decided: full of abstractions and indecisions. When he asked Pless to tell him about Adler's death, Pless complied. Then they talked about Stoke again: sex, yes, was the big problem, Pless repeated, yet the business of Stoke being a peeping tom was innocent enough; the breakup with that nurse, yes, was an important factor, and, yes, this and, no, that. Pless tried to keep his patience, yet it seemed to him that the colonel had no right to ask all this—not even about his own son—and that what happened between Stoke and Addie, Clive and himself was private and special information, in spite of all its ambiguities, and should be kept that way.

Also, the colonel's anger was waning. Back at the Blackstone as they lolled around the apartment, the colonel began to sink back into his petty stances. Time, Pless saw, and a lack of information were simply against the colonel; in a few more hours, surely, he'd give up and leave.

The colonel gazed out of the window; drifts of snow like white hedges had accumulated around the drab buildings below. Idly, he unpacked a few of his clothes and loosened his tie. "I thought Clive was going to pay us a visit tonight," he said as it grew late.

"No, not now," Pless said.

"Why not?"

"I saw him watching us when we came back from supper."

The colonel looked up sharply. "Watching us?"

"He was across the street." Pless realized too late that he shouldn't have brought this up. "He does this sort of thing. Keeps watch on me sometimes. I think he sometimes takes notes."

"Clive does that?"

"He won't come up because of you."

"Wait a minute, now, let's get this straight: he spies on you? Do you know what you're saying? What's with him?"

"It's one of his ways. Harmless. Believe me, sir."

The colonel sat down and ran a hand through his hair. "I don't know what to make of you," he said with milder exasperation. "Stoke looks into windows. Clive shadows his friends. What is all this? Listen, Pless, you remember Florida? All those years you were in high school with Stoke—the two of you always going fishing or riding your bikes around Fort Walton Beach? Those were good times, weren't they? You two were smart kids, very quick, but good troopers. Now what's happened? Am I *wrong* about how normal, how right things were then? Am I wrong about how god-awful things are now? Look, I know it for certain: *something* was wrong with Stoke because he *did* do that to himself. And something's wrong with you, too. I saw it in your face the moment I got off the plane."

Pless sighed. "It's madness. The nation is screwed up, the world is screwed up, and people flip out all the time; some of them try to withdraw into pure space, like Stoke, and death is a way of saying: see here, this was all serious after all: I was one of your bright young men and I didn't dig your way of life and so I'm gone from it."

The colonel watched. A pensive quiet seemed to settle over Pless; he moved over to the window, glanced out, became a pale silhouette against the gray of the night sky.

"Pascal said that man is like a reed," Pless continued. "Both man and the reed perish under the assault of the elements, except man can perceive his death. Well, that's the way some want it. I don't want to be the product of any particular psychological determinism and neither did Stoke, I suppose, nor Addie. Of course they acted out certain inevitabilities. Addie was ugly and haunted and neurotic and thought he suffered from a cultural lag—the way he couldn't make his Ozark years fit anything he ever did afterward. And Stoke just couldn't get himself under control—his misguided puberty. Oh, they probably didn't reason things out as much as they should have, but suicide was a form of control over things. They managed to push the last button that controlled their lives, so to speak."

"Sorry," the colonel put in. "I'm not quite with you."

"It must have been in both of them—both Stoke and Addie—for a long time. They must have turned it over in their thoughts a hundred times or more. Stoke was really sensitive, sir, I guess you know that. It must have been in him like cancer. He thought about it a long time. No one just yawns and stretches and says 'Oh my, I think I'll spring off that building today.' It comes after long deliberation—and then perhaps gets triggered by some small burden, some mishap—like Stoke getting caught at that window. But it's usually the sum of many terrors. Oh, the way the major went down: no one wants to go that way. He was victimized and never in control. The military used his good brain and reflexes on trifles and made him—he said this himself—a supersonic bus driver. They wasted him until he wasted himself. I know that's why he went daredeviling up there over the bay: because he felt stupid, finally, in that little suit, all zippered up. Playing soldier is no job for an adult, he told me. He wanted to read and think and use his resources, I believe, and, oh, I think he was a little jealous of me. Society was never going to put me on its production line, I said to him once. Time can swallow me up before that happens. Ah, see, this is something of what Addie and Stoke felt, too."

Pless looked down at the colonel sitting there, his face buried in shadow in the darkened room. When the colonel spoke it was in a tired and bewildered tone.

"I want to hear you out, Pless. Really."

"You don't understand what I'm saying, do you?" Pless asked him.

"Not exactly, no. But I want to."

"It's all right," Pless said, and he laughed in spite of himself. The colonel looked so pathetic sitting there, so unplugged, so comic.

··· 22

THE COLONEL ESCORTED PLESS to breakfast
the next morning and went on campus with him; he could feel
Pless regarding him with a wry, detached amusement every
minute, but he stayed beside him.

"Where are we going now?" the colonel asked.

"I've got to go to the lab," Pless said, grinning at him. "My
rats need me. I've got to give them water and clean the cages
and you can come if you want to."

"Laugh if you want to laugh. I'm staying with you."

"What for? This is too gross! What do you think I'm going
to do?"

"I don't know. I'm not sure of anything."

"Well, I'm just going over to Kelly Hall, to the lab."

They walked through the snow together, the colonel's nose
turning red. He felt chilled and alone and wondered at himself;

yet all that Pless did and said seemed like a thin deception, a subtle tissue which couldn't quite be peeled away from the reality underneath. Yet, maybe not. What if I'm wrong, he asked himself, and I'm just acting like a fool? By the time they reached the psychology labs, he decided on another tactic.

"All right," he said, "I have a few other things to do myself. How long are you going to be working in there?"

"A couple of hours. Go ahead and I'll wait for you. And don't worry, sir. You're still upset, I realize, but don't sweat it."

"You think I'm just distraught over Stoker still, don't you?"

"Yes sir."

"Well, maybe. But I'm going to worry, I promise you." As he turned to leave, he suddenly slipped on the icy pavement and went down hard. He caught the main force of his fall on his wrist and shoulder and grunted loudly as he hit. Pless came over quickly, helped him to his feet, but couldn't restrain a thin smile.

"Sorry, sir," he managed. "You hurt bad?"

"No, just fine," the colonel lied. He struggled up, his arm and shoulder aching. His hat was lying in a pool of slushy ice and mud and he reached down, humiliated, and picked it up. "Perfectly fine," he said. "See you in a couple of hours."

"You went down pretty hard."

"Go ahead with your duties," the colonel said as he walked away. "I'll be back soon."

He walked around the corner to the administration building, asking directions of a coed as he went, his soiled hat in his hand. Finding the right office, he went inside and spoke with a young secretary, drawing himself up, speaking with as much authority as possible, until she went off to find what he wanted. As he waited, his wrist and shoulder throbbed, but it was almost a relief: all his pain had located itself. More than anything else he hated anxiety, not knowing about things; that's why, he knew, going over to Saigon was finally important—so that he could see firsthand all the mess, so that he could somehow deal with it and not just imagine himself helpless before it. Also, he admitted, when Cassie finally left me it was better. I had a real enemy to fight then: loneliness. And in the same way I was grateful for that little newspaper story about a possible suicide pact: it gave me something to do about Stoker's death.

He stood waiting. Soon the secretary came back with the information he wanted: Clive's address. He wrote it down on a piece of paper and folded it into his coat pocket. Still hiding his hat behind his back, he thanked the secretary and went out.

The campus: strolling its icy walkways, he tried to fathom it. The business here, he reminded himself, is the flow of ideas, yet it's that flow I suspect. In spite of everything, it tortures me now. Although I had a good education myself, a free flow of good courses at old Vanderbilt, I worry over it. Is man incapable of the liberal imagination? Does that which nourishes also destroy—like a rich food that ulcerates the stomach?

He looked around him at the gray buildings, the withered stalks of ivy, the Gothic doorways.

The university clinic was packed with people, as though there was a local epidemic, but again he stood tall, waiting, trying to get a properly haughty look on his face, and soon the head nurse came over to see what he wanted. He cleared his throat and told her that he was Colonel Martin H. Stoker, USAF, and that his son was the one who had recently—he cleared his throat—killed himself, and that he was looking for a young lady, a nurse. He didn't know how he was saying it all. The words were painful, deep as the throb of his shoulder. But the head nurse knew exactly.

"Come back to my office," she said to him.

She was a large woman who spoke with a thick accent, one he couldn't place. Polish or eastern European, perhaps. But she wrote out a name on a memo pad for him and handed it across her desk. He was almost too weary to get up and leave and gave her a moment to ask him a question.

"Why did your son do it?" she asked. Her face was earnest and sincere and he wanted to answer her, but he realized that he would have to invent a reason.

"He was sad about his mother," he lied. "His mother died recently. But there are lots of reasons, as you can imagine, and that's why I wanted to have a talk with this girl."

"You'll find Laura helpful, I think. She's a fine student nurse."

"I hope so," he said, rising. "Thanks. Thanks very much."

Outside there was a light flutter of snow. It had been easy to manufacture Cassie's death, such an easy lie, that he understood how Pless and Clive and Stoke could lie so often and so easily; when one tried to talk out of confusion and pain a lie was pure. Also, everything was so awkward. This was a strange city, a strange thing to be doing, all ridiculous and uncertain. I look ridiculous in this uniform, he told himself, and with my dirty hat in my hand I probably look senile and a little odd, so damned odd that the nurse probably figured she *knew* why Stoke did himself in: because he was crazy like his old man, because nuttiness ran in his family. Maybe I am a nut, descended from old Grandfather Bo, also a nut, cuckolded by another nut, father of another, earning a nutty salary from a nutty military establishment. Vanilla wafers and daiquiris: that's what I wanted this morning for breakfast. I'm mad. Didn't enjoy those eggs and ham with Pless at all. Nutty as hell. Yet, there's something about Pless I can't reckon with, something deep as an underground river flowing between us, some low undertone.

He went back to Kelly Hall and stood around waiting. Students passed him and gave him stares, but he tried not to care. What, he asked himself again, if I'm wrong about all my hunches? Then I'm a fool, but no more a fool than I've been all my life: that's all, a mere fool. And if I'm right, oh, then, what a difference. He took the pieces of paper out of his pocket and looked at them. Laura. Also an address for Clive. Kimbark Avenue.

An hour passed and he waited, pacing the hallway and sitting in the lounge which bore an oversized portrait of a dowager donor named Mrs. Jerome Beecher. He sat looking at the portrait, his shoulder throbbing with pain, and finally went down to the men's room and took off his coat and shirt and looked at the swelling. Satisfied, he dressed again and went back to the lounge where Pless soon found him.

"I want to visit this girl," he said, pointing to Laura's name and address on his scrap of paper. "And I want you to come with me."

"Right," Pless answered, and he seemed to smile indulgently.

They started walking again, the colonel trying to read the numbers on the apartments and the street signs and Pless not helping him any.

"I think we ought to go this direction," Pless said after a while.

"Fine." They walked on, Pless letting them stay apart at a sardonic and uncooperative distance. The colonel didn't understand it, yet it confirmed what he felt: that something was going on, that Pless' innermost turnings weren't right. The colonel dreaded meeting this girl. It would be another awkward moment in which the distance would widen and he would become the fool, yet he hoped something—anything—would come of it. They walked in silence as the apartment buildings passed. In one window hung a service flag, World War II vintage. Graystone dwellings. The icy wind off the lake racked the colonel's swollen shoulder and his dread and sense of foolishness deepened, but he trudged on.

Laura's apartment was filled with students, all having lunch of sandwiches and beer. The young man who acted as host,

Max, introduced them around and a brief, reverent silence fell on the room while it was established that this was Stoker's father. The colonel felt conspicuous and out of place; he tossed his soiled hat on a radiator, accepted a beer, and insisted on keeping his topcoat on—so his medals wouldn't show. The wrong time, he said to himself. We should have called.

In the kitchen Laura was slicing roast beef. When Max brought Pless and the colonel for introductions, she looked up hurriedly, smiled faintly, and returned to her slicing. "Have something to eat," she offered, not looking at them. "This is just a little off-duty party. No one's going to classes this afternoon. Very impromptu. Have a few beers. There's plenty."

The colonel saw immediately that she wouldn't want to talk. As a result, he accepted a beer and moved away for the time being, nodding and smiling at the students who nodded and smiled at him. Pless looked calm and aloof and perfectly comfortable.

As he rubbed his aching shoulder, he saw another girl watching him. "Took a nasty fall on the ice this morning," he explained, and she said that the weather was getting worse and soon they were talking about the Chicago winters. He felt isolated and his eyes followed Laura as she toured the room with a tray of sandwiches. He didn't know what he wanted to ask her or how to begin, but felt she had something to tell him.

More than an hour passed. Waiting, the colonel watched Pless finish his second and third beers and a thought came to him: the boy can't hold his liquor; his mother says he's famous for not being able to take a drink. File that information away. En route home, perhaps. Get us a bottle to get skunked on. Something potent like an old MIG-21. Something to knock his tongue loose, yes, like the old Scotch and Drambuie. For a moment his thoughts drifted back to Saigon, to the *Sportif*, to dead Charlie Miller, to those tennis games all full of lobs and soft volleys. Miller got it over Haiphong.

The world is dead or dying. No it isn't either. Screw that notion.

Another student was mewing at him about Stoker, her voice low and distant. He tried to concentrate on what she said, but across the room he saw Laura and Pless looking toward him and talking together. Condescension showed in the fall of Pless' mouth. Together, they were closing him out.

"My son's things. Books and desk and all that, yes, I'm seeing about his belongings. Excuse me now, please." He made his way over toward Pless and Laura, trying to calm himself. The room was a trap of elbows and pathos, everyone stopping him this trip to say how sorry they were, and he had his way through the condolences slowly. Someone slapped him on the shoulder.

"What're you two talking about?" he managed, making his approach. He fashioned a smile and picked up another can of beer from a nearby table and handed it to Pless. "Have another, son," he said. "We have a long walk home."

"Hello, sir," Laura said, her greeting smile slightly wrong.

"Actually," the colonel began, hating his own deep, authoritative tone of voice, "there's nothing special I wanted to see you about, but I knew you were Stoke's girl friend, of course, ahem, that much was in the newspapers—ah, and I thought we might have a short talk." Disgusting. I'll never get through this. She doesn't want to hear a word of it, either, I can tell.

"We really didn't go together very long," Laura said, putting him off. "I didn't have a hint that he might—"

Max strolled over and joined them and the colonel looked up just in time to see a smirk on Pless' face, a small communication that all this was too much.

"Really?" the colonel asked, picking up Laura's remark. "You had no idea? No sign of what—"

"No, of course not."

"Well, no, neither did any of us. But I was wondering if

we could get together and talk anyway—just for a short while?"

"There's my guests right now," she said. Her words were a mild argument.

"Not right now, then. Later. Tonight or tomorrow?"

"I go back on duty in the morning."

"Tonight, then?"

"There're all these people. When will you be leaving?"

"I'm not sure. I do have to get back to the base. Listen, can I call you?"

"Good, you do that."

It was awful. Pless exchanged further glances with Max and Laura as the colonel fumbled for a scrap of paper on which to write Laura's telephone number. Everyone cooling it. All a mistake, he told himself. All that sensational publicity might have misled me, true, just as Pless insists it did. I'm an idiot for even standing here.

They traded goodbyes and friendly patter as he and Pless went slowly toward the door. Then another girl, a very pretty one, came in. New introductions. Parker, her name was. Like Stoke, he thought, she doesn't use her first name. Her cold hand fell into his and while Pless, Max and Laura whispered among themselves she reached up and spoke right into his ear: "There's something I want to tell you. I'm glad we met like this, but I want to tell you something. Can we talk?"

He looked at her openly. "I don't know," he said, and by this time all of them were on the stairway going down toward the door on the street.

"My hat," the colonel called after them. "I've got to get my hat." He grinned with embarrassment. "It fell into a puddle this morning and I've been trying to forget it."

It gave him the excuse to get back into the apartment with Parker as the others moved down the stairs saying their goodbyes.

"It's about Stoker," Parker told him suddenly. "I think it

· · · **271**

might have been just an accident with him, not suicide."

The colonel took her by the arm and led her into the kitchen. "What makes you think so?"

"He telephoned me that night," she said hurriedly. "Just a few minutes before he was supposed to have done it. I don't think anyone knows this because I kept waiting for someone to ask: Laura, the police, the newspaper men or someone. This was about eleven thirty, I remember."

"All right. What of it?"

"He asked for a date! And I said yes! We were going to a movie!"

The colonel pulled her farther into the kitchen, thankful for the noise of the others. It would be a short time, he knew, before Laura and the boys would come back. "Now tell me this again, slowly," he said.

"Don't you see what this means? This was just after he and Laura broke up—this was supposed to be the immediate motive behind his jumping. You may remember this from the newspaper accounts at the time: he was supposed to have suffered this big breakup."

"Of course I remember. Go on."

"But he wasn't so broken up over that. I don't think this was just a rebound call he gave me—one he didn't mean. It's a long story. We kissed right here by this refrigerator one night. At a party. Anyway, he called me—just minutes before he was supposed to do what he did. But I've been thinking all along that all this suicide business is wrong. Everyone jumped to conclusions—like with this Khroeler boy, who wasn't part of any conspiracy, who died a natural death."

"Where was he when he called?"

"I don't know. But he wasn't particularly unhappy."

"He gave me a call shortly before he died, too. I thought he sounded fine. Better than I ever remembered."

"I've kept all this to myself partially because of Laura. She's wrapped up in her Max now, yet I think she's a little romantic about what happened to Stoke, too—as though she really wants to think he did it because of her. But I just don't think that was it."

"When can we talk some more?"

"This is really all I had to say."

"Please. Later tonight?"

He agreed to call her later and moved out of the kitchen just as Laura came gliding across the room toward them. Max stood in the doorway talking to Pless, who was sipping another beer. The colonel delayed long enough for him to get several more swallows down. "Nice meeting you," he told the girls and he and Parker exchanged a glance. An ally, at last.

On the way back to the Blackstone they stopped at a liquor store and the colonel bought a quart of Scotch, a pint of Drambuie, two fifths of rum and some daiquiri mix.

··· 23

WITH DISAPPOINTMENT Clive watched them return to the Blackstone. The colonel still hung on, probably badgering Pless about the suicide pact, Clive presumed. It was the only bad thing about those newspaper reports: they let the colonel in. Otherwise, they were sweet to behold. Newsprint held its peculiar reality and in black and white there all of it had been for Pless to read: Stoker's fall, Addie's elaborate hanging exercise, the note, motives, interpretations, assorted fabrications, all parts of the greater game. In a way—assuming the colonel remained inept at putting things together—he would make his contribution to the reality. He would talk about Stoker and Addie and keep them on Pless' mind; he would be his usually stupid self and give Pless a pleasant intellectual advantage; he would add hysteria to hysteria. For hysteria was the necessary gambit—no matter if it was the frenetic, neurotic, jagged hysteria of Adler or the quiet, seemingly reasonable hysteria of Pless.

Clive stood across from the apartment building thinking all this and wondering what he should do. They had been to see the nurses: all right. One could always find out what went on there. Sometime soon, he supposed, the colonel would want to see him. Perhaps visit him unannounced and try to catch him off guard—though, of course, there was little chance of that. I think I've established the upper hand with the dear colonel, Clive allowed. Such a pleasure.

Unsure of what he wanted to do next, Clive went for something to eat. It was dark and cold when he came back; the Blackstone was studded with lighted windows, the sky had cleared, and the snow-covered streets caught the various colors of the evening. He waited only a few minutes this time before the colonel emerged, alone, and hurried off down the street. Though he wondered what Pless was doing alone, he elected to follow the colonel. He stayed at a safe distance until the colonel entered the nurses' apartment again.

Fixing himself in the doorway of an apartment building across the street, he waited. Silence grew around him and he began to shiver. Also, he worried that he hadn't done the right thing, that he should have taken the opportunity to visit Pless, but in the midst of this speculation a taxi suddenly pulled up across the street. The colonel and Parker dashed outside, hurried into it, and it sped away.

"Damn," Clive said aloud, stepping out onto the sidewalk.

He walked quickly back toward the Blackstone, his fists closed tightly in his jacket pockets as he went along.

Carefully, he made his way up to Pless' room and tried the door. Open. He paused, looked around, and stepped inside. The colonel wouldn't be coming back here, would he? No, he's gone off to needle that little nurse.

The apartment was dark except for a single lamp and he could hear Pless' soft breathing from the bedroom. Quietly, he went over and checked; Pless was there all right, gone off in a drunken sleep. Stench of whiskey everywhere. Credit the colonel with discovering a weakness.

Standing there watching Pless sleeping, Clive's frustration began to simmer so that he had to caution himself: there now, don't panic, don't worry, keep steady; everything is mystic and true and doesn't all coincidence and sweet fate work toward the greater game and isn't everything successful so far?

He tried to shake Pless awake, but couldn't.

"The car keys—where are they?" he asked, but Pless couldn't answer. Another small tactical error on the part of the colonel, leaving the car keys and going over to that little nurse afoot, but where were the keys? He searched the desk, the tops of tables. Finally he found them in Pless' trousers. Another effort to awaken Pless failed.

He helped Pless on with his clothes; handling Pless like a heavy sack, he jostled him partially awake. Pless groaned.

"Good! Come around, you sot." He laughed, and Pless, responding only slightly, answered with a frail grin.

Then Clive picked him up and carried him out.

··· 24

THE COLONEL ALLOWED PARKER TO
RAMBLE, to talk about anything she wanted because he
felt it all mattered, but she wasn't as much help as he had
hoped. He was determined to find an immediate key to everything that perplexed him, but things went slowly, ambiguously,
and his impatience grew. Also, they were sitting in the vacant
apartment of another student nurse, a girl who was on night
duty at the time, and Parker's short skirt provided a distrac-
tion and she was very pretty, though young, very young, the
colonel reminded himself, and he thought of Verna, from
time to time, and of the Kincannon girl in Vegas and tried to
summon all his fatherly instincts for Parker, difficult though
it was. Parker was perched in a window seat, her legs pulled
under her, while he shifted his sore shoulder around on the
couch.

"Stoke was a guarded person," she was telling him, "but he didn't have all the low tides some people believed. Since his death, I mean, a lot of the students have been manufacturing this character for him—a kind of moody young writer type. But I didn't see him that way. And, okay, he had some trouble finding himself, but I think he managed to cope. This was the *thing* about Stoke: he mostly knew himself. That's why I have a hard time believing he took his own life."

The colonel had tried to tell her about Pless and how he felt something was wrong; he had also told her about Addie's remark in Vegas, the announcement of their intentions, and had tried to show her his special knowledge in the matter which had brought him back to Chicago. Yet he didn't know if she understood or not; she seemed eager to help, but he detected a greater eagerness than he wanted from her, an excitement over the events of Stoke's death, and it was as if she talked out of an impulse to gossip, to talk just for the sake of talking. Also, it was Laura he really wanted to make talk. So he had dissatisfactions, but he listened.

Parker went out to the kitchen and brought a pot of coffee and cups. "I want to help," she said, sighing, "but let's admit it: I have limitations. I knew Stoke only a short time."

"Any conversation is helpful," he said, grateful that she admitted limitations.

"I just *don't* think he did it," she insisted. She poured the colonel a cup of coffee, bending down so that her faint perfume came to him. He watched her arms. Slender.

His shoulder throbbed and he thought of asking her to give him a little rubdown, but dismissed it.

"The whole notion of a pact," she said thoughtfully, "just doesn't make much sense either. Suicide, I mean, is such a personal and private act. It's something you usually crawl off and do by yourself, isn't it?"

"Sometimes people stand on high places for hours—to attract crowds," he answered. "But go ahead: what're you thinking?"

"Oh, I was just trying to think about everything that happened. How Stoke and this other student—Adler—did it. Wouldn't a pact be different? Something they would do together? Like a lover's leap? Wouldn't they get together so that their mutual misery would be strong enough to kill them?"

"I don't think there's much precedent for anything that happened. I've tried to think the same way. I don't know how to begin—just that I want a practical approach."

"How do you mean?"

"We should be playing detective, not philosopher. That's all I mean. And how to get at it: that's the question. Tell me, what do you know about Pless?"

"Wasn't he Stoker's friend for years?"

"That's right, but I know him in a different way. And, as I said, he won't let me in now. He's changed. I thought you might have another angle on him."

"Sorry. There's just his reputation. He was a real campus brain as an undergraduate, you know, and now he's a grad student. That's most of what I know. All Laura seemed to know about him was that he had a laundry room where he lived—where Stoke went to wash clothes."

"All right, skip him then. Go back to Stoke. Anything. Say what comes to your mind."

"Anything?"

"That's right."

"Well, I always wanted to go to bed with him."

The colonel stared into his coffee cup. "All right. Anything else? Try to free associate a little."

"Oh, he might have been drinking a little too much. The first time I saw him he was smashed. And then—oh, I'm trying too hard. I *want* to say something helpful, but I can't think of anything." She bit her lip and curled her legs underneath her again.

"Keep trying."

"Mainly, this: he wasn't hung-up. I've seen them all on campus, believe me, and so many of them make a whole career out of being hung-up! I'm not attracted to them! That was the thing with Stoke—and it's my strongest feeling in all this!"

"What about Laura? Tell me about her."

"She's all right—except when she has problems she adopts roles for herself. As a defense. After she split up with Max, for instance, she played the liberated female—and met Stoke about that time. In any case, I think they were good for each other."

"Adler, then. Did you know him?"

"Never met him. He called Laura the night of Stoke's funeral, you know, and wanted to see her. She agreed, but couldn't go through with it because she said she was just too emotional. The poor boy. Laura hated turning him down that night, but I understood. She had a lot of distress."

"There's someone else, too: Clive. Do you know him?"

"Clive? Yes, is he in the picture, too?"

"Somehow. I'm not sure. What do you know about him?"

"I just recently met him. Let's see, I'll have to think. The campus is huge and fragmented, you see, and the students all have lives of their own. Everyone living in apartments off campus. Tending their own work. But Clive, let's see, how shall I say it? I don't want to overstate this, but he really is fascinating. On one level he's all bluff and noise and seems like a little boy who wants to be demonic. Very melodramatic. Cocks his eyebrows. Glares. So self-serious about himself—so that I want to laugh at him. Yet, his eyes. He tries to be mysterious, you see, and he gets caught at it so that it's sort of funny, yet he really *is* strange."

"He appeals to you, too, then?"

"Oh, no, he's not at all sexy—not exactly. But I've watched Clive and have gotten absolutely mesmerized. Not at those times he's performing, curiously enough, but at other times: when he's watching everyone else and waiting and watching for his chance to leap onstage, so to speak. He's *so* melodramatic, really, and he likes to stir people up, say sensational things. A lot of students are like that, I mean, but he has a real gift for it."

"Yes, true," the colonel agreed. "What do you know about his family and background?"

"Nothing. Sorry again. I'm not very helpful."

"Yes you are. You said you met him only recently. Was he with Stoker?"

"That's right. At the same party I was telling you about. I've seen him on campus only once since then—a chance meeting. We talked a few minutes and he tried to impress me. He talked about South America."

"Do you know why I had us dash out to the taxi like that this evening?"

"Because of Clive?" She smiled in spite of herself.

"That's right. It was a small defensive maneuver on my part. I could have come for you in Stoke's old car, but I wanted to see if Clive followed me. He was! Shadowing me! So I led him a little chase, then we drove off and left him."

"Why would he do a thing like that?" Parker laughed nervously and pulled her legs tighter beneath her.

"There're quite a few pieces to this jigsaw, believe me. Just no picture, yet."

"Following you! I can't believe it!"

"Let me ask you something else about him: do you think Clive is particularly moody? Would he be the sort who would kill himself? Or could you make a judgment like that?"

"Not Clive, no, he'd never do it. He's too pleased with himself. He'd like the idea—because it's melodramatic enough— but he's just not the sort."

"Clive had a rough emotional life with his family—I know that much," the colonel offered.

"He's just not the suicidal type, though," Parker said, laughing nervously again. "Homicidal, perhaps, but not suicidal."

The colonel got up, restlessly, and went over to the window; he stood above Parker looking out, aware of her closeness, pondering. "Can you manage to go back to the Blackstone with me tonight?" he asked her quietly. "You can still be useful."

They took a taxi back to Pless' apartment. As they drove, the colonel sat with his chin resting on his closed fists, staring out over the icy streets. All my foolishness—if that's what it is—is among strangers, he told himself. This girl doesn't belong; she was merely the friend of a friend of Stoker's. His pathetic solitude struck him; no one knew anyone else in all this desperation. Perhaps this is what Stoke himself felt and why he dived into oblivion. For a moment, oppressed by this truth, the colonel's eyes went hot with tears and he turned away in the taxi so that Parker wouldn't see.

At the Blackstone they went up in the elevator and hurried to Pless' rooms. The place was dark and musty-smelling and only after they had gotten inside did they see the note pinned on the door. It was from the downstairs desk, a handwritten transcription of a telegram that had been phoned in. Verna was arriving at O'Hare within the hour.

"There's no one here," Parker called from the bedroom.

"No one?"

"All empty. What shall we do now?"

"Listen carefully," the colonel said. "Pless' mother will be arriving before long. Wait here. Can you do that?"

"Sure, anything."

"Good. Wait here and hold anyone who comes—don't let them leave again: Pless, his mother, Clive or anyone. This is very important. I'll be gone for an hour, maybe two."

"What are you thinking? What's going to happen?" Parker asked, her voice plaintive.

"I can't say what's happening or what I'm thinking or anything. I'm just making decisions. In my profession, that's usually the way we do things." He tried to smile at her and reassure her.

··· 25

THEY LEFT THE CAR in the mist and started walking down the shore alongside the lake. Small birds as deeply gray as the winter sky and the distant outline of the buildings hovered at the water's edge, fluttering, unwilling to touch down in the cold mud. Clive talked and Pless, still dazed and tipsy, held to Clive's sleeve for balance as they went, and as they walked they became a pair, silhouettes against the dull, early morning sheen of the water.

Weaving awkwardly, they went far down the strand, and it seemed to Pless that they traveled in peril, huddled together, the mists spooking them; it seemed like a long, barren, desolate peninsula—an uneasy place—and Pless listened to their footfalls in the gritty mud and shale. The vestiges of morning. Dark waves nearby. An unsteady head from too much drink. Clive's voice. Things are pleasantly uncertain, Pless decided, including our next few steps.

They had several conversations, bits of talk that Pless engaged in before his nausea and headache reduced him to silence again. "I want us to get some drugs now," he said once. "We've lived clean. We deserve some drugs."

"That's what you want now, is it? Drugs?" Clive was clearly in control, sober, and therefore in good humor.

"Yes, something quick. Like hashish."

"Jackie wanted to send me some goodies from the Near East just last year, but you know me: I never indulge."

"Right, not you."

"But I can get it for you—hash or grass or anything you want. Just two short blocks from the quad. There's plenty around."

"Yeah, I want it. You have to take it with me, though, okay? We ought to get stoned together, Cliver. We ought."

"Sure, if you want me to."

"We've done a lot together, haven't we? We could do that one more little thing." Pless stumbled, but grabbed onto Clive's sleeve and held on. He could feel the swell of the bicep underneath the jacket and it made him laugh nervously although he didn't mean to laugh.

Pleasantly uncertain, yes. As Clive talked, Pless went quiet again, holding on, his thoughts staggering off, trying to locate some serenity of memory, and, not finding any, settling for what he had: Clive's presence. Meeting Clive: he recalled that day. He went to a lecture over at Mandel Hall and there sat Clive, cocky, his chair tilted back against the wall as some dull little professor who had just come back from Russia with some sociological generalizations addressed a nearly empty auditorium. Clive tilted the chair, making its legs pop, and the lecturer gave him stern looks, then asked him please to stop, then asked him to leave. When Clive finally sauntered out, Pless followed; they went for a beer, laughing. The little prof had been too earnest, quick to digest and summarize, quick to moralize. The dullard made us an in-group of two, Pless concluded, and the inebriation began: lots of cynical talk, always in Clive's drumming overstatement; I looked for another sense of myself, for something other than those tough veneers I manufactured after the major's crack-up, and I let myself go, let the days pace themselves out to Clive's rhythms, and gave up my poses, those weary façades which Stoke always misread and admired. The binge, the coming forth. Scars on Clive's wrists, now, as we walk this dreary lakeshore.

"Sure, we probably *should* make the drug scene now," Clive was saying. "You're right: we've experimented and ought to keep on."

Pless nodded uncertainly. Restaurants and bars came to mind, all the late-night sessions after his experiments were finished, the rats tucked in for the night and the clocks of the campus towers had turned yellow against the sky.

"You remember the night Stoke zapped out, don't you?" Clive asked.

"Of course." The rainstorm: how was it possible to forget? Stoke had been with his Laura that night and they had played their parting scene and Stoke, sad of heart, bless him, had caught a bad case of the dooms. But more: he and Clive had also been together, and this was what Clive meant now. "We went walking, didn't we? Just like this."

"Not far from here, right. And got caught in the cold rain and drenched."

Of course, of course: yet recollection came unwillingly, tinged with disbelief. They had been out strolling, taking the air to avoid their studies, talking, and when the freezing rain started they dashed for Clive's place. The L-shaped room.

"It was just another experiment that night," Clive assured him.

Pless nodded. In that room, cold candles glowing, they had peeled off their clothes, shivering, teeth chattering as they smiled at each other, breathless. There were stacks of towels, all obviously stolen from Bartlett Gym, and the heater made a thin, whining noise.

"It has no meaning in the long run," Clive went on, "except that we did it: we tried a little experiment out there on the edge of ourselves, so to speak. We had the nerve to do it. Steady there, old heart. Isn't that right? We had the nerve, didn't we?" He grinned with benevolence and held onto Pless.

Another nod in reply. Towels everywhere, Pless recalled, all stamped PROPERTY OF THE UNIVERSITY, and Clive took a handful and started rubbing me dry. Our breath short, laughing and shaking with the cold because the damned radiator wouldn't start. Then a gigantic can of talcum powder; soft motes of powder drifted around us in a rosy, sickening cloud. A small matter, at first, all this, then frenzied: sprawling on the bed, Clive's equations dancing on the blackboard above us, wet towels asunder, drifts of talcum on our cold skin. Then: a slight experiment further, to be sure: my concentration wavered, and I said to myself, *why not?* and *who am I now and what can I stand?* and thought of Verna, yes, sweet mother, liquored and lost, and let him. And then fell hard asleep: one of my long deathdrifts.

"We'll never do that again," Pless said, still gazing at the mud along the shore as they walked.

"We'll never have to. Once is enough," Clive answered. "But it was an important *once*—we pushed on the frontier that's inside us. And, yeah, all right, so we turn to drugs now. If you want to, I will. Did you ever read about Leopold and Loeb here in the city?"

"Some. I know the story." Pless gagged and for a moment imagined that he would vomit, but held on.

"Murdered that child, remember? Steady there, Pless m'boy."

Birds called from overhead, swarming toward the water. Other times, all the hours with Clive: I would complain about the system sometimes and he would say, boldly, "You're a student—studying so you can work for the system." And I'd say, Oh, but I don't want to. At first I wanted to study psychiatry, I'd say, and help everyone who is sick and warped in the head, but now I don't think so. Now I diddle in the laboratory and that's all I want. And he'd answer, inevitably, "That's because you know that the whole society is sick and warped. The insane man is sane, Plesser, and, really, you ought to go around spreading psychosis like seeds. Twist minds! Teach chaos and darkness to the masses!" And we'd laugh, oh, we'd laugh in the hallways, our heels making echoes along those hallowed aisles where Compton and Mulliken and Michaelson and all those noble Nobel winners meandered. Clive working with maniac pleasure at his blackboard, clusters of digets flying from his chalk. Clive hulking over a table giving anarchist blueprints to us all, telling us how society is so corrupt that war is nearly pure and purging. Clive breaking my middle-class mentality. Birdcalls out over the water.

"It's not that they were interested in child-killing," Clive was still saying, speaking of Leopold and Loeb, jabbing his way toward another point. "They were just interested in pushing on the edge of their own moral and psychological tolerance. They were experimenting, too. Don't you see that, old trueheart?"

Birds everywhere now, coming out to greet the morning. Clive making his conversational points, drumming on. Books he had me read that I don't think he ever read himself: I remember them so well: Schumpeter's study and D. W. Brogan's *A History of Witchcraft in New Orleans,* atlases of Guatemala and Bolivia, Bullock's biography of Hitler, Marcuse, McLuhan, Goodman, Dwight Macdonald, John Hawkes, Nietzsche, and Stokely Carmichael. The stuff of an evening's talk.

"Don't you understand? Still drunk?"

"I hear you."

"I was talking about Leopold and Loeb. Were you listening?"

"Yeah, sure," Pless said absently.

"No, I don't think you are. So I'll say it—ah, how?—differently: since society is topsy-turvy, so are all our traditional values. War becomes peace, our natural state—just as George Orwell said. What once seemed evil becomes the norm. In fact, by doing evil—or what once seemed like it—and you remember our conversations about Genet last spring—a person can make a small affirmation. And to go around doing the conventional good simply means that a person capitulates to the institutional evil in our society."

Quoting me Orwell and Genet, Pless thought. Making his intellectual pitch, now, but naturally he's right about institutional evil: I think of Nellis, of all those bases where Stoke and I grew up. All shit.

"Even sex has become a part of our foul-up. It isn't even a positive anymore, not a life force. People are sexing themselves to death. And since it has become so foul, perversity works as a kind of strange purge: it at least brings us back to an examination of what sex means. Perversity—abnormal behavior, I mean—cleanses the air, so to speak. So it becomes a moral force."

Sex: ah, true enough, it's a great problem, though it was never particularly mine. What finally broke poor Stoke, I wonder? Did he make out with that nurse or not? Let's see, I get it once in a while from Elaine Roddy who comes down to the rat room and pushes on me with those big boobs while I'm busy dissecting or cleaning the cages. Lets me bang her right there on the dissecting table, she does, and says she wouldn't know it was me if things didn't smell like rat pellets. And last year it was Martha Bannington, always telling me she had to leave afterwards and go study. The girl scientist who screwed with her glasses on and pretended to think about fission and molecules while she did it. I've always had just enough, I suppose, and, true, when there wasn't enough I took things in hand. Poor Stoke even had guilt about that; couldn't even masturbate wthout putting on a grim face for a couple of days.

Asked me if I had ever had a homosexual experience. Sex has to be it: why he took his dive. Committed us all.

Pain is a form of pleasure nowadays, too, Clive was saying, but Pless didn't exactly listen. Great pavilions of clouds assembled in the distance and he watched those, less drunk now then spellbound, his mind adream. His stomach, though, rolled with a slight nausea. Very slight.

Pless could imagine himself and his father, birdlike, eagles again, soaring out above Lake Michigan and those winter clouds, spiraling higher, viewing the entire lake, the continent, the globe itself all dazzling with the sun on its clouds. If he had lived, he found himself thinking, he'd be a colonel now too. Stupid thought.

"Finally," Clive was saying, "all learning is ignorance. And I don't mean just the old platitude about the more you know the more you realize you don't know. I mean this is an irrational age and it's a great vanity to believe that you can have a rational approach. Everything is chaotic and magnificently relative. Events sweep all our careful judgments away. Like our colonel, the thoughtful military mind: he wants to stand up in the middle of a battlefield and make some cogent and humane judgment, but under those circumstances it's absurd and impossible. Once, perhaps, human history moved at such a slow rate that we could step back and make certain rational estimations, but now events come at us with amazing speed and in great numbers—everything all over the world modifying everything we do or think—so that our ground of judgment shifts under us. Static thought doesn't work because the world isn't static, Pless, and only another *act* really modifies anything. Only a radical action—so powerful and provocative that it has the power to modify everything—can make any difference."

All right, Pless said to himself, we can't make summations or recognize what's what or reckon with ourselves. Rationale is lost and passé. Life is a series of postures and sensations. Phenomenology. Event is truth.

"So how will you do it, then?" Pless suddenly asked, shooting Clive a look.

"Do what?"

"Zap yourself."

"Oh, I suppose I ought to do something entertaining. Take hold of my asshole and pull myself inside out. I've been working with my barbells again just in case I decide on that method."

Pless grinned.

"Or I could eat a bulldog," Clive mused. "Or suck a bed of ants. There're lots of jolly ways, Plesser, but the object, naturally, is to provoke and entertain my millions of fans everywhere."

They laughed and Pless announced that he was cold and wanted to return to the car, so they started back. Pless could feel the tiny tremor of nausea rise inside him.

"About the colonel," Clive said, his tone serious again. "Do you agree with what I said about him? You think I'm right?"

"About how he's out of touch? Right, I guess so."

"He's racked up with paradoxes and ironies, you know: he's a good man, but serves a system that's gone rotten; he's a good man, but one of the goddamned warrior class; he's a good man, but blind. He's back here to find us out, too, but he doesn't know what he's looking at and doesn't know what he's looking for. It's pathetic. But he's not like us, you see. He can't begin to have this sense of experimentation we've got—he couldn't imagine such a thing."

Imagine such. Talcum flakes drifting on the pillows. No, he couldn't imagine such a thing, and, oh, Pless felt, I wish I hadn't been in that particular scene the night Stoke jumped.

"Addie and Stoke really didn't know who we are either," Clive continued. "Stoker was hung up on sex and the immature shit of growing up. He was always an adolescent when you get right down to it, and I liked Stoke. He had charm, you know, and I know I liked him more than he liked me sometimes, yet he was struggling with something so *ordinary:* his puberty and his goddamned growing up. You were always beyond that, but he wasn't—and couldn't know you because of it. And Addie squandered himself in all his little neuroses—worrying about his physical appearance and his hillbilly parents and the fact that he wanted to be a dancer and couldn't. All that. He had his endearments, too, but he was weak and disturbed and his life was cluttered with small problems. Both Stoke and Addie were conventional—and could never conceive of experimentation beyond that boundry. You hearing me?"

"I suppose so, yes."

"You're still drunk, aren't you?"

"No, I'm better. See? I don't have to hold on." Wish I hadn't been in that particular scene on that particular night, though. Oh, sweet mamadear: you tipple because you need a tailspin now, don't you, and because life is so hard. We all need our dives at times; the major and Stoke both had death by falling. Think of it.

Pless gagged again, almost vomited, and Clive slapped him on the back and grinned at him.

"Put a finger down your throat, champ," Clive advised. "You'll feel better."

Pless agreed and jammed his forefinger in. Bile and Scotch whiskey. Damn the colonel for this, he told himself, and damn Clive for laughing while I do it. As he finished, he sat down on the cold, packed mud and dropped his head between his knees.

"There's something else I want us to discuss now," Clive said, squatting beside him and peering off at the horizon of water and sky.

"What now?" Pless sighed.

"Just another small frontier I think we ought to visit. A little something else to share," he said, still grinning.

"I can hardly wait."

"It's just this: have you ever given thought to murdering someone, Plesser?"

"Oh, Clive, stop it." Pless paused, waiting, a small premonition stirring in him. Here comes a put-on, he told himself. Humor him.

"Suppose we decide to take a life with us when we go?" Clive began, pausing, letting the silence gather. Pless felt the blood race along through the tips of his fingers, his temples pulse violently; though he knew Clive was winging it, faking him off, he felt caught in the swoon of words, and although he wanted to stand up and reject this line of talk, to tell Clive that he spoke just so much nonsense, he couldn't, and he did what seemed even to himself a strange thing: he laughed—a laugh, he realized, of encouragement.

"Could you go through with it?" Clive was asking him.

"How do I know?" He laughed again, nervously.

"Suppose I arranged for us to knock off someone we both know? Someone we have no particular malice for, but someone who would, ah, supply a bigger thrill, say, than if we just knocked off someone who was anonymous? How would that be?"

"Marvelous," Pless sighed again, defensively. Then a thought: he wants to kill off the colonel. Is that it?

"Did you say all right? Speak up, Plesser."

"Sure. Could we draw and quarter the victim, though? I've never seen anyone drawn and quartered."

"Good suggestion. Now you're getting into the spirit of it."

"Or boiled in oil? Or does oil really boil? I've never actually seen boiling oil."

"Good, keep on."

"Or we could see just what the poor victim could take— how much torture. That way we could observe ourselves and see how much pain we could bear to inflict. Do you think man's capacity for inflicting pain is inexhaustible, old top? Generally speaking, naturally."

"Definitely. Such fine ideas, Pless. Keep them up."

Pless went on, conning Clive, himself, amusing himself; his nausea seeped away and in its place came an old strange and nearly mysterious surge. Patches of memory, too: times when they had gone strolling over on black 63rd in that loud Negro brawl, sullen spades around them everywhere, Clive wearing his grin, a letter opener down there in the folds of his coat; other times, thick with somewhat doubtful confession, when Clive talked about Jackie and his family as the ground which had grown such a bad seed. Clive: my vision of him blurs, at times, but he's like a disturbing dream one wants to go back to.

"Suppose I arranged to kill a friend of ours, then?"

"Permission granted," Pless managed, waving his hand.

"Suppose then," Clive said, "I've *already* killed someone for us—already set an experiment in motion so that the game is to determine how we digest the fact of it!"

Pless looked at him. A lie, he told himself.

"Suppose," Clive said, standing and stretching, "I took care of dear Addie for us. Gave our pact a small helping hand. Suppose I went to the greenhouse in the snow that night, picked him up like the fat little twig he is, and cracked his skull on that fish tank? Set off the automatic window control afterward. Tied him up in that ridiculous rig. What if I did that for us?"

Pless' heart pounded. Lie. "The note was in his own hand. The newspapers reproduced it—it was his."

Clive smiled and waited, drawing a long breath. "Suppose," he said, finally, "it was Stoker who was part of our greater game, then? And on the night he got it, say, I left you asleep —you were stoned with your own awful sense of what you'd done, if you want to know—and went out and lured Stoke over to the Blackstone?"

"What should I imagine you did?" Pless asked softly, his voice just a whisper.

"Imagine that I left a note on his door in your name.

Imagine us on the roof and Stoke feeling unusually good, having straightened out his puny sex life at last, and imagine him walking along the edge of the roof, humming a little tune, imagine, making it easy for me so that I just had to supply a quick shove. Oh, Plesser, imagine his face: the fleeting recognition in his young eye as he went over, and, oh, he yelled my name as he went down. Tried to *incriminate* me! Would you believe it? But no one heard."

Pless stared up at Clive, who towered above him. Lie. Oh, please, a lie. Waves of nausea again.

"And you have to imagine even more," Clive said calmly. "That night last spring when all this really began—it was your timely suggestion, you recall?—and Stoke was all wide-eyed and Addie was trembling and blubbering and all of us were nervous and shifty. Well, the greater game was on. Imagine that I put four carefully scheduled numbers into that stocking cap, that I wrote out *two* on two scraps of paper and *three* on another two scraps and put those into the cap and, oh, imagine this: even palmed one of the goddamned threes! So everyone drew my numbers! My pattern was already at work, my rules, and I was leading us toward this moment, imagine, even then. Of course there was some lovely coincidence when you got the other number three so that I just had to kill off Stoker to set things in motion, just kill him a little bit, and then wait for Addie to follow his natural course on the heels of such a disaster. Addie was just so unstable, you know—and, therefore, awfully predictable."

Pless couldn't say anything. His head went between his knees again, and Clive squatted down beside him once more, hissing at him.

"Imagine it this way: things have worked almost magically in this experiment: the way you spoke right up last spring and suggested the pact, Addie's drippy hysteria which has added mood to it all, the way that Stoke seemed to arrange his life so that all the motives for his killing himself looked so neat and certain. Lovely. And now the results, the psychic storm: we see how much knowledge we can stand. Isn't that something? We see if we can hold all this knowledge of things—and of ourselves—in balance. What'd you think of that, Plesser? How do you feel?"

"Oh, Clive," Pless said, and he rolled over so that his face lay flat against the cold mud, his body curled. Lie, he pleaded with himself. Oh, God. And then, curiously, something came out of him he didn't want or expect, something that served to blow a deep fuse down inside him: he began to laugh again.

··· 26

THE COLONEL WENT OVER TO KIMBARK
AVENUE, found that Clive was also gone, then knocked
on the landlady's door until she opened up. He presented himself with his topcoat over his arm, his medals exposed, smiling.
"I'm Clive's father," he explained, drawing himself up tall.
"He doesn't seem to be in and I wondered if I could have the
key to his room and wait for him?"

It was a troublesome bluff which took several minutes to
complete, but worked. As the little woman finally turned the
key in the lock at Clive's room she was still exclaiming that
she didn't know Clive's father was in the army, that Clive
was such a dear and eccentric tenant, and that it was, gracious,
still before daybreak. She tittered and complained and searched
her chenille robe for the right key and fingered her small gray
mop of hair as she swung the door open. Successful. My

ribbons did it, the colonel told himself, as he closed the door on her, nodding and smiling as he shut her out, and he turned to face the L-shaped room.

It had a weird and funky odor, the smell of sweetish incense, and the look of a circus or a cluttered chapel of candles: littered with valuables and trash and marked with color. Candles everywhere: dotting the room like varisized wilted mushrooms. Candles on the bedposts, on the floor, on the window sills and tables. The colonel dropped his topcoat near the door and began his search, uncertain of just what he looked for or expected to find. But Pless had mentioned "notes" on their movements. And that was tangible enough, but what would they mean if he found them? And what else hid there? And would anything be substantial proof of anything, he wondered, or am I just eager to invent evidence now? He stood for a moment recollecting his investigating work in Vietnam, those inspections he made of the small villages where some restless and misinformed pilot had popped a few rockets or bombed by mistake. I was a military detective, then, he told himself, trying to write reports, true accounts. Truth.

He counted the amount of the weights affixed to Clive's set of barbells. One hundred and eighty pounds. He doubted that Clive really hefted that much. Next he perused the phonograph albums, mostly single instrument recordings of guitar, flute, balalaika. A neatly made bed. Everything had an unusually ordered look in spite of the fact that things were strewn around —almost as if the clutter were carefully arranged. A blackboard near the window was covered with equations and a thick layer of chalk dust. What was Clive's mysterious number? Some prime number that solved all the world's math problems, was it? Chess boards: three in all, he found himself thinking, and none of them mine. Clive probably swiped my missing ivory set—or else hid it so that I just can't find it. A stack of postcards: short messages scratched out on them from, yes, let's see, from places like Israel and Santiago, Chile. His father and sister, I suppose. He recalled the photograph which Clive showed him of the girl astride the beach ball, her tanned naked breasts falling loose.

In the desk drawer he found the .45 caliber pistol, loaded but greasy. A burnt smear of incense on the top of a table. Books. Mostly unused math texts, their spines still unbroken. A pot plant, withered, not unlike those in Stoke's apartment. A small roll of dollar bills and a roll of nickels.

I've got to hurry through with this, he reminded himself.

Next were the assorted scraps of notes and jottings, both innocent and baffling, and he was beginning to dislike himself for such looting, but kept on sifting and reading through them. Then he found the notebook. It seemed innocent enough, too, but in the back pages he saw that series of numbers, what seemed to be a time schedule and it took him only a moment to decide that the initials stood for Adler, Stoker and Pless and that these notations of hours and minutes were important. Hurry, he told himself. Hurry and think, think very hard.

As he stood there an overwhelming logic came to him. Does a suicide pact have a leader, he wondered, and if so does that leader go first, providing an example for the others by martyring himself or is he the last one to go, the one who stays alive to prod them on, the homicidal member? It suddenly became clear enough. Everything fell into place, so much that he even doubted its immense clarity, and he peered at that series of numbers and initials as if it could tell him everything with certainty. Then, just as suddenly, other thoughts came, the pieces of the puzzle falling together, and he thought of Clive's size and strength, and speculated if perhaps Clive killed Adler—odd, he thought, that the hands were tied behind the poor boy's back—and if he planned a monstrous death for Pless too. The room seemed to stink with evidence; everything verified his intuition. I've not come to Chicago for nothing, he swore to himself; I've not.

The door clicked, the knob turned.

"Oh no," the colonel breathed aloud.

Clive was suddenly there, facing him, and unable to hide his surprise. Yet his voice was cool.

"Hello there," he said in greeting.

"Your landlady let me in," the colonel managed. "I told her I'd wait for you."

Clive smiled, came in, closed the door. He was a giant, hovering in the room and grinning, and by the time he had taken off his coat the air seemed rich with hostility. The colonel felt his throat tighten and his voice, offering its explanations, seemed distant and hollow.

"I had to talk with you," he found himself saying. "About Stoker. In fact, I've taken the trouble to come back to Chicago just for that. And I've already been talking with Pless on this matter." He talked on, meanwhile watching Clive, who did not sit down, who didn't make a single gesture of friendship, and whose eyes were at work surveying the room, those eyes Parker had described, darting here and there where the colonel had been meddling. "You can understand my concern," the colonel went on. "And after all it *was* in the newspapers."

"The newspapers, yes," Clive echoed.

The colonel talked on, unable to stop. "Not that I fully believed everything the newspaper said," he went on, "but after Stoke and Adler, well, rumor is rumor and all that, but . . ." He tried to imagine how he sounded, but couldn't stop. Clive gazed around the room and his eyes fell on the opened notebook.

"No need to explain," Clive said assuringly, moving around the room. He seemed to sense every misplaced particle of dust and although he smiled the colonel could feel the air burning between them. "Of course you're upset. And you're thinking lots of things."

"It's perfectly natural. You'll have to admit that."

Clive said he understood completely. He moved beyond the

desk, picking up a letter opener: a long, thin, chromed dagger. He still grinned and the colonel was absolutely certain, certain of everything—though he realized he knew nothing in detail.

The problem was suddenly to get out and back to Pless. His instincts—whether military or not he couldn't fathom—filled him with a sense of danger. Meanwhile, Clive was still talking, beginning to con him again, grinning, and moving around the room like a slow and patient cat, that letter opener protruding from his fist like an oversized talon so that the colonel could scarcely pay attention to what he said.

Clive was still talking when the colonel interrupted.

"Where's Pless?" he gushed, even before he thought about how he might sound.

"He's all right," Clive assured him, still smiling. "He just dropped me off and went back to his place."

The colonel moved toward his topcoat, thinking what he could do, if necessary, and Clive was talking on, his voice cool and honeyed. Yet the colonel felt a threat, an unmistakable threat which made him doubt for a moment his own better judgment, and all the while he shot his eyes around the room looking for a weapon, anything to defend himself with. Steady, he warned himself, and he nodded, not hearing what Clive was saying.

"What exactly did you want to talk with me about?" Clive asked. The question pierced through the maze of the colonel's thoughts.

"What's that?"

"You said you wanted to see me. You said you arranged to wait here for me so that we could talk."

The colonel tried to read Clive's impossible tone. Nothing. He struggled to detect something, anything, and finally had to address himself to the question.

"There are a lot of circumstances to Stoker's death," he struggled to say. "I just wanted us to have a long talk. Perhaps now's not the time, though."

"As good a time as any," Clive said, and he came toward the colonel, slowly.

"Well, I don't know. It's been a long night. Perhaps we ought to get together later." He's going to attack me, the colonel felt; his eyes are fiery. He's going to stick that goddamned opener in me while he's talking and smiling.

"You're visibly upset," Clive was saying. "You've had all these troubles—and I realize that disaster has a way of blurring one's vision."

He was almost on top of the colonel and the colonel said to himself: oh, Jesus, I'll bet he said those same words to Stoke. I know he did. And now: what to do? Oh, shit, what now?

"Just keep away from me," the colonel snapped, not expecting the words to come out.

"What's that, sir?" Clive asked, grinning. He advanced another step, then another. His face was a mask of deception. "What do you mean?"

The colonel swung sharply.

It was a quick, stiff-armed judo chop to Clive's throat—one which started as a reflex, out of fear, but the colonel put his weight behind it as he drove forward. It landed with a sharp crack almost like the sound of breaking bone, dropping Clive to his knees, his eyes wide with disbelief, and the colonel said, "Oh, god, I'm sorry, boy!" Then, before that was fully out of his mouth said, "No, I'm not! Just keep away from me!" His doubts were suddenly gone, though he didn't know why, and in a near whisper he said, "I'm *not* sorry, you grinning bastard!"

Clive was on his knees, his hands grasping his throat, his eyes wide, and he obviously couldn't speak.

Stupefied by what he had done, the colonel grabbed up his topcoat and hurried to the door.

"I'll be getting back to you, son," he added, turning to Clive before he went out. "But in the meantime you hear me good: leave Pless alone and leave me alone. And I damn well mean it."

Although Clive was still on his knees with his hands at his throat, his eyes narrowed coldly in reply.

The colonel ran. By the time he reached the street uncertainty had encompassed him again and he felt that he had probably made another awful miscalculation, that it was all part of his grief and his inability to understand, that there was probably no reason to hit Clive. Yet he ran. Oh, Jesus, he asked himself, what have I done? After more than a block his stride slowed down and he headed for the Blackstone out of breath, not even speculating anymore, knowing only that he had to protect Pless, that he had to reach him as quickly as possible and protect him.

When he arrived at the apartment he was relieved to find Pless there with Verna; Pless was sullen and nervous with a glint of hysteria in his eyes, but he was there, safe, and for the moment it was all the colonel cared about.

··· 27

CLIVE'S CONFIDENCE had begun to ebb away and he stood alone in his room at the mirror, looking in at the size of the welt where the colonel had struck him, wondering what the colonel was stirring up back at the Blackstone, wondering about a fingerprint on the automatic window apparatus and about what small detail, if any, Pless might reveal. He felt mostly certain of Pless and convinced that what he had told Pless out beside the lake would have the desired effect, yet, if not, what then?

He nudged a few pieces around one of the chessboards, making a few indifferent moves, then went over to make sure again that the door was locked. He took off his pants and undershorts. Out of his desk drawer came the thick odor of oil from the .45 and he reached in, picked it up, checked its load, and tossed it gently in his hand. When they come, he found himself saying, I'll give them a few rounds through the door, fill them with splinters and lead and there'll be some big cop with tobacco on his lip and the colonel with warrants, but they won't know I have this until it's too late. Afterward I'll make my way to the roof, then Pless will show his face from behind a squad car, smiling, saying It's Me, Clive, Look, and I'll pump one right through his freckled face.

He put down the .45 and hefted his weights, grunting slightly. The muscles of his stomach tightened and he felt, yes, the pleasure of it, I'm the strongest man I know, stronger than God it took just a mere push to topple Stoke and down he went yelling my name it was like a creaming prayer to me. And Adler caught the force of my will: brainwaves traveling across campus to freeze his center in that psychic snowstorm and make him do it. I love to feel these weights going up, but my throat really hurts I feel the strain he really busted me good with that chop. I just didn't expect it, but you can't figure everything.

Dropping the barbells abruptly, he held his genitals and walked around the room lighting his candles. Then he danced for a moment, turning, starting a spin, but he was too nervous and worry scuttled it. Exotic words came to him: Parsee. Dervish.

He knew very well what he should do: that he should get dressed and go directly over to the apartment where they were probably sitting and talking about him, that he should confront them, stage another act for them, and blur the truth for them once more until they lost sight of the greater game again. It would be simple, he knew: Pless was in no condition to measure reality, the colonel, embarrassed at having struck that blow out of instinct, would welcome any explanation that would allow normalcy to set in. They would easily believe simple lies in preference to ornate and monstrous facts because they were incapable of the greater games, he assured himself. Yet, he couldn't muster his will at the moment. Perhaps it was the blow struck by the colonel; he felt temporarily stalled and anxious, as a result, and uneasy.

Impulsively, he drew on his pants again and searched his drawer for his address book. Then he went into the hall to use the house phone. Three calls, he told the operator, three long-distance calls: to Ankara, to Rio de Janeiro, to California. Yes, he realized the time required to make connections overseas and, no, this wasn't a pay phone, and, yes, he would take the call to Los Angeles first while they worked on the others. He gave the operator a Turkish number and the name of a hotel—the Plaza del Oro—in Brazil. Waiting, listening to the slow, nasal tones of the operator, he slid his fingers along the welt at his throat; his voice was slightly thin and it amused him: the good colonel almost knocked out my main artillery, he laughed, with his little attack on my voice box.

The line rang the California number once, twice, several times without answer. Strangely, he couldn't even remember his mother's new name. At last he clicked off and the operator told him that it might be several minutes before his overseas calls would go through. As he replaced the receiver, he immediately felt apprehensive about staying in the hall any longer, so went back inside where the familiar safe smell of candle wax greeted him.

Aunt Leslie: there was another possibility, someone else to call, but to say what? What would he say to any of them? Visions of his aunt, those cobwebbed bicycles in her parlor, the chocolate simmering on the stove flashed behind his eyes. He took off all his clothes again. Drawing the curtain to one side, he peered out; above the dead limbs of the campus trees the clock tower caught the dull rays of the morning sun as they came filtered through the hovering smog. He touched himself softly between the legs again, thinking, my old rod, yes, they'll catch you and cut you off today if we're not careful, but no great matter I don't use you anymore just an occasional wet dream, sure, and what are those dreams about? I sleep too deeply nowadays, deep and lost, and can't remember my dreams anymore Pless says that the act of waking up sometimes makes us forget our dreams and assured me I wasn't just lying there in my sleep with blank pages floating in my head, but what would they be: Jackie, perhaps, who offered it to me once, but we refused her, didn't we, old rod, we don't use ourselves up like that, we let our juices stay put. That's the whole trick: we don't get turned on by simple things at all sex seems so ordinary and that was the thing with Stoker: he used himself up being so bloody ordinary always wanting ass and having growing pains and wanting to write famous books, but for what and for whom? Pless, too, for that matter: he likes ideas and ideas always belong to someone else, they're always ordinary, too stale, and we don't go for that either. Anything that can be learned and used is really worthless and only action can't be calculated or predicted and that's why we'd rather do things I'm an artist in my way much more than Stoke ever was because I've written a small epic playing with real chessmen, taking a knight here and a pawn there.

Waiting for the phone in the hall to ring, he went over and burned all the incriminating notebook pages over his candles, letting the crisp ashes decorate the floor around his feet. Caught, he told himself, but not really, for legally they have nothing, no evidence; Stoke, legally, died alone and Addie even left a convenient note and his death created a certain verification of Stoke's death and now Pless is frantic, yes, and the colonel will always be explained as just a harassed daddy, emotionally tipsy.

Minutes passed and the phone didn't ring.

At the mirror, again, he looked at himself. It was his father's face, in part: the same brow, hairline, mouth. It made him think of how ordinary his old man's vices had been, how bleeding ordinary, and he felt, Oh, I was good at trig and higher calculus, but that would have been no life sitting among my equations all my days I'd rather have had that one time on the roof with Stoke or one such morning as this on the beach with Pless it was worth my whole life if they come and find me now and take me away and cut off my pecker and stick it in my mouth and shoot me like they execute everyone in Vietnam it has been completely worth it.

He looked deep into the mirror, posing, candlelight swimming behind him, and gave himself a sneer and a short laugh, yet knew such gestures for what they were: last, futile cons.

Those phone calls will never get through, he told himself. Just as well.

··· 28

PLESS SAT GAZING OUT OF THE WINDOW
as the colonel talked while across the room Verna and Parker
chatted, Verna's unopened suitcase nearby, and for Verna,
he realized, all this was too terrible and too direct and she
talked to that young nurse only because she had to withdraw
from what was really happening. Reality was too much with
her, and Pless supposed that this was why she hadn't come to
Chicago right away with the colonel: because if all the colonel
suspected were true it would just be too large a helping. Yet,
he couldn't blame her. He felt himself withdrawing. For several
minutes the colonel had talked on without response from
anyone. "You've made terrible mistakes," the colonel said,
drawling slightly, his voice moderate but edged with nervous-
ness. The colonel tried for control, but paced as he talked
and there was something of the friendly interrogator about

him—or a lanky Southern lawyer, perhaps, who was patiently building a solid case. "Our Stoker is dead and gone," he said, enunciating. "And I don't think you've really faced that fact. And Adler is dead and gone. But something inside you is tuning all that out. I'm here to help, Pless, but you're tuning me out."

It was true. Slowly, in spite of himself, as the colonel talked on, his thoughts went fumbling back in elementary reconstructions and he was saying to himself: yes, we went to high school in Florida, Stoke and I, and went fishing in the gulf and he gave me that expensive Randal knife and we were excited about coming up here to the university together, excited about getting admitted at such a good school, and we *were* together—careful of the tense now—for almost six years, all through our undergraduate courses and into our grad studies and then we met Clive and only six short months ago made that stupid pact (real or unreal: which hand has the coin?) except we really didn't make it, did we? It was all a put-on. I didn't even mean what I said that night and have wished a thousand times I hadn't, but there it was, I suppose: we were scratching our names out with Clive's smelly blood. Truth is an eel slipping out of your grasp, hurting you when you finally grab it. The night in the talcumed room: what of that? This morning along the strand with Clive saying those things: what of that? Talking with the colonel is impossible, of course, though I remember having wanted to—and why is that? Guilt? The weight of what's happened? What?

Parker's voice trickled in from across the room, saying, "I'm not really involved in any of this, you see. I wasn't Stoke's girl—it was Laura, my roommate. But I *knew* Stoke and liked him. Oh, I just didn't believe he could have done it; that's what I told the colonel and that's why I'm here."

Verna nodded at her, slightly distracted, and smiled. Parker actually had no business in the room, Pless decided; neither she nor Verna wanted any part of what the colonel was saying

—that was certain. The colonel's words were mostly accusations; Verna had perhaps suffered too much, Parker was young and perhaps hadn't suffered at all, so in both cases they weren't up to the truth. Yet Parker was especially out of place. Slightly comic. Sitting there prim and helpful.

"Listen to me, Pless, I want us to go slow with each other, but I want us to think together. Are you listening?" The colonel leaned forward, searching for Pless' eyes.

Pless bit his lip. His seams were coming apart any minute now, he feared, and he laughed slightly, that same thin laugh he had given Clive out on the beach a few hours ago. He knew it for what it was: a release, a substitute wail.

"You've opened your mind and let a lot of shit inside," the colonel said. "You've got to admit that to yourself now."

Pless could only smile, unable to answer. Verna, in turn, shot her son a helpless glance, her eyes saying: Oh, I'm Sorry, But I Just Can't Help. Distressed, she turned back to listen to Parker.

"Let's take our time in this," the colonel went on. "Let's go back and talk about the major. Are you hearing me?"

Pless nodded yes.

"When your dad went down at Fort Walton Beach—listen to this carefully—you started trying to live with the fact. Now it's hard to live with such a stupid and awful fact, and when any of us try we put up guards so that we're not completely swamped by how goddamned absurd things are. In your case, you played it very cool. I watched you all those months, son, and I saw how you played it—and partially admired you for it."

True again. He knew that he had folded into himself, that he was doing it this instant, too, although he wanted to hear the colonel; it was an art he had practiced for years. True, all true: he had turned to ice after the major's death; he had deliberately grown aloof and stoic and self-possessed and that was what fooled Stoker, for Stoke always imagined him completely in control, but the control was always a lie, just a means of keeping all the horrors in place. The act had even come between Stoker and himself, he realized, for Stoke remained warm and open and mostly unapologetic for his hangups. Their first semester at the university, for instance, Stoke became excited about the Gothic towers, the wise-cracking young profs, the whole scene, and I was just as excited, Pless admitted, but didn't let it show, and it didn't do our friendship any good. I wasn't giving myself at all in those days, just couldn't, all true, and reticence became a minor disease and silence overtook me. Perhaps it was the major's death: I resolved to not cry a single tear at the funeral and didn't—reminding myself, I remember, that I had to take care of Verna afterward and help her get back to Phoenix.

The colonel was still talking. "You've practiced a bad tolerance," he said. "You've been tolerant of too much shit, but now you've *got* to see that it can't go on! In a way, you shouldn't have tolerated the major's crack-up. You should've been mad at him—because he was a fool on that particular afternoon. And you should've been mad at the whole goddamned Air Force, for that matter, and at a country and a world where such a goddamned wasteful establishment is needed. And you should've been mad at yourself for not loving him more when he was alive, for not always being aware that he flew with death every day and that every time could be the last. But you know what? You stayed cool. And anger turned to guilt on you, Pless, and the guilt piled up and turned to shit."

Pless' eyes suddenly burned, but he knew he'd keep from crying. Yet he didn't know if he could stay in the room and listen any longer.

"And something has happened here, something between you and Stoke and Adler and Clive—and you've been tolerant of whatever it is."

"Oh, stop it, Marty," Verna sighed, getting up. "Can't you

see how he's getting? Can't you stop?" She was nearly in tears herself.

"No, goddammit, I *can't!*" he shouted. The room shook with his voice.

Sudden silence. Parker put a hand to her mouth, frightened, and Verna stood there, dumfounded, then looked away. It was almost as if she couldn't see them, as if she felt the pain in the room vaguely, but couldn't locate it. She turned, walked away, and poured herself a whiskey.

The colonel wiped his face on his sleeve and started again, patiently. "Something *did happen* with you four," he repeated.

Perspiration glistened on Pless' brow, his mouth quivered slightly, as if he might speak.

"Can't he have a drink?" Verna asked.

"He doesn't need one."

"Let him have one small one with me," she persisted.

"He can't hold his liquor, Verna," the colonel said calmly. "I want him to talk, if he will. Say something, can't you, Pless?"

Pless couldn't. He was acutely aware of Verna listening, her body taut and poised on the edge of the couch across the room, and of Parker listening, too, all wide-eyed, but too many images rose up to bury anything he might say, and he saw himself and Stoke on bicycles touring the streets of the Florida town at night, their wheels humming on the warm pavement, and he saw them arriving at the house through the stand of palm trees which lined the driveway and there in the living room sat Verna, the major, Cassie and the colonel playing cards, coolers at their elbows; or a picture of the beach flitted in his mind, Stoker standing out on the jetty fishing and never catching anything and being his usually clumsy self with his rig, snagging his clothes or tangling his line in the reel; and he saw Stoker sitting there at breakfast in Phoenix that morning before they drove back to Vegas and he remembered coming downstairs and what he felt, how he wanted to put his arm around Stoker's shoulders except that he couldn't and how he reached out with his fork, finally, and rapped hello on top of Stoke's hand; and he saw Stoke sitting there in the car as they drove back to Vegas, afraid, worried about the pact which they wouldn't talk about; I should have talked then and should have said, O, Stoke, no, that evening was just a lot of crap, but I said nothing, just sat there; my fault. O, help.

The colonel talked on, prodding gently, but he couldn't say anything, just couldn't. He would say it all, he knew, if it were possible: the bloody wastebasket, the stocking cap, Addie sniffling, but his thoughts fumbled themselves away and he felt himself chasing them, withdrawing, thinking: There have only been two men in my life and now they're ghosts and the girls have been sort of ghosts, too, every screw a casual, ghostly screw, and my relationship to Verna has been mostly objective and custodial, so what does that make me except a cold fish? The colonel talked on.

"There're things *I* know," the colonel was saying. "But first there are things *you* have to say. We have to find a beginning point together. If we can do that, I know we can unravel a lot of things."

It all sounded very logical, but Pless was thinking, O a cold fish, that's what, full of that strange objectivity that shuts me out. Recent illustration: that morning I went down to the railway express office when Addie's casket was being shipped back to Arkansas. Didn't even tell Clive about doing that. Just before the colonel's telegram, this was, and there on the platform I stood, my collar turned up against that cold wind, staring at that dumb, oversized box which the men on the dock couldn't find time to load, which just sat there soaking up my cold homage; never once did I say to Addie what I knew he wanted to hear, never, and, oh, I did call him that night when we had our little party up here, but then it was too late with too little. I should have said, Addie we can go from

A to B, that we can, or forget Clive, Addie, if you can't handle his little riffs, and forget the pact, hell, we were all drunk and acting silly that night.

"Oh, Pless, do help Marty out, *please,* if you have anything to say," Verna whined from across the room. She was somehow too comic.

"You must do it, Pless," the colonel kept at him. "Stoke's *gone.* You just have to."

Pless' eyes burned again and he felt the hot tears puddle on his lashes, but he knew he wouldn't say anything, that he couldn't; he hated Clive more than anything now, he supposed, but he could feel a cold indifference setting in between the colonel and himself, and he knew they'd never communicate if they tried a thousand years.

"You really ought to ease down now, sir," Parker put in, mildly professional. "I really don't think he's up to any more." A nurse doll, Pless said to himself. Just what we need.

"You want to have a good cry? Go ahead and cry, son," the colonel went on. "At least I know you're hearing me."

The tears burned and suddenly a noisy sob broke out of his mouth, a strange sound which fumbled his thoughts again and he felt, O, I've been impersonating someone for such a very long time, but the impersonation failed somehow and I turned cold. The sound he made was miserably stupid, but now he couldn't stop. Several minutes passed before he gained control. He felt weak and unsteady; his mouth tasted like metal.

"Now there may be something else in all this," the colonel said. "Something you may need to know."

Okay, Pless felt: he wants to save a remnant of Stoker for his memory. That's what he wants and I can't blame him for that.

"Are you listening?"

Pless nodded, but he really didn't hear and his thoughts were tripping and stumbling into: O, Stoke, why did you do it or let Clive? And Addie: why did you have to? He seemed to fill up with Addie's sad adrenalin and it pulsed and burned through his eyes and the miserable sound came out again. And he saw that oversized box at the railway office with the Arkansas address stenciled on it and he saw a hot montage, his head filling with: the dark, deep canyon at Hoover Dam, the goldfish tank, the cluster bomblet unit, rows of empty houses, suburbs with no people, wreckage of airplanes, the end of the world. O, Stoke.

"You just cry," the colonel said, dropping down on a knee beside him. "Be sick with yourself and sick with the world—which is sick itself, sure, we all know that—but don't think dying is any good. Let me tell you from my business, I know: dying is nowhere. You hear me?"

"Oh, Marty, not anymore," Verna pleaded.

"You hear me, Pless?"

Pless nodded impatiently.

"This is what I have to tell you, so listen good: Stoke might not have killed himself. He might *not* have done it."

Pless didn't look up.

"It might have been Clive. Your friend Clive. You may not understand what I mean—and maybe I don't myself—but that will come. Actually, I don't have any proof of anything. But I know I'm right about *some* of what I feel and I think we can find a beginning point together in this."

Pless suddenly laughed again, surprising even himself. He put his fists into his eyes and rubbed them dry. Smiling, he shook his head in curious disbelief, and although he didn't especially want to give the poor colonel another put-on, there it was, and he was saying, "You really think so, sir? You think you know who's to blame in all this?"

"That's right," the colonel said, encouraged that Pless spoke. "I do. I think Clive might know a great deal more than we suspect—and I have a great many feelings about it. Call it intuition, instinct. Some things I know."

Weak and feeling almost silly, Pless couldn't help grinning.

He put his fists into his puffy eyes once more. "Then I think you ought to confront Clive," Pless told him. "I think we ought to have a showdown. You believe in having show- downs, don't you, sir?"

"I've already seen Clive once—just a short time ago. I saw his notebooks and there's something there, I'm not sure what. We've already confronted each other, in a sense, but—"

"Oh, I think we definitely should go and see him again," Pless said gravely. "If we don't—for one thing—he'll prob- ably come to see us. If he does that, he'll know why he wants to see us, too, so perhaps we ought to go catch him off guard."

"All right, let's do it," the colonel agreed.

"Marty, no," Verna put in. "Not now. You're too upset and you'll—"

"Oh, we should definitely go," Pless added.

"Not you," Verna said. "I *know* you're too emotional."

"We've got to do something, goddammit!" the colonel told her.

"Not this!"

Suddenly they were all arguing about it, fussing and spitting at each other, even Parker, who was there, Pless decided, just out of morbid curiosity, and the colonel in the midst of it all was getting on his coat. Verna's freckles streaked with mascara as she argued and Parker came to her side and put an arm around her. Dutifully, Pless felt. The colonel was try- ing his best to be decisive, helping with coats, keeping a firm jaw.

"This isn't the right thing!" Verna yelled at them as they went toward the elevator.

"We've come to settle something!" the colonel shouted back. "Let's settle it!" His face was flushed and exhaustion was etched in his frown.

Then the two of them, Pless and the colonel, were cutting across the campus toward Kimbark Avenue, snow whooshing around their footsteps, Verna's voice trailing off behind them;

the trees were heavy with ice. Winter has begun in earnest, Pless was thinking, and months and months of it will follow now, drab snow gathering on the corners and in the quad so that when it finally melts the first green sprigs will almost startle you. He wasn't even thinking about where they were going or why and he observed things as if from a great distance, still, as if this winter and all the seasons leading up to it were being viewed from afar through a telescope; he had a sort of wry amusement toward it all, in fact. The colonel was talking, not really saying anything, and they reached the Midway Plaisance.

For the colonel the day was grim and too painful and he talked only to hear the sound of his own voice now, as if he were encouraging himself and his men in a mission. He was damned cold. His shoulder, still sore and swollen, throbbed slightly in the cold wind; frozen branches creaked overhead.

When they reached Clive's place and turned in, there it was: they looked up, startled, to see Clive's face at the window. It stopped them for a moment, then Clive let the curtain fall shut. The colonel felt his heart drumming as they went inside.

The colonel beat his fist on the locked door and yelled, "Open up, Clive! We know you're there! We saw you! Open up and talk to us!"

"That's right, Clive!" Pless echoed in a somewhat mocking tone. "You open up in there! We know what you've done!" It was all he could do to keep from laughing.

"I'll go to the landlady and get a key," the colonel said.

He left Pless standing there banging on the door and ran upstairs, but the landlady didn't answer; at her door, shaking the knob, he suddenly felt ridiculous again, for he heard Pless mimic his own desperation downstairs and he felt, oh, goddammit, I had to trust my instincts and do something, but I've been confused and I'm tired, so damned tired. Being there didn't seem like a good idea. The landlady was obviously not home and his mind, he sensed, numbed by a long, sleepless night, worked much too slowly.

Pless was driving his shoulder into Clive's door when the colonel returned, exaggerating the colonel's excitement, grinning.

"Easy now, Pless," the colonel yelled at him.

"Now you come out of there!" Pless screeched. He drove his shoulder into the big door again, but it didn't budge.

This is terrible, the colonel thought, and he knew he had to settle Pless down and he hated being alone with what he had to do and felt empty about Verna, who, as it turned out, couldn't face any of this, who would go back to Phoenix, he supposed, and drink a few more rounds and hide herself, and he didn't even care, and he hated Cassie for somehow she was mixed up in all this, and he hated Clive behind that door, but it was Pless he had to save and he felt Pless slipping out of his grasp completely now, sliding off into a region where they might never reach each other again, so he tried to take hold of the boy and pull him back, saying, "Easy now, just hold it!"

But Pless' eyes were glazed with confusion and he wrenched away and slammed into the door again.

Then came the shot. It was like a cannon—so loud that the colonel not only dived away, pulling Pless with him and falling, but he also covered his ears in fright, dumbly, like a child. Then just as quickly he realized that Clive hadn't shot at them as they sprang to their feet. He also knew what they would both see if they broke into that room, but they both attacked the door, driving themselves against it, and Pless was clawing and screaming.

The door wouldn't break open. It was an old mahogany door with heavy, dark panels and it just wouldn't yield, so that the colonel started kicking at it with the heel of his shoe.

"What have you *done?*" Pless was screaming now, and the colonel felt that Pless was screaming at him.

The colonel kicked again and the wood around the lock and knob splintered.

"Oh, God, what have you done?"

The colonel flew against the door again, forgetting his injured shoulder, and went dizzy with pain. He hadn't even remembered his shoulder, but now he slumped down on the floor beside Pless, and Pless—the colonel seemed only vaguely aware of this for a moment—was striking him. Everything seemed blurred and wrong and he didn't want in that damned room anyway because he knew what they'd see, and Pless was screaming at him and hitting him. Sharp little angry blows, not very painful, but distracting and meaningless, and Pless was crying out, "Oh, Clive!" over and over.

The colonel got to his feet again and kicked until the wood around the lock cracked and broke, then he wedged the door open.

And he was right about Pless not being able to take what he saw there, for there was Clive in all his brains and gore and fecal matter dotting the floor and walls, those wild candles beating and flapping their flames, and Pless was suddenly down there beside Clive, sliding over him, moaning, "Oh God, oh God, oh God in heaven!"

For a moment the colonel couldn't take it himself and he turned to the wall trying for control, trying to sort out the debris that seemed to surge into his mouth and mind. All his years seemed to seize him and everything spewed out: old Bo, Charlie Miller, his dear sister Neddie, sweet Stoker his heart's blood, all the absurd pain of his life, that almost familiar pain he had always wanted to make sense of, Cassie, those strange far lands where he had flown and served; all of it gagged and sickened him and he was lost in all his griefs in that moment before he turned around again and took hold of Pless.

"Stop it, son. Stop it now!" he finally managed, and he tried to lift him away from the mess.

"Don't call me *son!*" Pless snapped at him bitterly.

"Get up! Get to your feet!"

"Oh, Clive!" Pless wailed, and the colonel didn't understand what he was doing down there. Everything was confusion. "Oh my Clive, my dear Clive!" Pless wailed, and he wouldn't get up no matter how hard the colonel pulled at him, he wouldn't get up at all.